Eric Wilson
Canadian Mysteries
VOLUME 2

Books by Eric Wilson

The Tom and Liz Austen Mysteries

Also available by Eric Wilson

Eric Wilson
Canadian Mysteries
VOLUME 2

RED RIVER RANSOM

THE GHOST OF LUNENBURG MANOR

CODE RED AT THE SUPERMALL

ERIC WILSON

Harper*Trophy*Canada™
An imprint of HarperCollins*PublishersLtd*

As in his other mysteries, Eric Wilson writes here about imaginary people in a real landscape.

Find Eric Wilson at www.ericwilson.com

Eric Wilson Canadian Mysteries, Volume 2
Copyright © 2010 by Eric Wilson Enterprises, Inc.
Red River Ransom © 2006 by Eric Wilson Enterprises, Inc.
The Ghost of Lunenburg Manor. Text © 1981, 2003 by Eric Wilson Enterprises, Inc.
Code Red at the Supermall. Text © 1988, 2003 by Eric Wilson Enterprises, Inc.

Chapter illustrations for *Red River Ransom* by Derek Mah.
Chapter illustrations for *The Ghost of Lunenburg Manor* by Susan Tooke.
Chapter illustrations for *Code Red at the Supermall* by Richard Row.

All rights reserved.

Published by Harper*Trophy*Canada™, an imprint of
HarperCollins Publishers Ltd

No part of this book may be used or reproduced in any manner whatsoever without the prior written permission of the publisher, except in the case of brief quotations embodied in reviews.

HarperCollins books may be purchased for educational, business, or sales promotional use through our Special Markets Department.

HarperCollins Publishers Ltd
2 Bloor Street East, 20th Floor
Toronto, Ontario, Canada
M4W 1A8

www.harpercollins.ca

Red River Ransom. First published in paperback by HarperCollins Publishers Ltd: 2006.
The Ghost of Lunenburg Manor. First published in paperback by Clarke, Irwin & Co. Ltd: 1981. First Collins Paperbacks (a division of Collins Publishers) mass market edition: 1982.
Code Red at the Supermall. First published in hardcover by Collins Publishers: 1988. First HarperCollins Publishers Ltd mass market paperback edition: 1989.
These three books first published in this omnibus edition: 2010.

Library and Archives Canada Cataloguing in Publication information is available upon request.

ISBN 978-1-55468-823-4

Printed in the United States of America
RRD 9 8 7 6 5 4 3 2 1

Contents

Red River Ransom

Dedicated by Flo and Eric to the new generation:

Peiter Thorup

Tomas Thorup

Emily Villeneuve

Stephanie Villeneuve

Joe Villeneuve

Cole Wilson

Makenna Wilson

Ryley-Ray Wilson

Vance Wilson

Wren Wilson

1

"Here it comes," cried Tom Austen.

Gliding down on silvery wings, the sleek executive jet approached Winnipeg International Airport. It was a bitterly cold night in January, but that didn't bother Tom. Born in Winnipeg thirteen years ago, he knew how to dress for winter's worst.

Tom stood beside his father, Inspector Edward "Ted" Austen of the Winnipeg City Police, watching the jet's smooth descent. The plane's running lights gleamed in the darkness as it lightly touched down. Tom was excited because inside the executive jet was one of Hollywood's biggest names, Johnny Lombardo. The young star was arriving in Winnipeg to film scenes for his latest movie, *Kid Gangster*. Some Manitoba locations would stand in for Chicago, where most of the movie had just been shot.

Security was tight. Johnny's arrival time was a closely guarded secret. From the jet, he'd be driven by limousine straight to his headquarters for the Winnipeg shoot. The location was unknown, but much discussed.

Johnny Lombardo was only thirteen but he commanded top dollar. Everyone knew about his yacht, and the mansion he shared with his father overlooking California's blue Pacific.

"This is so awesome," Tom said. "Imagine seeing a major star in person!"

Inspector Austen smiled. "I'm impressed that Johnny Lombardo is one of Hollywood's biggest stars. At his age—that's hard to believe!"

Two people stood nearby. They were government officials representing Customs and Immigration. One had silver hair. He wore a parka with the hood down. "There have always been kid stars," he said. "Who was that girl, long ago? Shirley Dimple, or something like that?"

The Immigration official beside him shook her head. "Shirley Temple," she said, laughing.

The good-natured man chuckled at his error. "You know," he said thoughtfully, "I feel sorry for Johnny Lombardo. Sure, he's rich and famous, but there's a downside. I bet people are always wanting things. His autograph, his money."

Once again, Inspector Austen checked his watch. "As you know, three security guards are travelling with Johnny Lombardo."

Stamping their feet against the cold, they all watched with interest the approach of the dramatic-looking executive jet with its silver nose. Engines whining, the impressive aircraft rolled to a stop. As the pilot shut down the systems, a boy looked out a window. He had curly black hair and large dark eyes.

"Dad," Tom exclaimed, as the boy disappeared from view. "That's him. That's Johnny Lombardo!"

"Yes, indeed," Inspector Austen commented. "I'd know that face anywhere."

Tom shook his head in amazement. "I just saw Johnny Lombardo in person! Liz will be so jealous. So will Mom! Too bad they've gone to that tournament in South Dakota. They've missed the chance of a lifetime."

A black stretch limousine was powering toward them. "Hey, Dad, check out the fancy limo."

"It's here for Johnny. Other limousines are coming for his people."

"Say, Dad, where's he staying? Dietmar claims they've rented the entire Hotel Fort Garry."

Inspector Austen smiled, but said nothing.

"Can't you just tell me? Please!"

"We've been though all this, Tom. I'm sorry, but I'm not allowed. If the Mayor found out, I'd lose my job."

The door of the jet opened soundlessly and the Customs and Immigration officials boarded. Soon after, they came back down the stairs and drove away in a government car.

Then three tough-looking people left the jet. "Look at them," Tom whispered to his dad. "It's so obvious they're bodyguards."

The trio—a woman and two men—were dressed in black trench coats and wearing sunglasses, despite the late hour. The bodyguards swiftly scoped out the scene. Looking satisfied, the woman spoke into her cuff. Immediately, Johnny Lombardo ran swiftly from the plane to the waiting limousine. As the chauffeur opened the door, he touched his cap to Johnny. The bodyguards immediately surrounded the vehicle, assuming aggressive stances.

"Wait here, son," Inspector Austen said, "while I talk to them."

As Tom's father walked toward the guards, a woman and a man left the jet. She was about thirty, and most beautiful. Her sleek blond hair was cut short, curling close to her lovely face. Diamonds winked at her ears. She wore an expensive-looking blue parka with the words "Kid Gangster" stitched in white.

The woman's large brown eyes looked around alertly. "Brrr," she commented to the man. "This wind is colder than Chicago. I heard about the corner of Portage and Main in downtown Winnipeg. It's supposed to be the coldest place on earth, or something like that!" Her laugh was as pleasing as the sound of silver bells.

Seeing Tom, the man waved him over. He also wore a blue parka, open to the cold. He was about twenty-five, with large hazel eyes. His thick dark hair was razor-cut in a bi-level style that looked extremely high-maintenance. The man seemed very Hollywood, with his dark suntan and a heavy silver chain around his neck. He wore new jeans that looked expensive, shiny cowboy boots, and several large silver rings.

"I'm Zack Sanderson," he said. "I'm the producer of *Kid Gangster*." He glanced around the scene. "How'd you penetrate the security, kid?"

Inspector Austen spoke from behind Zack. "I can answer that. Tom is my son. I'm Inspector Austen of the Winnipeg City Police. I'm your local contact for police security during Johnny Lombardo's visit."

They shook hands. "Good to meet ya," Zack said.

The woman smiled at Tom and his dad. "I'm Johnny's manager, Sally Virtue." Her voice had a British accent.

"I love Johnny's movies," Tom said.

"I'm glad you're a fan, Tom. Would you care to meet him?"

"I'll say," he replied. "Thanks, Sally!"

Leaving Inspector Austen talking with Zack, they walked to the limo. Sally tapped on the window. "Johnny," she called, "there's a fan out here. Open up. Say hello."

The smoky glass powered down. A handsome boy smiled at them.

"This is Tom Austen," Sally explained. "His father's in charge of local security."

The boys shook hands. The same age and size, they were both handsome. Tom was a redhead, and Johnny had dark colouring. He had the well-groomed look of a young star and seemed very confident. "I like Canada," Johnny said. "It's a cool country."

"As well as a cold one," Tom quipped, making Johnny laugh.

"I've been on shoots up here before," he said. "Great crews, great talent."

"It's incredible to meet you, Johnny. Your movies are the best."

The star's smile was warm. His face was so famous. It

was amazing for Tom to actually meet Johnny Lombardo!

"Hey, Tom," he said, "you should visit the set. Watch me shoot a scene or two. Meet some movie people."

Tom could hardly believe his ears. "That's an awesome idea," he enthused.

Sally nodded her agreement. "I'll make the arrangements with Inspector Austen. I think he's scheduled to visit the set tomorrow morning. I'll suggest that Tom come along."

"I've got an idea," Tom said suddenly. "How about coming to my place, Johnny? Meet my friends, maybe play some snow football."

"That sounds great." Johnny looked hopefully at Sally. "Sunday's my day off. Okay if I visit Tom?"

"Not a chance, Johnny. Too many security concerns."

"But," Tom protested, "my dad will be there. He's in charge of local police security! It's the safest place Johnny could be."

Sally squeezed Tom's hand. "Oh, Tom, we'd love to visit. But it's just not possible. I know you'll understand." She climbed into the limo next to Johnny.

As the luxury vehicle glided away, Sally waved a pleasant farewell. Tom returned the wave, looking forward to seeing her again.

* * *

Back at the executive jet, Zack Sanderson was telling Inspector Austen about his lifestyle when Tom joined them. "Riding in that jet is a thrill, Inspector. Imagine travelling forty-five thousand feet above the earth's surface, eating a gourmet meal and watching the rushes from your latest flick. Meanwhile the other suckers are travelling on commercial flights, with all that airport security hassle."

"Is this your personal jet?" Tom asked.

"Nope. It belongs to Polygon Studios." Zack stared into the empty night. "No sign of my limo. Just my luck." He turned to Tom and his dad. "Come on. I'll show you inside."

The aircraft contained six leather chairs. The deep-pile carpeting was pale blue. The ceiling was high. They were able to stand up comfortably inside. Displayed on the bulkhead was the logo for Polygon Studios—an empty parrot cage.

On a cherrywood coffee table was a silver plate containing chocolate-dipped strawberries, beaded with moisture. Tom's mouth watered at the sight. Zack passed him the plate, and Tom bit in greedily.

Zack introduced the pilot, a man in his thirties. His name was Ebenezer Smith. Ebenezer sat in a light-weight wheelchair—both of his legs ended above the knee. His head was bald; his body had the bulk of a weightlifter.

"I'm from England," Ebenezer said, shaking hands. His grip was powerful. He smiled at Tom. "Been wondering how a double-amputee can fly a jet?"

"Well, yes, actually."

Ebenezer gestured at the cockpit, visible beyond a low divider. "The controls have been modified for my use."

"How do you board the jet?" Tom asked.

"Using a hydraulic lift," Ebenezer replied. "After losing my legs I learned to fly executive jets. A woman who learned with me later moved to Hollywood. Recently she got connected to Polygon Studios. They needed a pilot, and she remembered me. I started two weeks ago. Polygon's a good company to work for."

The big man smiled proudly. "This Falcon 900EX has all the latest gadgets. Computers, fax, satcom, digital datalinks. You name it, we've got it."

"What's your flight range?" Inspector Austen asked.

"Forty-five hundred nautical miles. Last week I flew this baby from Stockholm to Moscow without refuelling."

Tom glanced at Zack. The producer was slumped down on a leather sofa. A cellphone was pressed to his ear. "You want a meeting? Right away? But I'm busy. I'm producing a movie. Get real, man."

Zack listened to his phone. His face seemed to lose colour. He raised a hand slowly to his throat, looking shocked. "Don't threaten me," he said. "You can't . . ."

Zack stared at the phone. "He hung up."

"Who was it?" Tom asked.

Zack ignored Tom's query. He stared into space, then finally spoke.

"They can't do this," he said to himself. "I won't let it happen. They must be stopped."

2

Early Thursday morning, Tom and his father were heading for Winnipeg's Exchange District. Soon they would be watching Johnny Lombardo act for the cameras. Tom could hardly wait!

They were inside Inspector Austen's police car. Winter ruled—all was darkness. The wind howled past, shaking their vehicle. Bare branches danced above; in houses a few lights glowed, but not many people were awake at this early hour. An empty cardboard carton bounced across the road as their headlights followed swirling snow through the city streets. On the radio, the announcer reported a serious wind chill. The temperature was well below freezing.

Tom was talking about Zack Sanderson. "He's got some kind of problem, Dad. I think he's worth investigating."

Inspector Austen shook his head. A kind man, he loved his family. But his children's detective aspirations sometimes caused problems. "Tom, I'm putting my foot down. No more detective work for you and Liz. That's my final decision."

Tom smiled. "Okay, Dad. I hear you."

Inspector Austen parked at a busy Tim Hortons and they hurried across the windy lot as pellets of snow attacked their faces. Inside, the sudden warmth made tears stream from Tom's eyes. Everyone looked relaxed. They were reading newspapers or chatting together over steaming mugs. Waiting in line, Tom studied the people. He was constantly searching for the faces from his poster of Canada's Ten Most Wanted Criminals. When he found one, he'd help police make the arrest. That would be so great! For sure his picture would be in the newspaper.

They were joined by a handsome man aged about thirty. He had large, dark eyes and thick black hair, presently hidden under a toque with the logo of the Manitoba Moose hockey team. His smile was friendly.

"Uncle Timothy," Tom said, hugging him. "I'm glad to see you."

"Tim's going to the shoot with us," Inspector Austen explained. "We arranged to meet here."

"I'm excited," Uncle Timothy said with a grin. "I love movies."

"How'd you get here, Unc?" Tom asked.

"By bus."

Inspector Austen smiled at his brother. They shared the same dark colouring and handsome looks. "Still environmentally sensitive, Tim? Good for you."

Back in the police car, Inspector Austen hungrily attacked a cranberry-blueberry bran muffin while Tom and Uncle Timothy both sipped hot chocolate. They watched a pretty dark-haired woman hurry toward the doughnut shop, her arm linked with a man's. She wore sparkling jewellery and a stylish outfit topped by a leopard-patterned hat; he wore a black leather coat and dark trousers.

"They're obviously not locals," Tom said, noting that the man's coat was open to the cold. His flamboyant tie featured a large maple leaf against a white-and-scarlet background. "His clothes are way too light for this climate, and he hasn't bothered with a toque. You can be sure that guy hasn't experienced frostbite."

Inspector Austen sipped his coffee. "He's an author, in town visiting schools with his wife, Flo. Their picture was in yesterday's newspaper."

* * *

Several brick buildings with arched windows and old-fashioned awnings in the Exchange District had been chosen as the backdrop for the day's movie shoot.

"The Exchange District is perfect for this film," Inspector Austen said, parking his car in a police zone. Daylight had arrived, bright and cold. "Apparently the story is about hoodlums in Chicago in the 1930s. These buildings are from that time period. People once called Winnipeg the Chicago of the North."

"Why's the movie called *Kid Gangster*? Do you know, Dad?"

"Apparently Johnny Lombardo plays a boy with a gangster father who gets gunned down by rival thugs. The boy vows revenge. Pretty soon there's a killing spree."

Stepping from the car, Uncle Timothy shivered. "This cold! Months and months of it. I wish I lived somewhere warm."

Above them was a six-storey building with large letters that read "THE J. H. ASHDOWN HARD-WARE COMPANY LIMITED." "They're filming a shootout today," Inspector Austen explained. "Using blanks, of course. It's all done with special effects."

Tom stared at the sunny street. "Hey. It looks like the U.S.A. has taken over!"

Outside various buildings, the "Stars and Stripes" fluttered in the brisk morning breeze. Newspaper boxes offered copies of the *Chicago Sun-Times*, and licence plates on old-fashioned cars and trucks read "Illinois 1937." On a mailbox they saw an eagle and the words "U.S. Mail."

Tom noticed the movie's producer, Zack Sanderson. He was standing near a truck where food and beverages were available, holding a steaming container of coffee and chewing aggressively on some food.

A man of about thirty was talking to Zack. He had dark curly hair and seemed all muscle and bone. He was a menacing sight, with his thick sideburns ending in sharp points. The man's leather bomber jacket was open. His muscular body was packed into a T-shirt and jeans, and he wore sneakers.

Sally Virtue joined Tom and his dad. "Hi there," she said with a friendly smile. "I'm your personal guide."

The cold weather seemed to suit Sally. Her eyes were bright, her skin glowed. Seeing her, Tom's heart beat just a little bit faster.

The movie crew was busy; people hurried back and forth between large white trailers parked along the street. "The actors use those trailers for wardrobe and makeup," Sally explained, escorting them through the exciting scene. "The stars have their own trailers where they can relax between takes. Including Johnny Lombardo, of course. Usually he's got three."

Tom's mouth fell open. "Three trailers. For one kid?"

Sally smiled. "One is a combined schoolroom and office. Johnny's tutor is Ian B. Lawson. Ian's a nice guy. They've been together since Johnny started lessons. The second trailer is a fully equipped gym. Currently, Johnny's taking fencing lessons for a new movie called *Zorro and Son*."

Inspector Austen turned to her. "You're originally from England? I detect an accent. Possibly Manchester?"

"I'm impressed," Sally said, smiling warmly. "Yes, I grew up in a suburb of Manchester. A place called Weatherfield. Eventually I moved to Hollywood seeking fame and fortune."

"Did you get into movies?" Tom asked. "You're beautiful enough."

Sally smiled at the compliment. "Not as an actor. But I did meet some interesting people, including Roberto Stella."

"Wow, he's really famous! My mom likes his movies."

"I'd done some personal management in England," Sally explained. "Roberto hired me to guide the career of his son, Johnny Lombardo. So that's how I got into movies."

Tom stared at a passing girl. She was in her midteens, and tall. Her dark hair and eyes were very familiar to him. "Oh my gosh, that's May-Lin Chan, in person!"

Sally called May-Lin over and made the introductions. The young actor had arrived in Winnipeg to visit Johnny Lombardo. "I'm not appearing in this movie," May-Lin explained to Tom and his father. Her face was lovely, her eyes bright and intelligent. "My father and Johnny's dad are both actors, so our families are friends. Johnny gets lonely on these shoots, so I decided to visit. I'm not working right now so I flew up from Los Angeles in a private jet."

May-Lin turned to the pretty young woman at her side. "This is my friend, Jeneece Edroff. We're both good pals with Johnny, so Jeneece came along for the ride."

"I've seen you in some movies, too," Tom said.

Jeneece smiled. "Next I'll be co-starring with May-Lin in a remake of *Emma*."

May-Lin shivered with the cold. "This is so freezing!" She turned to Jeneece with a laugh. "I can't believe that Tuesday we were on the beach at Malibu."

Tom produced an instant camera from his pocket. "Would it be okay if we took some pictures together?" he asked hopefully.

May-Lin and Jeneece willingly agreed. Uncle Timothy did the camera work. Then, after some polite conversation, May-Lin and Jeneece departed. Tom watched them go, amazed at his good fortune in meeting them.

Making their way past large cables and cameras, huge lights, and other impressive movie equipment, Tom, with his father and uncle, arrived with Sally at a large trailer manufactured by the Winnebago company. "This is sometimes called a 'Winnie,'" Sally explained, ringing the bell. "It's where Johnny hangs out during the shoot."

Laughter sounded from within the trailer. Then the door of the "Winnie" opened. Tom saw a woman of about thirty-five. Her beauty was astonishing. She had long dark hair streaked with copper tones. The woman's green eyes were enormous. She was casually dressed in jeans and a thick woollen sweater with a Scandinavian design.

"Sally," she said, smiling. "How nice to see you."

"What are you doing here, Carmen?"

"I've got news from Roberto." Carmen slipped into a blue *Kid Gangster* parka. "Let's go for a stroll."

As the women walked away, Johnny watched from the doorway. He was lost in thought. Then, snapping out of it, he invited the others inside. The lavish furnishings included a leather sofa and chairs, a state-of-the-art entertainment centre, and a refrigerator, which turned out to be stocked with cold juice and bottled water. A large painting showed a surfer riding a big wave.

"Who was that woman?" Tom asked Johnny.

"Carmen Sanchez. She's an executive vice-president at Polygon Studios. Carmen and my dad got engaged recently. She's come to Winnipeg with information for Sally."

Outside the window, loud talk was heard. Tom saw two men cursing at each other and shaking their fists. One wore a baseball cap displaying a skull and cross-bones. Tom had noticed him earlier, talking to Zack Sanderson.

"Who's that guy?" he asked Johnny.

"Ivan," he replied, then shivered. "I don't like him. I've heard stories."

"What's Ivan's job?" Inspector Austen asked.

"He's a grip, sir."

"Meaning?"

"Grip is a movie word, Inspector. It refers to people who work with cables, lighting, cameras—that sort of thing. I think Ivan's way too pushy, but Zack Sanderson does the hiring. He fills the jobs, not me."

"Where are your bodyguards?" Tom asked.

"They're not needed here," Johnny replied. "The entire set is guarded. They're taking a break, and I don't miss them."

The boys lounged comfortably on a super-sized leather sofa while talking surfing and hockey with Uncle Timothy and Inspector Austen. Johnny and his dad had season tickets for the Los Angeles Kings and were major fans of the sport.

Then a strange yip was heard. Turning, Tom saw a small dog fashioned from metal. Lights glowed from its eyes, and whirring sounded when the dog moved its head.

Johnny laughed with delight. "Meet Rover—he's robotic." As Johnny punched commands into a control unit, Rover lifted a paw in greeting and then rolled over and did headstands.

Smiling, Johnny lifted the dog and kissed its shiny head. "I gave a bunch of these dogs to my friends," he told them.

The trailer's doorbell rang. Johnny opened the door to a young woman. "Thirty minutes, Johnny."

"Thanks," he said, then turned to Tom. "She's called an Assistant Director, or A.D., for short. If you'd like, Tom, I'll teach you the lingo."

The young star quickly slipped into a slick gangster suit, perfectly tailored to his thirteen-year-old size. "In this scene," he explained, "I make my first kill. There's a car chase, then a gunfight in the warehouse district. That's where Vinnie the Lip takes my bullet, right between the eyes. But you won't see any gore. That'll be added later, by computer."

"Are you in any real danger?" Tom asked.

"Not a chance," Johnny replied casually. "I'm worth a lot of money. My action is all faked, or done by a stunt actor. For me, it's a snap."

"*Kid Gangster* sounds pretty violent," Inspector Austen commented.

Johnny shrugged. "My father always tells people, if you don't like the violence don't buy the movie. Still, Inspector, you're right. It's gruesome. But that's what people want. Blood equals money at the box office. That's why these movies get made."

"Maybe so," Tom's father remarked, "but every day the police see the results of real-life violence. Kids crying their eyes out, entire families suffering. Today's popular entertainment makes that seem acceptable."

Uncle Timothy nodded. "I agree with Ted. To me, that's not what humans should be. We could make the world so much better."

Tom admired Johnny. Instead of getting annoyed by the criticism, he was listening.

"Possibly you're right," he admitted, "but there's no way I can change things. I'm just one person."

"John Lennon didn't feel that way," Uncle Timothy said. "He was a star, and he made a difference. He said, 'Give peace a chance.' Every year, that message goes out in his song worldwide. Your movies also have a global audience, Johnny. Think of the difference you could make."

But Johnny just shrugged and looked away.

* * *

Watching the shoot from across the street, Tom enjoyed the action. The highlight was seeing a 1937 Ford Model A slam into a building, then roll over and burst into flames. As the classic auto exploded, Johnny's stunt double escaped unhurt. Appearing totally casual about the dangers he'd survived, the double strolled nonchalantly away from the wreckage. He didn't even flinch when the burning vehicle's gas tank blew up with a thundering roar, sending orange-and-red flames shooting into the sky.

Johnny Lombardo was then filmed making the appropriate faces in front of a blue screen, as if he'd acted the scene himself. Later, computers would blend the star into the stunt. Watching the final movie, people would think Johnny Lombardo had been driving the Model A.

Later, Tom stood with Johnny at the craft services

truck. Known as the CST, the vehicle served delicious foods and beverages for the cast and crew, totally free of charge. The afternoon air was cold. The boys were drinking hot chocolate and eating chips. Tom was also munching on triple-layer carrot cake smothered in cream-cheese icing.

"This is so toothsome," Tom exclaimed between mouthfuls.

"Toothsome?" Johnny laughed.

"That's my sister's favourite expression."

"I like these flavoured chips," Johnny said, "especially salt and vinegar. You can't get them in the States." Johnny studied the wording on the package. "Cool how it's in English and French." He smiled. "Mom and I went to Quebec on holiday once. It was real fine. We liked the people we met."

Johnny flipped a coin in the air. "This is called a loonie, right? Because of the bird on it?"

Tom nodded. "Do you know what's on the toonie?"

"A polar bear," Johnny answered immediately with a grin, "and that's perfect for Canada."

"I've got a special edition loonie showing Terry Fox." Tom glanced shyly at Johnny. "Ever heard of him?"

"Sure," Johnny replied. "In fact, Dad and I help organize the Terry Fox Run in Malibu. We've had great turnouts and raised a lot of money for cancer research. That guy was an amazing athlete. Imagine running a marathon a day, and doing it with an artificial leg. Incredible!"

"My sister Liz knows everything about Terry Fox." Tom shook his head, looking glum. "You know,

Johnny, I really wish you could meet Liz. Are you certain about Sunday? You can't come to visit?"

The young star shook his head. "Sally said no, and she meant it."

Tom looked around the set, hoping to convince Sally otherwise. But she wasn't there, and neither was Carmen. Then he was introduced by Johnny to his stunt double, Jacob Herring. About twenty-five years old and a former professional jockey, Jacob was the same shape and size as Johnny, but his hair was scarlet, like Tom's.

"Most people call me Red," he explained. "I wear a wig when I'm filming Johnny's stunts."

Tom pulled out his camera. "Okay for a picture together?"

The stunt double's reply was unexpected. "Not a chance," he snapped. "I never pose for photographs."

The man walked briskly away. Johnny shook his head. "Red's a strange guy," he said, "but incredibly courageous. He makes huge money."

"How's he spend it?" Tom asked.

Johnny shrugged. "Red parties in Vegas. I've heard stories, but. . ." Johnny's voice trailed away. "I really shouldn't say anything more."

Tom jotted the details in his pocket notebook. "There's something strange about that guy. He makes me feel suspicious, but I don't know why."

3

On Friday morning excitement ruled in River Heights, a pleasant neighbourhood close to downtown Winnipeg. The place had been transformed by the energy of the film crew setting up outside Tom's school, Queenston Elementary. Many big movie trailers had arrived, and after much effort the classic red-brick schoolhouse was ready for fame.

Given time off from their lessons, students and teachers watched from behind barricades. Also present were many curious onlookers from River Heights. Houses in the neighbourhood were cozy. Each had its own yard. Large trees lined the street, their bare branches looking cold and forlorn.

Frozen flakes drifted from the grey sky. Caught by a gust of wind, they swirled past the three-storey schoolhouse. In the distance, the grips were taking a break. They stood beside the craft services truck, lined up for food. One was Ivan. His greying hair was cropped close to his bony skull. The muscular man bounced in his sneakers, keeping warm. His brown leather bomber jacket was faded and creased from years of wear. It was open, revealing a T-shirt reading "Show Me The Money." Tattooed on his neck was a butterfly. Ivan was speaking on a cellphone, his breath white in the air.

Tom studied the director of the movie. Like others on the set, Jordan Quicksilver wore a blue *Kid Gangster* parka. With his long neck he resembled a strange bird. His face was thin, and his hair was sparse. It was hard to believe that he was a genius, but that's what *Tribute* magazine had recently said in a cover story on the director.

The door of Johnny Lombardo's trailer opened, and three heavies in black trench coats and wraparound sunglasses stepped outside.

"Those are Johnny's bodyguards," Tom said to Dietmar Oban. "They arrived with him on the Polygon Studios jet."

"Did you get Johnny's autograph?" Dietmar asked. He had known Tom for many years, but refused to be impressed by his detective heroics. A good-looking boy with dark hair and eyes, Dietmar was known around Queenston School as an eating machine. He'd consume anything, anytime, anywhere.

"As a matter of fact, I did get his autograph. Also one for Liz. I didn't think you'd be interested."

"You're wrong, Austen. I could have sold it on eBay. Johnny Lombardo is a major star."

"He's the major star," Tom responded, once again annoyed by Dietmar.

The heavies checked out the area. As they did, excitement grew in the crowd. Girls were jumping up and down, anticipating the sight of Johnny Lombardo in person. The leader spoke into her cuff, the door of the big trailer opened, and Johnny Lombardo stepped out to cheers and screaming adoration. He smiled and waved as the girls whooped and hollered.

Johnny blew a kiss to them, then joined Jordan Quicksilver for a private conversation. As they spoke, their breath turned misty.

Zack Sanderson walked past. The young producer was studying a business organizer in his hand. Today his eyes looked sad, his shoulders seemed slumped. Tom called hello to Zack but was ignored. The man put away his BlackBerry, crossed the street to the CST, and began talking to Ivan.

Sally Virtue left Johnny's Winnebago. Seeing Tom, she came to say hello. He introduced his teacher, Mr. Stones, and the others in his class. Very tall and thin, Tom's teacher was well liked by everyone at Queenston School.

Someone called for quiet as the actors moved into position. Dressed for Chicago in the 1930s, Johnny wore a cloth cap, a woollen coat, breeches, and boots. Running up the outside stairs of the brick schoolhouse, the young star took his place at the top.

"In this scene," Sally explained to Mr. Stones and the students, "Johnny plays Tony Junior. His father, Big Tony, has died horribly. The mob wants to kill Tony Junior. We'll watch two gangsters approach the school, determined to kill the boy. They're in a car, being chased by the police."

Across the street a large camera began to move, rolling along metal tracks. Jordan Quicksilver yelled, "Action!" and Johnny started down the stairs.

At the same time, loud engines sounded and around the corner came a Ford Model A, with two old-fashioned police cars in hot pursuit. A man dressed as a mobster leaned out of the Ford, firing a fake machine gun at the cops. Then the gangster swung toward Johnny and unleashed another burst of fire. Leaping from the stairs, Johnny landed in the snow and rolled to the side.

"Cut," yelled Jordan Quicksilver. "Good work, Johnny." As the crew rushed around, preparing for another take, Johnny Lombardo brushed away snow. Then he strolled across the street toward the crowd of onlookers. The bodyguards were with him.

"Oh," cried the girls, "he's coming over!"

The friendly star was soon answering their questions and signing autographs, watched by Sally Virtue. "Don't get too close," Sally warned the girls, as they pressed toward Johnny.

On a street nearby, a white limousine stopped. Out stepped Carmen Sanchez, the strikingly elegant woman recently engaged to Johnny's father. She wore a white parka. Tom glanced at Sally. When she saw Carmen, her eyes narrowed. Her hands tightened into fists.

Carmen's arrival was also noticed by Jordan Quicksilver. Leaving the set, he hurried quickly to the limousine. Seizing Carmen's hands, he began speaking rapidly. Tom couldn't hear the director's words, but he sensed urgency. Finally, Jordan and Carmen got into the limousine. Its engine was running, but it remained motionless.

Tom turned to his teacher. "Hey, Mr. Stones, I need something from my backpack. It's in the classroom. I'll just be a minute, okay?"

Before the teacher could reply, Tom headed toward the school. He was careful to avoid the movie equipment, which seemed to be everywhere.

The building was empty. Even the office was deserted, with everyone outside watching the movie action. Tom cautiously climbed the stairs. His heart beat loudly. It felt strange, being alone inside the abandoned school.

At the top floor Tom paused, listening. From outside came the amplified voice of someone giving instructions. In his classroom, Tom opened his backpack. It contained a portable listening device, purchased with his Christmas money. The device was simple to operate, but very effective.

From a second-floor window, Tom looked down at the limousine. The idling engine puffed out small clouds of exhaust. Putting on lightweight headphones, Tom made adjustments to the PLD. Then he aimed the device at the limousine.

A laser beam struck the limo's rear window, then bounced back to a small dish beside Tom. The beam was unscrambled into an audio signal, which was transmitted to the headphones.

" . . . *marry Roberto*," said a female voice. "*So stop hassling me. No more e-mails. There's no point in arguing. Now please get out of the car, and let me go free.*"

Moments later, Jordan Quicksilver stepped from the limousine. As it powered away, he raised a fist and gestured angrily after the vehicle.

Tom heard the sound of footsteps. Someone else was in the school. Returning quickly to his classroom, he put away the listening device. As he did, the grip named Ivan entered a nearby room to work on a movie light aimed down at the street. Going closer, Tom peeked in the classroom door at Ivan.

The man's cellphone beeped. He checked the call display before answering.

"Yeah?" he said.

Silence.

"Yeah, I've seen you around."

Another silence.

"That's right," Ivan said. "I want half the fee up front. The rest gets paid when the job is finished. And don't make trouble or you'll regret it."

This time the silence was short.

"Let's meet tomorrow afternoon," Ivan said. "There's a place downtown called the Golden Boy Café. I'll see you there at one."

Soon after, Ivan finished his work and was gone. But Tom remained in his classroom, considering his options. Finally, he made a decision. Tomorrow at one, he'd be in action.

* * *

The wind was cold. Hard snow blew against Tom but he was dressed for the weather, and he felt good. He was seated on a park bench in downtown Winnipeg. Small, jagged icicles hung from the bench; snow covered the small park. Cars passed by, many in need of a wash.

Tom looked down at the Golden Boy Café from the park's highest point of land. Not long before, he'd watched Ivan enter the restaurant and sit down at a window table. The grip was clearly visible.

Ivan was talking to someone. This person was hidden from view but occasionally gestured with a hand. Then the sleeve of a blue *Kid Gangster* parka was visible.

Tom could hear every word spoken by the grip. Beside him on the bench was his portable listening device. "*From now on,*" Ivan said, "*totally ignore me on the set. Pretend we never met. You do your job and I'll do mine.*"

Then there was a muffled response, impossible to understand.

"*Wait a minute,*" Ivan said.

The grip stood up. The words "*Hasta La Vista, Baby*" were displayed on the black T-shirt he wore under his bomber jacket. Ivan quickly drank some coffee. "*Be right back,*" he said.

Using powerful binoculars, Tom watched Ivan in close-up. The man glanced in his direction, then walked away through the restaurant. At the back, he disappeared around a corner. On the wall, a sign read "Washrooms."

As time passed, Tom continued to focus the binoculars on the window. If only the second person would stand up and move around. Tom was hoping to make an ID. It might be someone he knew from the *Kid Gangster* shoot.

Suddenly a powerful hand gripped Tom's parka from behind. He was yanked back hard against the bench. Then the person seized his binoculars and tossed them away.

"Hey," Tom protested, as his binoculars disappeared beneath the snow, "those are . . ."

Tom looked into Ivan's eyes and fell silent. The man's nose was crooked, possibly broken in a fight. Close up, his face was hostile, the scary image of a scary man.

"Spying on me, kid?"

"No," Tom mumbled. "You see . . ."

"I carry defences," Ivan said in an unfriendly manner. "I detected the laser beam from your PLD. Then I spotted you up here with your binoculars. I left the restaurant by the back door and circled around."

Ivan clutched Tom's parka tighter. He leaned close, smelling strongly of garlic. "What's going on?"

"Nothing," Tom replied hastily. Luckily, the grip didn't seem to remember him from the movie set. "Sorry to be a nuisance. I got this stuff for Christmas, and I was just fooling around. I'm sorry, really sorry."

Ivan continued to stare at Tom. "Bother me again, and you're roadkill. Understand?"

Finally, the grip released Tom. "Stupid kids," he muttered, sliding down the snowy hillside. He ran quickly across the street, weaving nimbly past cars and trucks, and returned inside the restaurant.

Tom packed away his gear. He was shivering. He retrieved the binoculars from the snow, then headed for home. He didn't look back at the Golden Boy Café.

* * *

The next day was beautiful. Winnipeg looked its best. The sun smiled down, making diamonds of light glitter in the freshly fallen snow. All along Campbell Street, thick white flakes clung to rooftops and trees. Kids were outside playing with toboggans and sleds, while their parents shovelled walks and driveways. Above, the big sky was a brilliant blue.

The Austen family was walking home following Sunday church services. Liz Austen, aged fifteen, strolled with her dad. They shared the same dark eyes and hair, while Tom was a blue-eyed redhead like his mom. Judith Austen was a criminal lawyer. Her career demanded a lot, but she enjoyed sharing Sundays with her family.

"Oh my goodness," Mrs. Austen said, as they approached their home. "What's a limousine doing here?"

The long black vehicle was idling at the curb, sending clouds of exhaust into the cold air. Across the street, some kids had gathered to stare.

"Dad and I saw that limo before," Tom said. "It was at the airport, collecting Johnny Lombardo and his people. They flew up from Chicago in a Falcon 900EX. It's an awesome jet, Mom."

The door of the limousine opened, and out stepped Sally Virtue. Tom's heart beat faster.

"Tom," Sally said, smiling at him. "It's good to see you again."

He introduced his family. "Liz and Mom returned home yesterday from South Dakota," Tom told Sally. "Liz's team was playing in a volleyball tournament."

"How'd you do?" Sally enquired.

"Second place, out of eighteen teams."

"Congratulations, Liz." Sally turned to Tom. "Remember inviting Johnny to visit? Well, we'd like to accept after all. Johnny needs some downtime, away from all the heavy security and stuff. He gets sick of it, and I can understand."

"That's great news," Tom exclaimed. "But how'd you manage it, Sally? What about his security guards?"

"I figure the home of a Mountie would be a pretty safe place to visit," Sally replied, smiling at Inspector Austen.

"I'm not RCMP, Miss Virtue," he replied. "I'm with the Winnipeg City Police. But we're also pretty good at our jobs!"

Mrs. Austen smiled at Sally. "You and Johnny Lombardo are very welcome to visit. When will we meet him?"

"Any moment now," replied Sally.

She waved at the limousine, and out stepped an elderly man. Shaggy white hair hung from under an old-fashioned Sherlock Holmes cap. The man wore large sunglasses. Leaning heavily on a cane, he shuffled slowly forward. His frayed coat was not suitable for the cold, and his hands were bare.

"Oh my gosh," Tom exclaimed. "It's Johnny in disguise!"

Grinning, Sally pressed a finger to her lips. "Don't say anything until we're inside."

4

In the living room, Mrs. Austen switched on a gas fireplace. Flames popped into life, adding warmth to the scene. There was a big comfy couch and several armchairs. Red and white carnations were arranged nicely in various vases. A large coffee table was scattered with books, including mysteries and biographies, and newspapers like the *Winnipeg Free Press* and *The Globe and Mail*. Above the fireplace, a large painting showed a wilderness scene. Campers sat beside a fire. A loon floated on the lake, a chick on her back.

Johnny removed his wig and sunglasses, then was introduced to Liz and Mrs. Austen. They both seemed starstruck, but who wouldn't be? After all, they were in the company of Hollywood royalty. Grinning, he slapped Tom on the back.

"Today I'm just a regular guy. No security guards, no Assistant Directors pounding on the trailer door, no Zack Sanderson or Jordan Quicksilver making my life a misery."

"Okay to ask some friends over?" Tom asked his dad. "We could play snow football."

"Okay with me," Inspector Austen said.

Johnny looked at Sally. She hesitated, then nodded her approval. "Sure, that's fine."

Before long, several of Tom's friends had gathered in the yard for a game of snow football. Dietmar Oban was there, and so was Mohammed "Mountain" Hussein, the biggest kid in Queenston School. Mohammed's family had recently arrived in Canada and he was already a major hockey fan. Almost daily he wore an oversized Toronto Maple Leafs sweater to school.

Jesse Carveth and Cole Lenton were the quarterbacks. "Hey, Deet-mar," cried Jesse. "Get on the ball, eh? Quit dropping my passes."

On the next play, Jesse faked to Dietmar and then sent a perfect spiral deep to Johnny Lombardo. The boy leapt high for the catch, then followed with a spectacular diving touchdown into a snowbank.

Standing up, Johnny grinned happily at Tom. "This is a most excellent day, *amigo*. Many thanks for the invite."

"It's great that Sally changed her mind."

"Hey, Johnny," Dietmar called. "Watch this."

Dietmar removed his snowy toque, making steam rise into the bitterly cold air from his warm head.

"Wow, Dietmar," the star laughed. "You're on fire!"

Inside the house, the kitchen smelled of freshly baked sugar cookies. They'd been made by Inspector Austen, who wore a chef's hat and an apron with the slogan "Try My Kraft Dinner." He passed around a tray of the mouth-watering treats while Mrs. Austen served hot chocolate with small marshmallows floating on the surface.

The kitchen's "Wall of Fame" featured members of the Austen family, past and present. Tom's favourite picture showed his great-grandparents. They'd managed to get their family to Canada from a country where many people were poor. "When they first arrived," Tom told Johnny, "they lived together in one small space. The family built a house around themselves, one room at a time. They didn't have much money."

Mrs. Austen looked at Johnny. "My granny made her slips from Red Rose flour sacks."

"Ouch," he replied, grinning.

Johnny turned to Tom. "My father's family travelled to America from Calabria. That's in Italy. Grandpa was a stand-up comic. He even opened for Elvis in Vegas." Johnny looked sad. "Grandpa taught me lots before he died. I miss him."

Recovering his composure, Johnny went on, "I grew up in a mansion with movie stars for parents. As a kid I only remember work, nannies, tutors, attending gala openings, and posing for the cameras with Dad and my latest stepmom." Johnny shook his head. "I'm still at it. Always posing for pictures!"

"It sounds like an unhappy life," commented Mrs. Austen.

Johnny responded with a radiant smile. "Actually, Mrs. A., I love it. Fame fits me like a good jacket. That's what Tony Curtis once said. Now there was a smooth guy. Dad worked with him several times."

"Your name is Lombardo," Tom said, "but your Dad's is Stella. What gives?"

"When Dad broke into movies, names like Lombardo got changed. Stella means 'star' in Latin. It took Dad hours of searching through dictionaries to find that name."

"Well," Mrs. Austen said, "Roberto Stella will always be a star to me. What's he working on now?"

"Actually, Dad's retired from acting. So's my mom. They're divorced but still friends." Johnny bit into a sugar cookie. "Dad was a workaholic, movie after movie. Finally he decided to quit. He's in self-imposed compulsory retirement, golfing and gardening." The boy laughed. "I don't know if the retirement will last, but here's hoping!"

"You've got a great life," Tom said, feeling envious.

"There are some downsides," Johnny remarked.

"Yeah?" replied Tom, doubting him. "Like what?"

"Like the paparazzi."

"What's that mean?" Tom asked.

"Paparazzi are photographers. They're kind of like piranhas, you know? They make big money taking pictures of celebrities looking bad, like shopping in baggy clothes or yelling at each other in public."

"I've seen those pictures," Liz said.

Mrs. Austen nodded. "Me too."

"It's ridiculous," Johnny commented, "but they're part of our life. The paparazzi are everywhere. They even jump out of bushes. What's worse is they go after kids with famous parents. It's not fair. Family members should be off limits to the paparazzi. But who cares what I think?" He laughed. "Hey, I'm starting to rant. I'd better be quiet."

* * *

When the footballers left, they proudly clutched autographs from Johnny Lombardo. Many pictures had been taken.

Shortly after, Inspector Austen received an urgent call. Leaving Sally in charge of Johnny, he hurried outside to his police car. Moments later, siren wailing, it disappeared from sight.

Sally went into the kitchen to visit with Mrs. Austen, while Johnny went upstairs with Tom and Liz. The walls of Liz's room featured travel posters, plus some famous young stars, including Johnny himself. He said hello to Liz's budgie, named Stitches, then knelt beside a large cage where a big, healthy hamster was noisily chewing a carrot.

"This is Cuddles," Liz told the star. "I got her at the shelter."

Before leaving the room, Johnny paused at a poster featuring an ultra-famous teen sensation. "She was in a movie with me, playing my sister."

"We own that one," Tom said.

"She's in British Columbia right now, at an eating disorders clinic. She's being treated for anorexia." Johnny shook his head. "Chelsea's parents pushed her into movies when she was a kid. Her life's never been normal. Too much pressure."

Tom glanced at him. "You seem normal."

"That's because my parents are both movie stars. Stardom is a family tradition. One day, maybe, I'll teach my own children how to handle fame. But only if they're interested in getting into the business."

Liz looked regretfully at her watch. "I'm due at my friend Nikki's birthday party. I can't be late." She smiled at Johnny. "What a treat to meet you! Thanks for coming by."

Next stop for the boys was Tom's detective office in the attic. Outside the door, Tom showed Johnny a tiny wedge of paper in the frame. The paper was still in place, meaning no intruder had opened the door. Attached outside was a crude but effective warning: "KEEP OUT! THIS MEANS YOU."

"Don't take that personally," Tom commented to Johnny. "My friends are always welcome." He showed Johnny a collection of wigs and hats and various items of clothing. "These are my disguises."

Johnny was interested in everything, including Tom's poster of Canada's Ten Most Wanted Criminals. "I study faces," he explained, carefully examining the various villains. "I enjoy that aspect of being an actor."

"It's also important to a detective," Tom said.

Johnny took an iPod from his pocket. "This is a present for you, Tom, to thank you for inviting me over. It's got music by me and some guys—one's my cousin. We all live in Malibu. Anyway, our band's called TRM. That stands for Tanned Ruthless Manipulators. I hope you'll like our stuff."

Tom was thrilled to receive the gift. Turning to a bookcase, he grabbed a copy of *Monsterology* by Arthur Slade. "Here's a present for you, Johnny. This guy's a cool author, and I'm proud to say he's Canadian."

Just then, Sally arrived at Tom's detective office to suggest a limousine ride. "I bet you'd love that, Tom," she said, smiling. She turned to a map of downtown Winnipeg displayed on the wall. "Where exactly is the Forks?"

Tom pointed at the place where Manitoba's two major rivers joined together. "The Forks is a big park. There's lots to do there, summer and winter."

"Someone at the set mentioned it," Sally explained. "Apparently, they've got dogsled rides, Johnny. Feel like going? We could take Tom."

"Have you cleared this with Inspector Austen?" he asked.

Sally nodded. "I just phoned him."

"It sounds cool," Johnny said. "I'd better get into my old man disguise."

Tom shook his head, grinning. "I've got a better idea. Let's turn you into a Canadian."

* * *

Soon after, they were travelling downtown inside the limousine. The ride was smooth. Tinted windows kept the trio private. The luxurious seats were white leather. A small refrigerator was stocked with bottled water, juices, and healthy snacks.

Tom felt proud. He'd created a solid disguise for Johnny. On his head was a Manitoba Moose toque and in his hand was a mug from Tim Hortons. Johnny's parka was open; his T-shirt displayed the word "Eh?" in large letters. His backpack featured NHL hockey logos in a colorful design, and he wore snowboots discreetly displaying the maple leaf.

Tom sat on a jump seat, facing Sally and Johnny. Through the limo's back window he saw traffic, but he heard almost nothing because of the thick glass.

"Tell me about the Forks," Sally said.

"It's been a meeting place for centuries," Tom explained. "The Assiniboine River meets the Red at the Forks."

"Interesting names."

"Assiniboine is a First Nations name," Tom explained. "It means 'people who cook by placing hot stones in water.'"

"What about the Red River? Why the name?"

"That's the colour of the clay mud. For a long time the Forks was railway land, then it was declared a National Historic Site. The Forks is like a big park, you know, plus there are stores and a mall and even a TV studio."

Through the back window, Tom studied a silver SUV travelling behind the limo. A low-brimmed cap shielded the driver's face, but two pointed sideburns were visible. Tom was reminded of Ivan, the tough guy from the set of *Kid Gangster*. Was Ivan driving the SUV? The licence plate indicated that it was a rental. Tom scribbled the plate number in his notebook.

As he did, Sally watched. "You collect licence numbers? Is that some kind of a local game with kids? Back home in England, people collect train numbers."

"No, I'm just kind of an amateur detective, I guess. Does that sound strange?"

"Not at all," Sally replied.

Again Tom studied the SUV through the rear window. Sally noticed his gaze and turned to look at the vehicle. Then she asked, "What are the snow sculptures we keep passing, Tom? Is there some kind of carnival happening?"

He nodded. "The city's getting ready for the Festival du Voyageur. It's held every February. The Festival's kind of a treat, I guess, to help people get through winter."

Stepping from the limousine near the Forks, they put on sunglasses. Sally studied a snow sculpture being prepared for the Festival. The artist stood on an aluminum stepladder. Wearing a toque and a yellow parka, the black-bearded man was smoothing down a giant face carved from a huge block of snow.

"This is Aboriginal Woman," he called to them from the stepladder. "Walk around the sculpture and you'll also see Aboriginal Man and a Sun God."

"I like your work," Sally said enthusiastically, as they studied the large faces. "It's a shame it won't last."

"*C'est la vie*," the artist replied with a shrug.

A lookout tower dominated the Forks. Former railway buildings housed an indoor market, shops, and restaurants. Out on the frozen Red River, a horse-drawn sleigh passed by. Above the river loomed the one remaining wall of the St. Boniface Basilica, destroyed by fire in 1978. Snow-lined, shadowed, the enormous wall looked cold and lonely against the pale-blue sky.

Close by, yapping dogs raced around a snowy track, pulling sleds filled with happy kids and adults. The cold air pinched Tom's nostrils and filled his lungs with ice. In the distance was downtown Winnipeg and its skyscrapers; near by stood the railway station. Tom could see the silver passenger cars of *The Canadian*. It was waiting to continue its long journey across western Canada. A shiver passed through Tom as he remembered a scary time in a railway tunnel somewhere in the Rockies.

Their boots squeaked on the frozen snow as they followed a snow-packed pathway through the park. Lots of people crowded the scene. A toboggan bumped past, carrying children with bright red cheeks and shining eyes. Older kids also passed by, holding hockey sticks and figure skates.

At a concession stand they hungrily feasted on sugary Beaver Tails while Tom told Johnny and Sally about the fate of Catherine Saks on board *The Canadian*. Then, feeling full, they wandered toward the dogsled rides. Some of the animals were tethered; the air was noisy with their yipping, yapping, and yelping. Meanwhile, other dogs raced past with sleds behind, fiercely blowing clouds of white steam from their nostrils.

Tom turned to Johnny. "Let's go boarding."

Johnny grinned. "Excellent."

"I'll watch from here," Sally said, "and take some pictures. I'll e-mail them to Roberto."

The boys climbed a nearby snowy hill to a wooden platform, where kids waited with boards for their turn to race down. Here the wind was brisk, fluttering flags above them and making Tom's skin tingle. He pounded his gloved hands together, thinking about Johnny Lombardo at his side. If these kids knew the truth, they'd be so amazed!

Using boards borrowed from a couple of girls who were taking a break, Tom and Johnny enjoyed the slopes. Johnny had surfboarding experience and proved to be a natural.

After a number of runs they returned the boards to their owners. Standing with Tom on the hilltop platform, the star looked down at the nearby dogsled ride. "That looks like fun! Let's give it a try."

Slipping and sliding, the boys descended the snowy slope. At the bottom they posed together, grinning, as Sally took some pictures. "Roberto will love these," she said, studying the camera's screen.

"We're going for a dogsled ride," Johnny said.

"No, wait," Sally exclaimed. "Don't go yet."

"What's wrong?"

"Um . . . remember those sugary Beaver Tails? I've been here freezing, waiting for you guys, and thinking about those Beaver Tails. Come with me, please, and let's get some food. I'm starving!"

"Sounds good," said Johnny. "I'm mellow to anything."

"We could go inside the market and warm up," Tom suggested.

Sally shivered. "My blood's turning to icicles. California here I come, the moment we wrap shooting in Neepawa."

"After Winnipeg, you're filming out there?" Tom asked, as they started walking.

Sally nodded. "I'm going to Neepawa on Wednesday to check Johnny's accommodations. Margaret Laurence lived there. I love her books. She wrote about a stone angel in the Neepawa cemetery. I'm hoping to see it."

"Neepawa is also a First Nations name," Tom told Sally and Johnny. "It means 'the land of plenty.' "

Sally led them past a parking lot filled to capacity. Vehicles cruised slowly, their drivers hoping for a space. Then Tom suddenly focused on a silver SUV parked nearby—it was possibly the SUV that had followed their limousine.

The driver's door opened. Out stepped Ivan. There was an object in his hand. Tom looked at the object, trying to figure it out. Then he heard Sally shout.

"Police," she cried, pointing into the distance. "Look, Johnny! Look, Tom! They're coming!"

Close by, a police car was racing their way. Its siren was shrieking. Ivan leapt into the SUV and took off toward the exit.

The police car stopped and Tom's father leapt out. Running forward, he pointed at his vehicle. "Johnny, get inside immediately. I'm taking you out of here." Highly agitated, Inspector Austen gave the superstar a push toward the car, then turned to Sally.

"This trip shouldn't have happened, Miss Virtue. I didn't authorize it."

"I called your cell, Inspector."

"Leaving a message isn't the same as getting permission. My job is to keep your star safe. You are not helping me."

Sally's cheeks were bright. "I'm sorry," she murmured. Her large brown eyes, downcast, brimmed with tears. "I really messed up, and I'm really, really sorry."

Tom's heart melted for Sally. But Inspector Austen only said "Humph" as he gestured toward the police car. "Get in the car please, Miss Virtue."

Meekly, she obeyed.

Before getting into the car, Tom turned to his father. "What brought you here?" he asked.

"I phoned home," Inspector Austen explained. "Your mother told me about you and Johnny going to the Forks with Sally. I didn't want Johnny in danger, so I raced over here."

Tom told his father about Ivan's connection to the movie shoot.

"That's interesting information," Inspector Austen commented. "I'll follow it up."

"Maybe Ivan was planning to abduct Johnny!"

"Possibly," Tom's father replied. "But we could never prove it."

* * *

The next day, the shoot resumed near the corner of Sargent Avenue and Sherbrook Street in downtown Winnipeg. Several Winnebagos stood in the parking lot of a large food store. Other movie trailers were located on nearby streets.

In this neighbourhood, shops and cafés advertised international goods. Some of the residents were people who had immigrated to Canada from all over the world. Many of them were now standing behind police lines, watching the crew at work. American flags and patriotic bunting decorated the storefronts. Icicles sparkled from the bumpers of old-fashioned cars with Illinois licence plates.

Thanks to his friendship with Johnny, Tom was a guest on the set. The boys stood in line at the craft services truck, waiting their turn. Close by was Ivan, shovelling fries into his mouth. Chewing vigorously, the grip stared at Tom with unfriendly eyes.

A long white limousine approached along Sargent Avenue, then pulled to a stop. A woman hurried across the frozen parking lot toward them.

"Carmen," Johnny said, smiling warmly. "It's nice to see you."

"I'm heading home to L.A.," she said. "I've come to say goodbye."

"Manitoba's too cold?" Johnny asked, grinning.

Carmen shook her head. Pale sunlight touched the copper streaks in her hair. "I'm leaving," she said, "because I'm frightened. Someone's been calling my phone, then hanging up. The police checked for me. The caller's here in Winnipeg."

"But your phone is protected," Johnny said.

"I think maybe my personal codes were stolen. You know, from my purse."

"But who'd do that?"

Carmen shrugged, avoiding Johnny's eyes. "Nobody's perfect, including me. I've let some creeps get too close." Carmen rubbed the back of her neck. "I feel like someone's staring at me."

Tom gazed across the parking lot. The movie's director, Jordan Quicksilver, stood outside a Winnebago. His eyes were on Carmen. Seeing him, she trembled.

"This cold weather," Carmen said, forcing a smile. "It gives me the shivers."

Watched closely by Jordan Quicksilver, Carmen hurried back to the limousine. As it powered away, a second limo pulled to a stop. Its passenger was Sally Virtue. Leaving the limo, she waved hello to Johnny and Tom. Sally was on her cellphone. She walked to Johnny's Winnie and went inside, still talking.

Close by, someone belched loudly. Tom turned, expecting to see Ivan. But a different grip was the guilty party. Ivan was crossing the parking lot toward the Acropolis Restaurant on Sargent.

Tom hesitated, then decided to act. "Johnny," he said, "I'll catch you later."

"No problem," his friend replied, smiling. "Anyway, I'm due back on set."

Tom hurried after Ivan. Talking on his cell, the grip entered the Acropolis. Tom found shelter behind a parked car, then removed binoculars from his pack and focused them on the restaurant.

Sunny travel posters of Greece added bright cheer to the café, as did the checkered tablecloths. There were lots of customers, including some from the movie set. Ivan sat at a table, drinking coffee.

Time passed. Tom remained outside the restaurant, watching Ivan through the binoculars. The grip drummed his fingers on the table. He sipped at his coffee, then looked at his watch.

A car stopped beside the restaurant. Two men were

in it. One was Zack. Using the binoculars, Tom studied the second man, making mental notes on his close-cropped blond hair, scowling green eyes, and down-turned mouth surrounded by unsightly stubble.

Returning his attention to Ivan, Tom felt a shock of fear.

The grip had spotted him.

He was on his feet, staring in Tom's direction. He pointed a finger at Tom, then yelled something.

Time to leave!

Tom took off running. Making for the shelter of a nearby rooming house, he heard the restaurant door crash open.

"Stop, kid!" yelled Ivan.

Reaching the three-storey building, Tom pulled open the outside door and dashed inside. The lobby was small. Two chairs and a small table were chained to the wall. Scattered on the table were newspapers and magazines.

Tom took the stairs fast. Reaching the uppermost hallway he stopped, sucking air into his burning lungs. Somewhere behind a thin wall someone was thunderously snoring.

No sounds came from below.

Cautiously, Tom leaned his head over the railing. He could see to the bottom floor. Nothing moved, not a sound of pursuit was heard, but Tom still waited a long time before leaving the building.

What a close call!

5

Early Tuesday morning, the sky was unusually pale. Tom rode beside Inspector Austen in his police car. They were close to downtown, approaching Winnipeg International Airport through a neighbourhood of attractive homes. Their snowy yards were bathed in the strange, aquamarine light of winter's early dawn.

Tom thought about telling his father how Ivan was making life a misery. But it wasn't just Ivan's fault that there'd been trouble, so Tom decided to let it be.

"We're heading for the Western Canada Aviation Museum," Inspector Austen said. "It's located at the airport."

Tom nodded. "In grade four my class went there, on a field trip."

"I'd forgotten. Anyway, there's a shoot Thursday night at the museum, so I'm rechecking all security arrangements. I thought you'd enjoy tagging along, son. You're always so interested in police matters. Afterwards I'll drop you at your school."

"The museum's a cool place," Tom enthused. "It'll look great in a movie."

"Jordan Quicksilver told me it's perfect for his needs. They've even got genuine check-in facilities from the 1930s—"

"—and that Lockheed Electra 10A," Tom added.

Inspector Austen nodded. "The Electra was Canada's first passenger plane. It's perfect for the movie's time period."

"Will it be flying?"

"I don't think so, but check with Zack Sanderson. He'll be there today, along with Sally Virtue and some other movie people."

The Aviation Museum was located in the airport's original passenger terminal. In the parking lot they met an official named Bill Zuk. A friendly man, Bill had been asked by the museum to work with the movie people.

"In my other life," Bill said, smiling, "I'm an author. My books are about aviation."

Inspector Austen nodded. "I've read several of your works, Bill. I'm very interested in the history of flight."

A black limousine purred to a stop. Freshly washed and polished, the limo gleamed in the pale light of morning. The uniformed chauffeur opened the door for Sally Virtue and Zack Sanderson. Zack wore his blue *Kid Gangster* parka open to the cold. Tom sensed the producer was grouchy this morning. Unshaven, pouchy-eyed, Zack snapped his fingers at an assistant, who'd arrived in a second vehicle. "I need caffeine. Get me a coffee."

A second young woman approached Zack. She was studying the screen of a BlackBerry. "Mr. Sanderson," she said, her breath misting in the frosty air, "I've got a bunch of e-mails that need answering."

"Anything from Mitzi?"

"But of course," the young woman replied, smiling.

As they walked away, talking together, Sally turned to Tom and Inspector Austen. "Zack's girlfriend is named Mitzi," she said. "He got her into the movie business. According to Zack, Mitzi's the next great star."

Inside the museum, Bill Zuk showed them the original facilities. "Passengers checked in here," he explained, "then went outside to board their flight. Everything is vintage. The reception booth, the weigh-in scales. No metal detectors back then, and people smoked everywhere. Even on planes. Things have changed, eh?"

The hangar contained an impressive collection of classic aircraft. Dominating the scene was a McDonnell CF-101 Voodoo fighter jet, but a much smaller craft caught Inspector Austen's eye. "Say," he exclaimed, "is that a flying saucer?"

"That's a life-size model of the so-called Avrocar," Bill said, as they studied the small, circular craft. "Back in the 1950s, the Avro company tried making a real flying saucer."

"Did it work?"

Bill nodded. "The saucer did actually lift off the ground, but only waist-high. The test pilots nicknamed it 'The Flying Hubcap.' Eventually the project was cancelled. I designed this model of the Avrocar myself, for a documentary on the Discovery Channel."

Outside in the cold air, the Lockheed Electra 10A was being prepared for the shoot. The beautiful plane had been built in the 1930s and flown by Trans-Canada Air Lines, which later became Air Canada. On its nose was the Trans-Canada logo, showing the letters TCA over a red maple leaf design. Bill proudly smacked the Electra's body. "This plane looks silver, but it's not. The fuselage is actually highly polished aluminum under a wax coating."

Zack Sanderson looked at Inspector Austen. "For the shoot, we'll change the lettering to Northwest Airlines, which flew into Chicago back then. In the scene we're doing here, a Northwest flight has landed at Chicago for passengers on its way west. Tony Junior is at the airport, where his wealthy uncle is flying out. Once again, Tony begs his uncle to help. Once again, the cheapskate refuses."

Sally shivered in the icy wind. She watched a small plane buzz into the sky from a nearby runway, then pointed toward a fence. "What are those planes parked over there?"

Everyone turned to look at the row of large yellow aircraft with red markings. "Those are Canadair CL-215 water bombers here for servicing," Bill explained. "During the summer they're based up north at places like Gimli and Thompson, fighting forest fires. As you can see, this is a working area of the airport. It's not just a museum."

Sally looked at a parking space reserved for the air

ambulance service. "Does that service operate all over the province?"

"Yes," Bill replied. "There are air ambulances based in different locations. They fly into Winnipeg with seriously ill or injured people." He pointed to a nearby runway. "The jet lands out there, then taxis to our hangar. After that, the patient is transferred to a city ambulance for the ride to hospital."

Zack Sanderson suddenly turned to Bill. "I just thought of something! What if an air ambulance arrives during our shoot?"

"You'd have to stop filming," Bill replied. "But you'd only lose a few minutes."

"In the movie business, sir, time is everything. Couldn't the ambulance circle the airport or something, then land when we're finished?"

Bill Zuk shook his head. "Not a chance! Someone's life could be at risk."

"I guess you're right," Zack grumbled, as his mouth turned down at the corners. Under pressure, the producer tended to sulk.

Sally looked at Bill Zuk. "The crew will be filming near the hangar. Is there any risk to the crew?"

Zack glanced at Sally, annoyed. "The safety of cast and crew is my concern, not yours."

Sally shushed the young producer. "Let Mr. Zuk answer the question."

"Well, Sally, you're right," said Bill. "Should an air ambulance approach the hangar during your shoot, it would pass close to the crew. But it's a very unlikely event."

"Well that's just great," Zack whined. "An accident is all I need."

*** *** ***

Later that evening, Tom received a chance to stand in for Johnny Lombardo on the movie set. Zack Sanderson had phoned to offer the gig. Receiving permission from his parents, Tom eagerly accepted. Although it was a school night, they thought he shouldn't miss the opportunity.

Dressed for the cold, Tom left the house with his dad. "Johnny's regular stand-in has gone home to Florida," Tom explained to Inspector Austen, as they drove toward downtown Winnipeg. "There's a problem in his family. Johnny suggested me as the replacement. Zack agreed, and so did the union. They called it a special case. What a break for me!"

"Is the work difficult?"

Tom shook his head. "Sally explained that I just stand in front of the camera while the crew prepares the lights and sound. Then Johnny replaces me, and does the acting. Apparently I was chosen because I'm the same shape and size as Johnny."

"What about your red hair?"

"I'll be wearing a wig."

Inspector Austen smiled. "I'm proud of you, son. People will be wanting your autograph."

"Not as a stand-in, Dad," Tom grinned, "but maybe someday."

Driving swiftly through the night, they soon arrived at the VIA Rail station downtown. Ideal for a movie shoot about 1937 Chicago, the station had been built for the Canadian Pacific Railway early in the twentieth century.

Under the black winter sky, bright spotlights lit the scene. Big movie trucks lined nearby streets. The most popular was the craft services truck. This evening the CST featured traditional Manitoba foods, including cherry blintzes and blueberry verenekes. Some people were laughing and talking while stamping their feet against the cold. Others moved past with furrowed faces, intensely focused on the task at hand.

Sally Virtue waved from the doorway of the station. As always, Johnny's manager was both beautiful and friendly. "Hello," she said, greeting them. "You'll enjoy this experience, Tom, and bank some serious money." Sally handed Tom a large, blue bundle. "Here's a special present for you. It's a *Kid Gangster* parka."

"Amazing! That was my dream."

Inspector Austen smiled happily at Tom. "You're the lucky one."

"Are you staying, Inspector?" asked Sally.

Tom's father shook his head. "Other officers are in charge of security this evening. I've got some paperwork waiting at the office. Mountains of it, in fact. I'll return later for Tom."

"When Tom's finished," Sally said, "I'll call your cell. I've got the number."

"Yes," Inspector Austen replied. "I remember."

Tom hugged his dad goodbye. He could feel tension in his father's shoulders. "You worry too much, Dad," Tom said. "Try to relax, okay?"

Sally's cellphone purred. Walking away from Tom and his father, she talked quietly to someone. Twice she glanced toward Johnny's trailer, parked near the station. The shadowy area was in near darkness. Tom wondered if Sally was worried about the safety of her young star.

A limousine pulled to a stop. Out stepped the producer, Zack Sanderson. He wore a blue *Kid Gangster* parka. Once again it was open to the cold.

Tom remembered seeing Zack outside the Acropolis Restaurant, where Ivan had been waiting for someone. Had Zack also met Ivan at the Golden Boy Café? Tom needed some answers.

Zack approached, looking sour. "What is it?" he demanded, as Tom stopped him. "I've got no time."

"This will only take a minute."

"Yeah, sure. You sound like my dentist."

"Were you at the Golden Boy Café on the weekend? To be precise, Saturday at 1:00 p.m.?"

Zack Sanderson was looking annoyed. "Where's this leading? Come on, kid, cut to the chase."

Tom bravely pressed on. "At the Golden Boy Café, did you meet with a grip named Ivan?"

No response from Zack. He was staring hard at Tom.

"Please tell me," Tom said with determination, "what is your business with Ivan?"

Shaking his head, Zack walked away.

Sally watched him go, then turned to Tom. "What's going on?"

Tom quickly outlined his suspicion that Zack and Ivan were possibly engaged in some kind of conspiracy. But Sally surprised him.

"Unfortunately," she said, "there's something you don't know. Zack and Ivan are cousins."

Tom's mouth fell open. "Say what?"

"Zack got Ivan work on this movie." Sally looked pensive. "Ivan's recently out of prison. Zack's helping him go straight."

"Oh," Tom said quietly.

They began walking toward the station. "I'm a bit nervous," Tom confessed.

"You'll be fine," Sally replied. "You're much like Johnny. The same shape and size. The technical people only care about that."

A friendly Production Assistant escorted Tom into the enormous, old-fashioned railway station. It hummed with activity. Big movie cameras and hot lights and tall microphone booms dominated the scene.

"Now," said the P.A., "I'll explain the first scene we're filming tonight. Johnny enters the station, stops, looks around. That's it. Later we'll film him outside, arriving at the station. Movie scenes usually don't get shot in order."

In a dressing room, Tom was converted into a Chicago kid from 1937. He put on lace-up boots, knickerbocker trousers, a shirt and tie, and a winter coat of dark, rough wool. Wearing a black wig and makeup applied by an expert from Hollywood, Tom closely resembled Johnny Lombardo. It was an awesome look.

Under bright lights, in the centre of the station lobby, Tom was given a place to stand. "When Johnny films the scene," the P.A. explained, "he'll be wearing the identical outfit to yours."

Tom was asked to stand quietly at a certain place inside the station while the movie crew adjusted various spotlights, made measurements for sound, exchanged information with each other, and generally kept Tom waiting for a long, long time.

Finally the calculations were over. Tom saw Johnny enter the station. Taking off his blue parka, the young star waved hello to Tom.

Several times Johnny was filmed entering the station, his dark coat dusted with artificial snow. Finally Jordan Quicksilver yelled, "Cut." Hoping for a chance to chat with the star, Tom waited patiently while Johnny spoke to Sally Virtue.

"Hey, Tom," said Johnny, coming over at last.

"Hey, Johnny."

As they chatted together, Johnny exchanged smiles with a young background extra, who looked very attractive in her 1930s Chicago schoolgirl outfit. Then he turned to Tom. "Listen, could you help? Sally left some keys in my trailer. She asked me to get them during the break, but there's someone I need to talk to. Would you mind getting the keys?"

"I'd be delighted," Tom replied.

"Cool." Johnny handed Tom a key. "This opens the Winnebago. Apparently Sally forgot her keys in the restroom."

Johnny and the extra fell into conversation. Proudly putting on his blue *Kid Gangster* parka, Tom left the station. Outside, he took a deep breath of the cold night air. It was almost midnight, but the night's shoot was far from finished.

Nearby, someone moved away through the shadows. It was Jacob "Red" Herring, the man who did Johnny's dangerous stunts. Tom hurried past a lineup of trailers both large and small. Above, a few stars twinkled. He'd have loved to just sit in Johnny's trailer for a few minutes, relax, take a break, but Sally needed those keys.

As Tom approached Johnny's "Winnie" he saw the glow of lights behind drawn curtains. The white cotton billowed softly at an open window; someone was inside, lounging in one of the expensive chairs. Tom stood on tiptoe, trying to see into the trailer. The person was Zack Sanderson.

At that moment, a hand appeared from nowhere and a foul-smelling rag was pressed hard against Tom's face. He saw visions of blood-red skies and jagged mountains, then fell into dark shadows and never-ending silence.

6

When Tom awoke, his head was thick. His eyes hurt. He was in darkness. Wherever he was, he was being bumped and jostled, and he was moving fast. Putting out his hand, he touched a glowing fluorescent strip dangling before his eyes. The strip displayed the words "PULL TO RELEASE TRUNK."

Tom was inside a car trunk! If he grabbed the fluorescent strip, the lid would pop open. But he still couldn't escape. The car was going too fast.

He heard traffic sounds, and once the wailing of sirens. Finally the city noises ended and eventually the car stopped. Tom heard a voice. Muffled, it came from inside the car. The speaker was a man, and he was shouting angrily.

"I got the wrong person? Now you're telling me

what? Release him? Not a chance! I'll deal with the troublemaker. Right here, right now."

The words made Tom's hair stand on end. Fear gave him energy. He seized the fluorescent strip. The trunk popped open.

Tom scrambled from the car. The air was cold. Bright stars watched from above. The car had stopped on a quiet country road. In the distance Tom saw small houses with glowing windows. Close by was a dark cemetery where old tombstones leaned crookedly in the midst of snowdrifts.

The driver of the car was Ivan. He was alone. The grip stared in astonishment at the open trunk, then at Tom. He leapt from the car, mouth open, shocked at Tom's escape.

"Stop!" Ivan yelled. "Stop, kid!"

Tom took off running toward the cemetery. The metal gate squealed as he tore it open and raced inside. Adrenaline pumped through Tom, making him move in super-fast time. In the night, dogs commenced to howl. Tom ducked into hiding behind a large marble monument. Crouching low, he scrambled from tombstone to tombstone. The icy snow cracked beneath his feet, loud in the darkness.

Tom dashed across the snow to a low wall. Climbing over, he dropped into the snowy front yard of a small house with a porch. Somewhere in the cemetery, Ivan was crashing through the frozen snow. He was coming in Tom's direction, and coming fast.

Tom ran swiftly up the front porch steps. "Help," he cried desperately, pounding on the door. "Let me in. Please!"

A young man opened the door. He had curly red hair and a frizzy beard. He wore horn-rimmed glasses. In his hand was a newspaper. "Yes?" he asked.

"I need help," Tom cried. "Please, let me in."

"Of course." The man stepped aside, allowing Tom to rush into the house. Then he carefully locked the door. "What's happened? Is someone chasing you?"

"Yes," Tom exclaimed. "I was kidnapped by a man named Ivan. He's a grip on the movie. You've got to phone 911."

The man punched 911 into his phone, then looked surprised. "Hey! It's not working."

Tom grabbed the phone and shook it. But the phone was dead.

"Use your cell," Tom urged.

"I don't have a cellphone."

Then the lights went out.

Looking out the window, Tom saw Ivan. He was in a corner of the yard, beside a power pole.

"He's cut the hydro and phone lines to the house," said the man, sounding frightened.

"We have to do something," Tom said desperately. "If Ivan breaks in, big trouble."

"What's with the old-fashioned clothes? Are you from that movie about Chicago?"

"I'll explain later," Tom cried as footsteps sounded from outside. Tom looked out the window. Ivan was approaching the door. The handle turned slowly one way, then another. Then Tom noticed moonlight shining on car keys. "Yes," he whispered.

A loud thump sounded from the door. Ivan was knocking it down! The young man gazed anxiously at the noise, still clutching his newspaper. Quickly, Tom seized the keys from the kitchen counter and pressed the emergency alarm button.

Outside, a car's loud horn began to HONK HONK HONK over and over and over.

"Brilliant," the young man exclaimed. "Knowing my neighbours, they'll be phoning the police to complain. These people like things quiet."

The thumping stopped. Tom rushed to a window in time to see Ivan racing across the yard. Leaping over the cemetery wall, the grip ran swiftly away.

The man slumped down into a chair and released a loud sigh. "That was horrible." His voice was barely a whisper. "I've never been so frightened."

* * *

Soon after, police arrived. Medics checked Tom and then, sitting in the man's living room, he answered questions. Before long his father entered, looking worried, and joined in the questioning. Tom was able to provide the plate number for Ivan's car, which was from Avis, one of many vehicles rented locally by the movie production company.

Saying goodnight, the young man shook Tom's hand vigorously. "Brilliant strategy, Tom. Scaring him off with the car horn. Congratulations."

Driving home in a police car, Inspector Austen and Tom discussed events.

"The car was probably parked somewhere near Johnny Lombardo's trailer," the Inspector said. "Ivan chloroformed you, then drove you into the country."

"Ivan got the wrong guy. It was really dark outside the trailer. He thought I was Johnny." Tom gestured at his blue parka, and the 1930s costume he wore. "We were even dressed the same."

Inspector Austen nodded. "Ivan may have planned to keep Johnny prisoner and demand a ransom."

"He was talking to someone on his cell. I wonder who?"

Inspector Austen nodded. "That's the big question."

"Will you shut down the movie, Dad? Stop the shoot?"

"I've already talked to the mayor about that. He's afraid of negative publicity for Winnipeg. Producers might be afraid to make movies here. The mayor wants *Kid Gangster* to finish shooting Thursday night, as planned, at the Aviation Museum."

"Will the police still investigate my abduction?"

"Of course, Tom. But we'll keep it secret for now. We're concentrating our investigation on finding Ivan."

"What about the media?"

"We won't say anything until the movie company returns to California. I've authorized this as a security measure."

"Maybe Zack Sanderson will shut down the movie."

Inspector Austen shook his head. "No chance. I swore Zack to secrecy, then told him about your abduction. I said Ivan might have been after Johnny."

"What was Zack's reaction?"

"He brushed off my fears. That man is so arrogant,

but he's got the mayor on his side. Zack knows that the director, Jordan Quicksilver, desperately wants to use the Electra 10A. Quicksilver thinks Thursday night's scenes at the Aviation Museum will be the movie's strongest." Inspector Austen shook his head. "I just don't get it, Tom. Zack Sanderson is prepared to gamble the safety of his young star, just to keep the director happy. What twisted values."

"Jordan Quicksilver movies are very precise in their period detail," Tom explained to his father. "That's one reason why people like them."

Inspector Austen sighed. "Well, tomorrow night's the big hockey game. Johnny Lombardo will be there, dropping the first puck. It's a guaranteed sellout, and a security nightmare."

"Why don't you cancel Johnny's appearance at the game?"

"I tried to, but his people called a meeting at the mayor's office. Johnny was there, along with his heavies. I guess Johnny Lombardo is a hockey nut, because he was some upset." Inspector Austen shook his head. "Johnny got what he wanted. He's going to the game, and so is every available officer. The arena will be crawling with cops. We've got to keep that kid safe!"

* * *

The stands were jammed at the MTS Centre, where the local American Hockey League team, the Manitoba Moose, were playing the Cleveland Barons. As special guests, Tom and Dietmar were rinkside with Liz, in the very best section. With them was Uncle Timothy, wearing his Moose toque. He had a cowbell ready for use.

Tom wore his blue *Kid Gangster* parka. Johnny and his bodyguards sat nearby with the movie's producer, Zack Sanderson. Cameras were flashing from around the stands. Even though Johnny faced the pressure of dropping the opening puck in front of fifteen thousand hockey fans, it was Zack who was agitated. He kept glancing around the stands, then at his watch.

As promised by Inspector Austen, the place was thick with police. Those in uniform nervously scanned the crowd. Tom knew that undercover officers were also present. Kids ran past, taking a look at Johnny. Many wore hockey jerseys displaying the names of their favourite players. Tom looked at the advertising signs along the boards. Their colours were intense under the bright glare of television lights. The air smelled clean and cold.

The Manitoba Moose players burst suddenly onto the ice, receiving a roar of applause accompanied by the clanging of cowbells and the blaring of horns. The arena shook with the noise, vibrating with the raw emotions of the excited crowd.

A red carpet was rolled to centre ice, then a microphone dropped from above on a long wire. Out walked radio personality Al Ferraby to sing the anthems of the two nations. As he began "The Star-Spangled Banner" an American flag appeared on the JumboTron, far above the ice. Johnny solemnly placed a hand over his heart and proudly sang along.

Following the American anthem, Al Ferraby launched into "O Canada" with great emotion. As he sang, Canadian scenes appeared on the JumboTron. Red-coated Mounties rode past on beautiful horses, a young couple climbed the side of a mountain, and then a huge flag was seen, rippling red and white above the Peace Tower in Ottawa. All the while, an electrical charge of excitement vibrated in the crowd as the singer passionately built toward the final top notes of the anthem. By the time he finished, the throng was yelling and whooping in anticipation of the coming action.

Johnny stepped onto the carpet, producing even more excitement in the stands. The noisy fans were watched alertly by every police officer, but not by Johnny's three security guards. They slumped in their seats, scowling. The star had ordered the bodyguards to remain behind. He was embarrassed to be seen with his minders on the ice.

Waving to the crowd, the smiling star walked forward to shake hands with Al Ferraby. He also greeted the captains of both teams, posed for pictures, then dropped the puck to officially start the game.

Moments later Johnny was back, proudly clutching the official puck as a souvenir. "Good times," he exclaimed to Tom and Dietmar. Turning, he called to an assistant. "Get this puck framed for my beach house, okay? I want to remember tonight."

"Sure thing, Johnny."

The game was very fast, featuring great teamwork. Johnny followed the action closely. Then he laughed when the Moose mascot suddenly appeared in the aisle beside him. As the big woolly creature pumped up the crowd, the screen above flashed "MAKE SOME

NOISE! LOUDER! LOUDER!" Nearby, a young police officer watched the mascot warily. She was ready for trouble, hand close to her gun. Then the mascot moved off, and the officer relaxed.

Manitoba responded to the supercharged excitement by putting tremendous pressure on Cleveland. As the coaches yelled orders, the puck flew quickly from player to player. Then a loud *SLAP* from the blue line was followed by the *THUD* of the puck connecting with the Cleveland goalie's pads. Bouncing free, it was scooped up by Dean Anderson of the Moose. He faked, then calmly flipped the puck over the sprawling goalie into the waiting net.

A rolling blast of sound erupted from the jubilant crowd as Dean slid across the ice on his knees, one fist pumping the air, stick held high in triumph. Surrounded by other players, Dean skated to the bench for more congratulations.

When the game ended, Inspector Austen joined them rinkside. "So far, so good," he said to Johnny. "I'm your personal escort leaving the building. Other officers will surround us."

Johnny glanced at Tom, shaking his head. "I get tired of this stuff." Then he snapped his fingers at the security guards, still pouting in their seats. "Come on, earn your money. Protect me."

Inspector Austen turned to Zack Sanderson. "You're going ahead with the shoot at the Aviation Museum?"

Zack nodded. "Unfortunately, I won't be there. I really wanted to watch the Electra being filmed, but I'm needed in Neepawa for a meeting with the Mounties. After what happened at the train station shoot, we'll be upgrading the security for Johnny."

Inspector Austen turned to Johnny Lombardo. "My officers are ready. Let's go."

Johnny smiled at Tom and the others. "Life in the fast lane! See you."

* * *

On Thursday night, the movie company assembled at the airport's Western Canada Aviation Museum. The Lockheed Electra 10A waited proudly on the tarmac, its highly polished aluminum body gleaming under the powerful lights of the movie set.

Jordan Quicksilver was not directing tonight's shoot. Strangely, he was missing from the set. Tom heard some people say that Jordan was ill, while others suggested the neurotic director had major personal problems.

Instead of Jordan, the directing duties were performed by Chris Connolly. Chris was the movie's second unit director. He was responsible for filming scenes whenever Jordan Quicksilver was unavailable.

Once again Tom was the stand-in for Johnny Lombardo. As the crew prepared lights, cameras, and sound, Chris took Johnny away to discuss the next scene. They were watched carefully by Inspector Austen and Johnny's personal trio of heavies.

Many police officers were present, along with private security guards. Video cameras were in place, recording everything. One private company was using an infrared camera as an additional security measure. The camera could see in the dark. If something caused the power to fail, and the set lost its lights, the camera would continue to record the scene.

The shoot went smoothly. Johnny, as Tony Junior, and his evil uncle yelled angrily at each other during the filming, but when Chris called "Cut!" they started cracking jokes together. Joining them, Tom told a favourite. "This barber said to a kid, 'Do you want a haircut?' 'No,' the kid replied, 'I want them all cut.'"

As Tom laughed heartily, Chris approached. "One more take," he said, "then we'll wrap for the night."

"Sounds good," responded the actor playing the cheapskate uncle. Johnny nodded his agreement.

The shoot's First Assistant Director hurried to Chris, looking worried. "We've just heard that an air ambulance is inbound to Winnipeg. It'll touch down in one minute. We have to suspend filming."

"Fair enough," Chris replied calmly. "Move everyone back. We don't want an accident when that ambulance rolls past."

One of the grips laughed. "Just as well Quicksilver is missing tonight," she said. "He'd have flipped at the delay."

As people were herded out of danger, Tom decided to get a hot chocolate from the CST. Walking toward the truck, he saw Johnny's trio of security guards eating doughnuts together. Then their leader opened her cellphone. As she listened, her face creased into a frown. Shutting the phone, she turned to the men.

"Trouble at the hangar. The cops are guarding Lombardo, so we'll take this. Let's go, move it. *Move it!*"

The bodyguards ran toward the hangar. Feeling anxious for Johnny, Tom abandoned thoughts of hot chocolate and returned to the young star's side.

Out in the night, a small jet floated smoothly down to land. On it were the words "Manitoba Emergency Aero-Medical Services." Twin engines whistling noisily, the executive plane made a sweeping turn. Swiftly it rolled in their direction, then suddenly braked to a stop.

The windows of the air ambulance were dark, hiding the pilot from view. Tom glanced toward the hangar, wondering about the city ambulance that was supposed to be waiting for the transfer. No such vehicle was visible.

Johnny Lombardo's cellphone beeped. As he listened to the caller, his face grew serious. He glanced at nearby people, then began edging away.

Suddenly, Johnny broke into a run. He headed straight for the air ambulance. As he did, the door flew open. Out jumped a man. He wore a camouflage jumpsuit and combat boots. In his hand was a silver revolver. The man wore a mask of the famous movie gorilla, King Kong.

Before anyone could react, the man seized Johnny's curly black hair. Twisting it savagely, he dragged Johnny to the plane and stuffed the boy inside. Quickly following him into the jet, the man slammed the door.

It all happened in the blink of an eye. Then the jet was rolling away, engines screaming, quickly gathering speed.

"Hey," Inspector Austen cried, running after the plane. "Hey, come back here!"

The air ambulance was moving swiftly. Within moments it had powered down the runway and lifted off into the night.

Johnny Lombardo was gone.

* * *

Tom was devastated by Johnny's kidnapping. So too, it seemed, was the entire world. The media went crazy, and appeared to speak of nothing else.

Tom discussed his theories with Liz, and even tried out ideas on Dietmar. Police were trying to identify the pilot of the air ambulance. In the meantime, a ransom demand had arrived, and both the RCMP and the FBI were trying hard to track it to its source.

A few days after the kidnapping, the boys were still speculating. They were in the main terminal at the Winnipeg International Airport. With them were Tom's family. They'd come to wish Tom bon voyage. He was going to Hollywood! To his delight, he'd been asked to continue working on the movie. He'd received permission from his parents. This was a great opportunity, and besides, it would give him a chance to keep an eye on some of the crew members, like Zack and Ivan. Maybe he'd be able to find a clue to Johnny's kidnapping in Los Angeles.

Dietmar was deeply envious. "Just because you look a little bit like Johnny Lombardo," he grumbled to Tom, "they're filming you, instead? That's why you're going to California? To shoot scenes down there? Why you, Austen? Why not me?"

Tom shrugged nonchalantly. "I'm just lucky, I guess. Jordan Quicksilver wants me, so I'm going. I'll double for Johnny. But only long shots. I'll be a good distance from the camera. Jordan's got almost everything he needs. The movie will be finished soon. Hopefully

Johnny will get back in time to finish his scenes himself."

"They should use Jacob Herring. You know, Johnny's stunt double."

"Red would never do that kind of work," Tom scoffed. "It's beneath his dignity."

"Are you flying down in the studio's executive jet?"

Tom shook his head. "It's standing by at Johnny's estate in California. In case it's needed for the search."

"Is Sally Virtue going with you?"

"No," Tom replied, "and I'm disappointed. She's already in the States, talking to the media about Johnny."

"Where are you staying?" Dietmar asked.

"At a hotel called the Chateau Marmont. Someone said it's haunted. Uncle Timothy is going with me."

"Mom says his fiancée dumped him. Is it true? How's he taking it?"

"Not well," Tom replied. "Uncle Tim was hoping for kids—he wants to be a family man." Sighing, Tom changed the subject. "The movie company is paying for everything, including our meals. We can order anything off the menu. That's what Zack told Uncle Tim."

"So, they'll release *Kid Gangster*, even if Johnny is history?"

Tom shook his head. "Don't be a fool, Oban. Johnny Lombardo's not dead."

* * *

At the gift shop, Inspector Austen bought Tom a mystery for the trip. He also treated himself, purchasing a DVD of Robert Linnell's *Warriors of the Night*. "This is about Bomber Command in the Second World War. Your great-grandfather was the pilot of a Halifax bomber, Tom. He was on the winning side." Inspector Austen sighed deeply. "I'm going to watch this, and try to stop stressing about Johnny Lombardo."

"I've been thinking about what happened at the Forks," Tom said. "I'm sure Ivan planned to abduct Johnny that day."

"The FBI wants to question Ivan, but he's gone to ground."

"He's disappeared?" Tom said. "That proves my theory that he was the guy in the King Kong mask. They were definitely the same body type."

"The FBI tells me there's been another message from the kidnappers. They've started calling themselves the Red River Gang. They've doubled their ransom demand."

"How much is it?"

"I'm sorry, son. That's classified information."

"Come on, Dad! Be a pal."

Smiling, Inspector Austen shook his head. "Anyway, I'm very glad that your Uncle Timothy agreed to accompany you to California, Tom. I'm sure he'll keep you out of mischief."

"Anything more on the air ambulance?"

"As you know, it crossed the border and landed in North Dakota. It was found empty at a small airfield. Recent tire tracks in the snow were traced to a rental van. It's disappeared, but of course there's an APB on it. The FBI will find Johnny, you can be sure of it."

"How'd the kidnappers get the jet?"

"It was parked on the tarmac at Neepawa Airport.

Someone contacted the pilot by cellphone, said the ambulance was needed to evacuate a patient to Winnipeg. While the pilot was getting ready for the flight, a man in a King Kong mask sneaked on board the jet. He had a gun."

"That guy must have been Ivan."

"Could be," Inspector Austen replied cautiously. "He marched the pilot to an empty office inside a hangar, tied him up, and the air ambulance took off for Winnipeg."

"I'd love to know who was piloting the jet. Any ideas, Dad?"

Tom's father shook his head. "I think we're dealing with amateur kidnappers, son. They're inventing strategy as they go along. Quite frankly, I'm worried for Johnny Lombardo."

Inspector Austen pushed a button at the wood-panelled door of the airport's Executive Lounge. It buzzed open, and they saw Uncle Timothy waiting inside. Tom said his goodbyes, then entered the lounge. It featured expensive leather furniture, private work-stations, hockey on a big screen, plus free food and drinks. Tom felt hungry but didn't get a chance at the goodies. Instead, he and Uncle Timothy were rushed through corridors and breezeways to a waiting jumbo jet. Inside, Zack Sanderson and Jordan Quicksilver lounged in the executive section.

"Timothy," said Zack, "you sit with Jordan. He's an intellectual, like you. You'll enjoy each other." The young producer then nodded at an empty seat. "You sit here, Tom, beside me."

7

As their jumbo jet lifted off from Winnipeg, Tom looked down at the city. He saw the statue of the Golden Boy, perched on top of the Manitoba Legislature, and the Forks, where the Red and Assiniboine rivers joined forces. Then the city was left behind, replaced by the white prairie lands and the communities of rural Manitoba. Northwest of the city, out in that snow, was Neepawa, where the air ambulance had been taken. Who was the pilot of the hijacked jet? Was Ivan wearing the King Kong mask? Tom desperately needed to answer those questions.

He turned to Zack Sanderson. "Where is Johnny? Any ideas?"

The producer lifted his shoulders. "I haven't a clue."

"I've got some news," Tom said, watching Zack closely. "The kidnappers are calling themselves the Red River Gang."

Zack shook his head. "The media will love that name."

"It suggests the kidnappers know Winnipeg," Tom said. "The Red's one of our major rivers."

Zack didn't appear interested. He opened a copy of *Inside Entertainment* and began to read. Sunlight streamed through the window and onto Zack's hand, glittering on a large ring showing an airplane in flight.

"Where'd you get that ring?" Tom asked.

"It's a graduation gift from a school I attended."

"You mean a high school?"

Zack shook his head. "No, a different kind of school."

"What did you learn?"

Ignoring Tom, Zack returned to his magazine. Moments later, he was scowling, like a bear with a sore head. Zack was reading a report about Johnny's abduction. The headline shouted: "Movie to collapse?"

Under his tan, Zack's face was pale. Tiny droplets of sweat beaded his forehead. Seen close up, Zack's hair looked like it was colour-treated. This information could be useful. Tom reached for his pocket notebook, then decided to record the observation later.

"Bad news?" he asked Zack.

"They're speculating, Tom. What happens if Johnny is found dead? They're saying the movie might not get released. Johnny's fans would be offended. They could boycott the movie." Zack stared out the window. "That didn't happen when James

Dean died," he finally said. "Jimmy was a handsome young guy, fairly new to the business but already incredibly popular."

"My cousin Meagan's got a poster of James Dean."

"Jimmy died in the crash of his high-speed Porsche Spyder on a California highway. After his death, the studio rushed his new movie into wide release. *Rebel Without a Cause* was a gigantic hit! Everyone made a mint." Zack rubbed his hands together, relishing the thought. "Polygon Studios will be releasing *Kid Gangster*, you can be sure of that."

Tom seized on this. "Then you think Johnny's dead?"

The young producer shook his head. It was a swift, sharp motion. His hazel eyes narrowed. "No," Zack said vaguely, staring into space, thinking about something. "No," he repeated, this time with strength. "I'm sure Johnny is perfectly safe, and he'll be found alive."

"I watched Sally Virtue on the CBC news," Tom commented. "It was a press conference in Los Angeles about Johnny. She looked upset. I felt sorry for her." He looked at Zack. "Guess what? Sally's meeting our flight. She's driving us to the Chateau Marmont. Apparently it's a heritage hotel. That's where Uncle Timothy and I will be staying."

"Plans have changed, Tom. Sally's doing television interviews this afternoon. She's begging the public to help find Johnny."

"I understand," said Tom, "but I'm disappointed."

Zack gestured at his cellphone. "This morning I received a text from Sally. She asked a favour. You see, I'm staying at the Chateau Marmont myself. When *Kid Gangster* wraps, I'll be heading home to New York."

Zack leaned toward Uncle Timothy. "I'll take you and Tom to the hotel. When I'm shooting a movie in L.A., I always stay at the Marmont."

"Mind if I ask you something, Zack? I heard you were a contestant on 'Survivor.' Is it true?"

Zack grinned. His perfect teeth were Chiclet white. "Actually, that's how I got into the entertainment business. I developed a huge following on 'Survivor.' Lots of people recognized me, even in Thailand when I took a holiday there. You should have seen the e-mails! Bunches of chicks wanted to marry me. It was just amazing." Zack smiled to himself. "Actually, you know, I still get recognized. It's a cool feeling."

Jordan Quicksilver snorted. "I watched that program," he said. "You lied and cheated."

"But that's how the game is played," Zack replied indignantly. "Anyway, it's a shame I didn't win. I could have used the prize. It was a million bucks."

"Everyone needs a million," the director responded. "But personally I wouldn't cheat to get it."

* * *

The big jet descended smoothly toward Los Angeles airport. Zack pointed to a distant island surrounded by the sparkling ocean. "That's Santa Catalina. There's a cool song about that place."

In the distance were the glass towers of downtown Los Angeles. As the jet approached the runway, Tom saw palm trees and industrial buildings and small houses, many with swimming pools of a beautiful turquoise colour. He also spotted several baseball diamonds and the familiar yellow arches of a McDonalds before the big plane lightly touched down.

First to leave the jet were the VIPs from Executive class, including Tom. He was excited to be in California! From the plane they reached a glass-enclosed terminal with palm trees indoors and out. People looked healthy and self-confident. The "Stars and Stripes" hung from above, and the American flag was also seen on clothing and in shops where travellers were purchasing gifts and newspapers and books and music and movies.

As they walked through the terminal, Tom's uncle studied the scene with interest while occasionally saying hello to people passing by. He was youthful, and very handsome with his intelligent eyes and thick, dark hair. Total strangers exchanged smiles with him, and Tom wondered if perhaps his uncle might be discovered for the movies.

Eventually they reached the carousel where the luggage would be delivered. Tom tried to question Jordan Quicksilver about his absence from the Aviation Museum shoot, but Quicksilver hurried away without speaking. The director wore a silver bomber jacket and pulled a small wheeled suitcase. He carried his blue parka from the shoot in Manitoba. They saw him go outside, where Jordan was greeted by a man standing beside a minivan displaying the words "Burbank Flying School." The director jumped into the van and it drove away.

Beyond the terminal's towering windows, palm trees were silhouetted against an intensely blue sky. Their large fronds moved gently in unseen breezes.

People looked so West Coast with their tans and T-shirts, shorts and sandals. On a bench, a man was reading a book entitled *Anything Is Possible in California*.

Attractive young people passed with their luggage. Some gazed around nervously, while others seemed re-laxed. Uncle Timothy glanced at Tom. "They must come from all over the world," he said. "They're hop-ing to become movie stars. The poor kids. What chance have they got?"

"But some people succeed, Uncle Tim. Look at Michael J. Fox. When he arrived in Hollywood from Canada, he couldn't afford a phone to look for work as an actor. He used a pay phone in the street. And he be-came a huge star. It can happen!"

His uncle grinned. "I like your optimism, Tom. You know, I really admire the attitude of your generation. You're going to be great leaders for our society."

Tom smiled kindly at the comment. His uncle fre-quently became sentimental about life.

Standing at the luggage carousel, waiting for their stuff, Tom and his uncle and Zack watched a wall-mounted LCD screen. On it, Sally Virtue was seen. She looked great, as always, but Tom could tell that Sally was tired. Lines of fatigue showed beside her big brown eyes.

Sally was on CNN, telling Larry King about her ef-forts to locate Johnny Lombardo. The famous journal-ist held a document. The camera moved in on the words which were a bit uneven, as though they had been printed in some old-fashioned way, and not with a computer printer.

"This message was delivered today to the Los Angeles office of CNN," Larry King explained. "It's from the Red River Gang. Someone delivered it to our front door, then fled on a motorbike." On a grainy videotape, a bike and rider were seen escaping. They were shadowy shapes, moving fast. To Tom, the bike looked Japanese.

Sally leaned forward in her chair. "What's the message say, Larry?"

"If the Red River Ransom isn't paid, Johnny Lombardo will die."

"But that's barbaric! I'm shocked and appalled. Larry, the police, the FBI, the . . . I don't know." Sally slumped in her chair, totally disheartened.

Larry King shook his head in sorrow. "I don't understand these kidnappers," he told his viewers. "Roberto Stella mortgaged his Malibu estate to pay the ransom. Then this gang of thugs double-crossed him. They now demand much more money. Roberto has pleaded for time to finance this new ransom demand. He's devastated. All parents feel his pain, feel his sorrow."

Hunching forward, Larry King gazed with intensity at the camera. "More later, but first, our sponsors."

Tom felt anxious for Sally. "I'm worried," he said to Uncle Timothy. "She could be the kidnappers' next victim."

"But why? Sally's not wealthy."

"No, but now she's famous. Plus, she's trying to find Johnny. That could make her a target."

"I suppose it's possible. But still—"

Uncle Timothy was interrupted by a loud cry. Running toward Zack, arms outstretched, was a beautiful young woman. People turned to stare—in a terminal filled with eye-catching faces, hers was outstanding.

"Mitzi," Zack said. "Great to see you, babe."

Mitzi had large blue eyes and attractive blond hair streaked with pink. Her earrings were also pink, and so were her sneakers. Mitzi was dressed casually in white jeans and a T-shirt displaying a heart containing the name Bel Air. Meeting them, her eyes lingered for a moment on Uncle Timothy. Then she focused her attention on Zack as he immediately began discussing her career.

"I've got a photographer booked for later today," he told Mitzi. "I need more publicity shots for overseas investors. Bring that bikini I got you—the pink one." Zack turned to Uncle Timothy. "I'm raising money for a movie to star Mitzi. She'll be so beautiful on screen, and we'll be very rich." His eye dropped in a wink at Mitzi. "Right, babe?"

"Yeah, sure," she mumbled, avoiding his gaze.

As soon as they made their way outside, they knew they were in California. The sun beat down hard. Everyone slapped on sunglasses. "Warm air," Uncle Timothy said with pleasure.

"Good grief," Tom exclaimed, "it's so hot!" Sweat was forming on his skin. "But it's only February."

"We're having a heat wave," Mitzi said. The lenses of her pink-framed sunglasses were shaped like two hearts. In the sunshine, Mitzi's hair radiated beauty with its shades of gold and auburn.

As they waited for the limousine to arrive, Zack made phone calls while Mitzi and Uncle Timothy laughed together about something. Tom stood very still, trying not to burn energy. The heat was almost unbearable.

Finally the limo pulled up. Tom took a picture of Mitzi and then everyone climbed gratefully into the air-conditioned interior. Soon they were sipping ice-cold Pellegrino water as the limo purred away from the terminal building. Curious about everything, Tom stared at a large and unusual sculpture formed from the letters LAX.

Mitzi smiled at him. "That's the code for Los Angeles Airport."

Before long, the limo was humming along a freeway many lanes wide. Palm trees grew beside the road; beyond them, Tom saw office towers, apartments, and houses. Nearly every building displayed the "Stars and Stripes." All kinds of vehicles zoomed past—fancy cars low to the pavement, motorcycles with big handlebars and lots of chrome, limousines with various communications aerials, and many convertibles.

Uncle Timothy and Tom sat on a jump seat, facing Zack and Mitzi. The heart-shaped sunglasses were perched on her blond locks. Mitzi was cuddled into the young producer, but he didn't seem interested. Zack was making a cellphone call.

"That's right, man," he shouted, "and it's pink. You're gonna love the pix! I'll e-mail them, as soon as we've received your investment. Believe me, man, this movie will be boffo. You'll be making *mucho mucho* big bucks. Mucho!"

Zack ended the call and started another. Moving away from him, Mitzi looked at Tom. "I heard you witnessed the abduction, Tom. You're pals with Johnny, right? He mentioned you in his Winnipeg blog. But you probably knew." Mitzi's large eyes were the colour of a perfect summer sky. She turned them on Tom's uncle. "What is your occupation, Timothy?"

"I'm with Canada's number-one bank," he replied proudly.

"That's good," Mitzi said. "A bank is secure." She lowered her voice. "Let me give you some advice, Timothy. Stay in banking. You're attractive, you could get into movies, but don't. Okay? People will say anything, just to get you into the business. Listen to me— they're liars!" Mitzi gave a guilty look at Zack, but he wasn't paying attention. He was still on the phone.

"Of course she can act," Zack was saying. "She's just finding her chops, that's all. Be patient."

"I must say," Uncle Timothy commented to Mitzi, "you are the perfect movie star. You look like an angel, you're so beautiful."

She blushed at the compliment. "But I'm not a good actor, Timothy, and it's so difficult! All these people watch from behind the camera, the grips and everyone. When I miss a line, they shake their heads and makes faces. Then I get even worse!" Mitzi's large blue eyes filled with tears. "It's just awful."

"Then why are you doing it?" There was gentle concern in Uncle Timothy's voice. He reached out to Mitzi. Then he changed his mind and drew back his hand.

Mitzi leaned close to him. Zack continued to talk on the phone, totally ignoring them. "I got into this," she said quietly, "because I've always longed to make a difference in the world. Zack offered me stardom. I figured I could make things happen as a celebrity. Kind of like Princess Diana was an activist about AIDS and stuff like that."

"How'd you meet Zack?" Uncle Timothy asked.

"I was working in a Dairy DeLite near my old high school. Zack was on a shoot. He came in. We got talking."

Mitzi wiped away a tear. "Stardom isn't working out. Let's face it, I just can't act. Besides, this pink look is totally wrong. It's fine for some people, but not me. Pink was Zack's idea."

"Then what's your favourite colour?"

Mitzi smiled. "Green."

"Me too." Uncle Timothy gazed fondly at her. "So, what would make you happy?"

Mitzi cast down her eyes, then glanced shyly at him. "Being a mom," she said quietly. "That's my number one dream."

"It's a nice one," he said.

Mitzi smiled. "You're amazing, you know. It's like we've always been friends, like I could tell you anything."

"Perhaps we were in love," he responded, "in some other lifetime."

Mitzi reached to touch his hand. "That sounds so nice."

Zack snapped shut his phone. "We're arriving at the Marmont. Take care of my luggage, Mitzi. Tip the driver, but not a lot. I've told you before, you're too generous."

The main building of the hotel looked pleasingly old-fashioned. The air was heavy with the scent of tropical blossoms, and palm trees were everywhere. They looked so exotic to Tom's Canadian eyes!

Small cottages occupied the grounds of the hotel. Tom and his uncle were assigned one, not far from another occupied by Zack Sanderson. Inside their cottage, Tom and Uncle Timothy discovered a kitchen, a living room, two bathrooms, and two bedrooms. Switching on CNN, they learned that the search for Johnny and the kidnappers had spread out from North Dakota. Mention was made of the Red River Ransom, but the precise demand was not disclosed.

"I wonder where Johnny Lombardo is," said Uncle Timothy.

Their conversation was interrupted by knuckles on the outside door. To Tom's astonishment, standing on the porch was May-Lin Chan. The young movie star was grinning.

"Hey, Tom, I'm your L.A. guide. I got a text from Sally, asking if I'd show you around. You're expected at the studio tomorrow, but she says that today you're free."

"Totally cool," Tom exclaimed.

May-Lin asked Uncle Timothy to join the excursion, but he politely declined. "I've got e-mails waiting," he said, glancing at his laptop, "and then I'll go to the pool for a swim."

Tom opened his suitcase. "Say, May-Lin, I brought special-issue surfing shorts from Winnipeg. Any chance we could find a beach somewhere?"

* * *

May-Lin's vehicle was an H.E., meaning a Hybrid Electrical. It was sleek and low to the ground. With May-Lin at the wheel, the H.E. zipped through the busy streets of the huge metropolis. Tom stared at the people, the shops, the cars—it was all so exotic.

Reaching the heart of the city, May-Lin parked the H.E. "This is called the Walk of Fame," she told Tom. "See all those people, outside Grauman's Chinese Theatre?"

"They're looking at the sidewalk. What gives?"

"Over the years, famous stars have pressed their hands and feet into wet concrete here. They've also written their autographs."

Tourists crowded around the concrete hollows, having their pictures taken. "Here's Lassie," said May-Lin, pointing at paw prints in the concrete.

Tom was studying another set of prints. "These belong to Lucille Ball. Mom's got all her shows on DVD."

Enjoying themselves, the pair wandered the streets of downtown Los Angeles. Through a gate they stepped into a small cemetery called the Westwood Memorial Park. It was cool and restful, with high walls protecting against city sounds. "Most tourists don't know about this graveyard," May-Lin explained. "Many movie celebrities are here, including one of the most famous stars of all—Marilyn Monroe. Every day, without fail, flowers are delivered to Marilyn's crypt. It's been happening for decades now."

May-Lin and Tom drank fresh-squeezed orange juice at a sidewalk café. Young people were everywhere, yakking on cellphones, laughing with each other. People were dressed for comfort in surf shorts, patterned tops from Hawaii, baseball caps, and straw hats. Most wore sunglasses.

"What a scene," Tom exclaimed to May-Lin, after a deep swallow of the delicious, cold juice. Music thundered from a nearby music store, sounding good to Tom. "If I wasn't so worried about Johnny, I'd be having the perfect day."

May-Lin patted the back of his hand. "You're a good friend to him, Tom."

He reached for his wallet. "I've got something to show you. It's a picture of us together."

The photo of May-Lin and Tom was taken near Johnny's trailer during the shoot in Winnipeg. Two grips were seen in the background. "This guy," Tom said, pointing, "is Ivan. He's disappeared. I think he was wearing the King Kong mask."

May-Lin studied the photo. "I recognize that T-shirt Ivan is wearing. It's from a tattoo parlour called Jake's Place. Out at the Santa Monica Pier."

Tom was amazed and thrilled. "But, May-Lin, that's a fantastic lead! Listen, can we drive to Santa Monica? Right now? I want to check this out."

8

The enormous city seemed to never end—stores, palm trees, gas stations, apartment buildings, malls, restaurants, malls, more malls. Frequently they caught sight of the famous Hollywood sign, located high on the side of Mount Lee.

"Originally," May-Lin explained, "that giant structure said 'Hollywoodland.' It was made from telegraph poles. The sign was built in 1923 to advertise a new housing development."

They passed a small airfield, where single-engine planes buzzed into the sky. Tom thought of the Winnipeg airport, and the bitterly cold night when he'd first met Johnny Lombardo.

"That guy Ebenezer," he said to May-Lin, "can he be trusted?"

"You mean the pilot of Johnny's jet? I've heard he's an okay guy. Has anyone told you Ebenezer's story?"

Tom shook his head.

"Ebenezer's from England. He won Olympic gold in weightlifting, but they took away his medal."

"How come?"

"Ebenezer made a stupid choice. He got into illegal steroids. He was caught. Then, things got worse. The steroids produced blood clots in his legs, and he lost them both. They had to be amputated."

"That's horrible."

May-Lin glanced at Tom. "Ebenezer then trained as a pilot. Eventually Sally got him a job, flying for Polygon Studios."

Tom grinned. "That's just like Sally. She's so kind."

"That chick's going through a rough time," May-Lin said. "She was a great manager for Johnny, but now she's dumped. That's why Carmen flew to Winnipeg, just to tell Sally in person. When Johnny is found, and *Kid Gangster* wraps, Sally is finished as his manager."

"But she's stayed loyal to Johnny," Tom commented, feeling indignant. "Look how hard she's working to find him." Tom shook his head. "May-Lin, I'm so worried about her."

"How come?"

"Trying to find Johnny may put Sally at risk."

"Let's hope not."

The seaside community of Santa Monica seemed a relaxed place. They saw attractive older homes with their own gardens, and lots of pleasant shops. The sidewalks were busy with people enjoying another perfect day. Palm trees moved in warm breezes and flowers bloomed everywhere.

Approaching the ocean, Tom sniffed the delicious breezes. "Smell the salt," he said, grinning at May-Lin.

They parked the H.E. near the beach and walked to the famous Santa Monica Pier. "It's party central," May-Lin said, smiling as Tom stared at all the young people.

Very wide, the pier extended far out over the ocean. On the huge structure, palm trees swayed, and a Ferris wheel revolved as its riders screamed with pleasure. The afternoon sunlight glittered from the waves rolling ashore. Gulls swooped in the air currents, or explored the wet sand along the shore. On the beach, people lounged under large red and blue umbrellas. The day was golden, and so were the lucky ones enjoying the sand and the sea.

On the pier, music was everywhere. Multi-coloured helium balloons were attached to shops and floated above in the sunshine. People were pricing surfboards and souvenir T-shirts, cellphones and deck shoes. Kids rode a merry-go-round while their parents captured every moment on hand-helds. Lots of food was for sale, and Tom spotted a Playland arcade with loud games and players. There was so much happening! He couldn't take it all in.

Some people smiled at May-Lin, recognizing her, and a few said hello. Weaving through the noisy crowd, she led Tom to Jake's Place. The tattoo parlour occupied a small, open-sided tent. Beyond, the ocean sparkled. Souvenirs were for sale, and Tom immediately spotted a T-shirt identical to that worn by Ivan.

Jake was an aging beach boy with bushy white hair and a deeply wrinkled leathery tan. His Hawaiian shirt featured large red flowers and sailboats on a blue sea. Jake was listening to surf music. He was busy, applying a multicoloured dragon to a young woman's shoulder, but he paused to study the photo of Ivan.

"Sure, I know this guy. Folks call him the Pier Rat. For years he hung around here. This place was his home. He knows everything about it. Then he got into trouble with the law and disappeared."

"You tattooed Ivan?" Tom asked.

"Sure thing," Jake replied. "I put a butterfly on his neck. It seemed a strange choice for such a tough guy."

"It's a good way to invite a fight," Tom commented. "Listen, have you seen Ivan lately?"

"Nope," Jake replied.

As they walked away, Tom shook his head. "My third-degree needs work. We didn't get much."

"Placing Ivan at this pier is a good start to your investigation," May-Lin responded. "Let's try the Ferris wheel. Maybe we'll see Ivan from up there."

Unfortunately, they didn't spot the suspect. Nevertheless, they enjoyed the ride. The view of distant mountains was spectacular. Far below, white waves curled ashore. A powerful motorboat approached from the distance, then disappeared beneath the vast pier.

"You know," Tom said, enjoying the sparkling waves, "Pacific means 'peaceful.' This ocean lives up to its name."

May-Lin showed Tom family pictures stored on her phone. "Here's my favourite cousin," she said proudly about a young girl with long black hair. Displayed on the screen was the name "MeiXia."

"How's that pronounced?" Tom asked.

"Maysha," May-Lin replied. "It means 'beautiful summer.'"

Back with the vibrant crowds, Tom and May-Lin showed the picture of Ivan to several people without any results. Then they paused where a sidewalk artist was hard at work. A pretty young woman was paying for her portrait. She seemed pleased with the results.

"It's for my mom," she told them, "back home in Utah."

Tom showed his photo to the artist. "Do you know this guy?"

She nodded. "That's the Rat. It's a strange thing—there's a speedboat he always used, and I saw it today. After all this time. It went under the pier."

"Is anything down there?"

"The ocean, of course," the artist replied, "but there's also dry land. I once explored an abandoned boathouse under the pier, but it was just full of junk."

"What were you expecting?" Tom said, smiling. "Buried treasure?"

The artist laughed. "That's exactly what I was hoping for!"

Tom thanked her.

"May-Lin," he said, as they walked away, "let's check out that boathouse."

They left the partying crowd behind and went down to the beach in the direction the artist had indicated. To the right, they saw people taking it easy on the golden sands. To the left was the deeply shadowed underbelly of Santa Monica Pier.

The deck was supported by large wooden pilings. Sunshine slanted through the murky light beneath. The thin, golden beams revealed wet sand and clumps of seaweed. It clung to exposed boulders and the pier's wooden pilings.

At the nearby shore, a motorboat was tethered to a small dock. Above the waterline was an old wooden building.

"That's the old boathouse," May-Lin said. "Are we going inside?"

Tom nodded. Cautiously they approached the shabby structure. It had a door and two small windows. The shingled walls were stained green.

Tom tried the door. It creaked open.

Inside, their eyes slowly adjusted to the dim light. Sunlight struggled through the filthy windows, illuminating abandoned rowboats and surfboards, oars and bits of machinery, and old rope hanging in loops from the ceiling. Cobwebs were everywhere.

From nearby came a sound. Tom and May-Lin followed the noise, moving cautiously forward past old boats and piles of rusty machinery. Ahead of them, light seeped past a makeshift wall constructed from driftwood.

Behind the driftwood, a candle glowed. Tom and May-Lin saw a workbench. On it was an old-fashioned desktop printing press. Ivan stood beside the press, examining a document. Tom recognized the print style. He had seen it before, when CNN had broadcast a close-up of the message from the kidnappers.

They had to alert the police immediately! Signalling May-Lin, Tom pointed to the distant door. She nodded, and they scuttled quickly toward it.

Unfortunately, as it opened, the door produced a loud creak. Tom and May-Lin exchanged a frightened look, then ran from the boathouse.

Outside, Tom turned urgently to May-Lin. "Use your cellphone! Call 911."

May-Lin tried the phone, then shook it. "No signal."

"Quickly, run to the beach. Ask someone to phone for help. I'll stay here and keep watch. I'm hoping Ivan didn't hear that noise. If we're lucky, he'll be inside when the police arrive."

May-Lin raced away.

In the distant sunshine, people were enjoying the beach. Tom saw kids playing, and seagulls on the wet sand at the water's edge. Feeling very alone in the darkness beneath the pier, Tom studied the speedboat at the nearby dock.

Then he turned his attention to the boathouse. Moments later, Ivan's face appeared at a window. He looked around suspiciously.

Tom listened desperately for sirens, but he heard nothing except the happy sounds of music and laughter from above on the pier. Then the door of the boathouse opened. Ivan stepped out. In the dim light, his bony face looked especially scary.

Tom crouched low, heart pounding.

Then someone cried his name. "Tom Austen!"

Turning, Tom saw Zack Sanderson. Wearing a bathing suit, the young producer was running toward Tom. "Don't do anything foolish," he yelled.

Tom looked toward the motorboat. Ivan had run to it and was starting the engine. Before Tom could go in pursuit, Zack grabbed his arm.

"Leave Ivan alone," he ordered. "Let the police deal with this."

"But he's part of the Red River Gang! We mustn't let him escape."

"It's too late now," Zack replied, as the motorboat roared from the pier's dark recesses into the sunlight.

"Where'd you come from, Zack?"

"I was on the beach with Mitzi. May-Lin found us. I called 911, then came after you. I ordered Mitzi to stay with May-Lin, out of harm's way." Zack shook his head. "Too bad about my cousin. I tried to help Ivan, got him work as a grip, but he's just plain bad."

Soon the police arrived. They interviewed Tom and May-Lin at length. "Apparently," one officer told them, "Ivan came here to print ransom messages. He used an old hand-powered printing press. We also found a Kawasaki, hidden in the boathouse. We're pretty sure it's the same bike that appeared on the security video at CNN headquarters, when the first message was delivered from the kidnappers."

"Where could Ivan be hiding?" Tom asked the officer.

She shrugged. "There are a million and one possibilities."

"What about Johnny Lombardo? I don't suppose you found him in the boathouse?"

"There's no sign of Johnny himself," the woman replied, "but we did find a King Kong mask, and I'm guessing it was used in the kidnap. Our C.S.I. team will take over. They may find more."

"Let's hope so," Tom said. "The gang could get desperate. They'll be worried now."

* * *

Back at the Chateau Marmont, May-Lin said goodbye to Tom. Soon after, he was travelling in a limousine with Uncle Timothy. They were heading for Malibu, an upscale community for the very wealthy. Malibu was home to Blue Paradise, the oceanside estate of Roberto Stella and his son, Johnny Lombardo.

"We're invited to visit," Uncle Timothy explained, "because of your friendship with Johnny. His father is anxious to meet you, Tom. He wants to talk about Johnny, show you some scrapbooks. I imagine it'll be good therapy for him."

The quiet streets of Malibu were shaded by heavy tropical plants. Palm trees swayed above. No houses were visible. The estates of the rich lay behind high brick walls and large gates. The driver looked at Uncle Timothy in the mirror. "We're approaching Roberto and Johnny's estate. It's around the next corner."

The limousine suddenly swerved as a sports car approached from behind, then raced past. At the wheel was someone wearing a baseball cap and a silver jacket. Tom was unable to identify the driver. A woman was in the passenger seat. Tom glimpsed hair stylishly streaked, and silver earrings, before the car disappeared around a corner.

Turning the corner, they saw the car again. It had stopped, and the woman was getting out. Now Tom recognized her. "That's Carmen Sanchez," he said to his uncle. "She's engaged to Johnny's father."

Carmen looked elegant, as always, but she also

looked annoyed. She shouted something at the driver
of the sports car, then slammed the door. Tires screeching, the car leapt away.

Carmen watched it go, then hurried toward a heavy
gate protecting what Tom presumed was the Roberto
Stella estate. People immediately emerged from cars
parked along the street and ran toward her. They carried notepads and shouted questions about Johnny.
Others crowded aggressively around Carmen, taking
pictures from every angle.

"The paparazzi," Tom exclaimed.

The limousine driver leaned on his horn, giving the
mob a scare. "Move aside," he yelled, "we're expected
here."

Uncle Timothy opened his window. "Hi there," he
called to Carmen. "Are you going in? Would you like a
ride?"

"Yes," she replied gratefully, jumping into the limo.
"I've misplaced my entry key." The journalists continued to shout questions through the window, but she ignored them. "They're human jackals," she said to Tom
and his uncle. "Feeding on the misery of others."

Stopping at the gate, the driver faced a video camera. He answered some questions, then the gate swung
open. The limo rolled into the grounds, leaving the
noisy rabble behind.

Carmen turned to Uncle Timothy with a lovely
smile. "Thanks for the rescue," she said, extending her
hand in greeting. Silver bracelets jingled at her wrist.
Then she glanced at Tom. "Hello again."

Uncle Timothy told Carmen about their invitation to
meet Roberto. The limousine followed a paved drive-

way past endless lawns of velvety green and many colourful gardens. Water rose from large fountains, and Tom saw white statues situated along pathways.

"Those are Greek gods," Carmen explained.

At last the limo purred to a stop beside a two-storey mansion. It was white, with a red-tiled roof. Several electric golf carts were parked near the front door.

They stepped from the limousine. Somewhere nearby, surf could be heard rumbling ashore. Above the mansion, gulls rode the wind.

The front door opened. Out stepped a man wearing a butler's uniform. He informed Carmen that her fiancée was asleep and didn't wish to be disturbed.

Carmen turned to Tom and his uncle. "Let me check on Roberto," she said, then went inside with the butler.

Moments later, they heard the sound of an approaching vehicle. It was a luxury convertible, yellow in the sunshine with lots of gleaming chrome. Zack was at the wheel, Mitzi beside him.

Stepping from the car, Zack rang the front bell. "I'm here to see Carmen and Roberto," he told the butler, forcing his way past the man.

As the two disappeared inside, Mitzi shook her head. "Zack is way too assertive," she commented. Then she smiled happily at Tom's uncle. "How lovely to see you again, Timothy. Last night I dreamed about you, but I've forgotten what happened." She beamed her big blue eyes at him. "Maybe just as well!"

Tom smiled at Mitzi. "Blue Paradise is quite the place."

"I've got a great idea," she said. "Let's go for a tour. We'll use a golf cart."

Minutes later, they were underway. Mitzi was at the controls, with Uncle Timothy at her side. Tom was in the seat behind. The cart zipped smoothly along the winding paths of the estate. Several workers were tending to the splendours of Blue Paradise.

"The estate covers more than twelve acres," Mitzi explained. "Long ago, Blue Paradise belonged to a hugely wealthy movie producer. He was Roberto's great-uncle, and he loved to throw parties. Imagine all the stars of Hollywood gathered on these lawns, laughing and talking together. That's what used to happen. Then the producer died, and Roberto took over. Things are much quieter now. The place has a tennis court modelled on Wimbledon, plus an Olympic-size swimming pool."

Eventually they reached the cliffside. Mitzi stopped the golf cart at the top of a road. It curved down to the distant beach. Big waves rolled ashore, throwing white water into the air. The deep booming of the surf came clearly to their ears.

"Down there," said Mitzi, pointing, "is Johnny's beach house. It overlooks the water."

She put the golf cart into gear. Soon they saw open fields and distant hills. Behind a wooden fence and gate was a small airfield. Tom saw a hangar, parked planes, and a long, paved airstrip. "This airfield belongs to Roberto and Johnny," Mitzi explained.

The hangar's big door was open. Tom saw a sleek executive jet. "I remember that plane from Winnipeg. Dad and I got to see inside."

"The jet's here on standby," Mitzi explained, "in case it's needed for a rescue."

A wheelchair bearing a bald man rolled out of the hangar's inner shadows. Tom recognized him. "There's the pilot, Ebenezer Smith."

As they returned along a shaded pathway in the direction of the mansion, Tom noticed another golf cart in the distance. Carmen was at the controls. Seeing them, she immediately changed direction and disappeared into a thick stand of trees.

Back at the mansion, Mitzi offered to show them the greenhouse where Roberto grew prize orchids. Uncle Timothy eagerly accepted, but Tom declined. "Would it be okay," he asked Mitzi, "to try driving this golf cart?"

"Of course," she replied.

Chatting happily together, Mitzi and Uncle Timothy disappeared around a corner of the mansion. The moment they were gone, Tom started the cart. Soon he was rolling through the grounds of the estate, in search of Carmen. Why had she avoided them?

Eventually Tom came to an eight-car garage with living quarters above. Another golf cart was parked outside. Leaving his cart, Tom cautiously approached the garage. It had several large windows. Looking in, Tom saw Roberto's collection of classic cars.

Opening a side door, Tom stepped nervously into the garage. He smelled oil and gas and rubber. Then Tom heard a boy's voice. It came from somewhere above.

Johnny's voice!

What amazing detective skills—Tom could scarcely believe it. He listened to the voice. Yes, for sure Johnny Lombardo was speaking. Tom stared at the ceiling, uncertain what to do. He should call the LAPD, let the locals deal with the matter. But all he had was a suspicion. It needed confirmation.

Tom heard a second, muffled voice. Glancing around the garage he noticed stairs leading up. Tom began climbing the stairs.

9

At the top of the stairs, Tom cautiously opened a door. He saw curtains billowing at an open window, sofas and armchairs, a desk, a computer—

—and Carmen.

Seated on a leather sofa, Carmen was watching a movie. It was a remake of *Treasure Island*, starring Johnny Lombardo. That was the voice Tom had heard!

Tears were streaming from Carmen's eyes. Seeing Tom, she grabbed for a Kleenex and dabbed at her eyes.

"What's going on?" she demanded.

"Um . . ."

"Are you investigating me? Zack was saying you're a detective. Is that right?"

Tom nodded, feeling foolish. "I'm sorry to intrude. I, um, I . . ."

"What brings you here, Tom?"

"I saw you on a golf cart. You seemed to avoid us, so I thought . . ."

"You thought I was guilty of something?" Carmen smiled. "That's so cute. But you're right, I did scurry away. I wasn't feeling social." She turned off the movie. "Sit down, have a visit." She wiped away tears. "I'm feeling sad about Johnny. I'm so worried, but I can't let Roberto know. I save my tears for here."

Tom looked around the living quarters. The space was comfortable, with tropical flowers in vases and lots of books on the shelves. A collection of movies included all of Johnny Lombardo's hits. Seeing the familiar titles hit Tom hard. Like Carmen, he harboured deep fears for Johnny.

"I hope he's okay," Tom said, feeling choked. Then he tried to change the subject. "Who lives here?"

"I do," Carmen replied. "It's my temporary home, until I marry Roberto. He wanted to live together, but I said no. It's marriage or nothing, that's what I told him. My Nona—my grandmother—gave me that advice. She's smart—I listen to her. I'm living here until I tie the knot with Roberto."

Carmen poured ice-cold spring water for Tom. "The kitchen is small, but it's functional."

"Where are you from?" he asked.

"Oklahoma," she replied. "My friends all got married. Instead I took the bus out of there. I came to California and worked hard. I qualified as a pilot but eventually gave it up. Then I got into the movie industry. It's a tough world, but I love it."

"How'd you meet Roberto?"

"When the deal was announced for *Kid Gangster* a party was held at Polygon. Johnny's proud papa was there. We met, and a friendship was born."

"Now you're getting married. Congratulations."

"Thanks, Tom. You're very gracious, just like your uncle."

Saying goodbye to Carmen, Tom went downstairs. He looked at his watch, thinking about meeting Uncle Timothy, then studied the cars. Six were vintage, and one was ultra-modern. Possibly it belonged to Carmen. The car was a golden colour, expensive and low to the ground.

Tom was deep in thought, studying the cars and wondering what they might tell him about their owner. Roberto Stella had mortgaged his Malibu home to raise money for Johnny's ransom—would he sell his car collection as well? It must have been then that a man sneaked into the garage, because Tom heard a creak and saw an intruder climbing the stairs, moving slowly and stealthily. He wore jeans and a dark hoodie. A ski mask covered his face and leather gloves covered his hands. Tom had to warn Carmen!

Seizing a wrench from a nearby workbench, Tom threw it hard at a row of paint cans on a shelf. The wrench knocked two cans flying. Tumbling down, they crashed to the cement floor.

The loud noise startled the intruder. He ran down the stairs. Inside the mask, his eyes were visible. Tom recognized the eyes, but where from? Then the man raced from the garage. Tom hurried to the open door. He couldn't see the intruder, but he heard footsteps crashing away.

Carmen ran to join Tom. "What happened?" she demanded. Her voice trembled with fear. "I heard a terrible noise."

"Some guy was after you, Carmen. I saw him, on the stairs. He was masked."

Carmen stared at Tom. She looked badly frightened. "Okay," she said, "that's it. I'm not staying here. I'll move to the mansion. Roberto offered me a suite of rooms over there. I'm telling him yes."

"You'd better also contact the police, Carmen. You could be in serious danger."

Carmen suggested walking back to the house together. Passing the beautiful gardens, they paused several times to enjoy the heavily scented tropical flowers. Carmen didn't mention the stalker. On her cellphone, she learned that Roberto was unable to have visitors. "We'll have to make arrangements for another time," she told Tom.

* * *

Early Monday morning, a limousine delivered Tom and his uncle to Polygon Studios. The company occupied an enormous area in a suburb of Los Angeles.

Their ID was checked by security guards, then a big gate swung open. As they drove into the studio grounds, Tom was surprised to see a street of brown apartment buildings and small delis and other shops.

"This looks like New York City, but it can't be. We're in California."

Uncle Timothy smiled. "It's totally fake, Tom. Open those doors and you'd walk into empty space. They use this street to make movies about New York."

It was a busy scene. Actors strolled past dressed as cowboys, space travellers, even a giant chicken. The limousine soon reached Sound Stage Five, where Tom would be shooting his scenes. The building seemed even larger than an airplane hangar. All kinds of workers filled the place, busily preparing.

Between scenes, Tom found his way to the craft services truck. There he greeted people who remembered him from Winnipeg. Everyone had an opinion about Johnny and the Red River Ransom. Tom listened with interest but kept his own thoughts private.

The CST was serving smoothies made with fresh organic berries. They also offered other California favourites, including big, fat fajitas. Heavy on the salsa and sour cream, they were sloppy to eat with lots of finger licking. Tom loved this food!

It was an odd feeling for him to stand in for the missing Johnny Lombardo. Tom thought they might have closed the production out of respect for the young star, but one of the grips had an answer for that. "Movie-making is a hard-nosed business," she told Tom. "These productions cost a fortune to make. The studios can't let sentiment rule."

As the day's shooting ended, Carmen Sanchez arrived on the set. "My office is here at the studio," she explained to Tom and his uncle. "Now that Tom's finished filming, I'll show you both around."

Outside, the afternoon sun burned down fiercely. Nearby was an Old West town. Cowboys wandered around, and Tom saw horses at a hitching post outside a saloon. People in jeans and checked shirts strolled along a board sidewalk, spurs jingling on their boots. At the town's blacksmith shop, a child actor in a starched shirt and knickerbocker trousers shot an arrow into a target stretched over a bale of straw.

Grips and other workers were seen; bright lights shone as enormous movie cameras tracked the actors. Watching everything from a safe distance was a tour group, guided by a young woman wearing a green jacket and white slacks. The name "Polygon Studios" was stitched into a pocket of her jacket.

Climbing into a golf cart, Carmen gestured for Tom and his uncle to join her. "May-Lin Chan and her father are expecting us at Stage Sixteen."

Tom was delighted. "That'll be fun."

A huge number sixteen identified the sound stage where the duo were in action. As a young man, May-Lin's father had burst into fame starring in Hong Kong action movies. Then he'd arrived in Hollywood, where his charming demeanour and amazing stunts made his movies a great success at the box office. Lately his teenage daughter had joined him on screen, leading to even more good fortune.

Tom was thrilled to meet the famous man, and delighted to see May-Lin again. They posed for pictures, then May-Lin and her father returned to action. Tom and the others watched from the distance as the duo climbed a ladder to stand on top of a British double-decker bus. Beyond the bus, elaborate sets suggested a street in England. Props included a red telephone booth, a fake "bobby" directing traffic, and Union

Jack flags in the windows of several make-believe shops.

An Assistant Director watched with them. "In this scene," the A.D. explained, "the bus is racing through downtown London. May-Lin and her father are on the roof, escaping some villains. Just before the bus flips over, they leap to safety."

"That sounds dangerous," Tom said.

The A.D. nodded. "The Chans are fearless. They insist on genuine stunts—nothing faked with blue screens and computers. He's suffered some major injuries, but he keeps on going. Their movies are guaranteed box office gold."

Soon everything was ready. The bus driver was a stunt specialist wearing a crash helmet and a padded fire-retardant jumpsuit. "She'll be at the wheel inside a customized roll cage," said the A.D. "The double-decker has also been reinforced with steel to minimize impact. You see the passengers inside? They're dummies, but don't they look human?"

"Where'd you get the bus?" Uncle Timothy asked.

"Up north in Victoria, from a tourist company. It cost twenty grand. After this shoot we'll probably auction the bus on eBay. People will buy anything."

Exhaust fumes belched from the double-decker as the driver revved the engine. With May-Lin and her father standing on top, the bus picked up speed. Then Tom saw another vehicle, coming from the opposite direction. It was a black British taxi. Suddenly the cab swerved, forcing the bus to change direction. The huge double-decker raced straight at a delivery truck parked at the curb.

"There's a hidden ramp built into the delivery truck," said the A.D. "Watch what happens!"

On the street, pedestrians and shopkeepers scattered in all directions. They were stunt experts, trained to escape danger. As they ran, a grip released pigeons from a cage. The birds flew up, adding to the commotion, as huge cameras captured the excitement from several angles. On top of the bus, May-Lin and her father braced themselves for action.

Reaching the ramp, the double-decker lifted into the air. At precisely the same moment, May-Lin and her father leapt away.

"They'll land on giant air mattresses," the A.D. said. "They'll be fine!"

Tom watched, transfixed, as the bus flew sideways, wheels spinning helplessly. With a sickening thump the double-decker landed on its side. Sparks flying everywhere, it skidded to a stop.

On the set, silence. Everyone stared at the wounded bus. Then a cheer went up. The driver was safe! Climbing out, she pulled off her helmet and waved, grinning. With her sun-streaked hair the young woman looked very California.

"That was something!" Tom exclaimed to Carmen after they'd congratulated May-Lin and her father.

Returning with Carmen to Sound Stage Five, they said goodbye to her. "The limousine will collect you soon," she promised. "It'll take you back to the Chateau Marmont. By the way, Tom, thanks for helping with *Kid Gangster*."

Uncle Timothy went in search of a washroom. Left on his own, Tom wandered toward the Old West town.

The place was deserted—even the horses were gone from the hitching posts. Climbing wooden stairs to the boardwalk, Tom opened the saloon's swing doors. Inside there was nothing. Instead of a bar and a big mirror and round tables for card playing, Tom saw only wooden struts holding up the saloon's false front.

Tom walked into the make-believe barn. Cables snaked across the concrete floor; lights and cameras and other movie devices filled the space.

With the crew and actors working elsewhere, the set was creepily quiet. Tom's skin prickled. He felt as though he was being watched. He looked around, but no one was visible.

* * *

A muscular man crouched in the shadows of the fake blacksmith shop. His eyes stared at Tom. The man had a bald head, and silver earrings. He wore a black T-shirt, jeans and dusty motorcycle boots. Around his neck was a dirty bandana, hiding a distinctive tattoo.

Nearby was the bull's eye target, stretched across straw, and the bow and arrow. Reaching out, the man grabbed the bow. There was only one arrow, but that was enough. This time, he thought, the kid will die.

Carefully he threaded the arrow into the bow and raised the weapon. Sighting along the quivering arrow, the man took a perfect bead on Tom's head. He pulled back tight, then let fly.

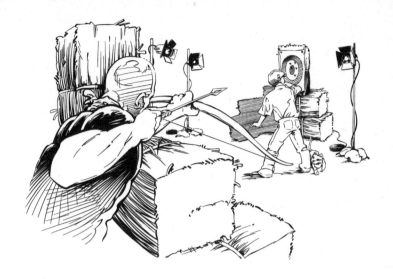

10

A cat ran to Tom. He bent forward, smiling. Behind him, the air hissed as something shot past and disappeared into a thick bale of hay.

Tom looked around, puzzled by the sound. The only person in sight was walking away—a bald man, with silver earrings and a dirty bandana around his neck. Then Tom knelt beside the little black cat. "What's your name?" he asked, feeling its rough tongue lick his fingers.

Tom heard voices. A tour group was approaching. These people were Asian; their guide spoke a language Tom couldn't understand. Grips and actors also appeared, and the set started getting busy.

When Uncle Timothy returned, Tom mentioned the cat.

"It must be a studio mascot," his uncle suggested. "Were you okay alone?"

"Sure," Tom replied, "but I was a bit bored. Nothing much happened."

* * *

Back at the Chateau Marmont, Tom enjoyed a swim. After a big meal, served poolside, he returned to the bungalow with Uncle Timothy. They both talked on the phone to the Austens back home, then decided to watch CNN. But there was nothing new about Johnny.

"I'm going outside," Tom said, "to sit on the porch."

Night had fallen, suddenly and swiftly. Pale blues and pinks streaked the western sky. Tom stretched out his legs, relaxing on a comfortable chair. Much of the outdoor area around the Chateau Marmont was in darkness. The cottages were shadowed by dark trees and shrubbery.

Above Tom's head, the thick leaves of palm trees rattled together in a light breeze. Beyond the hotel's dark grounds he could hear traffic, and people calling to each other. A warm wind carried the scent of tropical flowers.

Close by, the door of Zack's cottage slammed. Moments later, Mitzi hurried past. She didn't notice Tom. He thought she was crying. Going into the bungalow, Tom returned with his personal listening device. He aimed the laser beam at Zack's window.

The producer's voice came through, loud and clear.

"*No way,*" he was saying. "*If you don't play ball with me, I'll go to the police.*"

Silence from the bungalow. Then Zack laughed. *"You've got no choice. Co-operate with me, or go straight to prison."*

Zack's call ended. Tom gazed thoughtfully at the night sky. A large bird flew past, big wings beating against the heavy air. Who was Zack threatening, Tom wondered. Could there be a link to the abduction of Johnny Lombardo?

* * *

Tom and Uncle Timothy stepped from a limousine. Once again they were inside the grounds of Blue Paradise, the estate owned by Roberto Stella and his son, Johnny Lombardo.

Roberto had asked to see them. His beautiful fiancée, Carmen Sanchez, was at the front door to welcome Tom and his uncle. She wore sandals with a plain black dress and a silver necklace with turquoise earrings.

"I'm no longer living above the garage," Carmen told Tom. "That was a scary experience."

Tom nodded. "I was worried for you."

They entered the mansion. The ceilings were high and the walls were covered with many oil paintings.

"Roberto collects art," Carmen explained. "You see the blue painting under the spotlight? It's an original Picasso."

"Excuse me for asking," said Uncle Timothy, "but couldn't Roberto sell his art to pay Johnny's ransom?"

"He was about to do that," Carmen replied, "but it's no longer necessary."

Tom and his uncle glanced at each other—this was interesting news! Providing no additional information, Carmen gestured to a hallway. "The offices are in that wing of the mansion. Johnny's office is filled with flowers, sent by anxious fans."

"I can smell them," Tom said.

A uniformed servant appeared, pushing a wheeled cart loaded with cold drinks from around the world. Tom selected a tall, thin can of Italian soda. He was also offered snack-size thin-crust pizza, piping hot, and gratefully accepted.

"This is the life," he said, smiling at Carmen.

She showed them a dozen Oscars displayed inside a glass cabinet. "Did you know that Blue Paradise was built years ago by a famous movie producer who was a relative of Roberto's? He won all these Oscars."

"Has Roberto got any?" Uncle Timothy asked.

"Oh, yes. They're upstairs." Carmen gave a pleasing laugh. "Roberto uses them as door-stoppers."

Tom studied the golden statuettes, impressed to see such famous objects up close. "This display cabinet," he commented to Carmen, "is it secure? Surely these Oscars are very valuable."

"Don't worry, Tom. It's all taken care of."

One wall contained framed portraits of people striking glamorous poses. The autographed pictures were in black and white; the people's clothes and hairstyles looked dramatic but dated.

"A long time ago," Carmen explained, "these folks were movie stars. They were all friends of Roberto's great-uncle."

She turned to Tom's uncle. "This house has eight

bedrooms. It's more than 13,000 square feet. In the drinks lounge, the bar is fifty feet long."

"Very interesting," Uncle Timothy remarked, "but you know something? You could fit a lot of food banks into this space."

Carmen didn't comment. They entered the library. It was large, with leather chairs and sofas and glass-topped tables. In a corner stood a popcorn machine and a candy dispenser filled with colourful gumballs. Outside the windows was the gravel driveway, and the visual splendour of Blue Paradise's tropical gardens.

The walls of the library were panelled with dark wood. Lots of books were on the shelves. "Roberto loves mysteries and police stories," Carmen said, smiling fondly. "He's got the complete works of Michael Connelly, and they're all autographed." She gestured at a bookcase enclosed by glass. "He also has all of Shakespeare in leather-bound volumes." She smiled. "Unfortunately, they're not autographed."

At that moment, Roberto Stella entered. Tom recognized him immediately. "I'm so sorry," Roberto said, "to have missed you on your last visit."

Smiling, Uncle Timothy vigorously shook hands with the famous man. "It's wonderful to meet one of yesterday's great stars," he enthused.

Roberto Stella arched an eyebrow. "Suddenly I feel old."

But he didn't look it. Roberto had large black eyes in a scarcely lined, handsome face. His luxurious hair was swept back dramatically from his face. The star wore a burgundy silk shirt monogrammed "R.S.," dark slacks with a leather belt, and tasselled black loafers.

Roberto shook hands with Tom. Tears formed in his eyes. "Your smile, Tom, so like my Johnny's. I miss him, I miss my son."

"Johnny was a neat guy," Tom said. Then he blushed. "I mean, he *is* a neat guy."

"He'll survive," said Roberto. "My son has character." He looked at Uncle Timothy. "We all face adversity in life. Right, Timothy? We need strength to overcome our setbacks. A strong person makes good choices. Johnny will be making decisions that keep him alive."

Roberto's calm assurance made Tom feel better. "You mean, Johnny won't antagonize his kidnappers?"

"Exactly," Roberto replied. "We both took training from the police on how to survive a hostage situation. My son's smart, he paid close attention in that course."

Tom was staring at Roberto's watch. "That's quite something," he said admiringly.

The man smiled. "This watch was a gift from Johnny for my fiftieth birthday. It's very rare. Patek Philippe designed it in 1946. The watch is incredibly ingenious, a mechanical work of art. The revolving bezel includes the names of forty-one places worldwide."

"Anything Canadian?" Tom asked.

"Montreal," Roberto replied, "and the Klondike."

Tom's uncle studied the watch. "It must have cost Johnny a lot."

"You're right, Timothy, but you know what? Even if it came from the corner drugstore I would treasure this watch, because my Johnny is a son to be proud of."

Roberto asked Tom about Winnipeg, and the time he'd spent with Johnny. The man was eager for every detail, and seemed especially pleased that Johnny was a success at snow football.

"My boy, my boy," he said fondly, then turned to Carmen. "I must rest."

Saying goodbye, Roberto left the library. Moments later, they heard the whir of machinery. "That's the elevator," Carmen explained. "It goes up to Roberto's private suite, and down to the media room in the basement."

Her face brightened. "I've had good news. Friends of Roberto's have raised the additional ransom money. It can be paid in full. A message has gone to the Red River Gang."

"Does Roberto know?" Uncle Timothy asked.

Carmen shook her head. "I'm waiting to tell him. The final moments of a hostage situation are often extremely dangerous. I don't want to raise false hopes."

Looking out the window, Uncle Timothy's face brightened. Tom saw Mitzi and Zack stepping from the yellow convertible. Today she wore green, and had a confident air. Soon after, Mitzi entered the library with Zack. Seeing Tom's uncle, Mitzi grinned with pleasure. "I was hoping you'd be here!"

Carmen looked at Zack. "Roberto can't meet with you today."

"That doesn't matter," the young producer replied, "but listen, are the rumours true? I've heard the ransom will be paid in full."

"News travels fast," Carmen commented. "Yes, the story's true. But please keep it quiet. We're waiting for a response from the gang."

Zack looked out the window. "Look who's arriving. It's Sally Virtue. I wonder if she's heard the news?"

"Sally's driving an amazing car," Tom said. "What is it?"

The enormous vehicle was red, with a cream-coloured roof. Large, round headlights were mounted on the fenders. "That," replied Carmen, "is Roberto's pride and joy. It's a 1926 Rolls-Royce Phantom. It was originally owned by Mack Sennett, the genius behind the Keystone Kops comedies. He was a Canadian, by the way, from the Eastern Townships in Quebec."

"Why's Sally driving it?" Tom asked.

"The Phantom was on loan from Roberto. Now that Sally's finished as Johnny's manager, the car gets returned. She phoned me this morning and arranged to deliver the Phantom. She wasn't sounding happy."

"That doesn't seem fair," Tom said, "when Sally's been leading the search for Johnny."

"Pure grandstanding," Carmen replied, scornfully snapping her fingers. "Next she'll be selling her memoirs, *How I Saved Johnny Lombardo*. You wait and see."

Zack left the library without speaking. Mitzi immediately turned to Tom's uncle. "I'm really troubled about Zack. He's been acting so strangely. Listen, Timothy, may I get your advice? I need a friend to talk to."

"Certainly," he replied.

Uncle Timothy smiled at Tom. "Hold the fort, okay? I think I'll take Mitzi for a walk in the garden."

"Sounds good, Unc."

Soon after, Tom saw the couple emerge outside. Sunshine lit their faces as they talked intensely, not even glancing at the amazing Rolls-Royce Phantom. Then Uncle Timothy said something that made Mitzi laugh, and they strolled away together past banks of lush tropical flowers.

Only Tom and Carmen remained in the library. Her phone beeped. "It's a text message from Roberto. He says to meet him downstairs at the media projection room."

"I'll wait here," Tom said, "and explore the library. Maybe I'll find the collected works of The Hardy Boys in leather-bound volumes."

Carmen smiled at the joke. "I won't be long."

After she'd disappeared down the basement stairs, Tom examined the shelves. Then the butler entered.

"Excuse me, young man," he said in a snooty voice. "Master Roberto is tired, and has gone to bed. He cannot see you again today. Perhaps another time."

"But. . ." Tom bit back his words. Something was wrong—Roberto was supposed to be in the basement, not in his bedroom. Had a false message lured Carmen into danger? Was the butler involved in a conspiracy?

In the hallway, the man glanced at Tom. "The limousine is waiting at the front door."

"Is there a washroom handy?" Tom asked.

"A what?"

"You know—a restroom."

The butler inclined his head toward a nearby door. "In there."

"Okay," Tom said. "I'll meet you at the limo. Give me a few minutes."

Keeping the washroom door slightly open, he watched the butler walk slowly away down a long hallway. Then Tom slipped across the hallway to another door.

It led to the basement stairs.

Tom followed the stairs down to a dark and gloomy place. Except for the media room, the space was open plan. There was very dim overhead lighting, but it was difficult to see things. A lamp stood close by. Tom tried without success to switch it on.

Workout equipment was visible in one corner. Close by was a storage area for high-tech bicycles. The door to the media room was open. Tom saw three rows of stadium seating. Carmen sat there, facing away from him. She was very still, not moving at all.

Unexpectedly, an outside door opened. Tom smelled the ocean. Through the doorway he saw sunshine and greenery, but most of Tom's view was blocked by a man who was removing an electronic key from the lock. A dark hoodie hid the man's face. He wore a pale shirt and creased, corduroy trousers.

The door closed.

Moments later, the lights went out.

Plunged into darkness, the place was suddenly frightening. Tom's senses rose to full alert. Deeply aware of the basement's musty smell, he heard the magnified breathing of the intruder. Tom's heart thundered, an enormous sound in such silence.

The dark shadow of the man moved toward the media room. Reaching to the lamp, Tom slowly and carefully removed the light bulb. Then he wound up like a baseball pitcher.

"Carmen," Tom yelled, as he threw the bulb at a wall, "take cover!"

The loud *blam!* of the exploding light bulb was followed by the man's shout of surprise. Throwing himself toward the sound, Tom connected with the intruder's legs. The man went down hard, cracking his head against the floor.

The lights came on. Carmen stood by the switch, staring at Tom and the intruder. The man was unconscious. Close to his hand was a hunting knife.

Pulling the hoodie away from the intruder's face, Tom got a shock.

"Oh no," he exclaimed. "It's Jordan Quicksilver."

Carmen approached cautiously until she was close enough to see his face. She gazed sadly at the movie director. "Yes," she said quietly, "it's Jordan who's been stalking me. He's been crazy angry that I chose Roberto over him. Jordan is immature—he was a spoiled boy, and now he's a spoiled man. He doesn't like rejection. Jordan needs to get revenge."

Carmen pointed at the knife. "It looks like he planned to hurt me, Tom. I'm so thankful you were here to help."

"Was it Jordan in the ski mask? The guy I scared away?"

Carmen nodded. "I'm pretty sure the police will find out from Jordan that he was in the garage that day."

"He isn't involved in Johnny's kidnapping?"

"I doubt it," Carmen replied.

"Remember those strange phone calls you received in Winnipeg?" Tom said. "It was probably Jordan who called, trying to freak you out."

Carmen shivered. "When we were dating, Jordan must have gotten into my purse and stolen the telephone security codes. I guess he also took my entry key to Blue Paradise."

Tom stood up quickly. "You'd better get Roberto here, and the security guards. Jordan could wake up any time." He looked out the window. Nearby was a small metal structure with a door but no windows. "What's that for?"

"There's a staircase inside. It spirals down through the rock. It was installed long ago but no one uses it."

"How do people get down to the beach?"

"There's an outdoor staircase that goes down the face of the cliff."

"Would that spiral staircase take me to Johnny's beach house?"

"I imagine," Carmen replied, "but I've never used it."

"You know," Tom said, "I've got this strange theory. Maybe the Red River Gang has Johnny in the most unlikely place of all."

"Which would be?" asked Carmen.

"His own beach house," Tom replied triumphantly. "Who'd ever look there?"

For long moments Carmen was silent. Then she smiled. "You're one smart kid."

"I'm taking those stairs down to the beach house," Tom declared.

"No," Carmen declared. "You mustn't do that."

"Why not?"

"Because it's too risky. You could get hurt." Reaching out, Carmen tried to grab Tom. But he wriggled away, and rushed outside. Carmen didn't follow.

The metal structure was unlocked. The door creaked open. It was dark inside as Tom hurried down the staircase. Around and around the spiral he went, lower and lower, smelling the salty ocean. At last Tom reached another metal hut. Opening the door, he saw the beach and the sparkling waves of the blue Pacific.

Nearby was a beach house. The building was white, two storeys, with large plate-glass windows. Its red roof was topped by a big stone chimney; the grounds featured beautiful lawns and gardens, even a fancy pond where gold and orange koi fish swam lazily. Beside the house was an open garden shed. Tom saw ladders and rope and other equipment inside.

He also saw the cliff and a metal staircase. Two people were descending the stairs. Zack was one. He held a gun. It was pointed straight at Sally.

11

Seagulls swept past the cliffside stairs, crying, while the surf thundered ashore. Zack was gesturing at Sally with the gun, forcing her to move quickly.

The two reached the sand. Zack pointed at the beach house. He shouted something, but his words were lost in the booming of the big waves. Tom watched Zack and Sally run to the house. Sally opened a side door, and they entered the building.

Sneaking closer, Tom looked into the living room. He saw nice furniture, including two long sofas with blue and green and purple cushions. One wall was decorated with large photos of Johnny on the beach with his surfboard, beaming at the camera, looking totally carefree. Another wall featured framed souvenirs from the young star's movie shoots—photographs and objects, including police badges and some handcuffs.

Sally and Zack stood in the middle of the living room, talking urgently. Tom couldn't hear them, and he didn't have his personal listening device to use. He was frightened for Sally. Zack was waving the gun around.

Tom tried the side door—it was unlocked. Carefully he opened it. To one side, through a doorway, a kitchen was visible.

Zack's voice came from the nearby living room. "I just want to see proof," the young producer said.

Slowly and carefully Tom crept toward the living room. Seeing Tom, a look of astonishment crossed Sally's face.

Zack turned to stare at him. "Hey," he shouted. "What gives?"

Seizing a heavy flashlight from a desk, Sally hit Zack from behind. He grunted and fell hard. Running forward, Tom checked Zack's pulse. "He's alive," he cried.

Racing outside to the shed, Tom grabbed some rope. He returned quickly to Sally, who was just closing her cellphone. "You called 911?" Tom said. "That's great!" Working together, Sally and Tom tied Zack hand and foot. Moments later, they heard an approaching car. Tom saw the Rolls-Royce Phantom descending the gravel road from above. At the wheel of the big machine was a muscular man with a bald head and silver earrings. Tom recognized his face. He had shaved off his dark, curly hair and pointed sideburns, but it was unmistakeably Ivan!

Tom grabbed the revolver from the floor and ran to hide in the kitchen. "When Ivan arrives," he called to Sally, "get him talking. I'll do the rest."

Sally nodded. Her brown eyes were huge. She seemed overwhelmed by the whirlwind events. When the door opened, she attempted to smile at Ivan. "Hello . . . uh . . ."

"What's going on?" Ivan demanded, walking into the room.

Tom stepped forward, holding the gun. "I don't know what's going on, fella," he said triumphantly, delighted by Ivan's look of surprise and dismay, "but I sure hope this revolver doesn't go off. No funny business—my trigger finger is feeling itchy." Turning to Sally, Tom gestured at Johnny's wall of trophies. "Sally, quickly. Smash the glass, get those handcuffs. Then lock Ivan to the door of the refrigerator."

Within moments, Sally had cuffed a snarling Ivan to the big fridge. He yelled angrily at Tom and Sally, but Ivan was helpless and knew it. In the living room, Tom put the gun and the handcuff keys on a desk, far from Ivan's reach. "The police will want these," he said to Sally.

A strange noise came from above—it sounded like feet kicking a wall. Tom and Sally both stared at the ceiling.

In a corner, Tom saw stairs. He ran to them and started up. Moments later, he heard Sally climbing behind him. At the top, she joined Tom at a closed door.

The sound came from behind the door; it was a continuous *thump*, *thump*, *thump*. Cautiously opening the door, Tom looked in. He saw a big bedroom with floor-to-ceiling windows overlooking billowing white surf. In a corner was a closet door. The sound came from there.

Sally threw open the door. "Johnny, it's you," she cried, "and you're alive!"

Inside the closet was Johnny Lombardo, bound and gagged and obviously desperate to be rescued. Eyes goggling, the young star tried unsuccessfully to speak.

"Take it easy," Tom cautioned him. "You're safe now. We've come to rescue you."

A noise sounded from behind. Turning, Tom and Sally saw Ivan holding the revolver.

"Surprise," Ivan said, grinning. His jagged teeth were stained brown.

"But," Tom stammered, "but you were locked to the refrigerator. What. . . ? How. . . ?"

"I had assistance," Ivan replied. "You were stupid, kid. You left the handcuff keys behind, and this gun."

"Zack must have helped you," Tom exclaimed.

Ivan shook his head. "He's still unconscious."

"Then who . . ."

"No more talk!" Ivan waved the gun at Tom and Sally. "Get downstairs to the car."

"Are you partners with Zack?" Tom demanded.

"Shut up," Ivan snarled, grabbing Tom's arm. "Downstairs, fast."

Tom went down the staircase. He saw Zack unconscious on the floor, still bound with ropes. Tom's mind whirled, seeking means of escape. Sally was beside him—surely she'd find a way to save them both!

Outside, the sunshine was powerful. The red-and-cream Rolls-Royce stood waiting. Tom saw keys in the ignition. Here was his chance.

Faking a stumble, Tom fell forward. Taken by surprise, Ivan was pulled off balance. In the blink of an eye, Tom knocked the revolver from Ivan's hand. It sailed through the air, bounced off the Rolls and fell to the ground, spinning in the dust. Then Ivan grabbed Tom, and wrestled him to the ground.

"Sally," Tom yelled, "get the gun!"

Sally seized the weapon. Holding the revolver in both hands, she covered them. "Stop your fighting," she ordered. Her voice was strong. She was totally in control. "Don't move, or I'll shoot you dead."

Smiling with satisfaction, Tom stood up. "Okay, loser," he said, "you heard the lady. You're finished."

Getting to his feet, Ivan grinned. "Sorry, kid. You ain't the hero of this particular movie."

Puzzled, Tom looked at Sally. Then his heart leapt.

The gun was aimed straight at him.

"I'll say it again." Sally's voice was forged from steel. "Don't move, Tom, or I'll shoot you dead."

Horrified, Tom could only stare at Sally. "But . . ."

She turned to Ivan. "Thanks for bringing the Rolls."

"No problem. The keys were still in the ignition, where you left them." Ivan showed his stained teeth in a creepy smile. "I was glad you tossed me the handcuff keys. I didn't appreciate being cuffed to that fridge."

Sally gestured at Tom with the gun. "Get in the Rolls. You're my hostage. If you cause trouble, I'll kill you."

"But . . ."

"Silence!"

Moments later, the Phantom was underway. Ivan was at the wheel, Sally in the passenger seat. She kept the gun on Tom, who was in the back.

"I don't understand," he said bleakly. "You betrayed me, Sally. How could you?"

Sally shrugged. As the Rolls climbed the hill, she looked down at the sparkling blue ocean. "I loved being Johnny's manager, and I loved driving the Phantom. Then suddenly it was all gone."

"So you craved revenge."

"That's a bit harsh, Tom. I only wanted Roberto and Carmen to feel some pain, just like me."

"You also demanded a huge ransom, then doubled it."

"That's true. But don't forget, Roberto and his movie friends have pots of money. They can afford it. I decided to capture Johnny while I was still within his circle of trusted people. I hired Ivan, and we made our first try."

"In Winnipeg," Tom said, "at the Forks."

Sally nodded. "If your dad hadn't arrived in his police car, Ivan would have successfully abducted Johnny."

"But I could have prevented the grab."

"I planned to trip you, accidentally on purpose."

Sally studied Tom's face. "You were such a nuisance. Like at the Golden Boy Café, when I was talking to Ivan and you listened in with that gadget of yours. Or later, when I arranged to meet Ivan at the Acropolis Restaurant but you hung around outside. You messed up that meeting, Tom. I was annoyed, and so was Ivan."

"Good!"

"At the railway station Ivan grabbed you by mistake. That was stupid."

Ivan didn't react to the criticism. He was focused on the Rolls as it climbed the winding road.

"Then," Sally said, "Ivan tried to kill you with a bow and arrow. That was another mistake. Thank goodness the arrow missed you."

"Ivan tried to kill me?" Tom exclaimed.

Sally nodded. "At the movie studio, where he was working as a grip. I arranged fake ID for Ivan, and a new look."

"Why was Zack in Johnny's trailer at the station?" Tom asked.

"He'd arranged a business meeting with Johnny. Zack was never involved in my master plan."

"Were you the pilot of the air ambulance?"

Sally nodded. "Ivan hijacked the jet in Neepawa and I flew it to Winnipeg. During the flight I phoned the bodyguards and Johnny with fake messages. I told Johnny a kidnap conspiracy was unfolding. 'Trust no one,' I said, 'and run to the jet.'" Sally chuckled. "It worked."

Tom shook his head. "Ebenezer Smith told me a woman from England got him a job at Polygon Studios—she'd taken flying lessons with him. Later I learned you arranged for Ebenezer's job. That was a tipoff that you might have piloted the air ambulance, but I missed it."

"Too bad, Tom," Sally said, chuckling. "Back in the States we smuggled Johnny to California inside a rented van, then transported him to the beach house in Ivan's motorboat. Ivan stayed in the house, guarding Johnny."

"Why there?"

"It was the perfect hiding place. The police never looked for Johnny at his estate."

Sally sighed. "Arranging the ransom took longer than I figured, but it was worth the wait. In Switzerland I'll get my hands on the ransom money. It's enough for several lifetimes. My Swiss account has been opened using the brand-new name that appears on my forged passport. I'm also getting a changed look. I'll have facial surgery, shave myself bald, pierce my skin with metal decorations, and no one will ever know me."

"I'll find you," Tom vowed. "Wherever you go, I'll track you down."

"Not a hope," Sally said, laughing. The sound was no longer quite so pleasant to Tom. "Roberto and Carmen betrayed me. That's all I care about. Revenge is mine, and revenge is sweet."

"Did you plan to kill Johnny?" Tom asked.

"Only if necessary. The police will soon find Zack and Johnny, but by then I'll be safely out of the country."

"Me too," said Ivan from the wheel of the Phantom. "By the way, Sally, I want my payment. In full, and in cash."

She nodded vaguely. "When we get to Switzerland, Ivan, I'll pay you for sure."

Tom looked at her. "Zack figured out your scheme?"

Sally nodded. "He desperately needed large amounts of cash. Zack spends a lot of time gambling. He owed some gangsters big time. The mob sent an enforcer to Winnipeg, threatening Zack if he didn't pay up. Then

Zack learned I was behind the kidnapping, and tried to shake me down for half the ransom money."

"But," Tom said, "what proof did he have?"

Sally removed a small disc from her pocket. "Back at the beach house, I took this from Zack's pocket. You were outside, Tom, getting the rope. You didn't see."

"What's on the disc?" he asked.

"A guy in Winnipeg filmed it. He worked for a security firm. During the shoot at the airfield, this guy captured Johnny's abduction on video." Sally glanced at the disc. "The guard used an infrared camera, programmed to see in the dark. The camera captured me, piloting the air ambulance. It's on this disc."

"That guy sold it to Zack?"

Sally nodded. "I arranged to meet Zack at Blue Paradise. I planned to lure him to the beach house. I wanted the disc. I let him wave his gun around, thinking he was in control. But he wasn't."

"Why'd he go to the beach house?"

"Zack wanted to see Johnny in person, to be certain he was alive." Sally returned the disc to her pocket. "Zack figured we'd then escape to Switzerland, and split the ransom." She chuckled. "What an empty dream."

The Rolls-Royce crested the hill. Ahead was the airfield. Tom saw the hangar—the big door was open. Inside was the executive jet. Ebenezer's car was parked outside, but there was no sign of him.

The airfield was surrounded by a fence; directly ahead of them was a big wooden gate. Revving the engine of the Rolls, Ivan took the gate at a run. Wood exploded in all directions as the car smashed through, then raced across a field.

The Rolls-Royce skidded to a stop beside the hangar. Ivan pulled Tom from the car and shoved him through the open doorway. Inside the hangar, the Polygon jet stood waiting.

A door opened at the back of the hangar. Ebenezer appeared in his wheelchair. Seeing them, he looked surprised. Then he stared at the revolver with astonished eyes. "What's going on?"

Sally smiled. "You're flying me out. We're going to Switzerland. This kid comes too, as a hostage. Refuse to take us, and I'll blow you away. Then I'll pilot the jet."

Ebenezer raised his hands in surrender. "I am at your service." He wheeled to the jet, where a mechanical lift raised him to the door. Soon the twin jets whined into life.

"Move it, Tom," Sally shouted above the noise.

As Tom ran forward, Ivan also sprinted toward the jet. But Sally waved the gun and he stopped, startled. Tom hurried up the stairs, followed by Sally. Dropping into one of the fancy passenger chairs, Tom slapped on a seatbelt. Beyond a low divider, Ebenezer sat at the controls in his lightweight wheelchair. The pilot was speaking quietly into a cellphone. His eyes kept darting at Sally. She was at the open door, looking out.

Ivan stood near the jet, staring with disbelieving eyes as the stairs folded up into the jet, leaving him stranded. "Hey," he yelled, "what about my money?"

Smiling, Sally closed the door. Kneeling beside Tom, she pressed the gun's cold muzzle against his head. They both looked out a window at Ivan, who seemed very angry. His helpless fury caused Sally to laugh gleefully. "*Hasta la vista*, baby," she cried, and laughed again.

Engines screaming, the jet rolled toward the hangar's open door. The powerful plane began picking up speed. At the same time, they saw Ivan run to a control panel. A big metal door began dropping down from the ceiling.

"Faster," Sally screamed at Ebenezer. "Faster! He's blocking our getaway!"

"We'll never make it," Ebenezer cried, cringing back moments before the jet slammed into the descending door.

They were all thrown forward, but Tom's seatbelt saved him from harm. The Plexiglas windshield shattered, and Tom heard metal tearing apart as Sally screamed and Ebenezer yelled.

The jet screeched to a stop. Quickly releasing his seatbelt, Tom darted forward to Sally. She was unconscious. Reaching into her pocket, he removed the disc. "This is for the police," Tom told Ebenezer.

"No injuries here," the pilot said from the cockpit. "How about you?"

"I'm okay," Tom replied, "and I've got Sally's revolver. She dropped it when we crashed." Tom looked out the window of the mangled jet. "Oh no," he cried. "I can't believe it!"

Through the hangar's smashed door, he saw the Rolls-Royce. At the wheel was Ivan, escaping the scene.

"Don't worry," Ebenezer said, "the police are coming. I called 911 on my cell."

Within minutes, they heard sirens and very soon,

the hangar was filled with rescue personnel. The scene resembled the final moments in an action movie. Police cars and fire engines and ambulances were stopped at crazy angles, emergency lights twirling brightly, while police and FBI agents and people in combat gear were everywhere.

* * *

In the hangar's small office, a television screen glowed. People crowded around, including Tom. They were glued to a police chase carried live from a TV station's helicopter. Regular programming was suspended as viewers watched Ivan's desperate bid for freedom.

The Rolls-Royce was racing south on a coastal highway. The Phantom was easily recognizable with its white canvas top and big red body and wheels. Police vehicles were close behind. At the same time, from the helicopter, the television camera showed other officers crouched beside the highway. They were watching the Phantom approach.

Stretched across the road was a device that resembled a large belt. The moment the speeding Rolls crossed it, smoke exploded from its tires. The big car swerved in one direction, then in another.

Watching beside Tom, Ebenezer chuckled. "The Rolls just hit a spike belt. The tires have blown."

The Phantom was out of control. Smashing through a wooden fence, it skidded sideways across a green field and came to rest near a herd of grazing cows. The animals raised their heads to watch as Ivan leapt from the vehicle and tried to run, but there was no chance of escape. Police officers were coming from everywhere.

It was all over for the tough guy.

* * *

Tom returned home to Winnipeg, but he was soon back in Hollywood with Uncle Timothy. They were Roberto's and Johnny's guests, staying once more at the Chateau Marmont.

On a warm evening Tom and Johnny stepped from a limousine outside the Kodak Theatre, home to the Oscars ceremony. With them were Uncle Timothy and his date, Mitzi DeLite. Holding hands, the happy couple waved to the crowds. Johnny Lombardo and Tom both wore silk suits; they also smiled and waved as hundreds of cameras flashed.

From all over the world, the most talented people in movies were gathering for the presentation of the famous Oscar statuettes for the greatest achievements in film. The ultimate event for star-watchers, the show was being broadcast to a huge global audience.

A long red carpet led to the theatre. All along it, stars were being interviewed by television personalities. Johnny was collared by "Entertainment Tonight" while Tom continued on. It was a great scene!

Seeking celebrities for their cameras, the TV hosts jostled one another to gain the attention of the big names walking toward the theatre. In a clever move, the team from Canada waved a maple leaf flag at the stars—a ploy that worked. As Tom watched, a famous action star stopped to be interviewed by the host of "eTalk Daily," Ben Mulroney. Proudly watching the interview was the star's daughter, May-Lin Chan. Spotting Tom, she smiled prettily.

"My daughter likes your guy, Tom Austen," remarked the affable action hero. "You should interview him."

"We're about to," said Ben Mulroney, beaming. "Tom Austen's next for our camera." He waved at Tom. "Come on forward, young fella!"

Tom had been interviewed a lot recently. Once again he talked proudly about finding Johnny Lombardo at the beach house.

"Sally left hospital today," Tom told the television world. "Now she'll be living behind bars."

Ben Mulroney studied Tom's face. "Feeling nervous about your big moment tonight at the Oscars?"

"No, Ben. I'm cool, calm, and collected."

"Any plans for getting into show biz? Maybe as an actor? You've seen the lifestyle, up close and personal. What say you about movie stardom?"

Tom smiled. "It's not for me."

* * *

Inside the Kodak Theatre, Tom waited backstage with Johnny Lombardo. Large curtains separated the boys from the audience. They heard laughter as the host opened the evening with his clever take on the year in movies. Tom was really, really nervous. He pictured his family and friends in Winnipeg, gathered around their screens waiting for his big moment.

He mustn't mess up!

As Tom paced back and forth, Johnny grinned. "It's only a few words, Tom. You can handle this."

"The audience numbers in the billions, Johnny. One slip, and I'm toast. What if I accidentally say, 'And the loser is . . .' What then?"

"You're so funny, man. You can deal with someone like Ivan, but you're afraid to say a few words on TV." Johnny smiled. "It's easy."

"Yeah, sure. For you."

One of the show's assistants approached. "You're on next," she told Tom and Johnny. "Have fun."

Tom groaned. "I just want it over."

The curtains swept open. Tom and Johnny walked into the dazzling glare of television lights. Famous people sat in the large theatre, applauding as the boys approached the podium. The host, Billy Crystal, joked about their silk suits, getting some laughs from the good-natured crowd. Billy explained that Johnny had invited Tom Austen into the Oscars spotlight as a way of saying thanks to the young Canadian hero.

Johnny read aloud the nominees for Best Supporting Actress. Tom then ripped open a big envelope and announced the winner. He didn't mess up—the name came easily. Tom felt like shouting with pleasure and relief, but instead he walked calmly to the wings with Johnny and the winning actress.

As they left the stage, Johnny slapped Tom on the back. "Good work, pal! Say, how about visiting Blue Paradise tomorrow? Dad and Carmen want to thank you in person. Plus, a few friends are dropping by for surfing and beach volleyball. TRM will be playing some music."

"Sounds wonderful," Tom said.

"Ever tried surfing?"

Tom shook his head.

Johnny grinned. "Then I'll introduce you to the ultimate experience in sport."

* * *

The next day, after visiting with Roberto and Carmen, Tom and Johnny descended the cliffside stairs to the beach house. They hung out, discussing Johnny's capture and rescue, then gathered some gear. Finally Tom would be using the special-issue surf shorts he'd brought from home.

The boys began walking north. "We're following a secret trail," Johnny explained. "Only my father and I know about it. Before Dad, the secret was held by his great-uncle. That's why they both wanted to own Blue Paradise. This trail leads to an isolated point-break."

"What's that mean?"

"A point-break," Johnny explained, "is a rock formation that creates perfect waves. Over and over, they come rolling ashore."

"So that's why this place is called Blue Paradise."

Johnny smiled. "Exactly."

The boys reached a cove where huge breakers thundered in. The sound of the surf was unbelievable. Tom wanted to stand and stare, but he also wanted to learn some surfing!

Johnny was a good teacher. In the white-water mini-waves close to shore, Tom learned to stand and balance. The boys then paddled out, parallel to the point-break. From behind the break, Tom watched Johnny surf wave after wave. He was learning, and gathering his courage.

Then, it was time.

"Your wave next," Johnny yelled from his board. "You'll hear it coming, then just *go!*"

Heart pounding, Tom paddled hard to catch the wave. It was close behind. He felt deafened by the roaring water. "Don't look back," Johnny cried. "Paddle faster!"

Tom caught the wave on the lip, and the mighty water lifted him. For an unbelievable moment he looked straight down the vertical drop. Tom leapt to his feet and balanced, finding his snowboarding skills of real value.

Then, to his surprise, the ocean became his friend. The powerful wave carried Tom gracefully forward. The feeling was wonderful. All the fear of moments before became joy and exhilaration. He was alive, and it felt great.

* * *

Later, back at the beach house, Johnny hosted a party for Tom. Many in the good-natured crowd were famous actors. Tom was pleased to meet the celebrities, who praised him for helping save Johnny.

Some of the guests played beach volleyball—the best were May-Lin Chan and Johnny Lombardo.

"You know," said Jacob "Red" Herring as he watched the volleyball action with Tom, "no matter what Johnny does, he wins. I knew he'd survive the kidnapping."

"I guess lucky is a state of mind," Tom commented.

Red nodded. "Good fortune is what you make it."

"Will you be working on Johnny's next movie?"

"No," Red replied, "but that doesn't mean I'll be unemployed. Stunt people are always working." Red brushed at the sand with his bare toes. "Johnny has dropped the Zorro project. Instead he'll be shooting a surf movie in Costa Rica." Red shook his head. "I'm kind of surprised at Johnny. He's always enjoyed action films. Now suddenly he's into something peaceful. Apparently this one's strictly a fun story, without a single shot fired. I mean, what's going on?"

Volleyball over, Johnny and May-Lin joined them. Wiping his face with a towel monogrammed "J. L.," Johnny smiled at Tom. "What happened to us would make a great movie with a genuine happy ending. Dad's company could produce it for Polygon."

Tom was enthusiastic about the idea. So was May-Lin. "Have you thought of a title?" she asked.

"That's easy." Johnny smiled. "We'll call it *Red River Ransom*."

Tom grinned. "I like it!"

* * *

Carmen married Roberto at the Hollywood Bowl. They are happy together.

Johnny Lombardo joined the peace movement. In his latest movie he portrays his idol, musician John Lennon.

Sally Virtue served time at San Quentin Prison. Later, she ran unsuccessfully for governor of California.

Zack Sanderson is troubled by headaches and regrets.

Uncle Tim and Aunt Mitzi have twin girls. The family lives in Santa Monica.

Tom Austen remains a detective.

A Note From the Author

This story contains references to many real people, including the following:

Shirley Temple
Flo and Eric Wilson
Terry Fox
Elvis Presley
Margaret Laurence
Al Ferraby
James Dean
Michael J. Fox
Lucille Ball
Mack Sennett
Pablo Picasso
Ben Mulroney

Tim Horton
John Lennon
Tony Curtis
Arthur Slade
Bill Zuk
Robert Linnell
Larry King
Diana, Princess of Wales
Marilyn Monroe
Jackie Chan
Michael Connelly
Billy Crystal

The Ghost of
Lunenburg Manor

This book is dedicated to
Terry Fox.
And to the memory of my father,
R.S.S. Wilson.
Courageous fighters
against a common enemy.

1

"It's the ghost of the *Young Teazer!*"

The old man pointed a trembling finger at the fire across the sea. "It's come back, to haunt us all."

A group of people stood on the wharf, gazing through the darkness at the blazing light. The only sound came from waves washing against the rocky shore.

A light wind carried salty sea air to Tom Austen, a red-headed boy with many freckles, and his slim, dark-haired sister, Liz. "Who's this guy Teazer?" she asked the man.

"It's a ship, not a person. During the War of 1812, the *Young Teazer* was trapped here by the British navy. One of the men, knowing he was doomed to swing from an English yardarm, deliberately blew up his own vessel. They say it was terrible, how the sky exploded into flames and the crewmen screamed as they died."

"But how can we be seeing the same ship?"

"That's the strange thing, lass. Exactly a year after it blew up, the *Young Teazer* came back as a ghost ship. People saw a ball of fire sail across this bay, then suddenly flare up in a silent explosion and disappear. Since then, many have told of seeing the *Teazer* light."

Tom gasped in surprise. "It's gone! Did you see how it just vanished?"

The man nodded. "I'll be going home. We won't see the ghost ship again this night."

He turned away, and most of the others followed. As they left, their faces were briefly lit by the headlights of a car that came speeding out of the night.

"Here's Professor Zinck," said one of the people who remained, "but he's too late."

A man with a large oval stomach and a large oval face came quickly along the wharf. Besides a nose of remarkable size, his face included heavy glasses and a goatee bristling with short, black hairs.

"Have I missed it?"

"Yes, and it's a shame. You could have written about the ghost ship in your next book, Professor."

"Please tell me what happened."

After hearing several descriptions, Professor Zinck shook his head. "I'm sorry I missed it. The light may have been a prank, but I can't say for sure."

Tom looked up at the big man. "If you're going to investigate, sir, my sister and I would like to help."

Before the Professor could reply, a pretty woman with greying hair stepped forward. "Now, Tom, there's to be no detective work. Your parents want you to have a nice, relaxing holiday."

Professor Zinck gave her a puzzled look. "What's all this about, Shirley?"

Smiling, she introduced Tom and Liz. "Their parents have sent these two to my guest house for a holiday. They thought a fishing village like Stonehurst would be perfect, because Tom and Liz couldn't get mixed up in any mysteries."

The Professor chuckled. "There are lots of mysteries and strange events in Nova Scotia, but I guess I'd better not mention any."

Liz gave him an encouraging smile. "Won't you tell us just one, Professor? I'm sure that won't hurt."

Shirley gave Professor Zinck a warning look, but he chuckled again and pretended not to notice. "Would you two like to visit a haunted house?"

"Wow! You bet!"

Shirley shook her head. "I don't think . . ."

Professor Zinck laughed. "Now then, Shirley, these kids can't come to harm in my own home."

Tom stared at him in amazement. "You mean you *live* in a haunted house?"

The Professor nodded. "Come and meet my wife. She's actually seen the Lady in White who haunts Lunenburg Manor, where we live. Perhaps you'd join us for supper tomorrow, and Annette can tell you her story."

They walked along the wharf past piles of nets smelling of fish and salt, and stopped beside an expensive car. In the driver's seat was a woman who had hair and eyes as black as the Professor's. Smiling warmly, she agreed to tell them about the Lady in White the next evening.

"Are you frightened of ghosts?"

"I'm not," Tom said, "but my sister is scared of vampires."

"That's a lie," Liz protested.

"Well, you're superstitious. That's practically the same thing."

"It is not!"

Mrs. Zinck smiled at Liz. "If you want to be superstitious, Nova Scotia is the place to be. I've known hundreds of superstitions since I was a child."

Liz grinned and turned to Shirley. "I've heard some great ones here. Like this morning, when Wade started singing at the table."

"That boy!" Shirley said. "I know he did it to tease me, but now someone's life is threatened."

"Sing at the table, sing at a funeral. That's what the superstition says."

"Brrrr," Shirley said, rubbing her hands nervously. "Let's all go to my place for coffee and hot chocolate, and forget about singing at funerals."

Everyone piled into the car for the short ride to The Fisherman's Home, which was the name of Shirley's guest house. As they drove, Tom looked at Professor Zinck.

"What kind of books have you written?"

"Collections of ghost stories and superstitions, tales of buried treasure and shipwrecks. I love writing about the Maritimes because everyone here has a story to tell."

"Did you say *buried treasure*?"

"That's right. Pirates used to put into Nova Scotia before heading for Europe. Pieces of eight and other treasures have been dug up, and some say that Captain Kidd's wealth may be buried at the bottom of Oak Island's Money Pit."

"I've heard of Oak Island," Liz said. "Isn't that near here?"

The Professor nodded. "Why don't we visit the Money Pit together on Tuesday? I don't know if Kidd's gold is actually down there, but it's still a bizarre place to see."

"That would be great!"

Bright lights shone from the windows of The Fisherman's Home as Mrs. Zinck parked the car. Everyone walked toward the front door except for Shirley and Liz, who disappeared around a corner of the house.

"Brother," Tom said. "Liz is getting impossible."

"Where have they gone?" Mrs. Zinck asked.

"When we went to the wharf earlier tonight, we went out the back door. So Shirley and Liz are going in by the same door, to avoid bad luck."

"Maybe you should, too," Mrs. Zinck suggested.

"I'm not superstitious!" Pulling open the front door, Tom stepped inside and turned to Mrs. Zinck. "You see? The ceiling didn't fall on my head."

"That's not how superstitions work, Tom. Let's just hope you haven't jinxed yourself, or someone else."

"No way." Tossing his jacket at a chair, Tom went into the living room where two men were reading. One was Shirley's husband, Carl Goulden, who stood up to greet the Zincks, and the other was a paying guest named Roger Eliot-Stanton. Tall and bony, he had refused to answer any of Tom's questions and often spent long hours locked in his room.

"Hey, Mr. Eliot-Stanton," Tom exclaimed. "You should have seen the ghost ship! The sky exploded into flames, and you could almost hear the screams of the dying crewmen!"

Lamplight shadowed the deep hollows of Roger Eliot-Stanton's face as he looked up from his book. "There are no ghosts," he said, and then left the room just as Liz walked in.

"Maybe it's his funeral we'll be singing at," Liz commented.

When Carl had finished making the coffee and hot chocolate, he smiled at Professor Zinck. "Would you work the Ouija board with us?"

"A Ouija board!" Liz jumped up from her chair. "May I try it? Please, Carl! I'm sure I can summon spirits."

"I don't know, Liz."

"Please!"

Carl smiled. "Okay, you can give it a try."

As he lit some candles, Shirley went to get their children, Carla, Holli, and Todd. "A big group helps summon the spirits," she explained. "Luckily Wade isn't here, or he'd make fun of us all."

Liz sat down at the Ouija board, opposite Shirley. "Spirit of the past," Shirley chanted, "are you with us? Answer yes."

All eyes watched the board in the yellow candle-light. Somewhere in the house a clock ticked, and Tom was aware of the wind sighing through the trees, but there was no other sound. Seconds passed into minutes and then, with a terrible crash, the outside door flew open.

Shouts and screams were heard, then someone reached for the light switch. In the doorway stood the Goulden's teenaged son, Wade, his face shining with sweat.

"Hey, everyone," he said in an excited voice. "I just heard about the ghost ship! I ran all the way to the wharf, but it was gone. What was it like?"

Carl gave him an irritated look. "You've just scared everyone half to death, Wade."

"Sorry, Dad. Say, is it true you saw the ghost of the *Young Teazer*?"

"It's possible."

Wade grinned at Tom. "Hey, man, I'm surprised to see you sitting around. Why haven't you started your investigation of the *Teazer* light?"

"There are no ghosts," Tom said, trying to sound as haughty as Roger Eliot-Stanton.

Professor Zinck finished his coffee with a quick swallow. "It's getting late, my dear," he said to his wife.

She smiled at Tom and Liz. "I'll look forward to telling you about the Lady in White. My husband doesn't drive, so I'll pick you up tomorrow."

"Thanks, Mrs. Zinck. We can't wait to see your haunted house!"

After helping to clean up the kitchen, Tom went to his bedroom at the back of the house. For a while he sat at the open window, listening to the wind sweeping through the woods, then got into the bed and lay with his eyes on the dark ceiling.

What was the mysterious light out at sea? If it really *was* a ghost ship, had it appeared as a warning to beware of strangers? As for strangers, why had Professor Zinck been so quick to invite Tom and Liz to his haunted house, and even take them to Oak Island? Maybe an ancient curse hung over Lunenburg Manor, a curse that required the sacrifice of young blood.

Sighing deeply, Tom rolled over in bed. They'd been fools to accept an invitation from a stranger who could secretly be *anything*, even a vampire. With a shudder, he pictured the Zincks in the doorway of Lunenburg Manor, fangs glistening and black capes swirling as werewolves howled somewhere in the night.

Tom sighed again, and tried to think of a happier subject. As he began to drift into sleep, images of ghost ships and vampires loomed in his mind. Then, without warning, he felt icy fingers touch his neck.

2

Tom's eyes flew open.

Teeth chattering, he stared at his pillow in terror, waiting for the next touch of those ice-cold fingers. When nothing happened, he leapt from the bed with clenched fists, ready to fight.

The room was empty and still. Warm night air billowed the curtains, but nothing else moved as Tom waited for his heart to return to normal. Finally he got back into bed, but it was a long time before he fell asleep.

The next day Tom didn't mention the icy fingers, knowing how happy Liz and Wade would be to repeat the story when things got dull. But he did manage to laugh off his fears about the Zincks being vampires, and felt relaxed that evening as Mrs. Zinck drove them to the nearby community of Lunenburg. Expecting to see just another town, Tom was startled by its unusual beauty.

"What great old houses! Look at the spires on that one."

Mrs. Zinck smiled. "Lunenburg was founded in 1753 by settlers from Germany, and they brought a distinctive style of architecture with them. Do you see that house's dormer, overhanging the street? That's called a 'bump,' and they say it's a great room for watching what your neighbours are doing."

"This is fantastic. Like a fairy land," Liz said, staring at a house with gingerbread decorations around its gables. "I love all the flowers, and the bright colours of the houses."

"Look at that one," Tom exclaimed. "It reminds me of a wedding cake, with all those little roofs piled on top of each other. They could make a great movie in Lunenburg."

Mrs. Zinck laughed. "They already have. In fact, a company wanted to make a horror movie in our house, but we refused."

"A horror movie? How come?"

"I guess because it's old, and the tower makes it look a bit creepy."

They drove past brilliant-red buildings at the harbour, where gillnetters rode at anchor, then climbed a hill into a residential area where the streets were pleasantly shaded by old trees.

"Here's Lunenburg Manor," Mrs. Zinck said, as she pulled up in front of a large house with peaked windows and a tower.

"It *would* make a great horror movie," Tom agreed. "I'd give anything to live in a house like this."

"Even with a ghost?"

"Especially with a ghost!"

The windows of Lunenburg Manor were dark and menacing. Waiting at the door was a thin man with a heavily lined face.

"Welcome to Lunenburg Manor," he said, holding out a hand that felt brittle to the touch. "We've been expecting you."

Tom tried to smile, but the man's dusty voice and drooping eyes gave him a chill. Maybe he spent his nights in the cellar, creating the next Frankenstein out of spare parts collected from supper guests.

Tom stepped reluctantly into the hallway. On the wall was a sword, its silver blade reflecting the dying sun. Nearby was a faded picture of a runaway horse, with a rider whose eyes goggled in fear.

"The meal will be served in forty-five minutes, madam."

"Thank you, Henneyberry." Mrs. Zinck looked down the shadowy hallway, then went to a mirror and arranged her already perfect black hair. Again she looked down the hallway, then at Henneyberry.

"When are we eating?"

"In forty-five minutes, madam."

"Oh yes, I believe you just told me." For a second time, Mrs. Zinck's hands went to her hair without finding anything to do. "Henneyberry," she said after a pause, "I'd like to see how dinner's coming along."

He nodded his head, and shuffled along the hallway

behind Mrs. Zinck. As a door closed silently behind them, Tom looked at Liz.

"That guy could star as the phantom of the Rue Morgue."

"I think he's kinda cute, with his shiny head and perfectly rounded shoulders."

"What's wrong with Mrs. Zinck? She's started acting strange."

"Maybe she's worried about something."

"I'll bet she's going to check the soup in case Henneyberry's spiked it with cyanide."

"Listen, Tom, even if the soup tastes funny, you eat it. Don't do anything gross, like spitting it out, or Mom and Dad will be furious."

"Only if you tell them! Try it and . . ."

Liz raised a warning hand as the door opened and Mrs. Zinck emerged. With a bright smile, she motioned them toward a room where a grandfather clock ticked loudly.

"I'm sorry I kept you waiting."

"Are you okay, Mrs. Zinck?"

"Of course."

She cranked up her smile a few more watts, but it still looked unreal to Tom. Thinking about Henneyberry, alone in the kitchen with the soup, made the hairs on his neck tingle.

"Let's sit down, kids, and I'll tell you about the Lady in White."

"At last!"

The room was tastefully furnished with a thick Chinese carpet; red velvet curtains were looped beside the tall windows, and they saw elegant white candles in a candelabra above the fireplace.

"Many generations of people have lived in Lunenburg Manor," Mrs. Zinck said. "Two winters ago, I was awakened by the sound of a horse, galloping away into the night. Nothing unusual in that, perhaps, except that we checked the snow in the morning and there were no hoofprints."

"Could they have drifted in?"

Mrs. Zinck shook her head. "There was no fresh snow. Well, I decided it was all a dream, and had almost forgotten about it when I began hearing hollow knocks in my room. It was a strangely empty sound, and I can tell you it scared me, especially the night when I was awakened by the knocking and then had the covers yanked off my bed."

"Wow! What did you do?"

"I screamed. My husband came running from his room, threw on the lights, and found me shaking with terror. The covers were in a heap on the floor, and I can assure you it wasn't me who'd put them there."

For a second Tom thought he heard hollow knocks coming from somewhere above. His eyes rolled toward the ceiling. "Did either of you just hear a knocking sound?"

Liz laughed. "My brother has a 100-megawatt imagination, Mrs. Zinck. Soon you'll see him screaming down the road."

Tom's face went red. "This house gives me the creeps. It's almost like there's something evil here."

Mrs. Zinck stared at him. "You can feel it, too?"

"I can sure feel something."

For a moment she continued to stare, then turned to Liz. "Zinck is a German name, and both my husband

and I are descended from the original settlers of Lunenburg. You may have heard the term *poltergeist*, which comes from the German and means 'playful spirit.' At first we thought such a spirit inhabited the Manor, but later we decided it must be the ghost of a very sad person."

"What happened?"

"I began to notice the scent of roses, and one night I heard light footsteps in my room. They crossed to the closet, and there was something that sounded like the rustling of a petticoat, but I could see nothing, in spite of the bright moonlight. Then a week later I did see her, after some force had made me go up to the attic."

"*Made* you go up? All by yourself?"

Mrs. Zinck nodded. "A lady in a wedding dress stood by the attic window. Her head was bowed, and she was crying. I was filled with sadness, and was walking forward to comfort her when she vanished, leaving the room as cold as ice. For some reason I was no longer afraid, now that I'd actually seen the ghost, but I decided I had to learn her story. After doing a lot of research, I found out that a young lady who once lived here had been deeply in love with a man who left her and married another woman. Shortly after, the unhappy girl hanged herself in the attic of the Manor."

"Oh no!"

"They say that some ghosts are the spirits of those who have died tragically, and cannot find peace. I think the Lady in White wanted me to hear the sound of her lover, galloping away on horseback after he'd broken her heart, and then wanted me to learn her story so that someone in the Manor would know of her sadness."

Liz shook her head. "Men make me sick."

Tom's eyebrows rose dramatically. "Is that why your bedroom walls are covered with their pictures?"

"Every night I throw darts at those pictures."

"And every morning you kiss and make up. I've heard your rubbery lips going *Smack! Smack!*"

Mrs. Zinck laughed. "You two remind me of being young. I was always bickering with my brother." Looking a bit sad, she added, "The Professor and I have no children of our own."

The large shape of Professor Zinck appeared in the doorway. "Good evening. Have you heard my wife's story about the Lady in White?"

Tom nodded. "It's sad. I always thought ghosts were things to be scared of, not feel sorry for."

Professor Zinck looked at his wife. "It's almost time to eat, and there's still no sign of our other guest. Should I go up the hill, to see if he's prowling around the graveyard?"

"I don't think that's necessary, dear. Why don't you show Tom and Liz some of the treasures?"

"Good idea." The Professor pressed a button, and Henneyberry materialized in the doorway. "Please bring the leather case from the safe."

"If you wish, sir."

During the long wait for Henneyberry to return, an Irish setter with a gleaming red coat came into the room, sat directly at the Professor's feet, and raised its handsome head for patting. After receiving a generous helping of affection from Tom and Liz, the dog stretched out and instantly fell asleep. Raucous snoring filled the room, making Tom laugh.

"What's his name?"

"Boscawen, but we call him 'Boss' for short. The name comes from an admiral in the British navy."

Henneyberry returned, carrying a small leather case. Taking up a position beside the Professor, he watched Tom and Liz with narrowed eyes.

Professor Zinck ran his fingers over the leather case, enjoying its smooth texture, then placed it on a low marble table and snapped open the catches. There was a glint of gold as he took out a coin, and placed it in Liz's hand.

"You're holding a louis d'or, my dear. It's worth a pretty penny."

Liz twisted her hand, and the coin disappeared. Henneyberry gasped in shock, then nearly had heart failure as Liz reached up and found the coin behind his ear. The Zincks laughed heartily, and applauded.

"Just a little trick I taught myself," Liz said, bowing. "I'm glad I finally got to try it!"

Tom burned with envy. Not only had Liz secretly learned the coin trick, but she had found the perfect time to use it. "Do you want to see my numero uno card trick? It will amaze you!"

"Perhaps later, Tom." Professor Zinck dropped several gold coins in Tom's hand. "These come from the sea bed. It's estimated that five thousand shipwrecks lie off the Nova Scotia coast. The coins belong to a friend who dives as a hobby, and who recently came up with *this* splendid object from a wreck."

The Professor reached into the case, and lifted out a golden goblet sparkling with jewels. "Rubies and emeralds," he said, pointing to the gorgeous stones. "Amethysts and sapphires."

"It must be worth a fortune!"

"At least."

The Professor glanced toward the doorway, and his face broke into a wide smile. "Well, speak of the devil. Here's the owner of the treasure."

Tom turned, half expecting to see someone in expensive clothes and flashy diamond rings. Instead, he was surprised to see worn jeans, an old denim jacket, and a face that—with its thick black beard, fierce eyes, and deeply creased skin—needed only an eye patch to become the very picture of a pirate. The man's black eyes flashed straight to the gold coins in Tom's hand, making his heart pound.

"You going to take those home?"

"No, sir."

The savage black eyes studied Tom's face. "Go ahead. Put them in your pocket."

Tom walked nervously to the leather case. The coins clinked as he dropped them in, and he breathed a quiet sigh of relief as he knelt down to rub the Irish setter's head. Who *was* this person?

The Professor returned the goblet to the case. "Still trying to give your wealth away, my friend? What an attitude." Taking the stranger by the arm, he walked toward Liz. "Come and meet a young woman who has some interesting ideas about men."

Blushing, Liz held out her hand. "Hi. I'm Liz Austen."

"I'm Black Dog," the man said.

After introducing Tom, the Professor put his arm around Black Dog's shoulders and gave him a friendly squeeze. "Kids, you are privileged to meet one of Canada's great artists. A neglected genius, who will one day be hailed in the capitals of the world!"

The man looked slightly embarrassed, but didn't deny that he might be a genius. Henneyberry, however, snorted with contempt before closing the leather case and carrying it out of the room.

"Don't drop it," Black Dog called after him.

A mutter came from the hallway as Henneyberry shuffled away. There was an awkward silence, then Black Dog glanced at Tom. "Why didn't you pocket the coins?"

"Because they're yours."

"I don't want the things."

The Professor smiled. He poured richly coloured sherry into crystal glasses that he then handed to his wife and Black Dog. "A libation on the altar of good friendship," he said, lifting his glass.

"Cheers." Black Dog knocked back his drink, and smacked his red lips vigorously. "Always the best sherry. You people live well."

"So could you, Black Dog. Just cash in those coins and the goblet, and you'll be rich. Then you can be a full-time artist instead of wasting your life in a boiler room."

"I like my job. Besides, too much money is an evil thing. I want no part of those treasures, so they're yours for good."

Mrs. Zinck shook her head. "We're only keeping them safe for you, Black Dog. You need lots of money to finance your art, which is why you'll inherit everything we have when we die. Except for a bit of money left to Henneyberry and the Professor's brother, it will all be yours."

Black Dog turned to the Professor. "I've told you before, leave it *all* to your brother. I refuse it!"

Professor Zinck shook his head sadly. "My friend," he sighed, "when will you come to your senses? You deserve the money, not my brother. He broke my parents' hearts, so they left him nothing. They would want their riches to be left to a young genius like you."

"Rubbish."

Henneyberry's solemn face appeared out of the shadows in the hallway. "The meal is ready."

The Professor rubbed his big hands in anticipation, then held out his arm and led Mrs. Zinck across the hallway to the dining room. Liz waited hopefully for Black Dog to be as gallant, but he only helped himself to another quick sherry and left the room without offering her even a glance. "Men," she muttered.

"Let's eat," Tom said, hurrying across to the dining room. Large and dark, it was lit by chandeliers and orange flames that leapt in a marble fireplace. The Zincks were at opposite ends of a long table set with crystal and silver, which reflected the sparkle of candlelight.

"Please sit here, Tom." Above Mrs. Zinck was an unusual oval portrait of a man. One of his eyes looked straight at Tom, the other was focused on the fireplace. Tom tried to avoid the picture, but there was nothing else to look at except the twisted shadows thrown on the wall by a towering bamboo palm. Against his will, Tom remembered last night's icy fingers and he felt his neck tingle.

Tom looked at Mrs. Zinck. "My nerves are on edge. I guess because this house is haunted."

"Then perhaps I'd better not mention that we also have bats."

"*What?*"

She laughed. "They nest in the attic, and fly around the rooms at night. They're scary, of course, but the patterns they make in flight are really quite beautiful."

The Professor nodded. "They go *tssch-tssch* as they fly, and I swear they're laughing at the hopeless attempts Boss makes to catch them. Bats are very useful, you know, because they eat vast numbers of insects."

"That's okay, but how much blood do they drink every night? I'm too young to be a donor."

"You've been watching too many late-night movies, Tom."

Henneyberry grew out of the shadows, which seemed to be his favourite trick. The dancing candlelight made his lined face seemed especially long and solemn as he moved slowly around the table, placing a bowl of soup in front of each person.

"*Kartoffelsuppe,*" he said in Tom's ear, the muttered word sounding like an ancient curse. "Enjoy."

"Thanks," Tom said shakily, then waited for Black Dog to try the soup. When the man had done so—and not fallen to the floor clutching his throat in agony—Tom took a sip and discovered that the soup was delicious.

"Do you like it?" Mrs. Zinck asked. "The schooner crews often had this soup while fishing out on the Grand Banks."

Professor Zinck snapped his fingers. "I knew I'd

forgotten something. Next time the kids visit, we must offer them some baked fish tongues as a treat." When Tom and Liz stared silently at each other, he laughed. "Just joking, of course, but the schooner crews used to eat all of the fish: tongues, jowls, hearts. It was the most easily available food, do you see? But they also enjoyed lots of tasty goodies while out fishing, like apple schnitzel and pumpkin pie."

"Aren't you having any soup, Mrs. Zinck?"

She shook her head. "I must watch my diet very carefully. I'm a diabetic."

"Do you take insulin shots?"

"Yes," she said, then changed the subject. "Ah! Here comes the Solomon Gundy."

This turned out to be small pieces of raw herring, served with onion and a wedge of lemon. After the delicious *kartoffelsuppe*, Tom was disappointed when the herring had very little flavour. His taste buds were soon back in action, however, as Henneyberry produced an excellent haddock covered in crushed almonds and surrounded by slices of fried banana.

"Fantastic," Liz said, as she polished off her haddock. "I've barely got room for dessert."

Henneyberry made another silent entrance, bearing plates of deep-fried apple segments rolled in cinnamon. Each slice was crisp on the outside, and steaming-hot inside.

"What a feast," Tom said, pushing back his chair and rubbing his swollen belly. "Mr. Henneyberry is a genius cook."

"You're right, Tom," Professor Zinck replied, "and we're lucky he's here. An expensive Halifax restaurant tried to lure him away, but we kept him by raising his pay a bit. Not that money seems important to Henneyberry!"

As the Professor laughed merrily, Henneyberry's sad, wet eyes watched him from the shadows. Tom felt a surge of pity for the old man, although he couldn't tell why.

"Can we help with the dishes?"

"No thanks, Tom." Mrs. Zinck looked at her watch. "Perhaps I should drive you home now."

"Thanks for the great meal, Mr. Henneyberry."

For the first time that evening, the solemn face managed a smile. "Please come again."

In the hallway they were putting on their jackets when Tom noticed a bookcase containing a collection of volumes, each with the words *by Professor C. Zinck*. "Hey, neat! Here're all your books."

"What an output," Liz said admiringly. "I have trouble scratching together enough words for a single essay."

"Say, Professor Zinck, what's your first name? Is it something unusual like Caliph or Carim?"

He nodded. "My name certainly is unusual. It's Carol. You see, my parents failed to have the daughters they always wanted, so they stuck their two sons with girls' names."

Smiling, Mrs. Zinck hugged her husband. "I can tell you really like Tom and Liz. Only your closest friends know the truth about your name."

"You're right, my dear! It's been a very pleasant evening, and I'm looking forward to visiting Oak Island tomorrow with the kids."

"Thanks a million, Professor."

After saying goodnight, Tom and Liz went out into the darkness with Mrs. Zinck. Walking toward the car, she suddenly stopped and looked up at the looming black outline of Lunenburg Manor.

"Thank goodness you were here tonight!"

"Why, Mrs. Zinck?"

"Because it took my mind off my fears. Tom, do you remember saying you felt the presence of evil in the Manor?"

"Well, it's not that I was scared or anything, but . . ."

"I've always loved our home, but lately I've been so frightened. I have this terrible feeling that someone is about to suffer a horrible fate in Lunenburg Manor."

3

Early the next morning, Tom and Liz stood on the roadside at Mahone Bay, watching a man named Marty focus his camera on the three graceful churches that cast their reflections across the shimmering water.

"Got it," Marty said, then hurried back to his car. "Let's move out, kids. Time is short."

Marty's wife, Christine, burned rubber as soon as the rear door slammed behind Tom and Liz. Professor Zinck smiled at the couple in the front seat.

"Christine and Marty," he said, "let me thank you again for offering a drive to total strangers. When my wife was taken ill, I was afraid our trip would have to be cancelled."

"I'm glad Tom and Liz explained you were stuck for a ride," Christine said, her attractive eyes smiling at the Professor in the mirror. "We absolutely *must* shoot Peggy's Cove first, then we'll visit Oak Island with you to check out all this hoopla about pirates."

"After that we'll hit Chester and Hubbards Beach," Marty said, consulting a list of tourist attractions. Picking up his calculator, he punched in distances and checked these against his watch. The young New Jersey couple had arrived as guests at The Fisherman's Home the previous evening, and were determined to photograph every possible attraction before returning to the States.

"I love this place," Marty exclaimed. "Do you know that people never lock their doors here? It's amazing."

"And the scenery is magnificent," Christine said. "Look at the view coming up now."

The highway ran beside the sea. The deep blue of the water was separated from the pale blue of the sky by a distant headland, shadowed by the morning sun behind it. Close to shore was the silhouette of a girl in a rowboat, pulling in a net as her collie watched alertly from the bow.

"Let's get this scene," Marty said.

The car screeched to a stop. As Marty fiddled with his camera, Tom watched two gulls squabbling noisily over a tasty morsel. One of them lifted away into the sky, dipped and soared, then circled down to a log bleached white by the sun. Its smooth texture reminded Tom of the smooth leather case containing Black Dog's treasures.

"I hope Mrs. Zinck will be better soon, Professor."

He responded with a brief smile. "Thank you."

"You don't seem yourself."

"You're right." The Professor waited for the car to get under way, then looked at Tom and Liz. "Please forgive my mood. I had a forerunner last night, and it left me a bit shaken."

"What's a forerunner?"

"I'd rather not discuss it, Liz."

She stared intently at the Professor. "It's a superstition, isn't it? That's why you won't tell me. You think I'll faint or something."

He shook his head. "Of course not. The subject upsets me, that's all."

Liz gazed moodily at the passing scene. Marty's camera continued to click, and occasionally Tom yawned but all was peaceful until Christine suddenly swung the wheel. The car bounced and fishtailed along the highway shoulder, then swerved back onto the asphalt.

"What happened?" Professor Zinck shouted.

"Some jerk came speeding around the corner on our side. Boy, did that scare me!"

"Good driving, honey," Marty said, quietly. "You saved our bacon."

Sweat glistened on the Professor's forehead. He wiped at it with a shaking hand, then leaned forward to watch for more trouble. "I never should have come today," he muttered to himself. "First Arnold Smith, and now me."

"Professor Zinck," Liz begged, "*please* tell us. What is a forerunner?"

"It's a warning of approaching death."

"*What?*"

"Now, aren't you sorry you asked?" The Professor shook his head. "Some things are better left alone."

"What kind of warning? Do you hear voices?"

"No."

"Well, what then?"

Professor Zinck sighed. "Very well, Liz, I give up. I'll tell you about forerunners, and then let's drop the subject."

"Agreed."

"A person might hear three slow taps on the wall, and shortly after, someone in the family dies. Or a forerunner could take the form of seeing your own spirit. I heard of a woman who was passing a cemetery and saw a ghostly vision of herself, walking among the tombstones. She went home, gave away her possessions, and died shortly after."

"I can't stand it." Liz hugged her body, but kept her eyes fixed on the Professor. "Tell us more."

"Arnold Smith was a teacher who drove this way to school. One night recently, people appeared suddenly on the road ahead and he just missed hitting them. Arnold got out of his car, but they'd disappeared into thin air."

"How was that a forerunner?"

"A week later, Arnold himself was killed when his car plunged off the road."

"I don't get it."

"Arnold's car crashed at the exact spot where he'd seen the ghostly people. They were his forerunner, warning him that he was about to die."

"I feel faint." For a moment Liz stared at the Professor with wide eyes, then she remembered something. "What about *your* forerunner, Professor?"

"I won't discuss it, Liz, and that's final."

"You win." She smiled. "Thanks for telling us about forerunners. I guess I'll be listening tonight for three slow taps on the wall, but I just had to know."

"Hey folks," Marty said, looking puzzled, "why haven't we seen a Mountie yet?"

"There's one straight ahead."

"*What?*" He grabbed his camera. "Where? I don't see one!"

"In that police car."

"But he's wearing a brown uniform. And where's his horse?"

Tom laughed. "Mounties patrol in cars these days, and they only wear red serge for special occasions."

Marty lowered his camera. "What a disappointment! How can I face everyone back home without a picture of a genuine Mountie?"

"Check the legislative building in Halifax. There may be one there in dress uniform."

"Let's hope so." Marty looked at a highway sign, announcing the approach to Peggy's Cove. "What if this place lets us down, too? It may not even have a lighthouse. I'll be stuck with a bunch of empty film."

Christine gave him an affectionate smile. "I'm sure it's going to be beautiful, sweetheart."

This was an accurate prediction. The car entered a spectacular landscape of treeless land, empty of anything but the wandering highway and hundreds of huge boulders scattered everywhere. Some lay alone, others balanced against each other, resting exactly where they'd been left thousands of years ago by the melting of a glacier.

"In some parts of Nova Scotia the ice was two kilometres high," Professor Zinck said. "Here the glacier scraped away all the soil, exposing granite that is 415 million years old."

"Give or take a year," Liz quipped.

The Professor smiled. "There's Peggy's Cove, straight ahead. Don't the houses look fragile out on the granite?"

"You'd think the wind would blow them into the sea!"

Houses of bright blues and yellows and reds were perched above the waves. The village was dominated by a church spire and a lighthouse famous worldwide. Christine followed a lane that wound among the houses, needing all her driving skills to avoid the hundreds of tourists who clogged the village.

"That poor kid," Liz said, looking at a girl who'd stepped onto the porch of her house and been instantly photographed. "Imagine living in the middle of a tourist trap."

"This is fantastic." Marty grabbed his camera as the car stopped in a parking lot beside a tour bus from Ontario. "We're scheduled for thirty minutes here, so let's hustle."

The young couple hurried off. Professor Zinck wanted to rest in the car, so Tom and Liz headed alone across the granite toward the booming surf.

"Maybe the Professor's forerunner warned him not to walk out here," Tom said, pointing at a sign that cautioned *Swells and breaking waves may unexpectedly rise over the rocks and sweep you out to sea.*

Liz snorted. "You get full marks for imagination."

"Well, something is bothering Professor Zinck."

"Sure, he's upset about the forerunner, plus Mrs. Zinck being sick."

"Now, *that* is definitely weird. Just last night Mrs. Zinck told us she's frightened, and today she's at death's door."

Liz laughed. "She's probably got the flu, or a sore tummy from too much Solomon Gundy."

Tom jumped between two slabs of granite, then studied the many fissures, which seamed the rock like the face of a very old person. "I'll bet Henneyberry put something in Mrs. Zinck's food, and that's why she's out of commission."

"But why? You're always producing a theory before you have any proof. You should study the situation, watch the people, and only speak up when you've got an iron-clad case."

"You work your way, Liz, and I'll work mine."

As they approached the lighthouse, the wind carried the click of cameras and the shouts of tourists setting up pictures: *Move to your left—NO!—I said your LEFT! Can't you get that kid to smile? Hey, lady, you're blocking my shot!*

Tom sat with Liz in the warm sunshine until their time was up. Right on the minute, their car rolled out of Peggy's Cove past a final vision of a wharf, which was piled high with lobster traps and groaning under the weight of a multitude of cameras and their owners.

"Whoever designed this village must have received a big fat fee from Kodak," Liz commented.

Tom noticed a highway sign that had been riddled with bullets. Could this be a forerunner, warning him of his own death? Hoping Liz wouldn't notice, he got out his lucky coin and rubbed it vigorously. "I guess nobody's actually been killed there?"

Professor Zinck looked at Tom. "Killed where?"

"At Oak Island."

"Actually, five men have died while searching for the treasure that is supposed to be at the bottom of the Money Pit. In 1860 a man was scalded to death when a pumping machine blew up, then in 1963 four men were overcome by fumes while working in an excavation. The locals say only one more must die, and then the island will give up its secret. But of course that's just superstition."

"Sure," Tom said, trying to smile.

"Say Prof," Marty asked, "is it true that Captain Kidd buried his horde on Oak Island?"

"No one knows. Just before his execution, Kidd offered to reveal the secret location of his treasure in return for a pardon. He said there'd be enough gold to make a chain that would stretch around the city of London, but the authorities refused the deal and hung him."

"What exactly is this Money Pit?"

"It was discovered by a teenager way back in 1795. He was hunting on Oak Island and spotted an old ship's tackle block dangling from the branch of an ancient oak. The ground below had caved in slightly, so the boy figured something might be buried there. He came back with a couple of friends and some shovels. They made a discovery that led to what has become the most expensive treasure hunt in history."

"They found gold?"

"No, they discovered a circular shaft with walls of solid clay, and a floor of oaken planks. They ripped these out, and what do you suppose they found?"

"More dirt?"

"Exactly. Down they went, and soon they came to a second set of planks. When these were removed they kept on digging, and found yet another platform!"

"Those poor guys," Liz said. "How discouraging."

"Apparently they were very excited, because it appeared that something of immense value must be down there. Otherwise why build all those elaborate platforms? Eventually, with the help of others, the boys removed nine platforms and were down very deep when their shovels struck something hard which stretched the width of the shaft. The lads were convinced the treasure lay directly beneath, but it was getting dark so they climbed back up to the surface and spent a happy evening discussing how they'd spend their riches."

"What did they find the next day?" Liz asked.

"A shaft full of water." The Professor shook his head in sympathy with the long-ago treasure searchers. "They started to bale water, then used a pump, but the shaft remained flooded. Eventually it was discovered that the engineering genius who constructed the Money Pit had included a second shaft that angled out to the sea bed. This was designed to flood the Money Pit if strangers got into it, and the plan worked! The first searchers gave up, but many others have tried ever since. There have been twenty-one separate shafts dug, even though nothing has been brought up so far except three links of a gold watch chain."

Liz smiled. "What a great story. In a way I hope no one discovers the truth, because it's more fun to wonder what's down there."

Tom looked down the highway, where a sign with a

huge pirate indicated the turnoff to Oak Island. "The secret is safe until one more person dies," he said, with a doom-laden voice.

"You're becoming superstitious, Tom," Liz remarked.

"Yeah? Well, this place sounds creepy."

The car bumped along a narrow causeway toward Oak Island, which appeared peaceful enough. Another giant pirate, holding a treasure chest on his shoulder, stood guard with a cutlass outside a building marked *tickets.*

Christine parked beside a black van with two skulls on the rear door. They were crossing the parking lot when a familiar face emerged from the woods. "It's Roger Eliot-Stanton," Liz said. "You wouldn't think he'd be interested in Oak Island."

"I bet he won't even say hello."

Sure enough, their fellow guest from The Fisherman's Home passed them without a word. "Why *is* he here?" Tom said. "Maybe we should follow him."

Liz laughed. "As much as I dislike the guy, I can't believe Roger Eliot-Stanton is a criminal. He's just a tourist, like the rest of us."

Tom watched the long-legged man open a car door, then look their way. "Ah ha! He did see us. Why did he pretend not to?"

"He's just being rude," Liz replied.

They walked along a narrow dirt road through the woods past sweet-smelling evergreens, thickly carpeted ferns, and flowering bushes. A strange fear grew in Tom that danger lay ahead, but he overcame it by picturing the three boys as they walked across this very island centuries ago on their way to making such a great discovery.

"Do you believe in the Money Pit, Professor Zinck?"

"Something may be down there, Tom. One writer suggested it could hold the combined wealth of several famous pirates, including Blackbeard and Morgan, but of course that's just a guess."

"It's strange they would leave treasure behind on a deserted island without any guards."

"People say that after pirates buried a treasure, they often chopped off someone's head and threw his body down the hole so his ghost would be on guard. To this day, people here believe that buried treasure can only be dug up at night, and if anyone speaks during the expedition, the guardian ghost will be given the power to rise up and slay the treasure seekers."

"What a way to die," Tom murmured.

The road emerged from the woods at a bay with a rocky beach. A pink shell near the water attracted Liz's attention, and Christine commented on the cool breeze off the sea, but Tom's eyes were drawn to a nearby hill where a tall drilling rig stood dramatically against the sky.

"No one's there right now," Professor Zinck said. "I read in the paper that they're waiting for new equipment to arrive."

The group hurried along the beach and started climbing toward the rig. But then the Professor held up a hand, signalling a halt. "We're at the original Money Pit."

Confused, Tom looked around the hillside. Then he

spotted a few broken timbers surrounding a hole full of dirt. "This is *it?*"

The Professor nodded. "Are you disappointed?"

"A bit."

Tom stared down into the original Money Pit, then continued up the hill to the rig. It stood directly above a large steel pipe, which reached deep down into the earth. Tom dropped a pebble and heard it hit water somewhere below. Straightening up, he studied the rusty machinery, which was scattered around. The door of a tarpaper shack slammed back and forth in the wind that rushed across the hilltop, and a rusting car without wheels stood under a tree, but the scene was empty of life.

"This is like a ghost camp," Liz said.

"It's neat to think of all the people who've gone after the treasure. Just think, Liz, Captain Kidd's gold may be right under our feet!"

Professor Zinck came up the hill, puffing from the strain of the climb, but Christine and Marty weren't with him. "They've gone to take pictures of Chester," the Professor explained. "They'll be back for us in an hour."

"What else can we see?"

The Professor pointed toward a cove. "Down there is the 'G rock,' which was discovered in 1970. Maybe you can figure out what it means."

"Are you coming with us?"

"No, thanks. Climbing up and down hills isn't my cup of tea."

A letter G had been chiselled into the rock, but there was no way of knowing what it could mean. "G stands for gold," Tom suggested. "Maybe the treasure is buried here."

"G also means ghouls, ghosts, and goblins. Let's turn the rock over, and see what comes screeching out."

"Forget it." Tom skipped some flat stones across the ocean, then they started climbing the hill toward the rig. "We may be walking in the footsteps of pirates, Liz. Can't you just picture a ship with a Jolly Roger anchored in the cove, and men with eye patches and cutlasses climbing this very hill with treasure chests for the Money Pit. What drama!"

"I've had enough drama for one day, what with the Professor's forerunner and nearly getting killed on the highway. This place is getting on my nerves, Tom. I keep expecting a headless pirate to leap out at us."

There was no sign of Professor Zinck at the top of the hill. The whistle of the wind in the drilling rig and the banging of the tarpaper door made Tom feel lonely as he looked around for their friend.

"There's something wrong, Liz. I can feel it."

She nodded. "Where's Professor Zinck? He wouldn't leave without telling us."

Tom glanced at the scattered equipment, then tried to see into the darkness within the shack. He felt certain someone was watching them, and was about to tell Liz when there was a flurry of sound from the woods.

Whirling around, he saw a black raven rise above the trees and head out to sea. The sudden fright made Tom's blood pound through his veins and he watched anxiously as Liz walked past the machinery to look down the hillside. Somehow he knew that she would turn and call his name.

Liz whirled around, her face shocked. "Tom! Come here!"

With a feeling that he was living through a horrible dream, Tom stumbled over bits of rusty metal and machinery, then ran to Liz's side and looked toward the original Money Pit. Professor Zinck lay beside it, face down in the dirt.

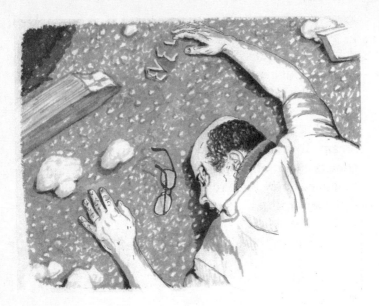

4

Tom and Liz rushed to the Professor, and found blood seeping from a wound in his temple. Gently they rolled him over, and Liz checked for a pulse.

"Look at this," Tom said, kneeling down. "He managed to write something in the dirt before passing out."

Clearly visible in the dirt were the letters EVEL. Liz looked at them, then stood up. "We've got to get help!"

They ran quickly through the woods to the ticket office, and breathlessly asked the attendant for assistance. Saying she had first-aid training, the attendant drove them back across the island in her Jeep, and the trio raced to the Money Pit.

Professor Zinck was gone.

"I don't understand," Tom stammered, staring at the Money Pit. "He was lying right beside it."

"Is this a practical joke?" the attendant said, frowning.

"No, ma'am. You can see the dirt's all mussed up, where Professor Zinck was lying. And look where he wrote EVEL."

The attendant returned to the Jeep, shaking her head. Feeling embarrassed and worried, Tom and Liz remained at the Money Pit to search for the Professor, but found no sign of him, either in the surrounding trees or the tarpaper shack.

"Maybe he was dazed," Tom suggested, "and wandered away through the woods."

"We could never search an island this big. Let's wait in the parking lot until Christine and Marty get back, and see what they think."

At the lot Tom and Liz paced anxiously, wondering what might have happened. Who had attacked Professor Zinck, and why had he then disappeared?

"That was a clue he wrote in the dirt," Tom said. "He was telling us he'd been attacked by evil, or something like that. He just spelled it wrong."

"A professor can't spell the word evil?"

"You've got a point. But I'm sure EVEL is a clue."

At long last, Christine and Marty rolled into the parking lot. Their smiles quickly left their faces when they heard the news, but Christine had a hopeful suggestion.

"Maybe he walked through the woods while you were fetching the attendant, and then talked some driver into giving him a ride home. If he was dazed, he might have forgotten about meeting us."

"You think he's gone back to Lunenburg?"

"It's possible. Why don't we drive there and find out?"

Although reluctant to leave Oak Island without the Professor, Tom and Liz agreed to check his home before contacting the police about a search party. When they reached Lunenburg, they were taken to the Manor by Christine and Marty, who waited outside in the car.

"Please be home, Professor," Tom said, as the doorbell echoed somewhere deep within Lunenburg Manor.

The door creaked open. "Yes?" Henneyberry said, mournfully.

"Mr. Henneyberry, is the Professor here?"

"Yes."

"Really?" Liz smiled, happily. "I don't believe it. We've been worried sick."

Henneyberry started to close the door, but Tom stopped him. "Please, sir, may we talk to Professor Zinck? We'd like to know what happened."

Henneyberry shook his head. "The Professor is not feeling well."

"How about if we come back later, after we see the police."

Henneyberry looked surprised. "Why are you going to the police?"

"Professor Zinck was attacked at Oak Island. We've got to report it. They'll want to question him, and start an investigation."

"I see," Henneyberry said, nodding slowly. "Well, come back here after you've been to the police."

Tom and Liz hurried down the porch steps, and had almost reached the car when Henneyberry called their names. As he beckoned them back to the Manor, they exchanged puzzled glances.

"What is it, Mr. Henneyberry?" Liz asked.

"I've decided that you should talk to Professor Zinck before seeing the police. He may want the officers to come here, and question you all together."

"That's a good idea."

"But do remember that the Professor's had a terrible shock. He's not himself."

Henneyberry led them into the shadowy hallway, then up the stairs. Light filtered in through stained-glass windows cheerfully decorated with flowers and birds, but the atmosphere was still gloomy as they followed Henneyberry's slow-motion steps to the top floor and along a dark hallway. At the end were some service stairs and a closed bedroom door.

"Wait here," Henneyberry whispered. He went into the bedroom, and shut the door.

"I wonder how Mrs. Zinck is feeling?" Tom said. His voice was shaky.

"I'm not surprised she's afraid of this spooky old place. When the Professor tells her about the attack, she's going to be even more worried."

Tom looked at an old painting of a cow in a field, then began pacing the hallway. At last, Henneyberry opened the door. "Don't be too long."

Musty hot air filled the room, and a fireplace threw dancing light on the walls. The Professor lay in a four-poster bed topped by an elaborate canopy. Beyond the bed was a circular alcove with windows looking down at the harbour and the boats riding at anchor.

Professor Zinck's head rested on a pillow. They saw a large bandage over his temple. Raising a weak hand, the Professor motioned for Tom and Liz to come forward.

"Many thanks for your concern," he said, his voice no more than a whisper.

"Who attacked you, Professor?"

"My mind's a blank. I remember talking to you near the drilling rig, and then all I have is a brief memory of riding in a car. Apparently I walked to the highway and flagged down a motorist, who brought me home. I can't remember anything else."

Henneyberry fussed with the pillow in an effort to make the Professor more comfortable, then poured him a glass of water. "The doctor says you'll be fine after a few days' rest."

"Professor Zinck, have you called the police yet?"

"I'm not going to."

"But why not?"

"It will upset my wife, who's already ill. First the police will come here, then there'll be a news story and the neighbours will be calling. Once started, it never ends. Do you understand?"

Liz nodded. "I see your point. But what about the attack? Shouldn't it be investigated?"

"I must think of my wife."

"Then *we'll* investigate it, Professor!"

He looked concerned. "I'd rather you didn't. There's been enough trouble."

"Don't worry," Tom said. "We can look after ourselves, and you've already given us a great lead to work on."

"I have?" The Professor attempted a smile. "Impossible."

"Do you remember writing EVEL in the dirt? We're sure it's a clue to your attacker!"

Looking pale, Professor Zinck frowned in concentration. "No, I'm sorry, but nothing comes back."

"You're straining yourself, sir," Henneyberry warned. "You should rest now."

"Perhaps you're right."

Liz smiled at him. "It's great you're safe, Professor. We'll try to find out who attacked you."

As they followed Henneyberry down the stairs, Tom pictured Mrs. Zinck lying ill somewhere in the house. Why was she suddenly so sick? With a shudder, he thought of her fears about the Manor. Were they about to come true?

The next morning, Tom tried to convince Christine and Marty to return to Oak Island in search of clues, but the young couple had only a few days' holiday, and they were anxious to see the Annapolis Valley. When Liz accepted Shirley's invitation to visit Lunenburg's Fisheries Museum, Tom had to stifle a groan. A *museum*, when there was a mystery to solve!

Happily, visiting the museum unexpectedly solved the problem of how to return to Oak Island. While boarding the schooner *Theresa E. Connor*, one of the historical vessels docked at the museum, Shirley called hello to a young man examining the dories on the schooner's deck. Introduced as Cap'n John, he turned out to be a friend of Professor and Mrs. Zinck.

"How terrible," he exclaimed, after hearing a description of the attack on Oak Island. "Is there anything I can do to help?"

"Would you drive us there, to search for leads?" Tom's eyes radiated hope.

"How about going by sea?"

"Fantastic. Let's get moving!" Glancing at Shirley's disappointed face, Tom realized he was being rude. "I mean, after we've seen this schooner."

Cap'n John agreed to the plan, then walked forward with them to the schooner's bow. His pride in Lunenburg was soon obvious, as was his love of the sea and the great schooners that once sailed from here to the Grand Banks of Newfoundland.

"Boys as young as ten went to sea as 'headers,' meaning their job was to cut the heads off the fish. They would get up with the rest of the men at 2 a.m. for breakfast, then row out in dories despite blizzards and howling winds. The tragedy was they often never returned. The bones of many men are out there still."

Shirley looked up at the signal flags snapping in the wind. "The greatest schooner of all was the *Bluenose*, which was built in Lunenburg and was world champion in the races they held for these ships."

"Say kids," Cap'n John said. "If you've got a dollar, I can sell you a terrific souvenir of the *Bluenose*."

"Great!" Tom produced a dollar, then frowned as Cap'n John handed him a dime. "What's this?"

"Your souvenir. On the back of that dime you'll see the *Bluenose* in full sail."

Tom stared in dismay at the coin, then the others burst into laughter and a grinning Cap'n John returned his money.

"Never trust a stranger with your cash," he said, chuckling. "By the way, Tom, there's a great picture of

Lunenburg and its schooners on the hundred-dollar bill. I can get you one for only $200."

The jokes continued until the tour was over, and they'd said goodbye to Shirley on the dock. Cap'n John led the way past the harbour's bright-red buildings to a dock where they climbed down into a skiff. With waves slapping against it, the skiff headed toward the many boats riding at anchor in the harbour.

"Which is yours, Cap'n John?"

Resting over the oars, he pointed to one with a sign reading *Island Tours*. "There it is," he said, smiling proudly. "I've converted it to take tourists out to visit some of the islands in Mahone Bay. Business isn't very good right now, but it'll improve!"

"What if it doesn't?" Liz asked anxiously. "Will you be ruined?"

The young man smiled, optimistically. "Let's hope not. I can always go to the Grand Banks on a trawler, but then I'd hardly see my family. Anyway, recently I've managed to rent my boat to locals a couple of times, so things look good."

On board the tour boat, Liz went into the cabin to watch Cap'n John start up the engine, while Tom sat in the stern, enjoying the lapping of waves against the hull and the light wind on his face. Nova Scotia sure was great, he thought, even if weird things happened here. The riddle of Oak Island, the superstitions and forerunners, the icy fingers that brushed his neck, and the attack on Professor Zinck—all puzzles that seemed to have no answers. What did it mean? Who or what was causing these strange things to happen?

The powerful engine came alive, and Liz emerged to sit in the sunshine as the boat headed out of Lunenburg harbour. Later, Tom and Liz went into the cabin where Cap'n John described his hobby of diving to ship-wrecks. "Recently I brought up a very special treasure. Buttons from an 1853 wreck. Buttons made from pol-ished stones of most unusual shapes. There's a precious green jade button that I'm saving for my little girl."

"I love the sea," said Liz. "It makes me feel so peace-ful. When I'm older I think I'll take up scuba diving."

"It's a great experience." Cap'n John looked out at a sailboat leaning far to starboard under the wind, then checked his chart. "We're not far from Oak Island. Look, over there."

Tom and Liz looked toward the shore, where the drilling rig on Oak Island grew slowly out of the waves. At Smugglers Cove they glided in over a trans-parent sea that revealed dark green eelgrass, waving gently below the surface. The beach was littered with jellyfish, shimmering brown blobs, which Cap'n John said were composed mainly of water.

As they followed a path toward the drilling rig, Cap'n John pointed out the damsel flies that darted around their dusty feet, then stopped at a plant with purple flowers and red berries. "Eating two of those berries will stop your heart."

"Impossible." Tom picked two berries, lifted them to his mouth, and started chewing. "You see? Noth-ing's happened."

Cap'n John gasped in shock. "Spit them out! They'll kill you!"

Tom opened his hand to reveal the red berries. "I

didn't forget your trick about the dime," he said, grinning proudly.

Cap'n John laughed and pounded Tom's back with a friendly hand. "You got me, fair and square! Now let's see what kind of detective you are."

Tom nodded, determined to find some clue to help their investigation. After checking the Money Pit, he climbed the hill to the piles of rusty machinery. What a mess! It would take *hours* to check through it, and he didn't know what to look for.

As he tried to think of an easier approach, Tom watched his sister carefully examining the ground around the tarpaper shack. He felt a little annoyed. If he didn't hurry up, Liz would find a clue and he'd look bad. Quickly, Tom began digging among the tangles of old buckets and ladders and tools.

Finding nothing but rust, he straightened up and tried to think. Where could an attacker have hidden yesterday? The woods, the shack, or inside the old wrecked car were the only possibilities.

The woods were too large to search and Liz was already inside the shack, but that still left the car. Suddenly hopeful, Tom headed toward it—just as Liz came out of the shack.

"Nothing in there," she said, sounding discouraged.

"Nobody's checked the woods," Tom suggested in a bright voice.

As Liz looked at the trees, Tom tried to find a route through the piles of machinery to the car. But he kept getting blocked, and he knew that Liz would think of checking the car at any moment.

"Say, Liz, isn't that something in the shack?"

"Where?"

"On the floor, way in the back. Looks a bit like a gun, or maybe a knife?"

Liz went inside the shack, and for a wild moment Tom wanted to slam the door and lock her in. Then he got free of the machinery, and dashed to the car.

"Tom, what are you doing? What's in the car?"

"Nothing!"

"Do you think someone was hiding in the car yesterday? What a brainwave!"

"Take off, Liz! This is my car."

Liz opened the front door, and watched Tom search around the pedals and under the seat. "Find anything?"

"Would I still be looking?"

"Let's try the back seat."

"Listen, Liz, this car was my idea. Take a hike!"

Liz tried to open the rear door, but the rusty metal screeched and refused to move. As she yanked on the door, Tom scrambled into the back seat and landed in thick dust. For a moment he was blinded, then he heard a rusty squeal as Liz got the door open. Wiping his eyes, he saw the glint of shiny metal on the floor. His hand flashed down, and snatched up a set of keys just as Liz reached for them.

"You shouldn't touch those keys, Tom! They may have fingerprints."

"Tough."

"Put them back on the floor."

"And have you grab them? Not a chance." Tightly holding the keys, Tom crawled out of the car. "Hey, this really *is* a clue, Liz! Look at the initials on the key ring."

"CZ." Liz nodded her head. "Those are Professor Zinck's initials. He must have been inside the car after the attack."

"But why?"

"I don't know, Tom. But this whole thing gets stranger by the minute."

"And scarier." Tom stared at the keys in his hand. "These are house keys—there's nothing for a car."

"I keep thinking about Mrs. Zinck," Liz said, "and the Professor's forerunner. I have this awful feeling that something terrible is about to happen and we won't be able to stop it."

Cap'n John's boat arrived in Lunenburg shortly before nightfall, giving Tom and Liz time to return the Professor's keys. At the Manor, they slowly followed Henneyberry up the tower stairs and along the gloomy hallway toward Professor Zinck's bedroom. Lying outside the door was his Irish setter, Boss, looking sad.

"What's wrong, boy?" Tom said, kneeling down. "Why aren't you inside, close to your master?" He pulled gently on the dog's collar, trying to coax it toward the door, but Boss held back, whining.

Suddenly Tom heard the familiar voice of Roger Eliot-Stanton, coming from behind the closed door. "I can make it worth your while. Name your price!"

There was a moment's pause, then Professor Zinck spoke. "I don't have a price. I will never agree."

The door banged open, and Roger Eliot-Stanton appeared. Briefly he paused, with firelight on his deeply hollowed face. Then, without saying a word to Tom and Liz, his long legs carried him away.

"I've never met such a rude man," Liz whispered. "What's he doing here, anyway?"

Tom shrugged.

The Professor managed a smile when they entered the bedroom, but he was obviously not himself. His eyes were strained, and his mind seemed to wander to other thoughts as Tom and Liz described their search at Oak Island.

"And Tom found your keys," Liz said excitedly, as Tom produced them. "It's a great clue, because the keys tell us your location after the attack."

Professor Zinck looked vaguely at the keys, then handed them to Henneyberry. "I'm in no shape to drive, so you'll have to do the errands."

"Very well, sir."

The Professor gazed into the fireplace for some time. Finally he seemed to remember that Tom and Liz were present, and turned to them with troubled eyes. "Have you enjoyed the company of an old professor?"

"You bet," Tom exclaimed, earnestly. "We just hope you get well soon."

"Of course, of course." There was a long silence followed by a sigh. "Life or death. What will the decision be?"

Tom frowned, wondering if the Professor was feverish. Henneyberry fluffed up the tired man's pillow, and tried to smile. "It will all work out, sir. Try to relax."

"Relax?" The Professor laughed, but it was a horrible sound that made Tom's skin crawl and he glanced in alarm at Liz. "Relax, you say? When life hangs by a thread?"

The creases around Henneyberry's eyes deepened. "There's nothing to worry about, sir. Leave everything to me."

Professor Zinck slumped down on the pillow. His eyes focussed on the yellow flame of a candle beside the bed. "How easily I could snuff that out."

Looking very worried, Liz reached out to touch the Professor's hand. "How is your wife feeling?"

Professor Zinck looked blank. "My wife?"

Henneyberry put a warning hand on Liz's shoulder. "Try to rest, sir," he said, then led Tom and Liz away from the bed. They had a final glimpse of the Professor's troubled face before the door closed, and Henneyberry shook his head.

"I've been terribly concerned, but the doctor says the worst will be over soon."

"How *is* Mrs. Zinck?"

"Not well, I'm afraid. At times she's delirious like the Professor, and says some very strange things."

As Henneyberry showed Tom and Liz to the front door, the bell rang and he admitted a woman dressed in expensive clothes. Obviously used to his slow pace, she refused to be led upstairs and hurried on alone. Without waiting for Tom and Liz to leave the Manor, an anxious-looking Henneyberry went after her.

"What's going on in this place?" Tom said. "The Professor's acting so weird."

"I wonder who that woman is? And why was Roger Eliot-Stanton here?"

"I don't trust that beanpole, Liz. Yesterday we saw him at Oak Island just before the attack, and today he's at the Manor. What's the connection?"

"Maybe he's. . ." Liz paused, and her eyes widened. "Did you hear that?"

"Hear what?"

Liz stared down the shadowed hallway. "I'm sure I heard footsteps," she whispered. "It was like someone on tiptoe."

Tom's body turned to ice. "Let's get out of here, Liz! I don't like this place."

"Look!"

At the end of the hallway, the door of the sitting room was slowly opening. As Tom and Liz watched, horrified, a white hand appeared, and beckoned.

5

Tom's heart pounded. "It's the ghost!"

"No," Liz said, squinting. "It's Mrs. Zinck. What does she want?"

The hand motioned frantically, then a warning finger went to Mrs. Zinck's lips as Tom and Liz approached. As they stepped into the room she closed the door, and turned to them with a haggard face.

"I'm so afraid!"

"What's wrong, Mrs. Zinck?"

"It's this house. Something terrible is happening here."

Tom remembered Henneyberry saying that Mrs. Zinck had been delirious. He wondered if she was hallucinating now. Then he recalled how frightened she had been of the Manor even before becoming ill.

"And it's the Professor," Mrs. Zinck said, drawing her bathrobe tight at the neck with shaking fingers. "He frightens me."

"But he's your husband," Liz exclaimed.

"Even so, I'm afraid of him. This morning when I went to his room for a visit he hardly seemed to know me, and just lay there muttering about life and death."

"We heard that, too."

"Then he demanded that I leave the room. He said I was making him feel guilty. Of all things!"

Tom looked at the grandfather clock, ticking in a corner of the lonely room. He wished he knew how to comfort Mrs. Zinck.

"I'm sure he'll be better soon," he said.

Mrs. Zinck smiled, but tears were in her eyes. "This afternoon, I went to see him. As I reached the bedroom, I heard the Professor making arrangements with Henneyberry for a lawyer to visit. That's the woman who just arrived."

"Why a lawyer?"

"My husband is removing Black Dog from his will. That's absolutely insane because he loves Black Dog like a son. I'm so afraid that some evil power has possessed the Professor, but what can I do?"

"We'll try to help, Mrs. Zinck."

Outside the Manor, Tom and Liz paused in the darkness to look up at the Professor's bedroom. Flickering firelight cast the long shadow of Henneyberry on the wall, and for a terrible moment Tom wondered whether the man was a demon who'd somehow taken control of Professor Zinck.

"That's stupid," he said aloud. "But there must be some reason for what's happening."

"You're right," Liz agreed. "So let's decide who'd want to harm the Zincks."

"Black Dog!"

"We just heard Mrs. Zinck say the Professor loves him like a son."

"But does Black Dog love the Professor?"

"Of course he does."

"Remember, Black Dog gets the Zincks' money if they die."

"You're just saying that because you don't like him."

Tom fell silent, refusing to give in, then gave a stone an angry kick as they started walking. "This is my case, Liz, so I don't care if you help, or stay home reading a book."

"*Your* case?"

"That's right. I found the Professor's house keys at Oak Island, and that puts me in charge."

"I saw those keys before you. I just couldn't get the car door open."

"Sure, sure. Anyway, I'm going to break this case wide open, with your help or without it."

They walked on in silence, until finally Liz glanced at Tom. "Okay, let's hear your argument against Black Dog."

"If the Professor knows that Black Dog attacked him at the Money Pit, it would explain why he's being removed from the will. And the Professor is terrified of another attack by Black Dog, which accounts for him raving about life and death."

"All right, I admit that *maybe* you've got something. Should we go to the police?"

Tom thought for a minute. "No, we'd better not. The Professor doesn't want the police involved, and we don't want him feeling any worse."

"Then what should we do?"

"I read in a detective manual that a good way to learn something about your suspect is to spring a surprise. Let's drop in on Black Dog tomorrow afternoon for an unexpected visit."

"Isn't that taking a chance?"

Tom smiled. "Black Dog works in the school's boiler room, doesn't he? What could be safer than a school?"

The confidence of Tom's statement was badly shaken the next day, however, when he learned that the school was located at the top of Gallows Hill. Climbing the hill, Tom and Liz found themselves in a cemetery full of moss-covered tombstones and twisted old trees.

Liz stared at an ancient building with narrow windows and pointed bell towers. "The school looks like something out of a horror movie." She looked at the fog, which had rolled in from the sea an hour before and was blowing through the trees like smoke. "What a day to be investigating an ancient school beside an old graveyard."

Liz watched the fog swirl past the school's towers. "You know what happens when Lunenburg kids fail a test? They get locked away in those towers, with spiders and rats to gnaw their bones."

Tom's determination to investigate Black Dog was quickly fading away. "Why don't we walk around the cemetery a bit, then try the school tomorrow?"

Tom studied a tombstone that showed a hand pointing to heaven and the words *Gone Home*. Nearby were two stones with the names of fishermen lost from schooners. He was becoming aware of how many Lunenburg people had drowned at sea.

Some mossy stones marked the graves of children. One family had lost several at birth, including twin boys. "That's sad," Liz said, leaning close to read the tombstone, which was covered with patches of mustard-yellow moss. "If they'd become grownup twins, I wonder if they'd have looked the same. You know, wearing matching clothes and all that."

Tom shrugged. "I've never seen identical adult twins."

Liz kneeled in front of a very old stone, which was dark with age. Engraved on it were lilies and the name of Mary Eliza Rudolf, who died in 1849 at the age of ten. "She was a Liz, just like me. I wonder what she was like?"

Leaving Liz to think about Mary Eliza, Tom walked around studying tombstones and trying to figure out the story of each person from names and dates. The name Zinck appeared often, and Tom realized how many generations of the family must have lived in Lunenburg Manor.

Raising his eyes from a black marble *Zinck* tombstone, Tom stared at the school, knowing that the lives of Professor and Mrs. Zinck could depend on their investigation of Black Dog. Now he felt brave and determined.

He waved at Liz, who was still in front of Mary Eliza's tombstone. "I'm going into the school!"

Standing up, Liz looked one last time at the old tombstone, then joined Tom as he approached the school. The only lights came from basement windows. Looking into the furnace room, they saw Black Dog staring into the eyes of Mickey Mouse. Then Black Dog turned away from the poster of the grinning mouse, and began pounding hot metal with a large mallet. He paused to wipe sweat from his forehead, then again the powerful blows rang out.

"What's he doing?"

Tom shook his head. "I don't know, but look at the muscles on that guy. He isn't skinny with his shirt off."

They found a basement door and knocked. Seconds later Tom and Liz were looking at Black Dog's fierce black eyes. Sweat ran down into the wiry tangles of his beard. "Yeah?"

"Uh," Tom stammered, "uh, hi there, Mr. Dog. We, uh . . ."

"We came for a visit," Liz said, with a big smile. "We're interested in your art."

"I'm busy."

"Can't we come in, just for a minute?"

"No."

Tom put his hand on the heavy metal door as it began to close. "Can we talk about the danger facing Professor Zinck?"

Black Dog stared at Tom for a moment, then stepped aside. "Come in."

They crossed a large room with a concrete floor and followed Black Dog into a brick-walled room with a huge furnace. Wind blasted down the chimney, making a loud *whooooo!* Then it died away for a few seconds before another gust repeated the alarming sound. Along the walls were brooms and mops and dusters, but Tom's eyes instantly spotted a container of *DEATH TO RATS* poison. A pulse throbbed in his throat.

Black Dog sprawled in a battered, old armchair, with one of his hands dangling close to the mallet on the floor. "What's this about Professor Zinck?"

Tom searched his mind for the right words. His reckless statement had got them into the school, but what should he say now? "We're afraid for the Zincks," he said at last, watching for Black Dog's reaction. "They face a great danger."

"Why come to me?"

Tom considered mentioning Professor Zinck's will, but knew that wouldn't be fair. "We can't tell you. But Liz and I will be keeping watch on the Manor. Would you help us?"

The man snorted. "I've got a job to do here, and my art. You've got me concerned for the Zincks, but I don't have time to hang around outside the Manor."

"Then we'll do it alone," Tom said, hoping this would warn Black Dog not to try anything. "We'll be there, night and day."

"*The eye that never sleeps*," Black Dog smirked. "That's the famous motto of the Pinkerton Detective Agency. Are you two in the same racket?"

"Maybe," Tom said, then quickly changed the subject. "How come you've got that poster of Mickey Mouse?"

Reaching for the mallet, Black Dog stood up. "I'm creating my interpretation of the icons of our culture.

Do you see this metal sculpture? It shows how I feel about Mickey Mouse, Charlie Brown, and Elvis Presley." With a savage swing, he brought the mallet crashing down on the metal. The room echoed with the blow, then it was repeated with even more force, making Tom and Liz cover their ears.

"What have you got against those guys?" Tom shouted.

Black Dog's laugh was sudden and unexpected. "Nothing! Can't you tell that this sculpture praises them?"

"No, I sure can't."

Again, the deep laugh. "Well, you're honest. I like that." The man seemed to have relaxed. Liz spoke up before he could swing the mallet again. "How old is this school, Mr. Dog?"

"Listen, kid, that's not my real name. It's Arthur Brown, but I call myself Black Dog because it's more interesting. This place was opened in 1895."

"Wow! Our school in Winnipeg isn't nearly that old. Would you show us around?"

"Okay, but only if you leave me in peace afterwards."

Putting down the mallet, he led them to a wooden staircase that creaked underfoot. They reached a hallway where the hardwood floors shone under a thick coat of wax, and exposed pipes crossed the ceiling in crooked patterns. Looking into a classroom, Tom was surprised to find it bright and cheerful.

"Hey, this place isn't bad. Look, Liz, you're featured on that list of French words!"

"Where?"

"Can't you see it says *la banane*?"

"Funny man," Liz said, looking annoyed because Black Dog had laughed. "It also describes Tom Austen as *le pain*, meaning he is le-pain-in-le-neck."

Black Dog walked down the hallway. "You want to see the next floor? It's condemned as a fire hazard." His footsteps echoed as they ascended into musty darkness.

When Black Dog switched on a light, Tom and Liz found themselves under the gaze of a magnificent eagle. Beside it in a display case they saw a dusty albatross, a hermit crab, and a snake with its red tongue sticking out.

Dusty desks and old textbooks were stacked beside the display case. Every sound echoed in this empty space, and the windows rattled in the wind. The school made Tom think of movies in which people were held prisoner in attic rooms.

"Is there an attic?" he asked, hoping the answer would be no.

"Right up there." Black Dog pointed at some narrow steel stairs. "From the attic you can get outside, and cross the roof to the bell tower." His scary eyes stared at Tom. "But that wind would blow you right off the roof."

"Don't worry, I'm not going to try it."

Liz poked her head into a storeroom, where a moth-eaten Red Ensign flag hung on the wall. "Hey, look at that fancy telescope."

"Leave it alone," Black Dog said sharply, as Liz walked over to the telescope. "That's mine and it's very delicate."

"I'm sorry," Liz said. She turned to a small oval window and looked at the cemetery far below, its trees bending under the wind. "This room must have an incredible view on a clear day."

Black Dog mumbled a reply and headed for the stairs. Clearly the tour, and the conversation, had reached an end. The grumpy man said nothing more, and within minutes Tom and Liz were standing outside the school in thick fog with night rapidly falling.

"Well," Liz said, "that was a dud investigation. We didn't learn a thing."

"No, but we scared Black Dog. He knows we're wise to his game." Tom pointed at the light that streamed into the foggy darkness from the furnace-room window. "Let's watch him for a while. He may panic, and try to get back to the Professor."

Keeping back from the window, they had a good view of Black Dog. After pounding his metal sculpture, the man began pacing the floor. Then suddenly he reached for a switch and the room went black.

Tom and Liz scrambled into hiding behind a tree and lay listening to the mournful cry of a foghorn somewhere in the night. What was Black Dog doing? Within seconds the basement door screeched on its hinges, then a lean figure stepped out of the school and hurried away into the fog.

"After him," Tom whispered urgently.

Stumbling past the tombstones, they managed to keep Black Dog in sight as he passed under streetlights before heading toward a row of elegant, old houses.

"He must be going to the Manor," Tom whispered.

"Those legs of his move so fast, we'll never keep up."

"We've got to."

For a few minutes it seemed they had lost Black Dog. Then Tom and Liz caught sight of him in a shaft of light from the window of a church. Quickly the man returned to darkness, and his footsteps died away.

Tom tried to see through the night, but it was impossible. The fog gripped the town, muffling every sound and hiding everything except the feeble glow of lights from porches and windows. Black Dog was gone.

"We've got to get to the Manor!"

"But where is it?" Liz said.

"Somewhere around here. This street, maybe, or the next."

Eventually they found Lunenburg Manor, but not before precious time had been lost. A single light was visible in the tower, but no one answered their urgent knocking. Finally Liz tried the door, and it opened.

"What should we do?" she whispered.

"Let's get to the Professor's bedroom and see if he's okay."

The house was in total silence. As Tom and Liz climbed the tower stairs the foghorn sounded, far away and sorrowful, but they heard nothing else until reaching the long upper hallway. There they heard the low whining of Boss, followed by creaking floorboards.

The Professor's door opened. Dancing light from the fireplace showed Boss lying in the hallway, then a thin man with blond hair came out of the bedroom and closed the door. He was visible in the hallway's dim light, then disappeared through the shadows toward the service stairs at the back of the house.

"Who was that?" Tom said.

"Not so loud! He might hear you."

Boss continued to whine as they tiptoed along the hallway to Professor Zinck's room. Inside, the coal fire burned silently, making strange patterns of light on the walls. Dark shadows hid the Professor's face as Tom and Liz went cautiously to the bed.

"Oh no," Liz said, leaning forward. "He's dead!"

"Impossible!"

Tom went closer, staring in horror at the Professor. For a moment he felt faint, then tears ran down his cheeks. "I don't believe it. He was our friend."

Liz was also crying. Firelight glistened on her wet face as she stumbled away from the bed, trying to control her sobbing.

Then suddenly, Liz knelt down. "Tom. Look at this."

"What is it? A clue?"

Liz held up a small bottle. "This is for insulin. Why is it here?"

"I don't know. Professor Zinck didn't use insulin."

Liz returned to the bed. "There's a pinprick of blood on his arm from a needle. *The Professor has been murdered, Tom.* Someone gave him an overdose of insulin."

"It was that blond man! We'd better phone the police."

Just then, a footstep sounded behind them. It was followed by the *phsssst* of gas being released from a capsule. There was no smell, but suddenly Tom's nose and throat were on fire. He sank to his knees, struggling to breathe, then saw yellow bombs exploding inside his eyes. Next came darkness, as smooth and luxurious as velvet.

6

Thunder awakened Tom.

He was aware of cramps in his stomach, and his entire body ached. Even the muscles of his eyes hurt as he opened them and looked around a small room.

Liz was asleep on another bed. Using some water Tom managed to get her awake, and they went outside. Above the door, a sign said *Rest Easy Cottage*.

"What's that noise?" Liz mumbled, still half asleep.

"I think it's thunder, but there's no rain."

"Where are we?"

"Some kind of resort. There're other cottages, and some picnic tables. We'd better find the office."

A woman looked up with a smile as they entered the office. "You're awake early. Are you the new kids in Rest Easy Cottage?"

"We're . . ."

"Your father forgot to sign the register last night. Would you ask him to stop by?"

"Our parents are in Winnipeg," Liz said impatiently. "That man who posed as our father is probably a killer."

The woman smiled. "And I'm probably Cinderella."

Tom leaned over the counter. "We're serious! Last night Professor Zinck was murdered, and we think his killer is the man who brought us here."

"Did you say Professor Zinck?" The woman looked horrified. "But, I know him. He can't be dead!"

"Sadly, it's true," Liz said. "Can you tell us where to find the police?"

The woman walked slowly to the window and stood looking out. "I can't believe it. The Professor was such a good man, and so kind to people."

"Is the police station close by? We're anxious to get there."

The woman turned to them with sad eyes. "The police are in Lunenburg. We'll drive there as soon as my assistant gets to work."

"If this isn't Lunenburg, where are we?"

"You're at the Ovens."

"What's that?"

The woman looked at her watch. "Go outside and follow the signs. Be back here in thirty minutes."

Outside the office, Liz started crying. "The Professor's dead, Tom. I don't want to look at some stupid ovens."

"We might as well. It's something to do."

"He knew he was going to die," Liz whispered, shivering. "Remember his forerunner?"

"We've *got* to find that blond person," Tom exclaimed. "He brought us here. But why?"

The thunder grew louder as they reached the top of a cliff. Dark clouds lay over the sea, and a strong wind drove white waves toward them. From below came the constant booming of thunder.

"Look, Tom, there are caves all along the bottom of the cliff. The thunder's coming from the caves."

Steps had been built into the cliff. Tom and Liz cautiously climbed down, then entered a cave. A platform looked down on seething, green water rushing in from the sea. Jagged rocks hung from the cave roof like sharp teeth, and the thunder came in deafening claps.

"I see what causes it," Liz shouted above the noise.

Tom watched the next wave surge into the cave. The green water was squeezed between the narrow rocky walls, then forced its way through a small opening into a hidden cavern. Moments later there was a terrible BOOM as the wave smashed into the walls of the cavern.

Foam and white water hissed out through the opening, followed by a blast of wind that tore at them. "It's strong enough to knock us into the water," Tom shouted. "This place could be a death trap."

"Especially if a wave swept us through that opening. We'd be squished to death."

"Let's get going! I've seen enough."

At the top of the cliff they watched a trawler heading out to sea. "It's coming from Lunenburg," Tom said. "I remember noticing the caves along this cliff when Cap'n John took us to Oak Island."

"How do we get back to the office? There's more than one path."

The path they chose wound through the woods to a grassy hill overlooking a cove. As they gazed down at surf pounding on a rocky beach, Liz grabbed Tom's arm.

"Look! There's Black Dog!"

The man sat on a beached motorboat at the far end of the cove, staring at the big waves. A tote bag was at his feet, and his hair looked wet, but there was no apparent reason for him being there.

"What should we do, Liz?"

"I don't know. It's your case."

"Black Dog scares me, especially now the Professor's been murdered. He may be partners with that blond killer."

"Let's go question him. If he really is involved with the murder, we'll soon know."

"Do you think it's safe?"

"Sure. He can't hurt us, not in broad daylight."

Black Dog's eyes never left the waves, even as Tom and Liz approached him along the rocky beach. He seemed deep in thought, but finally looked up after Tom coughed noisily.

"What are you kids doing here?"

"We don't know. Maybe you've got a blond friend who can tell us."

Ignoring the anger in Liz's voice, Black Dog watched spray fly from a big wave as it smashed down on the rocks. "Get lost."

"Sure we'll go. Straight to the police."

"What for?"

"Stop acting innocent! The Professor's been murdered, and we're going to tell the police everything we know."

Black Dog frowned. "What did you say?"

"We know it was murder, and we know about the insulin."

"The Professor is *dead*?"

"You're a good actor," Liz said scornfully. "Maybe the police will give you an Oscar, or maybe a life sentence."

"The fools!" Black Dog slammed his fist against the boat. "I warned them!"

Seizing the tote bag, he broke into a run. Tom went after him, but his feet slipped on the rocks, and he couldn't keep up with Black Dog's long-legged run. The man disappeared into the woods, and Tom waited unhappily for Liz to join him.

"I guess we blew it, letting Black Dog escape like that. We should have called in the police to arrest him."

"On what evidence?"

Tom shrugged. "He looks guilty, and he acts guilty."

"We'll need a lot more than that. I wonder if he really has got a blond friend?"

Tom's eyes lit up. "Or maybe it's a blond wig."

"Should we tell the police about Black Dog?"

"Not without any proof. We'll have to watch him ourselves, and see if he makes a slip."

Shortly after, they reached the Lunenburg police station and were astonished by the uproar their arrival caused. Then they realized they'd been missing all night. After telling the police what had happened, they learned that Professor Zinck's death was thought to have been caused by a heart attack, but the coroner would now check for an insulin overdose.

The Gouldens quickly arrived at the police station, relieved that Tom and Liz were safe. Then Carl stated, in very clear language, that their detective work was over.

"But what about the Professor?" Tom protested. "Don't you want his killer found?"

Shirley nodded. "Of course. We're terribly upset about the Professor's death, but I'm sure the police will find the person responsible."

"The police? They thought Professor Zinck had died of a heart attack!"

"Now, Tom . . ."

"I'm sorry," he muttered. "I just wish we could have a chance to break this case."

"Forget it, Tom, or your vacation will be ruined."

"Impossible, not when there's a murder to investigate."

Liz nodded her agreement, and Tom knew she wasn't ready to give up the case either. Back at Stonehurst they met secretly, and agreed *somehow* they would return to Lunenburg the next day, if only to make sure that Mrs. Zinck was safe.

Still feeling upset about the Professor, Tom went to bed early. Then, as he was falling asleep, he felt icy fingers brush against his neck.

Leaping out of bed, he looked out the window just in time to see a shadowy figure slip away through the trees. Then something on the ground caught his eye. Looking down, Tom saw an ice cube.

An ice cube? Suddenly a part of the puzzle was explained, and Tom returned to bed feeling a whole lot better.

A hand shook Tom awake. "It's 5 a.m.," Carl said. "Time to go fishing."

Tom groaned and tucked his head further under the covers. Then he remembered how he and Liz had begged Carl to take them fishing, and how they'd promised to get up at 5 a.m. without any complaints. Finally he crawled out of bed, pulled on his clothes, and went yawning into the kitchen.

Carl smiled from the stove, where he was pouring mugs of steaming tea. Liz and Wade were at the table, eating toast piled with jam. From somewhere in the house came the sounds of heavy snoring.

"Who's that?"

Wade laughed. "It's Roger Eliot-Stanton. Isn't that a gross sound?"

"Who is that guy, anyway? Why's he here, just hanging around? Doesn't he work for a living? I'd like to check him out."

Carl gave Tom a warning look. "Don't you remember what I said yesterday about giving up detective work?"

"I guess so," Tom muttered.

"Let's concentrate on the fishing. There's a beautiful night outside. The weather should be fine."

Tom hoped good weather meant the sea would be calm. Everyone had predicted he and Liz would be seasick, and he wanted to prove them wrong. Even so, he couldn't help studying the mariner's prayer on the wall:

O, God,
Thy sea is so great,
And my boat is so small.

They walked to the wharf past sleeping houses and stacks of lobster traps. Although it still seemed like the middle of the night, the waterfront was alive with activity. Even the seagulls were wide awake, wheeling and screaming above the little boats as they headed out to sea, their path through the darkness marked only by red and green running lights and the low growl of their engines.

Carl and Wade stopped beside some other fishermen to discuss weather conditions, while Tom and Liz walked on to the wharf. The moon had faded to pale white, shining above a lighthouse on the rocky shore.

"I hope Mrs. Zinck is okay," Liz said. "I've been thinking about her all night."

"We should go and see her soon, to be sure she's safe. I want to tell her how awful I feel about Professor Zinck dying."

"Carl and Shirley are driving to Lunenburg tonight. We could get a ride from them."

"Good idea. They can't object to us visiting Mrs. Zinck."

"Let's hope not." Liz looked at the pink light creeping into the eastern sky, and a stray gust of wind tossed her black hair. "Going to be seasick?"

"No way . . . I hope."

Soon they were roaring out to sea in the gillnetter, leaving a deep wake behind. Tom and Liz sat in the stern, a chilly wind on their faces, and watched Carl and Wade prepare a net with expert fingers. After leaving the harbour mouth, which was marked by a big rock covered with seagulls and hammered by waves, they headed into rougher seas. For a few minutes Tom thought he would be sick, then his body began adjusting to the swells and he learned how to anticipate the cold water spraying back from the bow.

"When's lunch?" he asked, delighted that he'd be able to eat it.

Carl laughed. "About seven hours from now."

"Brother!"

Tom looked at Liz in dismay, wondering how he would survive the boredom. But soon the action began in earnest, with Carl and Wade hauling up a long net from the sea bed and working quickly to untangle each fish.

"What kind are those?"

"Haddock," Wade answered, throwing one into a wooden crate on the deck. "Watch them come up through the water in the net. They look all silvery."

Liz leaned close to look at the fish, then smiled at Wade. "You must really like it out here."

"I do. It feels good sharing the work with Dad, and learning about the sea from him."

Tom couldn't help envying Wade's skill as a fisherman, and admiring his bravery in facing the open sea. "Doesn't it scare you?" he asked. "Being so far out here, in this tiny boat?"

"Sometimes," Carl said. "I've been fishing for a quantity of years, and lost some good friends. They're gone from life so suddenly, you understand. Already this year eight men and women have drowned from their boats along this coast."

"It's sounds awful."

"Sure it is, but those who survive the terrible storms and certain death, why, they change. Somehow they're stronger and prouder, for what they've overcome."

"Shouldn't you quit while you're still ahead?" Liz asked.

Carl shook his head. "Not the way I love this sea. You should be out here when the whales are around. They leap clear out of the waves and make rainbows in the air."

"Have you ever seen a shark?"

"Lots of blue sharks here in the summer. Some fellows brought one on board from their net, thinking it was dead. But it woke up fast, and slashed off Ben's arm. He screamed all the way to the hospital. Six hours, just screaming."

"How horrible." Feeling sick, Tom scanned the waves, searching for the deadly fin that could be slicing their way at this moment. "About what time do we go home?"

Wade grinned. "Thinking about sharks, Tom?"

"Of course not. I just don't want to miss the soap operas this afternoon."

"I hear there's a new one called *As Tom's Stomach Turns*. Our hero is out on a gillnetter, and starts barfing when he notices the boat is always rising and falling, rising and falling, rising . . ."

For a ghastly moment, Tom felt his breakfast coming up as Wade's hypnotic voice droned on. Then the crisis passed, and Carl straightened up from the net, rubbing his back. "Weather's changing. We'll haul one more net, then head for in. I'd say there's a heavy nor'easter coming on."

Liz studied the cloudless sky. "How can you tell it's changing?"

Wade smiled proudly. "Dad's been fishing since he

was fourteen. Not much he can't tell you about weather and tides and currents. He's a real Bluenoser."

"What's that mean, anyway? Everyone in Nova Scotia talks about Bluenosers."

Carl laughed. "If you came out fishing in December, you'd soon be one yourself. It's so cold on the sea that fishermen's noses turn blue."

"So that's it!"

"Now, let's have a mug-up." Carl opened a Thermos, then passed around haddock sandwiches. "These are some good," he said, biting into one. "You two heard about Devil's Island?"

"No, sir."

"Well, it seems the government owns a nice little house on Devil's Island, and anyone can have it for free. But there's nobody yet who's tried it and stayed. They say a fisherman lived there long ago. His wife and six kids died in a fire while he was out on his boat, and now his ghost roams the island looking for them."

"Dad's got some great ghost stories," Wade said, grinning. "Say, Tom, when are you going to investigate the ghost of the *Young Teazer*? Everyone in Stonehurst is waiting for your solution."

"Don't worry, Wade. I haven't forgotten."

The snack was over too quickly, and they headed for a fluorescent buoy that marked another set of nets. As he helped haul them up, Wade untangled an ugly brown fish and threw it on the deck beside Tom. Blowing angrily through its mouth, the fish stared at him with eyes that bulged from two bumps on its head.

"That's a sculpin. A gang of bikers visited here, and took one home to mount on their clubhouse wall."

Wade picked up the fish to look at its warted body and the horn growing out of its head, then threw it overboard. "Man, that thing is evil looking."

Evil. Tom's mind flashed back to Oak Island, where Professor Zinck had written EVEL after being attacked. If only they'd worked out that clue, perhaps the Professor would be alive today.

"Maybe it's part of someone's name. Or a set of initials."

Liz glanced at Tom. "Talking in your sleep?"

"What did EVEL mean, Liz? And what about the Professor's keys? I'm sure we missed an important clue in that."

"You know what upsets me? I have a sickening feeling that another person's life is threatened, and yet we can't do anything. And I'm sure the killer is someone we know."

As the gillnetter headed for port Tom thought about each person he'd met since arriving in Nova Scotia, and how each could benefit by the death of Professor Zinck. Possibilities tumbled inside his head, as plentiful as the seagulls that tumbled and shrieked behind the boat, fighting for the scraps that Carl and Wade threw overboard as they cleaned the haddock.

"You were right about the weather," Liz said from the wheel, which she'd asked to try. "Those are meanlooking clouds on the horizon."

"Yup," Carl said. "It's breezing up some."

Breeze is hardly the word, Tom thought, as a wind slammed in from sea just after they reached port, making the gillnetters dance at anchor, and pounding the rocks with huge breakers. They hurried home, getting there just as the first rain blew around their heads.

"Were you seasick?" Holli asked immediately.

Carla turned from the piano. "I bet they were!"

Sprawling on the sofa, Wade grinned. "I've never seen such a green face. Why, we only just put to sea and . . ."

"And Tom was just fine," Carl said from the kitchen. "Now, Wade, I have something to discuss with you."

The grin dissolved. "What is it, Dad?"

"Charlie Oxner says he caught you loading a raft with wood last night. Were you planning to set it on fire, and float it across the harbour?"

"Well, um . . ."

"Answer me!"

Wade lowered his head. "Yes, I guess I was."

"So that 'ghost ship' we saw the other night was just a burning raft?"

"Yes, Dad."

"Floated across the harbour by you?"

Wade nodded, his eyes on the floor. "Am I in trouble?"

"You can bet on that. When your mother gets home we'll discuss your punishment. For now, you can go to your room."

As Wade left, Tom smiled happily. So the ghost ship had only been a prank arranged by Wade. The gag had fallen on its face, but there was another score to settle. Just be patient, he told himself, and Wade will truly *suffer*.

After getting a handful of fresh blueberries from the kitchen, Tom sat on the sofa to listen while Carla sang hymns. It felt good to have survived the fishing trip, especially when Shirley returned from Lunenburg and also wanted to know if they'd been seasick.

The only person who didn't ask was Roger Eliot-Stanton, who came out of his room shortly after. He surprised everyone by complimenting Carla on her singing, then sat down beside Tom with a book.

Tom shifted away, and continued reading a newspaper article headlined *Tragic Death of Professor Carol Zinck*. "It doesn't say anything about an insulin overdose. Maybe the police are keeping that quiet, to avoid alerting the killer."

Roger Eliot-Stanton's eyebrows rose in a thin line. "What's this about an insulin overdose?"

Tom hid his face behind the newspaper. "Nothing," he mumbled, furious that he'd revealed secret information.

"The police suspect insulin killed Professor Zinck?"

"Who can say?" Tom muttered.

Tom's face remained hidden until he'd stopped blushing. Even then, he didn't begin feeling better about his mistake until he'd gorged on a big meal of chili and homemade brown bread, followed by a bowl of blueberries, huckleberries, and blackberries smothered in whipped cream. Somehow the food made him feel good, even about facing the Manor on such a stormy night.

As they drove into Lunenburg, Shirley looked carefully at Tom and Liz. "You're only planning to visit Mrs. Zinck?"

"Yes."

"No detective work?"

"You can count on us."

"That's not an answer." A blast of wind shook the car and thunder crackled. "We don't want another search party, especially on a night like this."

"No need to worry about us," Tom said, as the car pulled up in front of Lunenburg Manor.

"I'm not convinced," Carl commented, watching Tom and Liz get out into the storm. "Now, don't be late meeting us."

"No sweat," Liz said cheerfully. "We'll be perfectly safe."

"Let's hope so," Tom murmured, looking up at the Manor just as lightning flashed across the black sky, its jagged light reflected briefly in the dark windows of the tower. A clap of thunder followed, and cold rain lashed their faces as they ran to the shelter of a big oak in the yard.

"I think the power's out. No lights are showing."

"Even so, Mrs. Zinck is probably home. Let's go knock."

"The power's out everywhere," Tom said, stalling for time. "I can see candles in those other houses, but not in the Manor."

"You really messed up today, Tom."

"How?"

"By telling Roger Eliot-Stanton about the insulin. What if he's involved in the murder?"

"You're right, it was a dumb mistake." The rain was soaking Tom's clothes, making him feel miserable. "By the way, where is Roger Eliot-Stanton tonight? Did you notice?"

"He went to his room after dinner. But he could be anywhere by now."

"What a thought."

Tom looked up at the Manor, trying to locate Mrs. Zinck's room, then his eyes went to the looming dark shape of the tower. As lightning burst across the sky, Tom suddenly saw the horrifying image of Professor Zinck at a tower window, a silent cry on his lips.

7

"Did you see that?" Tom gasped.

"What?"

"I'd swear I just saw the Professor's ghost, haunting this place. Let's get out of here!"

Tom ran. Lightning and thunder exploded above his head, but all he could see was the terrible vision of the Professor's face, crying out. Finally he stopped running and gasped for breath.

"Tom!"

Somewhere in the night, Liz was calling his name. Summoning strength, he returned her shout, and moments later she came out of the darkness.

"You ran like the wind, Tom! I couldn't keep up."

"It was horrible, Liz. I'll never forget that face."

"Do you see where we are?"

Liz waited for a lightning flash, then pointed at a row of wet tombstones. "Look, up beyond the cemetery, some lights are on. How come the school's got power?"

"It must have its own generator. Let's go see Black Dog."

"What? Are you crazy?"

"Liz, we've got to do *something*, and Black Dog is our only real suspect."

"You're going to see him now? On a night like this?"

"That's right." Tom turned toward the cemetery. "Coming?"

"What'll you say to him?"

"I don't know, Liz, but I have this awful feeling that Mrs. Zinck is in real danger. We *must* grill Black Dog and force him to make a slip. Then the police can arrest him, and Mrs. Zinck will be safe."

Liz looked at the trees bending low under the wind, which shrieked across the hilltop. "I don't like it."

"Wait here, then." Tom went into the cemetery, trying not to notice the branches clattering above the dim shapes of the tombstones. He wished desperately that Liz would come, too, but he wasn't going to ask her again.

"Tom! Wait for me."

With a sigh of relief, he stopped. "I thought you weren't coming."

"First I had to count slowly to ten for good luck."

"We may need it."

Together they walked through the cemetery, doubled over against the wind. The lights from the school beckoned them on, but before they could reach it Liz seized Tom's arm.

"Listen! Did you hear that?"

"What?"

"Three slow taps. That's our forerunner, Tom!"

Liz's eyes were wide with fright, and Tom's own heart was pounding wildly. Then he saw two swings in the school's playground, slapping against each other in the wind. "There's the tapping," he said. "You see, we're not about to die."

Tom led the way to the school's basement door, but there was no answer to his knock. Opening the door, he called Black Dog's name but got no reply. They tiptoed toward the furnace room, casting anxious glances at the shadowed corners. "Black Dog's not going to leap out at us," Tom said, with a feeble laugh. "He's probably upstairs, cleaning the boards or something."

"My heart's in overdrive. It may never recover."

With a sudden *whooooo!* the wind blasted down the furnace chimney, making them jump. Mickey Mouse was still on the wall, waving a white-gloved hand, but where was Black Dog?

Upstairs, they went through the hallways calling his name and nervously checking each classroom. But they were all empty, which left only the condemned floor above.

"Why are we doing this?" Liz said. "We're supposed to be at the Manor, protecting Mrs. Zinck."

"We can't quit now. Besides, Black Dog's our major suspect. He's the only one we know of who's got anything to gain from the Professor's death."

Arriving on the top floor, they were greeted by a

lizard, which grinned wickedly from a display case. There were still old desks and stacks of dusty texts, and the windows still rattled and banged in the wind, but this time there was no Black Dog to stop Liz from examining the telescope.

"It's trained on the harbour. This thing is so strong, I can practically read the boat names when the lightning flashes."

Tom went to her side, and stood looking down at the cemetery far below. For some reason he remembered the graves of the twin boys, and the discussion that had followed.

"Hey," Liz exclaimed. "I think I just saw Mrs. Zinck."

"Impossible."

"I can see a skiff with a motor, heading out toward the boats in the harbour. There are two people in it, all bundled up, and I'm pretty sure Mrs. Zinck is one of them."

"Let me see."

Tom squinted into the telescope, and was surprised at its strength. Even spray could be seen, flying over the boats, which strained against their anchor cables. Shifting the telescope slightly, he saw a skiff disappearing behind a boat, which heaved in the stormy seas.

"I just missed seeing who's in that skiff. But do you want to know something weird? I think those people are aiming to get aboard Cap'n John's boat."

"What can that mean?"

"I don't know, but it makes me nervous. If someone *is* after the Professor's money, they may want to get rid of Mrs. Zinck, too. What should we do?"

"I'm not absolutely positive it was Mrs. Zinck in the skiff, so let's find out if she's at the Manor. If not, we'll have to call the police."

"I just hope she's okay."

They raced downstairs and out of the school. The rest of the town remained in darkness, and they stumbled down several wrong streets before realizing they were lost. Liz went to a house and got directions, but these proved to be wrong. Then they learned from another house that Lunenburg Manor was ten blocks away. Finally Tom and Liz reached it, wet and exhausted and very frightened for Mrs. Zinck.

Trying not to think about what he'd seen in the tower window, Tom knocked on the door. Eventually it swung open, revealing Henneyberry's sad face.

"Yes?"

"Mr. Henneyberry, please let us in. We're really worried about Mrs. Zinck."

"But she's asleep."

"We've *got* to see her! Otherwise we'll have to ask the police to make sure she's safe."

"Very well, then. If you are that upset."

Henneyberry stepped aside and they went into the hallway, where a single candle flickered on a table and the air was filled with groans and creaks.

Liz looked at Henneyberry. "When did you last actually *see* Mrs. Zinck?"

"Earlier this evening. Perhaps two hours ago, just before the power failed."

"So she's been unprotected since then?"

This suggestion seemed to annoy Henneyberry. "I haven't left the Manor at all, in case she needed me."

"But what about the service stairs in the back, Mr. Henneyberry? Could someone have crept up those stairs to her room without you knowing?"

"It's possible." Henneyberry gazed at Tom and Liz, no doubt wondering why they were so upset. But then he managed to smile. "All right. Since it's so important to you, you can see Mrs. Zinck."

"Terrific," Tom said, starting for the stairs.

"Just a minute. Let me go up first. She'll want to awaken properly before seeing you."

"I guess you're right." Tom tried to hide his impatience as Henneyberry picked up the candle, then put it down and went slowly to a closet. "Excuse me, sir, but what are you doing?"

"The hallways upstairs is drafty, so the candle could blow out. I'll need to use a storm lantern."

Moving at a maddening crawl, Henneyberry opened the closet door, looked up at the shelves to locate the storm lantern, then went along the hallway to get a small velvet chair. Returning to the closet, he climbed on the chair to reach the lantern, then got carefully down and took the chair back to its former place. Finally, after dusting the storm lantern and searching his pockets for matches, Henneyberry got the lantern burning and plodded up the stairs.

During all this time Tom paced the floor, trying not to worry about Mrs. Zinck and desperately fighting thoughts of the Professor's ghost. Finally he flung himself down on the velvet chair, but the seat was wet and he returned to his pacing.

"He's taking so long, Liz! I'm going *mental*!"

"Let's go upstairs."

Holding the candle that Henneyberry had left, Liz started up the tower stairs. A bolt of lightning lit up the stained-glass windows, then thunder crackled across the sky. Rain rattled against the windows as the Manor groaned under the storm's attack.

Reaching the top floor, they found no sign of Henneyberry. "This is where Mrs. Zinck has her bedroom," Liz said. "Why can't we see the light from the storm lantern?"

A sudden draft gusted down the hallway, blowing out the candle. Total darkness surrounded them, and Tom's heart beat fearfully as he thought about Mrs. Zinck.

"I'm sure she's out in Cap'n John's boat. Let's get out of here, and go tell the police. This place freaks me!"

The black air and the groaning of the Manor were almost more than Tom could stand, and he crashed down the stairs in a near panic with Liz right behind, her breathing harsh and frightened. A light came from below. Tom cried out in alarm as they rounded the final bend in the staircase and stumbled to a halt.

A man wearing a thick blond wig was waiting for them in the hallway below, one hand covering his mouth and nose with a wet cloth. He held up a capsule and there was a *phsssst* of escaping gas. As fire filled Tom's throat, he stared into the man's eyes.

"It's you," he gasped, before he slid into darkness.

8

Tom's body tumbled one way until it struck wood, then flopped back against metal. Creaks and rattles filled his ears, and there was a rushing sound he couldn't identify.

He opened his eyes and saw Professor Zinck lying nearby. An engine thudded somewhere near Tom's head, filling the air with fumes. As Tom slowly woke up, he realized that he was inside Cap'n John's tour boat, which was fighting its way through heavy seas.

Tom flexed his aching muscles, then slowly sat up. The big engine pounded in the middle of the cabin. Slumped on a bench near it were Liz and Mrs. Zinck, both staring unhappily at the man at the wheel.

Henneyberry.

The blond wig made him look ridiculous, but a pistol tucked into his belt made him look deadly. Tom's eyes went to Henneyberry's feet, which were soaking wet from the rain. Then he remembered the wet velvet chair at the Manor. Henneyberry had lied when he claimed to have been indoors all day and night, since his feet had soaked the chair.

Where was the man taking them? The rain-lashed darkness outside the windows gave no clue, and Henneyberry was silent as he concentrated on the boat's struggle through the stormy seas.

Tom glanced at Professor Zinck lying on the deck, then his heart leapt in terror. The Professor's eyes had flickered!

There was no further movement, and Tom was sure Henneyberry's knock-out gas was still playing tricks with his brain. Then a giant wave smashed against the boat, rolling it to one side. As Tom struggled for balance, he saw the Professor open his eyes.

Mrs. Zinck cried out, and stumbled to her husband's side. "You're alive! It can't be possible, but you're alive!"

Professor Zinck mumbled a reply, then shook his head and managed to sit up. He hugged his wife with tenderness, but when his eyes turned to Henneyberry they burned with rage.

"You'll pay for this, Henneyberry."

The man laughed. "Say your prayers, Professor. You and your missus aren't long for this world."

"Don't be a fool. You won't get away with it."

Henneyberry smiled, then twisted the wheel to take the boat straight into a towering wave. Tom was thrown sideways, then he tumbled across the deck toward Henneyberry's feet. Looking up, he saw the pistol in the man's belt. Could he reach it?

Liz seemed to read Tom's mind, for she distracted Henneyberry with a question. "How can Professor Zinck be alive, when we saw him dead?"

"Very simple. The man who died was the Professor's twin brother, Evelyn."

"I should have known!"

"A while ago Evelyn came to me with a plan for getting the Professor's money, and I agreed to help in return for a large cash settlement. The first step was to attack Professor Zinck when he was away from the Manor, so his wife couldn't interfere."

"So you waited for our trip to Oak Island?"

"Yes. After the attack we hid him in that abandoned car until no one was around, then returned him to Lunenburg by boat and kept him prisoner in the Manor's tower. Meanwhile, Evelyn pretended to be the Professor."

"So that's why both Mrs. Zinck and Boss were afraid of him."

Sea water crashed over the boat, forcing Henneyberry to battle the wheel, but he was back in control before Tom could find the courage to grab the pistol.

"Then came part two of our plan," said Henneyberry, apparently not guessing why Tom remained so close to his feet. "The lawyer was summoned, and the will was changed to leave everything to the Professor's brother instead of Black Dog. Now all the money would be his, but only if Professor and Mrs. Zinck died in an unfortunate accident."

"That you were going to arrange?"

Henneyberry nodded. "But Evelyn got cold feet. He was upset at the thought of murdering his brother and Mrs. Zinck, and finally decided to tell the police what we'd done. That would have meant a long prison sentence, for kidnapping the Professor."

"But surely that's better than murdering someone!"

"You forget, I'm an old man. If I'd gone to prison for kidnapping, I'd have died there. So I tried to convince Evelyn to continue with the original plan. When he refused, I killed him with an overdose of insulin."

These words were spoken quietly and without emotion, which shocked Tom. He couldn't understand how the man was able to speak so easily about murdering someone, but he knew that meant he could as easily kill again. Henneyberry had to be stopped. Again Tom eyed the gun, and waited for his chance.

"So," Henneyberry said with a sigh, "there I was, stuck with the Professor in the tower room. What should I do? Finally I decided that the Zincks could still have an accident, and I'd slip out of the country with Black Dog's fancy goblet and a few other treasures from the Manor's safe."

"What accident are you talking about?"

The evil man laughed. "You'll know soon enough. It won't be long before I'll be sailing down the coast to Maine. Cap'n John won't get his boat back, but that can't be helped . . ."

At that moment, an enormous wave crashed broadside into the boat. There was a scream of metal, the lights went out, and frightened cries were heard as people were tossed violently through the darkness.

Tom's head hit something and for a moment bells rang inside his head, then he opened his eyes. Somehow the boat had righted itself, the lights were back on, and the pistol lay on the deck close by.

As Tom reached for it, a foot came out of nowhere and pinned his wrist to the deck. "No you don't," Henneyberry said, picking up the gun. "No kid is putting me in prison."

"Henneyberry, listen to me." Professor Zinck's voice shook with tension. "Forget this crazy plan and I'll give you all of our money."

"Sure, and then you'll tell the police I killed your brother. If you hadn't given me such rotten pay, Professor, none of this would be happening. But now you'd better say your prayers."

Henneyberry looked out at the storm. As he did, Liz caught Tom's eye and he realized she had a plan.

"Mr. Henneyberry," Tom said, trying to keep the man talking, "why did you take us to that cottage at the Ovens?"

"To give myself time to think, and to prepare an alibi. I told the police I'd been out for a long walk, then arrived home to find the Professor dead of a heart attack."

Tom's mind whirled as he tried to think of another question. "Were you the person Liz saw rowing Mrs. Zinck out to this boat?"

"That's right. Then, when I went back to get the Professor, you kids arrived at the Manor. I planned to sneak away and leave you there, but then I heard you talking upstairs about going to the police and I decided I'd better bring you along on this trip. You're such nice kids, it's a shame you have to die."

Tom stared in horror at the man, knowing now that he meant to kill them all. Hopeful that Liz knew how to stop Henneyberry, Tom glanced her way and saw that she was leaning over the engine. Suddenly the thudding stopped, and the engine died to silence with an unhappy hiss. The boat began to wallow dangerously in the waves.

"What happened?" Henneyberry looked at the silent engine. "What's wrong with this thing?"

Tom grabbed a bench, and held it tightly as the boat reeled and shuddered, completely at the mercy of the storm. Desperately he prayed that Liz knew what she was doing.

"I guess the engine's not working," she said, raising her voice against the howling wind and the pounding of the waves against the hull.

Henneyberry's face was white as he stared at the engine. "I can't fix it! I don't understand those things."

"I know what's wrong," Liz said.

"Then get it going!"

"First open the cabin door, and throw your gun overboard."

Henneyberry's hands shook as his eyes darted between Liz and the engine. Clearly he knew he was finished without the gun, yet he feared the storm even more. As he hesitated, the boat lurched and groaned, then rolled almost onto its side. When it righted itself, Henneyberry staggered through the cabin and grabbed the door handle. He took the gun from his belt, then faltered.

"Do it," Professor Zinck shouted. "Otherwise you'll die with the rest of us!"

Henneyberry pulled open the door. Spray and rain lashed his face, and from somewhere close by came the unbelievable roar of constant thunder. As the gun went overboard and Henneyberry slammed the door, Mrs. Zinck trembled in fear.

"It's the Ovens! That's what he planned for us."

"Start the engine," Henneyberry screamed at Liz, his voice terror stricken. "We're almost into the Ovens!"

Another wave pitched the boat onto its side, and Liz had to grab for support as she struggled to fit the distributor cap back into place. Every eye was on her while the boat reeled under each blow from the storm, and the thundering roar grew louder.

"There," Liz said in relief, as the engine came alive. "We're safe now."

Henneyberry stumbled forward, grabbed the wheel, and got the boat back under control. Opening a drawer, he lifted out a revolver.

"Luckily I brought along a second gun," he said, pointing it at Liz. "Now get away from that engine!"

Tom tried desperately to think of another means of escape as he watched Henneyberry head the boat into the waves and then lock the wheel in place. Waving the gun with ugly menace, Henneyberry gestured at the Zincks to stand up.

"You're going for a little trip into the Ovens."

"Give us a chance, Henneyberry. Please!"

"Get out on the back deck. You kids go with them."

The Zincks reached for each other's hands, and went together onto the stormy deck. Tom blundered slowly through the cabin, hoping that he could somehow knock Henneyberry down or grab the revolver, but there was no opportunity before he reached the deck.

The roar of thunder from the Ovens was like the constant blasting of huge guns. This sound, combined with the shrieking wind, convinced Tom that the end had come.

A spotlight shone from the roof of the boat, gleaming on Professor Zinck's face as he turned to shout something at Henneyberry. Tom couldn't tell whether this was a final plea for mercy, or a cry of hatred, as the wind tore the words from the Professor's lips and sent them whirling into the darkness.

Henneyberry also shouted without being heard, and gestured at the skiff on the deck. The Zincks seemed finally to accept that Henneyberry would show no mercy, and with brave faces they lifted the skiff over the railing. As it tossed on the sea they climbed down into the little boat, and again reached for each other's hands.

With his gun, Henneyberry waved Liz across the deck toward the skiff. At that moment, the spotlight's glow was cut as something black slithered along the cabin roof and plunged toward Henneyberry.

"No," he screamed, his anguished cry rising above the storm. Vainly he struggled to free himself from the black shape, then screamed again.

Liz seized Tom's arm and pointed in the direction of the skiff. "It's broken free!"

Whirling around, Tom saw the skiff drifting away into the darkness. The terrified Zincks were waving and shouting from the skiff, but their words could not be heard over the roar of the Ovens.

"Climb to the cabin roof," Liz yelled at Tom. "Keep the spotlight on the skiff, and I'll try to steer the boat that way."

With icy fingers, Tom seized the ladder mounted outside the cabin and struggled up to the roof. Head down against the rain and spray that stung his body, he crawled toward the spotlight. Grabbing its handle, he swung the spotlight around and swept the seas in search of the skiff.

The beam picked out a wall of green water surging toward the boat. "No," Tom cried, gripping the spotlight as the boat rose over the wave, hung in the air, and slammed back down into the sea. He shook water from his eyes, then watched the spotlight beam travel along the black cliffs and raging surf that marked the location of the deadly Ovens.

Then Tom saw the Zincks, clinging to the skiff as it rose to the crest of a wave and disappeared down into a trough.

"We're coming," he yelled, even though he knew the Zincks couldn't hear him.

Liz must have seen them, too, for the boat turned and battled through the tossing seas in their direction. Tom kept the spotlight trained on the Zincks, trying not to hear the roar of the Ovens.

The boat rose over a foaming green wave and headed straight down toward the skiff. For a terrible moment it seemed as if the two vessels would collide, then suddenly they were alongside each other and the Zincks grabbed the tour boat's railing.

"We did it," Tom shouted in relief. "They're safe!"

As he shone the spotlight on the deck, helping the

Zincks find their way to safety, a figure dressed completely in black rubber moved forward into the glare and helped Mrs. Zinck over the railing, then did the same for Professor Zinck. When they were both safe, the figure in black turned from the railing into the full glare of the spotlight.

It was Black Dog.

9

A few days later, Tom was taking his sixteenth ride on the Tilt-A-Whirl, a machine that spun his body and scrambled his brains. "Fantastic," he murmured weakly, as the machine stopped its gyrations and he staggered away.

"Going again?" Liz asked. "You need five more rides to break my record."

"I'm going . . . I'm going to be sick." Covering his mouth with both hands, Tom stumbled toward a washroom. Much later, he emerged on shaky legs and saw Liz riding the Tilt-A-Whirl, smiling happily as her hair whipped back and forth across her face. Feeling his stomach rise, Tom turned away to stare at the people crowding the midway of the Lunenburg Fisheries Exhibition.

"I guess I win!" Liz grabbed Tom's arm, hustling him to a food stand that reeked of burnt onions and frying meat. "For my prize I want an oyster burger and a giant Coke."

"What a combination." Tom shelled out the money for Liz's prize, then closed his eyes as she gobbled the food. "You must have a cast-iron stomach."

Wade Goulden appeared out of the crowd, grinning as usual. "You're looking green, Tom. Did the merry-go-round upset your little tummy?"

"No, but the sight of your mug is spoiling my digestion."

"Too bad you're feeling sick, or I'd challenge you to a lobster-eating contest."

"Any time, Wade, any time."

"By the way, Tom, there's a rumour going around Stonehurst that a certain detective is scared of the dark. Surely it's not true?"

As Wade quickly disappeared into the crowd, Liz shook her head sympathetically. "You should get that guy."

"Don't worry," Tom replied grimly. He pointed at a nearby booth. "Let's go see the scallop-shucking contest."

At the booth, experts with flying fingers swiftly opened and emptied the pretty shells taken from the sea bed. "Look at that judge," Tom whispered. "He's a clone of Roger Eliot-Stanton."

"Imagine two copies of that guy walking around. You know, I still find it hard to believe that Roger Eliot-Stanton is just another tourist visiting Nova Scotia."

"You're right, but what's his story?"

"Maybe he's here for a special contest to pick the Rudest Man in the World." Liz looked at the shifting patterns of adults and children streaming through the exhibition grounds, then grabbed Tom's arm. "There's Black Dog over at that weight-guessing booth. Let's go say hello."

Tom shrugged. "Okay, but only because he saved our lives."

"What a hero he was."

"I still don't understand where he found the strength, when he's got a body like Dietmar Oban. He's so thin, I bet he has to move around in the shower just to get wet."

"Your jokes are a RIOT, Tom. Rotten, Idiotic, Oafish, and Tupid."

"Tupid?"

"Yeth. And they thtink, too."

Laughing, Tom and Liz hurried through the crowd to the booth where a young woman was studying Black Dog in an effort to guess his weight. But, like Tom, she misjudged the man's appearance, and was forced to part with a kewpie doll when her guess was too low.

Seeing Liz, Black Dog smiled and handed her the prize. "Take this home, as a souvenir of your Lunenburg adventure."

Liz gazed at the kewpie doll. "Do you really mean it?"

"Sure thing," Black Dog said, then looked at Tom. "Sorry, but there's no gift for you."

"Then could you give me some answers?"

"What's on your mind?"

"Well, to tell you the truth, I always suspected you were the person behind all the strange events at Lunenburg Manor. If you weren't pulling off a crime, what *were* you doing?"

Black Dog laughed, and squeezed Tom's shoulder with a hand that was surprisingly powerful. "Appearances are deceptive, Tom. Just because I have a black beard doesn't mean I'm Blackbeard, or some other villain. I'm just another artist, struggling to succeed."

"But what about that morning we met you at the cove, near the Ovens? When we told you the Professor was dead, you shouted *the fools—I warned them* and went running off. How come?"

"It was the police I was upset about, because I thought they'd let the Professor be murdered despite my warnings. Do you remember visiting the school and saying the Zincks were in danger?"

"Sure."

"I was already worried about them, so your suspicions forced me to act. After you left the school, I went to the police station and warned them to watch Henneyberry. But they didn't take me seriously, because everyone in town knows that I've been feuding with Henneyberry for years."

"Why?"

Black Dog laughed. "I've never met anyone so fond of asking questions! Anyway, to continue, I was talking to Cap'n John one day and he mentioned that Henneyberry had asked if his tour boat could stand up to heavy seas."

"I guess so he could put the Zincks overboard off the Ovens, during a storm."

"From then on I used my telescope to keep an eye on the tour boat. Unfortunately, I was in Halifax when the storm struck, but I got back just in time to spot Henneyberry taking you kids and Professor Zinck out to the boat. I alerted the police, then drove to the cliff above the Ovens to watch for the boat coming out from Lunenburg."

"Did you see it?"

"Yes, but there was no sign of a police boat in pursuit. I started to panic, because I knew Henneyberry was up to something terrible. So I ran to the cove, grabbed one of the motorboats that I rent when I'm scuba diving, and headed out to sea."

"Wearing your black scuba-diving suit for warmth?"

Black Dog nodded. "I could see the lights of the tour boat through the storm, but my motorboat couldn't catch up. Then, for some reason, the tour boat stopped moving and I was able to get close to it."

"That's when Liz killed the engine, and forced Henneyberry to throw his gun overboard."

"By the time the tour boat was going again, I was alongside. I grabbed the rope at the bow, managed to make my boat fast, and then struggled on board. I crawled along the cabin roof, saw what was happening, and made my leap at Henneyberry."

"Superman to the rescue," Tom said, laughing. "You sure had everything under control by the time the police boat reached us and Henneyberry was arrested."

Liz looked at Black Dog. "How'd you get so strong? Was it from scuba diving?"

"That's right. I started to build up my muscles, then got hooked on it. You kids should try it some time. If you like adventure and mystery, there's no detective work like searching for wrecks and their treasures."

"Sign me up," Tom said. "Say, I guess that explains why you were at the cove that morning. You'd been scuba diving."

"And that's where I'm going now." Black Dog waved. "Before you leave Lunenburg, be sure to drop by the school to say goodbye."

Liz gazed after Black Dog until he was lost from sight. "There goes the greatest man I'll ever know," she said wistfully.

Tom laughed. "What about Cap'n John? You seemed to think he was pretty great, too."

Liz's face lit up. "Do you suppose he's here?"

"Maybe he's in that building with the displays of fancy equipment for tracking fish. Want to go see?"

"Okay, but what about the Ox Pull? I don't want to miss that, or the Queen of the Sea contest. Not to mention a few more rides on the Tilt-A-Whirl."

They headed toward a large crowd that had gathered for the Ox Pull. Standing with the Zincks watching the event were Carl and Shirley, who smiled in greeting.

"The Ox Pull is a big attraction at Maritime exhibitions," Shirley said. "This is total muscle power!"

"Is it like a tug-of-war?"

Carl shook his head. "You see that team of oxen? They're about to be hitched to a cart with a dead weight of over three thousand kilos. If the team can manage to shift the cart forward, it will win the contest."

The smooth brown coats of the two enormous beasts shimmered and rippled as they were led into place. Brass bells clanged at their throats as they shook their great heads and prepared for the challenge. The teamster, standing before them, reached out a hand to one of their curved horns and shouted a command. The animals dug their feet in, the wood of their yoke groaned, and the cart moved slowly forward to loud applause from the audience.

"How are you feeling?" Tom asked the Zincks.

"Fully recovered," Mrs. Zinck replied, smiling. "I found out I was ill because Henneyberry was putting something in my food, to keep me out of action. After the murder he increased the dose, so I was too feeble to go for help."

"I knew it, Liz. Didn't I say he was poisoning the food?"

"I have to admit you got that one right."

Tom looked at the Professor. "And now I know why you wrote EVEL in the dirt."

"I was attacked at the Money Pit by Henneyberry and my brother, who rushed into hiding when they heard you two coming. I was too weak to get away, so I tried to write the names of my attackers in the dirt. Unfortunately I passed out after writing the first letters of Evelyn's name."

Tom shook his head. "I should have figured that out, especially since I knew your twin brother had a girl's name."

Liz nodded. "And we'd even discussed adult twins, that day in the cemetery."

"Oh well. You can't win them all."

Liz grew thoughtful. "So I guess the forerunner that you told us about was really your brother?"

The Professor nodded sadly. "At the time I thought the vision had been of myself, but it was my twin who was doomed."

The group headed toward a building that throbbed with the amplified music of a hillbilly band. Liz imitated the wild motions of a berserk fiddle player, then grinned at the Zincks.

"I love those country sounds. Say, Professor Zinck, did you hear that Tom swore he saw your ghost? Talk about running scared!"

"It's true," Tom exclaimed. "I'm sure you were at the tower window, during the storm."

"You're right, Tom. I'd broken free of the ropes that Henneyberry had tied me with, and started shouting for help when I couldn't get the window open. Then Henneyberry rushed into the room, and put me out with a gas capsule."

"Visiting the Manor always freaked me. Those creaky floors, and the time when Evelyn had secretly taken your place and was acting so strangely. He was muttering about life and death, I guess because he couldn't stand the thought of murder."

"Poor Evelyn."

Liz was now nimbly plucking an invisible banjo. "I'll tell you a clue we missed. It happened when we returned your car keys after finding them at Oak Island."

"Car keys? But I don't drive."

"Exactly! They must have actually been your house keys, but Evelyn just said he was in no shape to drive, and gave the keys to Henneyberry. We should have known your place had been taken by an imposter, who didn't know that you don't drive. It also showed that Henneyberry was involved, because he didn't say anything about Evelyn's mistake."

Inside the building, a mob of people was packed around a stage that shook and quivered with the electronic vibrations of the music. The soaring beauty of a fiddle carried the song to its close, and the crowd cheered wildly.

Suddenly, a pirate leapt onto the stage. As his cutlass flashed, the band cowered back and the audience gasped. Then Roger Eliot-Stanton hurried from the wings and approached the microphone.

"Ladies and gentlemen," he cried, holding up his hands for quiet. "Thank you for participating in a small experiment. Your fear of this pirate shows that I have selected the right person to play Captain Kidd in my next movie."

Excited chattering broke out, then died away when the pirate made threatening gestures with his cutlass. Roger Eliot-Stanton motioned the pirate to his side. "My friends," he said. "May I present the silver screen's next superstar!"

With a flourish he pulled away the pirate's eye patch and false beard. For a moment the crowd was shocked into silence, then wild whistles and cheers broke out as Cap'n John grinned and waved his cutlass in the air. When the noise finally ended, the band returned to its playing and the two men came down from the stage.

Tom and Liz pushed forward among the crush of locals to congratulate Cap'n John on becoming a celebrity. Hoping to question Roger Eliot-Stanton, Tom elbowed a path to his side.

"Are you a real movie director?"

"Yes."

"Are you actually going to make a movie about Captain Kidd?"

"Yes."

"Will you be filming at Oak Island?"

"Yes."

"Is Cap'n John really going to star?"

"Yes."

"Are you looking for a second star?"

"No."

Obviously the man had no eye for talent, and Tom lost interest in asking questions. But Liz wanted some answers, too.

"How'd you meet Cap'n John?"

"I chartered his boat to do some location scouting. As soon as I saw him, I knew that the great Eliot-Stanton had made another fabulous discovery."

"You were at Lunenburg Manor once, saying the Professor could name his own price for something. What did you want?"

Roger Eliot-Stanton smiled, and his face came close to looking pleasant. "Thanks for the reminder, young lady. I'd forgotten about that unfinished business."

"But what did you want?"

"The Manor would be a perfect location for some scenes in my movie." Sliding close to the Zincks, Roger Eliot-Stanton allowed his smile to grow wider. "Perhaps you'd agree to my company using the Manor? I would pay you handsomely."

Professor Zinck laughed. "The money doesn't matter. You can have the Manor for free, but there's one condition."

"What's that?"

The Professor nodded toward Tom and Liz. "I have two good friends who would love to do some acting. Do you suppose you could find them something in your movie?"

Roger Eliot-Stanton's smile faded. Then he wrapped his arms around Tom and Liz. "Of course! These kids are my buddies. There's nothing I wouldn't do for them."

Wriggling free of the bony arm, Tom looked at Professor Zinck. "Thanks a million, Professor. I hope that both of you will visit us at our Hollywood mansion."

Mrs. Zinck laughed. "We'll both be there for sure."

Later that night, a silver moon looked down on two figures moving silently through the black forest. Somewhere in the darkness an owl hooted, and a small creature rustled through the underbrush, but these sounds were ignored by Wade and Tom as they followed the faint outline of a path leading to Phantom Cove.

The two were after buried treasure. As everyone knows, such treasure can only be dug for at night, and in total silence. But there was another legend that both boys could not help thinking about: *If blood was shed by pirates burying their booty, then it must also flow before the gold and jewels can be dug up.*

Tom shivered, imagining the terrible eyes of the spectral pirate who might be guarding the treasure at Phantom Cove. He glanced at Wade, wondering how brave his companion felt.

A moan came from somewhere in the night.

Wade's steps faltered, but Tom pushed bravely forward. For a moment it seemed he would have to go on alone. Then Wade hurried to his side and they continued their silent journey.

Again they heard the moan, a fearful sound that grew louder and louder until it filled their ears.

Then they saw it.

On the path directly ahead stood a headless body, wearing a white suit that seemed smudged with the dirt of the grave. Moonlight shone on the horrible creature as it slowly raised its arms, moaning.

Wade screamed. The shriek of terror vibrated in his throat, filling the air. "*Help! Murder!*" he cried, then broke into a swift run and was gone. For several minutes his screams were heard, fading away into the night, and then all was silent.

Except for Tom's laughter, which went on for a long time. He turned to the headless body with a grin. "That's the last time Wade will reach through my bedroom window with icy fingers. Revenge is sweet."

There was a muffled reply, then Liz pulled away the black velvet that had covered her head. "What fun," she exclaimed. "One night soon I'm going to try haunting someone else. I wonder where I could find a nice juicy victim?"

"Don't even think about it!"

Liz laughed wickedly. "I can't wait, dear brother."

Code Red at the Supermall

For my niece Julia Wilson,
so new to our world.
And my friend Stuart Buchan,
gone much too soon.

THE INDOOR SEA

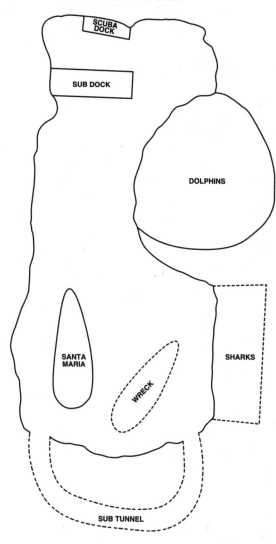

WEST EDMONTON MALL

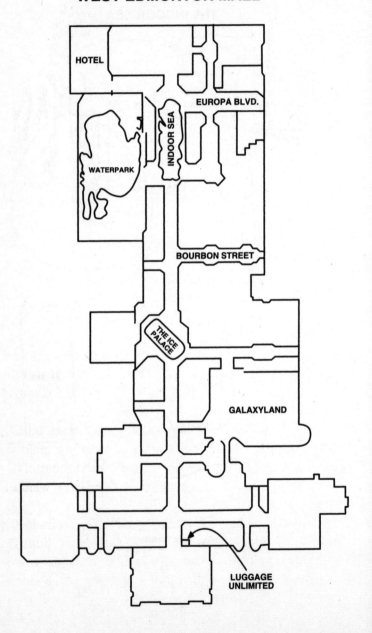

1

The shark came out of the darkness, moving swiftly toward Liz Austen.

She stared at the deadly teeth and stepped back with a gasp. As the shark reached the glass wall of its tank and swept away, Liz glanced at the people standing nearby, wondering if her fear was obvious.

They were all in a dark underground cave. Behind one glass wall the sharks circled in their big tank; on another side of the cave penguins preened themselves, while crocodiles with gleaming yellow eyes watched their visitors.

Leaving the cave, Liz hurried up some stairs to the marble corridors of the West Edmonton Mall. Sunlight poured down from domed windows high above, warming shoppers who strolled past some of the 828 stores.

The sun sparkled on the blue water of an indoor sea where subs moved slowly past a Spanish galleon, lighting up the dolphins performing spectacular leaps in their pool beside the sea.

Behind a high glass wall was the World Waterpark, where girls and boys strolled on a beach under palm trees, kids surfed the big waves and others plunged down an amazing collection of waterslides that were intertwined like green and blue snakes.

Nearby, Liz saw a store called Lots of Fun Stuff. It featured a display of stick-on tattoos, which the owner explained were very realistic. "They'll come off, of course, but you need to follow my special, printed instructions."

"I like the bats," Liz said. "Their eyes are really scary."

Consulting her map of the mall, Liz decided to visit Bourbon Street, a replica of the famous tourist attraction in New Orleans. It featured restaurants like the Café Orleans facing a street of cobblestones and benches. Lights twinkled above, suggesting a night sky, neon signs glowed outside the restaurants, and realistic mannequins stood on second-floor balconies above the crowds parading past.

A girl named Susan waited for customers at a row of old-fashioned shoeshine chairs. Like Liz, she was 16. "The money's good and it's a great summer job," Susan laughed, "but sometimes I get homesick for Nova Scotia."

"I miss home, but I sure love this place."

"How much longer are you staying?"

"Until this weekend. My Dad's teaching a course to the mall's security guards. After that," Liz pouted, "we fly home."

"Did you say he's an inspector in the Winnipeg police?"

"That's right. He's . . ."

"Liz, something's wrong!"

"What do you mean?"

"Listen!"

From speakers hidden in the ceiling, an urgent voice was saying, "*Code Red, Bourbon Street. Code Red, Bourbon Street.*" Susan quickly put away her brushes and polishes. "Code Red is the maximum alert for security guards. There's some kind of trouble here in Bourbon Street."

Liz looked at the people strolling past. "Who's going to tell them?"

"The guards will be here any second and they'll clear everyone from the area."

"But what about the Code Red? We won't know what it's about!" Liz stepped closer to Susan. "I have to find out what happened. Is there anywhere I could hide?"

Susan hesitated, then looked at a nearby booth. It was decorated with the signs of the zodiac, and the promise to reveal your *past, present and future.* "The fortune-teller's away and she left me her key. You could hide in there."

"Great!" Liz saw security guards at the entrance to Bourbon Street asking people to leave. "Hurry, Susan, hurry." Then, safely inside the booth, she called from the darkness, "Thanks a million! See you tomorrow."

"Let's hope so."

Crouching against the wooden wall, Liz listened to the guards clearing people from the area. As the Code Red continued to sound, a curious hush fell over

Bourbon Street. A few minutes later Liz's heart skipped when she heard her father's voice saying as he approached, "A package?"

"Yes, Inspector Austen," someone replied. "We've alerted the local police, but we'd like you to take a look right away."

"The robot can't get up there?"

"No, sir. Whoever planted this thing made sure a robot couldn't get near it."

As the voices faded away, Liz slowly raised her eyes to a crack in the wall. Through it she saw neon lights glowing along the street, now deserted except for several security guards. They stood in the distance with arms crossed and faces creased into frowns as they watched her father step onto the balcony above the Café Orleans.

Kneeling, he cautiously reached toward a package wrapped in brown paper. Liz was certain it was a bomb.

2

Moments later several police officers ran into the Café Orleans, just as Mr. Austen stood up from the package, a smile of relief on his face. The situation looked under control, so Liz raced from the booth and up the restaurant stairs. Grabbing her father, she hugged him. "Are you okay, Dad? Can I help you?"

"Liz, how did you . . . ?"

"I'll tell you later, okay?" She looked at the police officers studying the package. "How'd the security guards learn about the bomb?"

"An anonymous tip over the phone."

"A man or a woman?"

"Impossible to say. The caller's voice was deliberately muffled."

"Didn't they leave a note beside that thing? Demanding a ransom or something?"

"Nothing."

"Why do you think it was planted on the balcony?"

"Normally a robot would be used to investigate the bomb, so there'd be no risk to anyone. Whoever left that bomb wanted to make sure that the robot couldn't be used."

"So that's a real bomb? Not a fake?"

"It's the real thing all right, but there's one unusual thing about it. A key wire wasn't connected. I realized right away that someone was sending a serious message by planting this bomb."

"What do you mean?"

"One message: This person's an expert because that's a sophisticated device. The bomber's saying that, for now, no one's going to get hurt. But we can expect there will be more trouble, probably with minimum danger at first. The bomber's motive may be to hurt the mall without firing a shot. I'm only guessing, of course, but we've certainly got a strange character on our hands."

* * *

Just then a tall woman with the striking eyes and high cheekbones of the Cree Indians approached. She smiled as Liz was introduced by her father. "Cathy Winter Eagle, meet my daughter. I'm very proud of Liz and her brother Tom."

Liz hugged her Dad. He was tall and handsome, with black hair and eyes, and she was proud of him, too. "Pleased to meet you, Inspector Winter Eagle."

"Inspector? I'm impressed you noticed."

"Your uniform has the same number of pips as my Dad's."

As the pair discussed the case, Liz glanced around the restaurant's upper floor, wondering how the bomb had been smuggled onto the balcony. The entire floor was empty, and there was no trace of whoever had planted the bomb. For a moment she looked at a grill in the wall, enjoying the feel of the cool air that blew through it. There was a door right beside it, but when she tried the handle it was locked.

Back downstairs, after they had left Bourbon Street, Liz asked her father what would happen next.

"Cathy will use the police computer to search out names of previous mall employees who've been fired, also any troublemakers who've been banned from the premises." He looked at the inspector. "Have you got a few minutes? I'd like you to meet my wife."

She looked at the officers who'd begun fingerprinting the scene. "They'll be busy for a while, so that's a good idea."

Still talking about the incident, the trio made the long walk through the gigantic mall to the hotel at its far end. "My room's really fabulous," Liz said to Inspector Winter Eagle. "Do you want to come and see it on the way to my Mom and Dad's suite?"

"Certainly."

The elevator came to a stop and the doors opened. They stepped into a corridor with dark mirrors and a red HOLLYWOOD sign. In Liz's room, neon stars glowed on walls blacker than ebony and tiny lights twinkled in the deep-purple carpet. "Those are fibre optics," Liz explained. "Neat, eh?"

"You bet."

On another floor they entered a marbled hallway lined with pillars. The word ROME was in gold letters on the wall, backlit by a soft red glow.

"I've heard of this hotel's theme rooms," Inspector Winter Eagle remarked to Liz, "but I didn't know the hallways are also themed to fit the rooms."

"On the Polynesian floor, the rooms have Jacuzzis with volcanoes beside them that actually belch steam!"

Mr. Austen opened a door at the end of the hallway. "We're here as guests of the mall while I'm teaching a course to the security personnel. My son's friend Dietmar came with us, too."

The inspector gazed at the thick carpet's rich burgundy colour, which was repeated in the spread that covered a round bed enclosed by sheer curtains. Nearby, potted plants hung above the huge marble tub. Beside it was a statue of a Roman serving maid, in her hand a golden spout through which water plunged when the bath was filled.

Mrs. Austen was working at a desk. She was tall with blue eyes, and had hair the colour of flames. "Ted's told me lots about you, Cathy, so I'm glad we're finally able to meet," she said to the inspector with a warm smile.

Suddenly the hallway door opened and Liz saw her brother, and a second boy of about the same age. "Uh oh—here comes trouble in the form of Dietmar Oban. When you shake hands with him, Inspector, beware of him greeting you with a hand-buzzer."

"He looks nice."

"Appearances can be deceiving."

Tom was tall for 14. Like his mother, his hair was red, his eyes blue. Dietmar was shorter and rounder, with brown hair and eyes to match. He seemed excited about something, so Liz watched him warily as Mr. Austen poured refreshments into glasses. Then she got distracted by the conversation about what the bomber's motives could be. As the others discussed various possibilities, Liz took a sip of bubbly spring water and then almost choked when she saw a fly in the glass. She screamed and the glass dropped from her hand, then Dietmar sprang forward to retrieve the plastic fly.

"So that's where I left the little devil."

"Tom Austen," Liz said, as the others chuckled. "If you invite this odious creature on any more holidays, you can count me out."

Smiling, Inspector Winter Eagle looked at her watch. "I'd better get back to that bomb investigation. They'll be finishing off the preliminary stuff—picture taking, dusting for fingerprints—so I can really get started on my investigation." A beep sounded from her belt, followed by a static-filled voice speaking in police codes. "There's a problem at one of the mall's stores. It's probably not connected with the bomb incident, but I'd better check."

"May we come?" Tom asked.

"Sure."

Soon everyone but Dietmar was descending in the elevator. "That guy," Tom laughed. "Can you believe he'd rather watch TV than witness a police investigation? He's such a couch potato I could probably sell him to McDonald's." Then, as the doors opened onto the lobby he added, "But he's fun with that weird sense of humour."

"He's different," Liz said. "I'll sure admit that."

In the mall, neon store signs were reflected on the green surface of the indoor sea. Surrounded by a rocky shoreline and the brightly lit stores, the sea was dominated by the *Santa Maria*, a replica of the galleon that carried Christopher Columbus to the New World.

"People aren't allowed on the *Santa Maria*," Liz said. "It's a real ship that was made in British Columbia, and then shipped here in pieces and rebuilt. But there's nothing inside except a huge tank of tropical fish."

"Have you been on board to see them?"

"No, some kids in the mall gave me that scoop."

"Why the fish if nobody's allowed on the *Santa Maria*?" Mr. Austen asked.

"Because of the submarines." Liz pointed at a yellow conning tower rising above the surface. The vessel was creating small waves as it slowly moved forward through the water. "Those are real subs. The trip goes around the edge of the sea and passengers look out the portholes at all kinds of tropical fish in underwater tanks."

"Plus the ruins of the lost civilization of Atlantis," Tom added. "It's totally realistic."

"Where does that tunnel go?" Mrs. Austen pointed at a dark opening in the rocky wall surrounding the sea.

"That's how the subs change direction," Tom replied. "They go into the tunnel, make a loop and come out that portal below us."

"I'm dying to see inside the tunnel," Liz said, "but it's out of bounds for visitors." She looked down at a flipper-footed figure in scuba gear swimming silently among the underwater plants of the indoor sea. "Wouldn't that be fun?"

"Say, we'd better get moving. The inspector's already out of sight."

Liz took out her map. "She said the store's called Luggage Unlimited. It's at the far end of the mall. Believe it or not, that's eight city blocks away."

Mrs. Austen smiled. "We should rent one of those electric carts for weary shoppers."

"Or hire one of the mall's rickshaws! What a way to arrive at the scene of the crime."

A small crowd had gathered at Luggage Unlimited outside the yellow police tapes that blocked the entrance. Escorted by Inspector Winter Eagle, the Austens entered the store. At first it appeared normal. Suitcases stood in careful displays, attaché cases were arranged to appeal to the business shopper, and soft leather purses had been hung in neat rows. But, further back in an upper display area, there was terrible damage. Purses were slashed, suitcases twisted and useless, and pictures had been torn from the walls and smashed underfoot. Tom and Liz saw an officer questioning a man and woman who wore the traditional clothes of India. Then they became aware of the graffiti spray-painted around the walls.

Paki, the savage words said. *Go home, Paki. We don't want your kind. Pakis out!!*

3

The next morning Tom and Liz were still upset as they had breakfast at one of the mall's restaurants. "Why are some people so cruel?" Liz said to her parents. "It's *terrible* to hurt others like that."

"Racists are afraid," Mrs. Austen said. "Afraid of change, afraid of strangers, afraid of anything that threatens their narrow world." She pushed a strand of hair out of her face. "After we get home I'll be in court on a hate-mail case. I don't think I've ever been so angry about anything since I became a lawyer. I just can't believe some people can be so ignorant."

"I just wish I could *do* something," Tom said. "It was horrible last night at the luggage store. I felt so helpless."

Mr. Austen squeezed the back of Tom's hand. "You and Liz were great. When we were asking questions you really showed the Gills that you cared about them." He lifted a coffee cup to his lips. "Besides which . . . Ouch! That's hot."

Tom grinned. "Remember how I bugged Mom until she quit smoking? Now I'm going to work on you about drinking coffee. Your love affair with caffeine must stop!"

"He's right," Liz said. "Besides, that cream you put in your coffee turns to leather once it hits your stomach."

"Where's all this stuff come from?"

"Health class, of course. It's got the best videos in school."

Dietmar nodded. "She's right, Mr. Austen. Ever seen close-ups of lungs dripping tar? Every smoker in school was butting out at noon hour."

"It's hard to believe kids your age smoke," Mr. Austen said as he shook his head. "The world's gone haywire."

"Want some more bad news?" Liz spread some jam on a thick slice of toast and took a bite. "Mmmmm, that's good. Anyway, Dad, hang on to your cane. The next big fad may be tattoos."

"*What?*"

"You know, those weird designs on peoples' . . ."

"I know what a tattoo is, Liz. But you're telling me . . . ?"

"That kids are getting into tattoos. Isn't that right, Dietmar?"

"Maybe, but I haven't . . ."

"I don't believe it," Mr. Austen interrupted. "What'll the next fad be? Lobotomies?"

Mrs. Austen patted his cheek. "Remember your blood pressure, dear. Now just drink your coffee and try to relax."

Tom glanced up at the skylight as a cloud drifted past, momentarily blocking the sunshine. They were surrounded by greenery, from plants in bamboo pots to ferns spikier than a rock star's hair, to the 14 trees he'd counted below. The restaurant was shaped like a horseshoe, with an open space at its centre; one floor down were the tables, fountains and trees of a fast-food arcade.

"I love this place," he said.

Liz nodded her agreement. "Dad, is there anything new on the bomb?"

"Nothing major, but the police figured out how the luggage store was broken into. They've recommended the owners install an intruder detector in the showroom—the Gills said they'd get one right away."

"How'd the break-in happen?"

"Apparently there's a vast open space above all the stores. It's a huge, dark crawlspace—there's barely room to stand up in it. Apparently street kids used to sneak around up there at night. They'd lift out ceiling tiles, drop into stores to steal things, then escape through the crawlspace. Security thought they'd solved that problem, but somebody must have found a new way into it. It looks like that person's responsible for the damage to Luggage Unlimited."

Mrs. Austen poured herself some water from a jug. "I understand the Gills found the mess when they opened the store in the afternoon. Why were they so late opening the store?"

"A family emergency at her sister's farm. They were both needed, so the store was closed for the morning."

"So," Tom said, "that racist creep knew it would be easy to break in." He looked at the waitress who was approaching with more coffee. "Did you hear what happened yesterday at Luggage Unlimited?"

"Yes, I did. It was disgraceful." She turned to Mrs. Austen. "I enjoy seeing you folks every morning. You'll be here for a while, won't you? I'll bet those security guards are really glad that you're here to help."

"You mean because of that bomb being discovered?" Mrs. Austen shook her head. "We're not leaving. My husband says there's no immediate danger, so that's good enough for me. That crazy person who left the bomb will be eating every meal behind bars soon."

"Let's hope so. I've been working here since the mall opened and I love it. Plus, my relatives are arriving from Hungary next week to see this place. I don't want anything to go wrong while they're here, but I guess I'm just overreacting."

"Hey," Tom said, "they've actually heard of this mall in Hungary?"

"Sure. People from all over the world—even Siberia— have sat in that booth."

"Fantastic." He took out his notebook. "What a great addition to my trivia about the mall." He made notes, then glanced at the others. "Here's another test: You know those chandeliers we've seen around? How many lights in each?" When no one could answer he said, "Two thousand. Next question: How many people work here?"

"That one's easy," the waitress said. "Fifteen thousand. But if lots of people hear about yesterday's trouble or if there are any more bombs, people might be afraid to work here. You've got to catch that bomber fast, Mr. Austen."

"You're right." He drank the rest of his coffee. "Which reminds me, I'm meeting Inspector Winter Eagle in 15 minutes at Bourbon Street."

"May we come, Dad?" Liz asked.

"Sorry, sweetheart. This meeting's only for senior police brass and officials from the city and provincial governments. There's lots of important people worried about the bomber."

Tom stood up. "Well, Dad, seeing that you've got everything under control, I'm going to try to find out who's hurting the Gills."

Mrs. Austen touched his hand. "Be careful."

"It's okay, Mom, I'll stay in the mall." He looked at his notebook. "Know how many security guards this place has?"

She nodded. "Fifty, but I say it again: be careful."

Tom kissed her cheek, then looked at Liz. "Want to come?"

"I can't. Yesterday I met someone really nice and told her I'd meet her this morning."

He turned to Dietmar. "How about you? Or will it be another morning in front of the soaps?"

"Nope, I'll come with you." Dietmar shovelled a leftover muffin into his mouth as he stood up. Then he pulled a paperback out of his hip pocket. "Here," he mumbled to Liz through the muffin, "I forgot to return it earlier. Sorry, I got food on page 56."

"Thanks a lot," Liz grumbled, flipping to the page. "I hope it's not . . ." For a second her eyes bulged; then a scream ripped through the restaurant when a black spider tumbled from the book into her lap. As people turned to stare, she leapt from the booth, slapping frantic hands at her clothes. "Where is it? Where is it?"

"Right here." Dietmar knelt to pick up the spider. Stroking its little plastic head he murmured, "Poor pet, all those nasty screams must be upsetting. Shall I take you home to the joke shop?"

Liz grabbed for the water jug but was restrained by her mother. "Take it easy, sweetheart. Do any damage and his parents could sue." Then she looked at Dietmar. "Relax with the gags, okay, or I may have to lean on you."

"Sure thing, Mrs. Austen."

Grinning, Dietmar left the restaurant. Tom gave his sister an apologetic shrug, then hurried out of the restaurant after a brief, hungry stare at the display of Black Forest cakes and *gâteaux au chocolat* being prepared for lunch. Together with Dietmar he descended an escalator to the indoor sea, where brilliant sunshine streamed down onto the white sails of the *Santa Maria*.

"See those cannons?" Tom pointed at the deck. "You'll want to know they're fakes."

"Why should I want to know that, Austen?"

"To impress everyone back home with your knowledge of the supermall. Otherwise you'll be telling them that it's shaped like a TV screen."

"I've seen lots of things."

"Sure! The Drop of Doom, the Mindbender and the Sky Screamer."

"That's enough."

"Our walkabout this morning will do you good. With me as your guide you'll see amazing sights. Besides, maybe we'll hear something about the attack—

there are hundreds of kids around this mall. Someone must have heard rumours."

"This reminds me, and not happily I might add, of our little excursion to Blood Alley Square in Vancouver. I hope this isn't going to be a repeat."

"Not a chance." Tom moved along the railing to get a better view of the dolphin pool on the far side of the sea. "Compared to this mission, Blood Alley Square was a picnic."

"Then forget it."

Tom grabbed his arm. "Come back here! I'll protect you."

Dietmar laughed. "Only until we meet a pitbull terrier. Remember walking to school last winter when that one came charging at us across his yard?"

"I didn't think he was chained."

"You sure went up that tree in a hurry."

Over at the dolphin pool a trainer appeared through a door in the rocky wall that overlooked a small beach and the water. The excited faces of the dolphins immediately appeared from underwater, squealing for treats from the pail the man had just set down. As he made hand signals the dolphins disappeared under the surface, then leapt together from the water. For one splendid moment they glistened in midair, then plunged back beneath the waves. A moment later they were back to receive their reward, and the man continued to toss fish into the dolphins' mouths as he coaxed them to slide further up on the beach. Finally, when they had slipped back into the pool, Tom and Dietmar continued walking.

"I'd like that job," Dietmar said. "Dolphins are great."

Inside a video arcade coloured lights flashed like

alien eyes and the haunted mechanical voices of the games called out challenges. They watched a boy wearing glasses play for a while, then Tom asked if he could join in.

"You're going against Manitoba's finest," he warned. "Want to risk it?"

"This arcade's my summer home," the boy said. His teeth were thick with braces. "This game is my girlfriend."

"Too bad about the luggage store," Tom said as images whirled on the screen and his hands moved nimbly. "I guess you heard?"

"Sure."

"How do you feel about what happened?"

The boy shrugged. "Not good, but what can you do?"

"Any idea who did it?"

"The Skull. Everyone knows that."

"Who?"

"There's a guy around this mall who calls himself the Skull. He's got a shaved head and the brainpower of a slug. Steer clear of him—he's real mean and his hero's Adolf Hitler. Get the picture?"

"Sure." Tom looked in amazement at his score. "Wow, Oban, do you see that? A *Guinness Book of Records* qualifier."

"It's beatable," Dietmar said with a shrug.

The boy wearing the glasses nodded. "Your friend's right. Watch my moves."

Minutes later Tom and Dietmar walked out of the arcade, stunned by the score achieved so easily by the boy. From somewhere in the mall came the sound of music, booming down the corridor and making shop windows vibrate. They hurried toward it and joined a crowd outside a huge bookstore. On a raised platform a band was performing, fronted by a teenage boy in T-shirt and jeans. One hand on his guitar, one on the microphone, his eyes were closed and sweat poured down his face as he sang about losing at love.

"It's the Rock the Mall contest!" Tom moved closer. "This must be Creatures of the Night. I heard they're a great band and it's true!"

"What's the Rock the Mall contest?" Dietmar asked. "Nobody told me about it."

"The hottest new talent in the West is in this contest. There are musicians competing all over the mall this week. The winner gets a video contract, plus a trip to Hamilton for the national finals."

"Why weren't we invited?"

"Because our band belongs in a garage, which is why we only play there. If you came to more rehearsals maybe we'd get somewhere."

"Then don't rehearse Saturday mornings. I'm still asleep."

They stayed for the entire show, then reluctantly moved on as it ended. "*I wanna be a star*," Dietmar exclaimed. "I wanna be on the cover of *Rolling Stone*." With his hands playing an imaginary guitar, he side-danced along the corridor while shoppers stared and shook their heads. A little girl holding a balloon watched gravely, thumb in mouth, then presented the balloon to Dietmar.

"Thanks, kid!" He grinned at Tom. "She knows true talent."

"Hey!" Tom shouted at Dietmar as he started walking away. "Give her back the balloon!"

Not far away another crowd had gathered beside a bamboo cage, where two tiger cubs rolled together in a mock battle. For a moment they paused, gazing at the people with enormous and gentle eyes, then returned to their game.

"I feel sorry for them," Dietmar said. "Stuck in a cage."

"The mall owns a game farm. The animals spend a lot of time out there."

"Okay folks," a woman said from beside a camera. "Who wants a picture taken with a tiger on your lap?"

"She must be crazy," Dietmar said. "Who'd spend money on that?"

"I would."

Taking out his wallet, Tom stared at the thin collection of bills. "Where'd it all go?"

"Remember those five trips on the Mindbender yesterday? They didn't come cheap."

"Sure, but . . ." Tom counted his money. "Are there pickpockets around?"

"The defective detective," Dietmar snorted. "Since when do pickpockets only take some of your cash?"

Tom shrugged. "I guess you're right. I've been spending too much." Taking out a bill, he paid the woman for a picture and sat down. Her assistant opened the cage and lifted out a cub. "They've just had a bath, so they're a bit crabby."

"I don't care, I love cats!" The cub was on his lap just long enough for Tom to stroke the soft fur, then the shutter clicked and the tiger was returned to its cage. When the picture was ready Tom studied the cub's face before putting it safely away.

"What a great souvenir!"

"Keep spending your money like that, Austen, and there'll be nothing left for gifts. By the way, what're you taking home for me?"

"Why would I do that?"

Dietmar shrugged. "It seems the thoughtful thing to do."

"I got Mr. Stones the perfect gift yesterday. A key chain with the logo of his import. Have you seen the store that sells nothing but car accessories?"

Dietmar shook his head. "I'm getting hungry."

"You just had breakfast."

"So what? I just heard my stomach complain. Let's get something at the Ice Palace."

"Okay, but I want to learn more about this guy who calls himself the Skull."

They reached the Ice Palace a few minutes later. The size of a regulation NHL rink, it sparkled under the sunshine that poured down from high-domed skylights. "Those windows are computer controlled," Tom said. "Somehow they keep the temperature constant in here." Stores on two levels surrounded the rink, and a lot of people were standing at the railings, watching the skaters.

"The Oilers practise here. During the summer sometimes they even have exhibition games between a few Oilers and guys from other teams. There's one this Friday night, but I doubt you're interested."

"Not when I can watch *Wall Street Week*."

"That money programme? What's so interesting about it?"

"Pretty soon I'll be investing in stocks and bonds. I want to know which ones make megabucks."

"You're probably right. So what do you recommend?"

"That we get some food."

At a nearby stand they bought Coney Island hot dogs, and sat down at a table by the rink. Munching silently, Tom and Dietmar stared at figure skaters swirling past, wearing fancy costumes. When they'd finished eating, Tom turned to a boy about his age who was sitting at the next table.

"You ever heard of a guy who calls himself the Skull?"

The boy shook his head, but the question got a reaction from a couple of older boys who were sitting nearby with their feet up on a railing, hands in the pockets of their leather jackets, and boredom on their faces. Hearing Tom's question they turned to stare at him, then at Dietmar, then at each other.

"Hey you," one of them said to Tom. "Come here."

4

Tom hesitated, then walked over. "Yeah?"

"How come you're asking about the Skull?"

Tom looked at the boy's hostile eyes. "You know him?"

"Maybe. Why's it important?"

"Where can I find the Skull?"

"He's around." The boy flicked his cigarette onto the ice. "Why?"

"I'm just curious." Turning, Tom walked away. "Come on," he said to Dietmar, "let's get moving."

"Gladly!"

As they left the Ice Palace Tom glanced at a store window. Reflected in the glass were the two Neanderthals, following close behind. "Interesting guys."

"I'll say! Now we're in trouble, thanks to you asking questions."

"We're perfectly safe. This mall's got lots of security guards walking around in disguise and besides, we've struck pay dirt. Those two losers actually know the Skull."

"Sure, and they're following us. What possible use is that?"

"I don't know. Maybe they'll meet the Skull and we'll get a look at him."

"This is turning into a real fun morning, Austen."

"It could be worse. What if the soaps were all reruns?"

"Where are we going now?"

"Luggage Unlimited. I want to tell the Gills what we've learned."

On the way to the store they paused to watch another band performing near a group of fountains that gushed upwards from a marble pool, the water lit by orange and blue and red spotlights. "There's 43 individual fountains," Dietmar said, after counting them. "Put that on your list." He watched Tom make a note, then added, "That'll cost you, by the way. I don't research trivia for free."

"Forget it!"

"I'll expect a cheque by tomorrow, at the latest."

A few minutes later they entered Luggage Unlimited, where a boy their age stood behind the counter. His smile was friendly. "Hi," he said. "My name's Neil Raj Gill. Need help finding something?"

"Not exactly." Tom introduced himself and Dietmar, then explained he'd been at the store the evening before. "You weren't here, but I met your parents. I've got some information they might want."

"My mom's working today. I'll get her."

Mrs. Gill came from the office with a puzzled frown. "You've learned something?"

"It's nothing definite," Tom replied, "but someone called the Skull is probably the person who broke in here last night."

Neil Raj nodded. "I've had some trouble with him before."

"I'll phone the police," Mrs. Gill said. "Can you give them proof, Tom?"

"No, Ma'am. Just rumours."

"I'll tell them anyway."

As she placed the call Neil Raj looked out the window. The two punks were watching the store, hands in the pockets of their leather jackets and scowls on their mean faces. "Those two hang out with the Skull. I've seen them all together."

"They've been following us," Dietmar said. "It's giving me the creeps."

"Me too." Tom looked at Neil Raj. "I wouldn't mind losing them. This store's got a back door, right?"

"You bet. Follow me."

As they walked through the store Tom noticed that all signs of damage had been removed. The suitcases stood in neat rows, the walls had been freshly painted and there were new pictures. "It must have taken all night to fix things so quickly," he said. "Are you worried it'll happen again?"

"That's not likely." Neil Raj paused in the upper display area to point at a tiny red light flashing from a small plastic device on the ceiling. "That's our new intruder detector. If anyone moves in here at night, *zap*. A siren starts wailing and a message flashes to security headquarters and the police. The guards can have this place completely blocked off within two minutes."

"That's still 120 seconds," Tom said. "Enough time for him to escape."

"Maybe so, but at least the store won't be trashed."

Mrs. Gill joined them. "The police thanked me for the information, but they need some kind of real proof." She smiled at Tom. "You're very kind to help."

"I wish I could do more."

Neil Raj looked at his mother. "Okay to take an hour off? Heather's singing in the contest and I want to be there, cheering." After she'd given her permission he turned to Tom and Dietmar. "Want to come? I'd like you to meet Heather."

"She's your girlfriend?" Dietmar asked.

"No, she's 18. I play streetball with her brother, so she's kind of a friend."

They entered a storage area at the back of the store. Cartons were piled on shelves that reached to the ceiling, brooms and a vacuum cleaner stood in one corner, and cool air blew from a vent in the wall.

"I just thought of something," Tom said. "The police figure the intruder dropped down from the ceiling, but maybe he came through that air conditioning vent."

Neil Raj pointed up at a ceiling tile. "See those scuffs and scratches? Those were fresh last night, and the air conditioning grill didn't show any sign of damage."

"You're right. So much for my theory."

They entered a long corridor where nothing could be seen but the back doors of other stores. "This leads to another part of the mall," Neil Raj said. "It's a perfect route to slip away from those gorillas who were following you."

Tom looked up at the big aluminum shaft that carried air conditioning to the stores. "I'm still suspicious about those ducts. They're big enough to crawl through and they must go everywhere in the mall. It's the ideal secret route."

Dietmar smiled at Neil Raj. "I've listened to this stuff for years, ever since he discovered Frank and Joe Hardy. Now he reads le Carré, but it's still the same old story—hidden clues and villains crawling through air conditioning ducts. Tell me about it!"

Neil Raj laughed. "I'm surprised you two are friends. You're totally different from each other."

At the end of the corridor they stepped through a doorway back into the mall. Tom breathed a sigh of relief as he was once again surrounded by people. "I guess I was more nervous than I thought. Hey, what's that gizmo? I haven't seen it before."

A two-storey device nearby was producing a cacophony of sounds: *BONG! BONG!* and *BLAM—BLAM— BLAM* and *TING! TING!* A crowd had gathered around to watch billiard balls follow a twisting route down, twirling around and around in long spirals, triggering hammers that struck against gongs, striking brass cymbals, and performing other noisy tricks before being lifted to the heights to begin the journey anew.

"Bizarre," Dietmar laughed. "What strange genius created that thing?" He looked at his watch. "Say, how about a quick trip on the Mindbender? Have we got time before your friend sings?"

"Sure, let's go for it."

After a quick walk they passed through the arched entrance to Galaxyland, the indoor amusement park. Music played loudly, people jammed the sidewalks and a giant swing swirled above, but the scene was dominated by the Mindbender. Fourteen stories high, the roller coaster's triple loops were coiled like a sea serpent, and rose so far above them that the tops were barely visible under the sloped roof.

"Let's get moving!" As Tom ran toward the ticket booth he watched a car drop straight down with everyone inside screaming. "I can't wait! This thing is amazing!"

Minutes later they were in a car and he was rapidly changing his mind. "I can't do it," he moaned as it began moving. "I want out."

"You say that every time, Austen. Besides, it's too late," Dietmar yelled. "Here we go!"

The car rapidly climbed straight up toward the roof. People were screaming by the time they reached the top; Tom's knuckles were white on the safety rail. Then the car fell. Straight down, a terrifying drop into emptiness, the wind loud in his ears; then the car abruptly reached bottom and roared up inside a loop. Over they went, upside down, and flew to the heights again, before falling once more. Everyone on the ride was yelling and screaming with excitement.

With an ear-splitting screech of brakes, the ride finally ended. Everyone staggered out, shaking their heads in disbelief. Neil Raj stood on one leg and pounded the side of his head. "I feel like I've got water on the brain."

"You're out of focus," Tom said. "So's everyone else."

"Come on," Dietmar yelled. "The Drop of Doom's next."

"Not until my stomach feels normal."

"I'll stay with Tom," Neil Raj said. "We'll go play some games."

"Okay. I'll meet you guys there."

They were both good at Speed Shifters and equally useless at Championship Darts and Vegas Prize Ring. Then someone approached. He was a bit older than they were, with mean eyes and a totally shaved head. Beside his mouth was a long, ragged scar.

The Skull.

Just behind him stood the gorillas in leather jackets. "Yeah?" he said to Tom. "You're looking for me?"

Tom swallowed. "Uh . . . yes."

"So?"

"I'm . . . well, you . . . someone said you knew something. About what happened last night." Tom paused, but the Skull didn't speak. "You know, at the luggage store."

At that moment Dietmar appeared at Tom's side. "What's going on, Austen?"

"Just a little trouble."

The Skull looked at Neil Raj, then spat on the ground. "*Pakis.*"

"Hey," Tom said. "That's pretty . . ."

Neil Raj moved between Tom and the Skull. His hands were clenched into hard fists, but his voice was calm as he said, "Listen you. About that word *Paki*. It's ugly and it's ignorant. Besides, my family came from India, not Pakistan, and I was born in Vancouver."

Silence.

"Did you trash my parents' store?"

"Get lost."

"I'm sure it was you. Leave our store alone."

"You're giving me orders, Paki?" The Skull signalled to his friends, who moved closer. "That's not such a good idea."

Dietmar looked at Neil Raj. "Come on, let's get out of here."

"In a minute."

A man in a golf shirt and slacks approached the group. "Good day, gentlemen." He showed them a photo ID card. "I'm a security guard. What's going on? Things look a little tense here." When nobody spoke he pointed to the nearest exit. "Why don't you all move along?"

The Skull gave Neil Raj a dirty look, then walked away with his friends. As Tom and the others left by a different exit, Dietmar released a sigh.

"Wow! That was tense."

Tom looked at Neil Raj. "Do you think there's a link between the bomb found at the Café Orleans and the break-in at your store?"

"No. I'm pretty sure the Skull trashed our store, but he's not bright enough to get his hands on a bomb. Besides, what's his motive? I think the bomber must be someone with a grudge against the mall or something like that. And you've got to have brains to figure out how to make a bomb, and get it in here without being seen."

A series of ponds divided the corridor they were following. Coins gleamed underwater, fountains gurgled and palm trees reached to the skylights above. At the Ice Palace they rode up in a glass-walled elevator while watching the skaters make swirling patterns on the ice.

Stepping out of the cage they saw a crowd gathered around a platform. A golden-haired girl had just finished a song and the audience was yelling its appreciation. The girl grinned, her big eyes shining.

"She's really cute!" Dietmar said.

Tom looked at Neil Raj. "You actually know her?"

He shrugged, grinning. "Yup."

Heather's band wore stetsons and red satin outfits; she was in a white skirt and shimmering silver blouse. Picking up her guitar, she started a country song that had the people stomping their feet and clapping their hands.

"She gets my vote," Tom yelled as the song ended and everyone cheered.

Liz appeared out of the crowd, smiling. "Isn't Heather great? She's the girl I met yesterday."

After Liz was introduced to Neil Raj they listened to a final song. Heather took a bow, then came down off the stage to sign autographs and talk excitedly to the people who surrounded her. Finally Neil Raj brought her over to meet Tom and Dietmar. Her blue-green eyes were very large and beautiful.

"Great show," Tom said. "Congratulations."

"Thanks! Could you imagine if my band actually won the contest?"

"You'll do it," Dietmar said. "How about an autograph?" He borrowed Tom's notebook, ripped out a page and handed it to Heather. "Please include the year."

"Sure, but why?"

"It makes the autograph more valuable. Some day that scrap of paper will finance my first BMW."

"What a lovely thought!" Heather turned to Neil Raj. "I'm sorry about the store. I'll phone your Mom and Dad today to see how they're doing."

"Thanks, Heather. Maybe . . ."

He was interrupted by the arrival of a worried man in a rumpled suit. "Heather," he said, "there's a photographer here from the *Journal*. Can you pose for her?"

"Sure." She looked at the others. "This is Mr. Sutton. He's my manager."

"Hi there." He gave them a brief nod, then turned to Heather. "Come on, kid. We need the publicity. Save the socializing for later."

As they walked away Dietmar looked at his watch. "Hey, I'm outta here. It's almost noon and I'm not in front of the tube. Today Samantha and Robert find out about her uncle's fortune from the lawyer. I can't miss the show."

After Neil Raj made plans to go watersliding with Tom, he left for the store. Liz was leaning over a railing watching the figure skaters when Tom turned and smiled at her. "So what's the secret?"

"Huh?"

"You're excited about something. I can tell."

"You're right! I've got a date for Friday. His name's Chad. Heather introduced me."

"Where are you going?"

"To Galaxyland."

"What's this guy like?"

"Don't worry, I'll be okay."

"Want me and Dietmar to come along as chaperones?"

"*No!!*"

Laughing, Tom suggested they look at the piranhas. They walked along beside the curved upper railing to a large aquarium where the deadly fish swam among green ferns. Tom leaned close to the glass feeling brave as the tough little faces gazed back at him. "They don't scare me."

"Read that sign," Liz said. "*Feeding frenzies occur when blood is drawn.*"

"Now they scare me."

"This glass reflects well. I just saw someone take our picture."

Turning, Tom saw a man wearing glasses walk away. Attached to his belt was a leather pouch. "Is that a holster?"

Liz shook her head. "He put his camera in it." She looked at Tom. "Feel like following him? He was watching us earlier and making notes. And I'm sure I've seen him before."

"Okay, let's . . ."

Tom paused, looking puzzled. The music had suddenly stopped and all the speakers around the rink were silent. Then a voice urgently announced, "*Code Red, Code Red.*"

5

After a brief pause the announcement was repeated, but this time with a store's name included: *Code Red, Full Fathom Down*. "That place isn't far," Liz said, quickly consulting her map. "Let's get moving!"

People stared as they raced through the mall, unaware that the secret warning of a maximum alert was the cause of their mad dash to Full Fathom Down. Arriving there at the same moment as the security guards, Tom and Liz were surprised to see Inspector Winter Eagle already inside the store.

"We've got another bomb," she said. "Your dad's dealing with it."

"Should we leave?" Tom asked as security guards began clearing the area.

The inspector shook her head. "Naturally we don't want shoppers around, but your dad says this bomb isn't set to explode either."

"Was a wire left disconnected, like the first one?"

She nodded. "More bad news for the mall, but at least no one's been hurt yet."

"How did you and Dad get here so fast?"

"We were questioning people at stores in this corridor when we heard shouts." She glanced at a man slumped in a chair at the back of the store. He was about 30, with a fleshy nose and thin brown hair. Shock had drained his face of colour. "That's Benn Dunn, a sales assistant here. He discovered the bomb and ran out of the store, yelling at people to clear the area."

On display around the walls were face masks, flippers, oxygen tanks and other gear for scuba lovers. A poster showed divers plunging from a yacht into the aqua waters of a tropical paradise, while another pictured some people on a dock at the mall's own indoor sea. Tom and Liz walked through the store with the Inspector as she explained, "Benn Dunn found the bomb in the storage area at the back. It was either planted there overnight or some time after the store opened this morning."

"Wouldn't he have seen it carried into the store?"

"Not if it was hidden inside something."

In the cluttered storage room cool air blew through a vent in the wall, and big shelves were filled with cartons and scuba equipment. Mr. Austen stood near the tiny washroom, where a package was visible under the sink. "The red wire tells the story," he said. "The explosives are connected to that alarm clock, which was rigged to detonate them at exactly noon. But again this time the red wire was deliberately not attached. The bomb couldn't have exploded."

"The bomber didn't forget to do it?" Tom asked.

"Not a chance. This person is an expert."

Tom looked at the area set aside for staff to relax; sitting in a chair was a handsome man in his early 30s, with a good tan and hair bleached blond by the sun.

"My name's Christopher Dixon," he said. "I'm the manager of Full Fathom Down. Your dad's been telling me about your exploits in the past. I hope you're going to help too."

"Thanks, Mr. Dixon. We . . ."

"Please, call me Christopher."

"Do you have any idea how the bomb got into your store?"

"The back door's a possibility. It connects to a service corridor where deliveries are made, but it was locked all yesterday and this morning."

Tom glanced at his sister and saw that her eyes had glazed over as she stared at the man. Shaking his head, he asked, "What about the ceiling tiles? Could the bomber have dropped into the store that way?"

Before Christopher could answer a woman appeared in the doorway. She was about 24 years old; the dramatic black of her hair was matched by the colour of her eyes and the silk dress she wore. Gold jewellery shone on her fingers, and at her neck and ears. She extended a hand to Inspector Winter Eagle. "I'm Carroll McAndrews, owner of this store." Turning to Christopher the woman said, "You're okay?"

"Sure, I'm fine. But trouble like this isn't going to

do the mall any good. What'll we all do if people stop shopping here?"

"Father won't let this situation continue—he'll make sure the mystery is solved." Carroll looked at Inspector Winter Eagle. "My father has several stores in this mall."

"I know. It was the talk of Edmonton about how much money he paid to set up and furnish the stores."

"It wasn't his money."

"What do you mean?"

Carroll hesitated, then shrugged. "Well, I guess it's no secret. A couple of years ago Father was in San Diego on holiday and happened to meet a wealthy woman who lived there. Apparently she was involved with some local, but the guy was poor as a church mouse. He couldn't match Father's gifts of long-stemmed roses and jewellery. Before long she dumped the local, and suddenly I had a stepmother."

"She married your father?"

"That's right." Carroll shrugged. "But I hardly know the woman. We only met once, at the wedding in California. She's terrified of flying, so she's never been to Edmonton. Father visits her whenever possible, but in my opinion it's not much of a marriage."

"Your father used her money to set up stores in the mall?"

"Correct. It was always his big dream to be part of the supermall." She glanced around at the scuba gear. "Then he arranged this store for me. I guess it was supposed to make me happy."

Mr. Austen looked at her. "Edmonton seems an odd location for this kind of place."

"Not really. Our scuba club dives in the indoor sea every morning before the mall opens for business. Plus there's oil money in Alberta, so wealthy locals holiday in the world's scuba capitals with equipment purchased from my store." She looked at Christopher. "This man's the reason why my store's so successful. He knows the sport inside out."

Inspector Winter Eagle looked at him. "How long have you worked here?"

"Since Carroll opened the store, about four months ago. I came to Edmonton to dive the indoor sea and decided to stay. I got a job guiding visitors around the mall, then met Carroll and she asked me to be manager of her store." He looked at the Inspector. "I'm really angry about the bomber. I'd like to find the person who's responsible."

"Don't take the law into your own hands, Mr. Dixon." Inspector Winter Eagle looked at the notes she'd been making. "What about Benn Dunn? What's his story?"

"He's only been here about a month," Carroll replied. "He appeared out of nowhere, some kind of a drifter, but he's a great diver. The customers really respect his advice."

"I've got an idea," Tom said to Carroll. "Maybe the bomber's motive is to get revenge against your dad. If his stores suffer financially maybe he'd be ruined."

"Nope. My stepmother has lots more money in the bank. Besides, why would someone want to hurt my father?"

"I'm not sure. Maybe . . ."

Tom was interrupted by the arrival of a huge man in the doorway. He stared at his thick white hair, fierce eyes under bushy brows and bronze skin that had been seared by a lifetime of sun and wind. Towering above them all, he wore an expensive cowboy hat and a three-piece suit perfectly tailored to his body.

Inspector Winter Eagle broke the silence. "This is Carroll's father, Danniel McAndrews."

Mr. McAndrews scratched a match on the sole of his cowboy boot to light a cigar. After briefly inspecting the bomb he asked for details of the investigation and then, as smoke stung the others' eyes, he said, "Last year nine million people visited this mall. Lots of people already know about yesterday's scare, and more are going to hear about today's discovery. You know how easily people panic. Find that bomber fast, Inspector, or we'll be lucky to have nine visitors next year." He turned to Carroll. "Hang out some sale signs. Business will take a real nose-dive now, unless we do something."

"I'll make my own decision about a sale, Father. It's my store, remember?"

"This place was set up with my money and became a success because of my expert advice."

"Then why don't you run it, too? I can go back to diving in the Caribbean. I hate what owning a bunch of stores has done to you, Father. You're trying to build an empire and it's the only thing you care about."

When the big man didn't reply she sighed. Then she looked at Tom and Liz. "Ever tried scuba?"

Liz nodded. "Yes, we've both got our certificates. Any chance of diving with your club?"

"Maybe." She picked up a speargun from a shelf. "I was wondering if you'd be in the market for some good equipment like this. I'll give you a special discount."

Liz shivered. "We took lessons on using a speargun, but I hate them."

"Too bad." Carroll pretended to take aim at a carton. "I love these things." Putting down the speargun, she walked into the display area and the others followed. More police officers had arrived and one was questioning Benn Dunn, who was staring at the floor with sullen eyes.

Seeing Inspector Winter Eagle the officer said, "This man won't cooperate."

"Why should I?" Benn Dunn muttered. "I haven't broken any laws."

Christopher stepped forward. "A crime's been committed right here in our store. I want you to help these officers."

Benn Dunn flashed him a look of intense dislike. "I have to take your orders all day, but not this time."

A red glow spread under Christopher's tan. "You've got to help them."

"I told them the facts once. I don't have to answer the same questions again."

Tom glanced sympathetically at Christopher, then turned toward the front door, where a woman of about 20 was trying to get past a security guard. "My boyfriend's in here! He could have been killed!" With surprising strength for her size she pushed aside the guard and ran to hug Christopher. "Oh, Chris," she sobbed, her cheeks glistening with tears. "I was so worried! I heard the news on the car radio when I was driving to work. I almost drove off the Whitemud."

Gently freeing himself, Christopher smiled down at her. "I'm sorry you were scared." Turning to the others, he said, "This is my friend, Lisa deVita. She's one of the mall's dolphin trainers."

Carroll had been watching the other woman through narrowed eyes. Now she said, "Late for work again, Ms. deVita? I'm surprised my father doesn't have you fired."

Mr. McAndrews shook his head. "Not when we've got such a great dolphin show. But my daughter's got a point, Lisa. Why are you late for work?"

"I slept in."

Carroll shook her head. "Why's it so difficult to get reliable employees these days? If I . . ."

"Listen lady," Lisa interrupted angrily. "One more remark like that and you'll regret it!" Letting go of Christopher she walked to the door and turned to stare at Carroll. "Another thing: you keep your claws off my man or *you'll be sorry.*"

As Lisa stormed away Liz followed. Tom stayed in the store a few minutes more, then went into the mall to find his sister. When he did, she was smiling.

"Guess what, brother?"

"Major information?"

"Nope. A chance to see backstage at the dolphin show. Lisa deVita's one of the trainers and I just got permission for a special tour. Not only that, she's part of the scuba club and she's invited us to dive tomorrow morning. The club's got equipment we can use."

"Terrific! Say, what's with Lisa and Carroll? Are they both in love with Christopher?"

"It looks that way. They don't exactly get along, do they?"

"I'll say. Sparks must fly whenever they meet."

* * *

At exactly seven the next morning Tom and Liz stood on a small dock. Soft sunlight from far above touched the sails of the *Santa Maria* and made the blue water look cool and inviting. As Lisa deVita prepared the equipment and chatted to other club members, Liz studied the coral and make-believe crabs beneath the surface. "Whoever designed this mall should get a trophy. Everything looks so real! I love those statues and the pottery. Do you think Atlantis ever existed?"

"If it did, I feel sorry for the people when it sank," Lisa replied. "But the people around here don't seem to be having much luck either. I hope they find the bomber fast."

"I wonder if Carroll's father is upset?"

"Probably not. He's pretty self-confident." Lisa glanced at her watch. "Mr. McAndrews and Carroll will arrive at 7:15 A.M., on the dot. He's the world's most organized person and she's totally under his thumb."

The pair did arrive exactly on time. After brief words of greeting, father and daughter prepared in silence and plunged beneath the surface. Then Benn Dunn appeared, along with Christopher, who hugged Lisa and brushed her forehead with a kiss. "I've been doing a little investigating. I may even find the bomber before the police do."

"Oh, Chris, be careful! I can't bear the thought of anything happening."

After Christopher and Benn Dunn had dropped into the sea Liz stared across the water. "The sharks are hungry this morning. I can sense it."

Lisa smiled. "Want to cancel your dive?"

"Not a chance."

Tom and Liz waited for Lisa's thumbs-up signal. Then they tumbled into the water to enter a silent paradise where green plants swayed beside starfish clinging to jagged rocks. Tom motioned to Liz, pointing at a porcelain vase lying among the rocks; not far away were the statues of enormous temple dogs, their eyes staring forever at the waters that covered the lost treasures of Atlantis. Slowly Tom and Liz swam among the ruins, then turned to explore a treasure chest lying on the sandy bottom. They swam past gently moving strands of seaweed and pieces of jagged coral, then Tom almost choked with horror.

A shark was coming straight at him, ready to strike.

Desperately, Tom lifted his hands in a hopeless attempt to protect himself. But when the shark reached the glass wall of its tank it veered away, its body so close that every mark on the dark hide was visible. Turning, Tom saw that his sister's eyes were huge inside her mask. Motioning, she led them away from the sharks toward the *Santa Maria*. Through a glass wall they stared at a big grouper and other fish in the tank, then they swam to its stern where a realistic model captured a long-forgotten battle between a powerful sea-snake and some kind of aquatic dinosaur.

Then, as Tom and Liz began swimming toward the ribs of a sunken wreck, a figure in scuba gear appeared from its shadows and rose rapidly toward the surface, trailing a swarm of bubbles.

6

Reaching the surface, Tom and Liz tore off their masks. "That diver's in trouble," Tom yelled. "Where is he?"

"Over there, swimming toward the submarine dock. He looks okay now."

"It's Christopher! I wonder what happened?"

Within seconds Tom and Liz were with him. As other divers reached the dock Christopher showed them the wreckage of his air hose. "It was deliberately slashed! I could have drowned."

"What happened?"

Christopher glanced at Benn Dunn, who stood on the dock with sullen eyes. "We did the sub tunnel, then I signalled Benn that I wanted to explore the undersea wreck. There isn't enough room in there for two divers, so I swam into the wreck alone. I'd just entered some deep shadows when my air hose was slashed."

"But how?"

"I'm not sure—it happened so fast. I saw a hand and a piece of coral, then bubbles erupted around my mask."

"The attacker used a piece of coral to cut the hose?"

"I think so. No one in the club wears a knife."

A short time later, Lisa surfaced. When she heard the news there was an astonished silence, followed by an intense hug for Christopher.

"Get out of Edmonton, please! Take a holiday, I'll pay for it, just *escape*. Please!"

He laughed. "You think I'm a wimp? Come on, Lisa, drop the subject. I can take care of myself."

Soon after, Carroll and her father emerged from the water and were quickly told what had happened. Mr. McAndrews was furious at the latest bad news and left the area in a hurry. When he had gone, Carroll turned to the other divers.

"I'm sure it's one of you who's causing all this trouble," she said. "But whatever your scheme is, it won't work. I promise you: *It won't work*."

* * *

Tom was still talking about the air hose when he and Neil Raj reached the World Waterpark and bought tickets. "Who could have done it?"

Neil Raj watched a security guard check inside their sports bags, then wave them inside. "I don't know," he said as they entered the big locker room. "You said the sea was full of divers. They all had the opportunity."

"Sure, but they aren't the only possibility. What if some unknown person snuck into the mall early this morning when it was deserted? It would only take a couple of minutes to get into scuba gear and then hide underwater in the wreck."

"That's true, but why?"

"That's what I'm going to find out."

The air inside the waterpark was humid. Palm trees grew all over and they could hear the distant sound of waves rolling ashore on the artificial beach. Kids swirled down inside the translucent skins of the many enclosed waterslides and others were on a tree-lined volleyball court nearby. One of the teenagers watching them had a familiar face.

"Oh no," Tom said, "there's the Skull. And he just saw us."

"So what?" Neil Raj grinned as a loud horn blasted in the distance. "Hey, surf's up! Come on!"

Racing to the beach they plunged into the heart of a breaker and came up spluttering and laughing, then swam into the surf being created by a wave machine hidden under a waterfall at the pool's deep end. They body-surfed for a while, then headed for the beach. As they did, Tom saw the Skull and his two friends waiting for them.

"We've got company."

"Ignore them," Neil Raj replied as they waded ashore.

"Okay, but it won't be easy."

Grabbing their towels, they walked to a pair of empty beach chairs under a palm tree and sat down. The ugly trio followed to stand above them. Their chests were pasty white, but muscular.

"So!" The Skull stared at Neil Raj. "My first day here in months and you decide to spoil the view. So why don't you get out of here before I completely re-arrange your face?"

Tom looked across the water at a lifeguard standing on a platform. He was close enough to hear a yell for help, if he was needed.

"Why don't you guys leave us alone?" Tom said.

The Skull turned his cold eyes to him. "Shut your mouth. I don't like cops and I don't like their kids."

"How'd you know . . ."

Neil Raj raised a warning hand. "Ignore these guys. They'll go away before too long." He settled himself more comfortably on the chair. "Isn't that roof an amazing sight? Those arches are huge."

The Skull stepped closer. "Get out of here, Paki."

Neil Raj looked at him with steady eyes. "Not . . . a . . . chance," he said slowly. "Get the message?"

The Skull put his foot on the side of the chair and shoved it over. Neil Raj sprawled to the ground, then stood up rubbing his elbow. "You're pathetic," he said to the Skull. "Come on, Tom, let's go try the slides."

The others didn't follow, but they yelled a couple of insults as Neil Raj and Tom went to the stairs and began climbing. "Jerks," Neil Raj muttered.

"It was great how you handled the Skull. He was doing everything he could to get you mad."

"I know, but fights don't solve anything, and I'd never give that guy the satisfaction."

"I've been learning karate," Tom said, "but those guys still freak me."

"Me too," Neil Raj agreed.

At the top of the Blue Bullet slide Neil Raj sat down and waited for the go signal. "*Geronimo*," he yelled, disappearing down the tube. Tom waited for his green light and then let go, falling swiftly down, with the cascading water roaring in his ears. Then he was swallowed by a tunnel where he fell much faster; tiny blue lights above his head blurred together as he twisted down and down before falling through daylight into the pool where Neil Raj was waiting.

"Good times!" Tom yelled.

Then he saw the Skull and his friends. They were leaving the waterpark, but Tom was sure they'd meet again.

* * *

More than 50 mirrors surrounded Heather and Liz as they took an escalator to the mall's upper level. "Did you hear about the scuba diver?" Liz asked.

"Sure. Actually, I know Christopher."

"Really? How's that?"

"I was in his scuba store once and he was flirting with me." Heather smiled. "I told him to try someone his own age."

"Did he get angry?"

"No, he just laughed. Then we started talking. Since then we've often met for coffee. He's really interested in my career. He thinks I can be a megastar." She smiled shyly. "That's my dream, but Mr. Sutton doesn't agree."

"Who's Mr. Sutton?"

"My manager. You met him yesterday."

"Oh. Yeah."

"Mr. Sutton's always talking about one step at a time. He didn't want me to enter the Rock the Mall contest."

"But why?"

"He doesn't want me recording yet. In his opinion I need another year of building my voice."

"That seems a long time."

"I know. Christopher says the same thing. I don't think he approves of Mr. Sutton as a manager."

"Do you think Carroll's in love with Christopher?"

"Of course."

"Do you think she'll get him?"

"Only if Lisa deVita meets with an unfortunate accident." Heather looked at the stores that surrounded them. A man wearing a tuxedo was seated at a grand piano in the corridor, playing quiet melodies. "Know something? There are 55 shoe stores in the mall. Think that's enough choice?"

"Never too much choice in shoes!"

"I've got an idea! Let's window shop for our weddings."

They went into a store that sold bridal gowns and accessories. Mannequins were reflected along the mirrored walls, beautifully gowned for weddings they would never attend. A woman with a warm smile welcomed Heather and Liz, then left them alone to try on hats with veils and long white gloves.

"I like all the pearls," Heather said.

"And the lace."

"I know someone who's having eight bridesmaids when she marries."

"Eight?"

Heather nodded. "Remember that guy Chad?"

"I guess so! We've got a date tomorrow. You set it up, so don't forget to come!"

"I'll be there, don't you worry. Anyway, I've only met Chad once but he seemed friendly. I know his sister. She's the one who's having eight bridesmaids."

"Some wedding."

They decided to have lunch and walked to an outdoor cafe at the Ice Palace where the tables overlooked the ice. Heather and Liz ordered quiche Lorraine and spring water, then looked down at the rink.

"Hey," Liz said. "There's Chad."

He had curly black hair and was wearing an ice dancing costume. A female dancer and a grey-haired woman were with him on the ice. "She must be their coach," Liz said. She watched with fascination as Chad and the girl rehearsed with the woman, whirling around the ice. "I can't believe he's an ice dancer, and he's so good."

"Someone told me that's his cousin."

"His partner? That's great."

When the rehearsal ended they nibbled their quiche and a delicious salad while discussing the attack at the indoor sea. "You look for means, motive and opportunity," Liz said. "The villain has to have all three."

"So, who qualifies in the scuba club?"

Liz thought for a moment. "Well, any of them could have broken off a chunk of coral. So they all had the means, plus the opportunity."

"Don't they swim in buddies?"

"Sure, but two people could be in this together."

"You still need a motive."

Liz nodded. "I've been thinking about that. There's

been an underwater attack and a bomb left in Christopher's store. Both within 24 hours of each other. Why?"

"Some guy's got a grudge against Christopher."

"Or some woman. There's lots in that club." Liz thought for a minute. "What about someone not connected to the club? *Anyone* could have been underwater, waiting in the wreck for Christopher."

"You mean someone who got there early?"

"Sure, before the club members arrived. Quickly into scuba gear and quickly into the water. It's perfect, because of course the police would probably suspect the club members."

Liz saw a man approaching. He was wearing an old-fashioned suit that she thought was kind of strange. When he sat down at the table she remembered he was Mr. Sutton, Heather's manager.

He immediately began talking business. Heather smiled apologetically at Liz, then listened to Mr. Sutton's ideas about a road trip to Spokane and Seattle. As they talked Liz glanced at the nearby tank of piranhas and saw Christopher Dixon looking at the fish. Then he noticed her and smiled. As he walked over Mr. Sutton saw him approaching and stood up.

"Here comes the man with all the great ideas for your career. If you don't mind, Heather, I won't bother listening this time."

"But you just ordered strawberries and whipped cream."

"Share them with your friend." He pulled out some crumpled money and threw a bill on the table. "See you at rehearsal tonight. Be on time."

As he walked away Christopher sat down, smiling. "Two pretty faces! May I join you for a few minutes, before I get back to the store?"

"Sure," Heather said. "Are you okay after that attack?"

"Yes, but I'm certainly not going to just sit back and forget it happened."

"What do you mean?" Liz asked.

He turned to her with determined eyes. "I don't get mad, I get even. I'll find the person who slashed my air hose. That's a promise." He smiled at Heather. "Fabulous performance yesterday! Someone told me about it. The inside story is you're going to win the contest."

"Wouldn't that be great?"

"You're going to be a star, Heather. The only question is when. Tomorrow or five years from now?"

"Mr. Sutton says I need to build a strong foundation or I'll burn out fast. Kind of like a shooting star."

"Well, who knows? Mr. Sutton's made it clear that he doesn't like me or my advice. Maybe he's worked a long time in the music business but that doesn't mean you couldn't get a new manager."

"I suppose so."

"One more thing. Always think gold."

"You're a great cheering section."

"How's the food?" Christopher looked at the strawberries Mr. Sutton had ordered. He covered them with whipped cream and tried one. "Nice," he said, offering the dish to the girls. "I managed a restaurant near Sea World once. It had a nice view, but watching ice dancers while you eat is kind of unique." Turning from the rink he looked over Liz's shoulder at someone in the corridor, then glanced at his watch and put the strawberries down. Liz turned to see Carroll approaching with her father.

"Well," Carroll said, "here you are! I needn't have worried—just look for pretty girls and there you are. You should be back at work, Christopher."

He stood up. "Come on, Carroll. No need to stomp on me. Taking an extra five minutes isn't a major crime."

"You're right. Sorry, I'm really on edge."

As Christopher, Carroll and her father walked away Liz got out some money. "I'd like to know more about the McAndrews. Come on, Heather, let's pay our bill and see where they're going."

* * *

Soon they reached the indoor sea. There wasn't much of a crowd so only one sub was taking people on trips. A young attendant in a naval uniform saluted Mr. McAndrews as he went on board the sub with Carroll.

"Been on the trip?" Liz asked Heather.

"Sure, it's great."

"Feel like going again?"

"Okay."

They bought tickets and joined a small line of people on the dock. Then a hatch opened in the conning tower and Mr. McAndrews looked out.

"Hi sir," Liz said. "Can we get in that way?"

"Sorry, this is the emergency exit. Visitors enter through the hatch at the stern."

They went below to a double row of seats facing big portholes. As Liz and Heather sat down, Mr. McAndrews closed the emergency exit and stepped down into the cabin. Joining Carroll at the forward end of the sub he quietly spoke to her, while gesturing at various gauges.

"Why are they on board?" Liz said. "They're not tourists."

The stern hatch closed with a hollow thump. The air was warm and sweat beaded on Liz's forehead. She looked out at silver bubbles rising past the porthole, and saw an artificial crab clinging to the dock. Next to it she could see a fisherman's boot tangled in make-believe seaweed.

Mr. McAndrews looked at the passengers. "Good afternoon, folks!" He introduced himself and Carroll, then said he was in charge for this journey. "This will be a dangerous mission," he warned, as the sub moved slowly away from its berth. "We're going in search of the missing research sub, SR2."

The radio crackled as a voice said, *"You have clearance out of Bravo Bay, Admiral McAndrews."*

"Aye, aye," he replied. Then he looked at the others. "During the mission we'll be passing the ruins of Atlantis, that lost gem of civilization. We'll see fish from all over the world, perhaps even some sharks. Now everyone into position, and be watchful."

Liz and Heather leaned forward. They could see the portholes of another sub and its brass propeller. It was large and looked dangerous. They passed a circular glass tank in which little red fish swam, then saw a big grouper in its tank under the *Santa Maria*.

Mr. McAndrews was speaking quietly to his daughter, but she didn't seem to be listening. Instead, she was staring out a porthole, but wasn't concentrating on the view. Liz was sure something was troubling Carroll. But what could it be?

Everyone fell silent as the sub entered a tunnel. "Dangerous waters," Mr. McAndrews said ominously. "What's that to port? Is it the remains of the SR2?" Everyone leaned toward the left portholes, where they saw a make-believe sub crushed in the tentacles of a giant sea squid.

Suddenly Mr. McAndrews cried out. "We're under attack! We've lost our power!"

As the sub went dark someone screamed. Lights flashed on the control panel and Mr. McAndrews shouted excitedly about taking evasive action, then the sub glided out of the tunnel into peaceful waters. Mr. McAndrews was grinning after the adventure in the tunnel but Carroll's eyes were on the steel deck at her feet.

Liz looked out a porthole and saw the ghostly vision of the sunken wreck where Christopher's air hose had been slashed. She shivered, glad that he'd escaped with his life.

Then she looked toward the stern of the sub at a man in glasses who held a pocket notebook and pen.

He, too, was studying the wreck through a porthole. Determined to find out why, Liz stood up and walked toward the man.

7

The next morning Liz was shopping with her mother on Europa Boulevard. It was like a street in Paris, with pastel-coloured buildings side by side. Only a few people were on the tree-lined boulevard, but they were enjoying a great act in the Rock the Mall contest.

Rock Moves featured Ewan and Fiona Taft from British Columbia. They danced the length of the marble corridor, singing into small hand-held microphones while their band played under a street lamp that had hanging flower baskets.

After the act finished, Liz pulled her mother into a nearby store. "Know who owns this? One of the Edmonton Oilers! Maybe he'll be here."

The polished aluminum ceiling glowed with spotlights that shone on denim jackets and jeans. "Know what, Mom? They buy old clothes and turn them into these jeans and jackets." She smiled at the pretty girl behind the counter. "Hi, we're here to have lunch with Mark."

She laughed. "Take a number. You're the fourth girl today to try that act." She smiled at Mrs. Austen. "But I don't blame them for trying."

Mrs. Austen looked at a portrait of the handsome hockey player in his Oilers uniform. "If that's him I don't blame them, either."

"Will he be playing in the game Friday night?" Liz asked the girl.

"Unfortunately, no. He's at a celebrity golf tournament back east."

"Too bad." Liz tried on a jacket with a white satin kitten sewn on the back. "The game should be great, Mom. It's Edmonton against Calgary, but with only a few guys from each team, plus some local talent."

Back in the mall they looked in the window of a jewellery store at a necklace of miniature gold hearts and a ring inlaid with diamonds. "Who can afford all this?" Mrs. Austen said. "You'd need to own a money machine."

"Or a lot of credit cards." Liz went to the window of a nearby store where a pink hand-knit sweater graced a mannequin. "Can you imagine what would have happened if one of those bombs had gone off?"

"One more bomb or even a bomb scare, and we're heading home."

"Oh, Mom!"

"I know you love it here, sweetie, but I'm getting nervous. That scuba diver could have drowned! I'll have to talk to your father."

Liz looked at two men cleaning the brass rails nearby. Tom had reported there were people who spent all day every day polishing them. Everything about the mall was so fantastic and now, suddenly, they might be going home.

"I still haven't found Aunt Melody a present. I'd better get it really fast."

Mrs. Austen smiled. "Don't sulk. Nothing's been decided."

Liz looked in a window. "Wow, Mom, there it is! The perfect gift for Aunt Melody." A tiny crystal piano turned slowly under a spotlight, dazzling her eyes with beams of coloured light. She hurried into the store, then left quickly after learning the price.

"Never mind," Mrs. Austen said. "It was a nice thought."

* * *

Near the rink they leaned over some stairs to look down at benches several floors below. People were changing into skates but Liz couldn't see Chad. "He's an ice dancer, you know."

Her mother smiled. "Yes, you've told us several times." She touched Liz's hair. "Time goes by so fast. Sometimes I wish you and Tom were back in diapers so we could watch you growing up again."

"*Diapers*? Mom, please! People might be listening." Liz glanced at the stairs, hoping Chad wasn't coming up from a rehearsal. "Please be more discreet with your comments, Mother. I *am* 16."

Laughing, they went into the International Marketplace. It was like a narrow street in a foreign country, crowded with stalls selling dragons of pale green jade, tigers with gleaming fangs and the tiniest carved elephants they'd ever seen. There were also booths selling sugar baby mini-doughnuts, souvenirs of the mall and the chance to have your portrait taken in a gold rush outfit.

"Mom, a palm reader!" Liz pointed at the booth. "I have to know about my date with Chad!"

A bearded young man welcomed her to his table, then explained that reading her palm was like reading her mind. "The lines are like a map. I'll tell you what I discover."

They closed their eyes for two minutes, saying nothing. Then he studied her palms. "Your head line shows a thirst for knowledge. This trident means fame, fortune and honour if you follow your heart. But here," he said, pointing at a line, "I see confusion."

"You mean about what's been happening with the bombs? You're right, I'm really confused."

He shook his head. "Negative energy has entered your life recently. That's what's confusing."

"You mean someone I've met at the mall isn't very nice? Who?"

"I can't say that."

"What's going to happen?"

He smiled. "I'm not a fortune teller."

He continued with the reading, but Liz found it difficult to concentrate. Later, before having lunch with her mother, she stopped to throw a coin into a fountain. "Storm clouds are gathering. I can feel it in my bones."

"Storm clouds can't reach you, darling. This is an indoor city, remember?"

"There's more than one kind of storm."

As they entered Bourbon Street Liz looked at the shoeshine chairs, but Susan was gone. A small sign said CLOSED. A couple of people were talking at the far end of the street, but no one else moved under the lights that twinkled in the dark ceiling.

"I'm getting depressed," Liz said. "Maybe some food will help."

They chose a small table outside a café and were given menus. Mrs. Austen made her choice, then asked, "Heather arranged your date?"

"That's right. Her boyfriend knows Chad."

"He's seventeen. That's a year older than you."

"Don't worry, Mom, I'm not running away with him! It's just a minor little date, and Heather and her boyfriend will be with us."

"I don't call it minor when you're this excited." Mrs. Austen patted her hand. "Just remember one thing—you deserve the best."

"It'll be a great time! We're going to Galaxyland and then lunch and then the waterpark."

"Heather seemed very mature when I met her. Is that because of her music?"

"I think so. She travels a lot with her band, but she's also in university."

"In Edmonton?"

"Sure, she lives with her family. They're travellers, too. She was named Heather because her Dad loves Scotland."

"That's nice." Mrs. Austen waited for the waitress to take Liz's order, then said, "Oysters for me."

"Oysters?" Liz stared at her. "Are you serious?"

"Of course. Besides, you had them in PEI."

"I had ONE oyster in PEI. The first and last of my life." Liz fiddled with a glass, then said, "I hope Heather wins."

"Why is a country band in a Rock the Mall contest?"

"Haven't you heard of k.d. lang? Heather's got the same sound."

"Oh. Well, I guess I'm out of touch."

"Heather could be a major star, but there may be a problem."

"What's that?"

"Her manager. That guy, Mr. Sutton. He's moving her career really slowly. Christopher says Heather should be performing in Nashville by now." She started her Caesar salad, then looked down Bourbon Street. "Hey, there's Mr. Sutton now. He's talking to Benn Dunn. Maybe he's a customer at the scuba store."

"He doesn't seem the type."

"You can never tell."

A few minutes later Benn Dunn walked toward the mall and Mr. Sutton came along the avenue. He looked up at the balcony where the first bomb had been discovered, then studied a New Orleans taxi parked on the cobblestones before finally noticing Liz. Slowly he came across the street, staring at her.

"Haven't I met you before?"

"Sure, with Heather." Liz introduced her mother, who invited Mr. Sutton to join them.

"Okay, but just for a few minutes. Heather's got a rehearsal downtown and I don't want to be late." He ordered a coffee, then smiled at Liz. "I bet you enjoy this place."

"That's for sure. But it's more fun when there's lots of people."

"Yeah, it looks like those bombs might have started to hurt business. But Mr. McAndrews has lots of money, so he'll survive. I was in the navy with him. After that he went into furniture and now expensive stores, and I went into the music business." He showed them a hole in his shoe. "That's been the story of my life, but now everything's going to be fine."

"Because of Heather?" Mrs. Austen asked.

"You bet. That's a golden voice, Mrs. Austen, and it means my big chance at last. I've had other good singers, but they peaked too fast. A single hit, then they fizzled out. By the time Heather hits the top she'll have a solid foundation. She'll be around a long time." He stirred his coffee with a plastic stick, then suddenly snapped it. "Certain people think I'm a bad manager for Heather. They think she should be an overnight sensation. That's bad advice."

"I'm sure that's true, Mr. Sutton."

"Believe me, Mrs. Austen, it's very true. Heather's going to the top and she's going there my way."

* * *

After lunch Liz and her mother went to the dolphin show. There were lots of seats, but only a scattering of spectators. Bright store signs reflected on the pool's green water, which was held back by a glass wall. The dolphins could be seen underwater, playing among the sunbeams, and then powering up to leap high above the waves.

Mr. McAndrews arrived to watch the show and joined them. "Good afternoon," he said, sitting down. "Attendance is pretty low today, isn't it? Management has decided to only run one sub ride." He looked at the yellow conning towers visible at their berth in the sea. "But that won't stop my morning journeys."

"What do you mean?"

"I'm ex-navy, Mrs. Austen. I was in subs for years until I decided to earn some real money in business. I've never lost my love for those things, so I've made a special arrangement with management. Every morning before the mall opens I go for a solo journey. Being all alone in that silent underwater world sets me up for the day."

"How do you feel about the bomber?"

"A kook for sure. Nothing makes sense! Why bombs that don't explode? Why the scuba attack? Why the silence from the bomber? No notes, no phone calls, no demands for a huge payoff. It's beginning to drive me crazy."

"Something will happen soon. I'm sure of that."

"Does Carroll like subs, too?" Liz asked.

"Sure, my daughter loves being underwater. Scuba diving's her big hobby."

"But what about subs?"

"Well, she's not wild about them, but I've been taking her on trips, teaching her how the things work. I'd like her to follow in my footsteps at the mall." For a few minutes he looked at the dolphin pool before adding, "Unfortunately Carroll's got a mind of her own. She's spent time in the Caribbean and wants to go back there. She was never enthusiastic about me setting up a store for her. Now she wants out."

"That's a shame," Mrs. Austen said. "You must be feeling a bit down these days."

"You're right, and that's why I'm here to watch the dolphins. They always make me feel better. I think our show rivals the one at Sea World in San Diego."

A poolside door opened and Lisa deVita appeared beside a man Liz hadn't met. She clipped a tiny microphone to the N.Y. JETS sweatshirt she wore over her wet suit, and introduced herself. "With me is our chief trainer, Ken Nguyen. These dolphins were born in the Gulf of Mexico. They'll live to about thirty-five, right in this pool."

"Wow." Liz grinned at her mom. "Imagine spending your entire life at the West Edmonton Mall."

As Ken began telling the audience some information about the dolphins and how they lived, Lisa walked slowly around the edge of the pool, looking at Liz in the stands. "I remember now—you're the girl who requested a special tour. Come and meet Mavis." When Liz reached the pool she was given some instructions and then, as Lisa made circling motions, a dolphin rose out of the water to be patted. "Wow," Liz exclaimed as she hurried back to her mother. "What an experience—her skin's rubbery and she smiled at me!"

Mrs. Austen hugged her. "They've got your kind of spirit, darling. No wonder I enjoy watching this show."

Some of the dolphins' stunts were spectacular and they were applauded enthusiastically by the small crowd as the show ended with them circling the pool on their sides, slapping the surface with grey flippers. "I want that trainer's job," Liz grinned. "I wonder what's backstage?"

"Maybe you'll find out. She's waving you forward."

Within minutes arrangements had been made for a tour, which Mrs. Austen declined. "I brought some paperwork from Winnipeg that I haven't finished, so I think I'll get back to it."

"Your mom's nice," Lisa said, as she opened the door to an inner pool. "We can isolate a dolphin here for a medical examination."

"Do you ever swim with them?"

"Whenever I get the chance."

"What's it like?"

"They're shy. They circle around, watching, zapping out their sound waves. After a while they start playing."

"Lisa, may I ask you a personal question?"

"Sure. What do you need to know?"

"Are you engaged to Christopher?"

"Well, I'm not sure. He's talked about marriage, but so far no ring and no announcements. My family's getting restless. They want to start planning the wedding." She laughed. "I'm not *that* anxious, but I hate uncertainty."

"How's Carroll fit in?"

"She worries me. I hate to say it, but maybe she's the reason for no ring."

"She's moved in on Christopher?"

"Kind of. When he first started working at the mall as a guide he joined our scuba club. We started dating. Then Carroll came home from a long holiday in the Caribbean. One look at Christopher and, bingo, he was the manager of her new store."

"Has he dated her?"

"No, but he's a natural flirt. That just encourages Carroll. I try to act like I don't care, but I do."

In another room Lisa filled a pail with dead squid. "You know something? When Christopher's air hose got slashed I was really upset for him. But something else bothers me."

"What's that?"

"My scuba outfit is identical to Christopher's, and I swam through the wreck just before he did." She looked at Liz with huge, dark eyes. "I think the attack was meant for me."

* * *

Ten minutes later Liz was still asking questions, but Lisa couldn't offer any proof. "It's just a feeling," she said. "But I'm nervous anyway."

"Have you told the police?"

"Sure. They wrote it down, but that's all."

Walking down some metal stairs, they entered a corridor where their voices echoed, and there were pipes and air-conditioning ducts high above. After following a confusing route they reached an open space with a low ceiling and concrete walls. Before them was a huge tank, with waves moving on the restless surface.

"I'm nervous," Liz said. "Where are we?"

"Don't worry, we're perfectly safe." The trainer stepped onto a platform above the tank. Reaching into her pail, she tossed dead squid in different directions. The water erupted immediately as thick snouts burst forth, revealing razor-sharp teeth that tore the squid and slashed at each other's hides. As Lisa continued to throw squid Liz stared in horror at the sharks fighting each other for the food, then said, "I'll wait in the corridor."

"Okay."

Eventually Lisa joined her, smiling cheerfully. "These are only lemon sharks, you know, not great whites."

"Sure Lisa, but they're scary anyhow. Scary, scary, scary."

Lisa collected another pail of food and they went upstairs to the mall to feed the fish in the *Santa Maria*'s tank. At the railing around the sea they looked across the water at the galleon.

"See that two-headed serpent?" Liz pointed at the bow. "It's really bad luck for the *Santa Maria*."

"But it'll never be in a storm."

"That serpent is still bad news." Liz looked at the crow's nest high above. "Imagine if one of those Spanish sailors came through a time warp to the present. What would he think of the view from up there now?"

"That he'd really found a new world," Lisa laughed. "You've got an imagination like mine."

Christopher had arranged to meet Lisa, and was waiting as they approached the *Santa Maria*. He kissed her, then smiled at Liz. "How's the bomb investigation?"

"Slow."

"I'm close to learning something. I already have a name, but I need proof."

"*Who is it?*"

"Sorry, not yet. But I should know something soon."

Lisa put her arms around Christopher and looked up into his blue eyes. "Please, Chris, be careful. I get so worried."

He hugged her, then looked at Liz. "You were just at the shark feeding?"

"Yes, but how'd you know?"

"Your face is still the colour of chalk. Those sharks give me the creeps, too, but Lisa loves them. She's crazy about anything that swims."

Liz looked at the dark entrance to the sub tunnel. "What's that steel catwalk for?"

"It runs the length of the tunnel. If a sub ever got stuck in there the passengers could escape out the conning tower, then follow the catwalk to the mall."

"Any chance of taking a look in the tunnel?"

"Sure."

Their voices were muffled in the darkness. Cool air blew from air-conditioning ducts and the black water was calm. Liz imagined a sub moving silently past, the orange light flashing on its conning tower.

"I wonder . . ."

"What?" Lisa asked.

"Just . . . well, what if a sub did stop in here? Someone could sneak out the conning tower and into the water in scuba gear. No one in the mall would see."

"But why do that?"

"I'm not sure. It's just an idea."

Outside the tunnel they walked to the *Santa Maria*. As Liz stepped onto the deck a cloud crossed the sun, throwing a dark shadow across the galleon. She shivered and was glad when the others joined her. The sun returned, but soon they descended a ladder into more darkness.

"This is the hold of the *Santa Maria*," Lisa said, switching on a bare lightbulb. The yellow glow showed a floor of rough planks and a low ceiling. There were shadows all around. Below them was a tank lit up by hidden lights, where exotic fish moved among the green ferns.

"It's nice and cool in here."

"The *Santa Maria*'s connected to the mall's air conditioning system."

"Those groupers are something. Only a mother could love a face like that."

"How about the stingrays? I've petted one."

"Better you than me." Liz looked at the tank's glass wall. "That's the sea out there, right?"

Lisa nodded. "People in the sub can see these fish."

"I was on that trip just yesterday." Liz hesitated, then added, "Mr. McAndrews was on the sub. So was Carroll."

She watched Christopher closely, but he didn't react to the woman's name. He was looking into the tank, watching a grouper patrol its territory. But Lisa turned to look at Liz.

"Funny you should mention Carroll," she said. "I was just thinking about challenging her to a duel. We could fight it out underwater. Spearguns at 50 flipper-paces, or something like that."

"Are you still jealous of her?" Christopher asked.

"I didn't think it showed." Lisa looked up at him. "Don't you think it would be an interesting duel?"

There was a smile on her lips, but not in her eyes.

8

In Tom's hotel room he lay on the floor, reading. Dietmar was watching TV. He was sprawled on the bed, which was in the back of a Ford pickup truck. There was a smaller bed in the cab, and a traffic cop stood over the Jacuzzi. On the walls and ceiling were traffic signs and lights.

Dietmar turned off the television. "You know Europa Boulevard?"

"Of course. We were there an hour ago."

"Oh yeah, I forgot. Anyway, I . . ."

"That boulevard is like Paris."

"You mean with all those balconies? You know, I've been thinking about them. That would be a long fall."

"Sick, Oban."

Dietmar jumped off the bed. "Listen, how about playing Pebble Beach? My treat."

"What's going on? You hate golf and you never buy for me."

"Not true, Austen. Anyway, how about it?"

"Sure, okay." Tom closed his book. "Let's get going."

"I'm not quite ready. I need 30 minutes, okay?"

"Why?"

"I met this girl, and I want to invite her. I'm going to her mother's store to ask her."

"Use the phone."

Dietmar shook his head. "I'll walk. I need the exercise." He went into his room, which was connected to Tom's, and closed the door. For several minutes Tom heard him moving around, then all was quiet. He thought about the girl Dietmar wanted to invite, then turned on the television.

He was watching a game show when the phone rang. "Tom," Dietmar exclaimed. "It's me."

Tom sat up. "What's wrong?"

"I'm in Europa Boulevard! I think I know who the bomber is! Meet me here as soon as . . ."

"Dietmar, who is it?"

"Not over the phone! Get down here fast!"

"Where will you be?"

"I'm not sure, but look for a woman with red hair. She's my contact and . . ."

The line went dead.

Tom stared at the phone, then hung up fast. Grabbing his room key, he raced down the hallway to the elevators.

As he waited, jiggling the key in his hand and pacing the carpet, he was joined by an elderly couple.

"Canada's such a different country," the lady said to Tom. "There's no hotel like this back home."

"Where you from, boy?" the man asked.

"Winnipeg."

He held out a hand. "So was my Granddaddy. Shake, cousin."

Finally the elevator reached the lobby. Tom raced to the indoor sea, flew past the *Santa Maria* and up the escalator to Europa Boulevard.

But there was no sign of Dietmar. At the far end of the boulevard someone sat under the hanging flower baskets of a Victorian lamp-standard, but no one else was around. Tom walked slowly past a store with denim jackets in the window, then looked back toward the *Santa Maria*. Where was Dietmar?

Suddenly a scream rang out.

Where had it come from? Tom turned, staring, as people ran out from several stores. Then a sales assistant pointed up.

"There! On that balcony!"

Tom looked at the top of an elegant old building. Something or someone was up there. He could see a big mop of red hair.

"Don't jump," he yelled. "I'm coming up! I'll help you."

But it was too late. The figure leaned out further and everyone saw a T-shirt with wide stripes of vivid colours. The crowd screamed and scattered as the figure toppled off the balcony and fell, tumbling through the air to smash into the marble corridor.

Running forward, Tom looked at the victim.

Blue buttons for eyes. The nose a black button. A mop for hair.

Everyone was staring at him. "Hey, this isn't my gag." Tom raised defensive hands. "Don't blame me. I'm not involved."

There were some angry mutterings, until a sales assistant laughed. "Let's relax, folks! It made a real change from a boring day. I'll phone the custodians to clean it up."

Tom decided to tell Neil Raj about the fake suicide, and hurried through the mall to Luggage Unlimited.

His friend laughed as he heard about Dietmar. "He picked the perfect time for it, with the mall so deserted. On a normal evening he could have injured some shopper or a tourist."

"You closing now?"

Neil Raj looked at his watch. "Five minutes."

"Great. How about the Mindbender? Should we . . ."

Neil Raj looked out the window. "Not again!" He smashed his hand against the counter top. "When will it end?"

The boys in the leather jackets were back. Two of them stayed in the corridor, while the Skull came into the store. Without saying anything he stared at them.

"Something I can do for you?" Neil Raj said.

The Skull shook his head. He walked to a display of attaché cases and studied one, then dropped it on the floor. He kicked it to one side, then dropped a second case.

"Please leave the store," Neil Raj said.

A nine-year-old boy came in the door. He had some money in his hand. "Hi," he said cheerfully. "I want a present for my mom's birthday."

Tom looked at the Skull, who was staring at the boy. Neil Raj said, "Sorry, but the store's closed."

The boy looked at his watch. "The sign says you close at nine. That gives me two minutes."

"Nothing I can do about that." Neil Raj smiled regretfully. "You can't come in."

"False advertising! Our teacher told us about that."

With a tight smile on his face, Neil Raj escorted the boy out of the store. He watched until he was safely down the corridor, then came inside and looked at the Skull. "Okay, I'll say it again. It's time for you to leave."

The Skull reached inside his leather jacket and took out a can of spray paint. Neil Raj walked quickly to the phone, but the Skull leapt forward and ripped the cord from the wall. For a moment the two faced each other, then Neil Raj glanced at Tom. "Let's go. I'll phone security from one of their hot lines in the mall."

As his friend walked out of the store Tom saw the Skull looking at a picture on the wall. It was a family portrait of Neil Raj and his parents. Raising his hand, the Skull sprayed red paint across the picture.

Tom sprang at the Skull, hitting his wrist with a karate blow. The paint can fell to the floor and bounced away.

"You stupid . . ."

The Skull looked out the window. Neil Raj had stopped a security guard in the corridor and was gesturing toward the store. As soon as the guard spoke into his two-way radio the Skull's friends melted away around a corner.

"There goes your army," Tom said. "You've had it."

The Skull ran toward the back of the store. Tom hesitated, then realized the guard couldn't reach the store in time to catch him. Running swiftly through the upper display area, he raced into the storage room.

There was no sign of the Skull.

Tom couldn't find the light switch. In the gloom a machine was running with a low hum, a tap dripped and someone was breathing. Tom walked forward and, just as he'd found the switch, something was smashed across the back of his head. With a cry he fell to the floor, and lay shaking his head trying to fight the pain.

Looking up, he saw the Skull above. He'd reached the top of a shelf and was pushing away a ceiling tile. Just as the Skull pulled himself up into the darkness Tom staggered to his feet and started to climb the shelves to the ceiling. The air was musty as he pulled himself into the crawlspace. Faint light glowed from stores below and he could hear the crackle of the security guard's two-way radio as the man ran into the luggage store.

"Up here," Tom yelled. "In the crawlspace."

Then he heard the Skull, scrambling away into the darkness. Moving cautiously, Tom followed the sound until he saw a dim shape ahead.

"Take off," the Skull hissed. "I've got a knife."

"I doubt it. You'd have used it before now."

"Take off!"

"You're caught. There's spray paint on your fingers and three witnesses, including that kid. Maybe you . . ."

The Skull came at him out of the darkness, hands outstretched and snarling. They fell together, fighting until a flashlight beam cut the darkness. "Over here," Tom yelled to the security guard as he pinned the Skull to the floor. "You stupid jerk! You're finished now."

9

After being questioned by the police, Tom walked through the empty corridors toward the hotel.

The mall was a different world with all the stores closed. Behind the glass wall of an aviary a flamingo stood on one leg watching him with a tiny eye, while others slept with their beaks buried in pink feathers. At the indoor sea spotlights glowed under the dark surface, revealing the shapes of broken statues and the outline of the wreck where Christopher had come close to losing his life. After walking to the end of the sea, Tom followed a path among bushy plants to a railing at the water's edge. Beneath the surface he could see the sharks circling in their brightly lit tank, a strange and frightening sight in the silence of the mall.

Back at the hotel he found his parents pacing the floor.

They were pretty upset and were telling him exactly what they thought when Dietmar walked in with a happy grin. "Hiya, Austen! What happened in Europa .. ?"

Mrs. Austen held up a hand. "Hold it right there, Dietmar. We've just had a call from Mr. McAndrews. He heard about your stunt in Europa Boulevard and wants you sent home."

Dietmar turned pale. "Really?"

Mrs. Austen nodded. "It took all my courtroom skills to change his mind."

Grinning, Dietmar shook her hand. "You're a pal."

"You may not think so tomorrow."

* * *

Soon after the stores opened next morning Mrs. Austen returned to the suite with a pizza-shaped container and sent Tom to wake Dietmar. It was a long time before the two returned.

"This guy sleeps like he's in a coma. I could have driven a fire engine past the bed without him noticing."

Dietmar yawned. "I watched movies until six a.m., and I can hardly see."

"I've just bought a present for you, Dietmar."

"Thanks, Mrs. A. What did it cost?"

Tom snorted. "Do you measure everything in dollars, Oban? Sometimes you act like you're only a bit smarter than a bag of nails."

Mrs. Austen gave Dietmar the container. "Like so many things in the mall, this holds a world record."

"I've eaten bigger pizzas, Mrs. Austen."

"Just open it."

Dietmar cracked the lid to reveal an enormous cookie with writing on it that said *You're grounded.* "You've got to be kidding!"

"Care to bet on that?"

"Do I get to eat the cookie?"

"As long as you don't forget the message."

"Great! My favourite game show's on this morning, so I'll eat this thing while I watch it." He looked at Tom. "Call for me around two, and we'll go to the waterpark."

Mrs. Austen raised a hand. "Dietmar, you'd better turn that cookie over."

He gave it a spin, then stared at the words written on the back: *for two days.* "Grounded for two days? But we're at the West Edmonton Mall!"

"Next time you'll be grounded for life."

* * *

An hour later Liz arrived outside Galaxyland for the double date. Heather was with her boyfriend, Marc Hewitt. He was good looking and so was Liz's date, Chad Fleetwood, who was a nice dresser and wore a jacket with the name of his skating club on the back.

Inside the amusement park, Liz looked at the boats on the small lake, and at the miniature train. "This place is truly amazing. Imagine having an entire amusement park inside a shopping mall."

"You're right," Chad said. "And the Mindbender's waiting for us."

"The triple-loop roller coaster? I'm not crazy about riding that."

"You'll love it."

"I've done it once. That felt like enough."

Heather and Marc wanted to ride the Orbitron so they agreed to try that first. Soon they were experiencing massive acceleration. Their cars rapidly rose and fell, bouncing them up and down, forward and back, as the girls screamed and their hair whipped around their faces. "Wow," Liz gasped when the ride ended, "that was great!"

At the washroom she and Heather combed their hair and checked themselves in the mirror. "I can tell Chad likes you," Heather said. "You're doing great."

Liz grinned. "I'm a nervous wreck."

"Just relax and enjoy yourself."

After riding the bumper cars and winning a couple of plush velvet animals, they reached the Drop of Doom. Looking like the steel structure that stands beside space rockets at the launch pad, it rose high above.

Chad turned to Liz. "Scared of that thing?"

"No. Why?"

"The Mindbender scares you."

"Where'd you get that?"

"You're afraid to ride it."

"That's not what I said."

"Good, because that's what we're doing after this ride."

Liz looked at his blue eyes. "Maybe I'll do it. I haven't decided yet."

"Not maybe," Chad replied. "For sure."

Liz turned toward the Drop of Doom. "Come on, I'll buy this one."

"Nope. I'll get the tickets." Pulling out his money, Chad walked to the booth and soon they were being strapped into a small cage at the foot of the steel structure.

"Good luck," the attendant said. "Imagine you're about to step off a 120-storey building. That's what the ride feels like." Grinning, he stepped back. "I'll give you a free second ride if you survive this one."

Suddenly the cage began to rise. For a moment Liz closed her eyes, then looked down. Far below, a solitary tourist was aiming a video camera in their direction. Quickly the woman grew smaller, then with a crash the cage stopped at the top of the blue steel.

Rolling forward on small wheels, it stopped over eternity. Liz moaned, then everything fell away as the cage plunged down, faster and faster, while the metal wheels roared in their tracks and soundless screams erupted from her throat.

Suddenly the cage changed direction and slammed to a stop. As the attendant leaned into the cage to release them he asked, "Going up again?"

"Forget it," Chad groaned. "My stomach's still on the 95th floor."

"I won't argue with you," Liz said as they staggered away from the ride to join Heather and Marc. "That thing's a killer."

"The Mindbender's next."

Liz looked at the nearby roller coaster. The triple-loops rose so high that it was difficult to see their tops. While she watched, a red car came swiftly out of a loop, its riders screaming with delight, then roared straight back up into the heavens.

"Wicked."

"I'll get the tickets," Chad said.

"I don't think I'll go." Liz pointed at a nearby bench.

"I'll wait here for you guys. Watch for me waving!"

"Hold it." Chad raised a hand. "You're riding the Mindbender."

"You keep ordering me to ride the thing. What if I don't want to?"

"You're with me."

"Hey," Liz said, her voice trembling. "Hey, this is turning into a mess. I'll just go sit down."

"If you do," Chad said, "the party's over." He stared at her, saying nothing more. His eyes were a vivid blue, with wonderful long lashes.

"Listen," Liz said. "This is getting crazy. I'll sit this ride out, okay? I'll see you guys after it."

"Forget it. You're coming with us."

Liz looked at Heather and Marc. They were watching, and so were several other people. "Come on, let's drop this insane argument. Okay?"

"It's not okay," Chad said. "I spent a lot of money on you today."

For a moment Liz was quiet. She looked at him, then at Heather and Marc. Suddenly her whole body shook with anger. "Here," she said, pulling some money from her pocket. "Here's a refund."

Chad stared at her without saying a word. Then he turned and disappeared in the direction of the roller coaster. Liz turned to Marc and Heather.

"I've gotta go. See you tomorrow, okay?"

"Sure, but . . ."

"Can't talk! Sorry!"

Liz hurried through the amusement park on legs like rubber. She didn't see or hear anything, she just walked fast, wanting to get out of Galaxyland. At last she

reached the mall and saw people looking in store windows. As she walked along the polished marble, thinking about Chad, she saw some fountains ahead. They
seemed to be dancing in time to the Blue Danube Waltz.

"Wow," she whispered as she watched the water.
"I'm *really* glad I did that!"

10

That evening Tom and Liz were eating in a huge arcade, surrounded by booths that sold food from many places. There was salad from Greece, tortillas from Mexico and teri yaki from Japan, but they were eating hamburgers from McDonald's.

"So," Liz said, "do you think I did the right thing?"

"Of course! That guy's a jerk. What did Heather say?"

"She phoned my room an hour ago. She said she was really sorry it happened, but she thinks what I did was great."

Tom looked at his watch. "Hey, it's getting late. All the good places will be taken."

"Too bad Dietmar's still grounded. I bet he's sorry he has to miss this."

Mr. McAndrews was among the people walking through the mall to the Ice Palace. "This is great," he said to Tom and Liz. "An exciting game and more crowds than I've seen since the bombs started."

"I hear Cayley Wilson's playing tonight," Tom said. "Is that true?"

"You bet. I organized this game as a summer exhibition and Cayley said he'd play. So are some of the other Oilers, and several players from the Calgary Flames. They all agreed to play despite the bomber."

"Could you get me Cayley Wilson's autograph?" Tom asked.

"I can do better than that. How'd you like to meet him?"

"I guess so!"

Mirrored stairs led down to a basement area with Coke and video machines lining the walls, a skate shop, and doors leading to various dressing rooms. One of them featured the Oilers' logo; Mr. McAndrews went inside and returned a minute later with Cayley Wilson. He was tall, with blond hair and green eyes.

"It's good to meet you," he said with a friendly handshake. "Mr. McAndrews tells me you're crime busters."

"Sort of," Tom said, while Liz smiled shyly.

"What's been your biggest case so far?"

They talked for a while, then Cayley signed autographs and returned to the dressing room to prepare for the game. After thanking Mr. McAndrews, Tom and Liz followed some stairs that curved up to the Oilers' bench, beside the rink.

"Look at the crowd!"

The railings on both levels were jammed with fans. Most waved OILERS banners, but there were a lot of red flags being waved by Flames' supporters who'd driven north from Calgary. Tom and Liz went through a low gate into the crowd and managed to work their way to Heather's side. She'd saved them places by the railing.

"What excitement!" She grinned. "I bet this is better than a Stanley Cup final."

A roar from the crowd greeted the Oilers as they stepped on the ice, followed by the Flames. A few announcements were made, then Mr. McAndrews dropped a ceremonial puck and left the ice, waving to the crowd with his stetson.

Within seconds the play was directly in front of them. Two players fought for the puck in the corner, then it sprang loose toward Cayley. Picking it up behind the net, he began a move to the right. Then, in mid stride, he changed direction and broke to his left. The Calgary goalie was taken off-balance and watched helplessly as Cayley slipped the puck into the net.

The Ice Palace erupted with cheers from the Oilers' fans. People all around the rink yelled and stamped their feet and waved flags until the action resumed. Then, just after the players had swept past Tom, he looked at the upper railing and realized he was being watched.

Leaning close to Liz he whispered, "Someone's staring at us. Upper railing in sunglasses. Is that a wig he's wearing?"

"The one carrying the skates? It could be a she in that bulky coat."

"I think it's a he. Why's he watching us, not the game?"

"She's leaving."

The person in sunglasses pushed through the crowd to the glass-walled elevator. It descended to the lower level, then the strange figure disappeared down the curving stairs toward the dressing rooms.

Heather looked at them. "Hey, you're missing all the action! This is a fantastic game."

"Would you save our place?"

"Okay, but it won't be easy."

The Oilers on the bench were leaning forward, watching every move. The noise of cheering was really loud as Tom and Liz followed the stairs down to the changing area. It was empty.

"Is she in the skate shop?" Liz asked.

Tom tried the door. "Locked. What about the dressing room?"

"Also locked." Liz glanced up the mirrored stairs that led above. "There, look!"

The person in sunglasses was at the top of the stairs. One hand held a skate, the other was adjusting dark curls. "That's a wig for sure," Tom said. "Who is he?"

"And why did she come down here?"

"The skates! He's only got one now!"

"Then where's the other one? Is it hidden down here?"

Quickly they looked under benches and on the tops of the video games without finding it, then noticed the skate sharpener. Tom raced to the machine, fumbling for coins, and soon the small door slowly opened to reveal a skate within. A ticking sound could be heard and wires were visible inside the skate.

"The red one's connected! This isn't a false alarm!"

"We've got to warn people."

Tom and Liz raced to the stairs that curved up to the Oilers' bench, where they found Cayley Wilson wiping his face with a towel. "Calgary just tied the score," he said. "Why were you downstairs? You're missing a great game."

As soon as Tom explained, Cayley swung over the boards onto the ice. The referee blew his whistle, signalling a penalty, but Cayley quickly skated over to the announcer's booth and grabbed the microphone.

"Sorry folks," he said through the speakers, "but the game's over." There were a few groans, then everyone fell silent. "There's a bomb threat. Please leave the area immediately."

* * *

Tom and Liz were soon back at their parents' hotel suite watching television coverage of the incident. The cream-coloured outside walls of the supermall were shown on TV as the cameras panned over the watching crowds and the many police vehicles. Finally, Inspector Winter Eagle made the announcement everyone was waiting for.

"The bomb has been safely defused, thanks to Inspector Ted Austen of the Winnipeg Police."

"When will you make an arrest?" a reporter shouted.

"I've just issued a warrant."

"What? You're about to arrest someone? Who?"

"I can't reveal that."

As the questions continued Mr. Austen came into the room. He kissed his wife and gave her a big hug, then looked at Tom and Liz. "Pack your bags, kids. You're going home."

"I was afraid of that," Tom said.

"I've been checking flight times," Mrs. Austen said to her husband. "The first plane is tomorrow afternoon."

Mr. Austen congratulated Tom and Liz for discovering the bomb. "Want to know something strange? That thing wouldn't have exploded for six hours."

"Did the bomber need that much time to escape?"

"Possibly, but that's a long wait in the skate sharpener. Anyone might have found the bomb." Mr. Austen loosened his tie. "We found initials inside the skate."

"What were they?"

"B. D."

"Benn Dunn!"

Mr. Austen nodded. "He worked in the store where a bomb was discovered, he was Christopher Dixon's scuba partner when the air hose was slashed, and when we ran his name through the computer earlier, we found out that he's served time in prison. The police have issued a warrant for his arrest."

The phone rang. After a brief conversation Mr. Austen hung up, shaking his head. "That was Inspector Winter Eagle. The police went to Benn Dunn's store to make the arrest, but he was gone. Then they tried his apartment."

"What did they find?"

"Nothing." Mr. Austen looked at them. "Benn Dunn has disappeared."

* * *

"Our last morning at the West Edmonton Mall!" Liz

stared at the long corridors of marble, trees and fountains. "Our last walk to the World Waterpark."

Tom nodded. "We're lucky Dietmar broke Mom and Dad's hearts with his plea to say farewell to the waterslides."

"That's right, Austen," Dietmar grinned. "You owe me."

Passing the submarine dock they waved at Mr. McAndrews as he lifted the hatch on the conning tower. Climbing down a ladder, the man disappeared into the sub to begin his solitary morning journey around the indoor sea. "What a lonely guy," Liz said. "I feel sorry for him."

Outside the locker rooms they met Neil Raj, who thanked Tom again for his help at the luggage store and invited them to his house to try a curry dinner. "The best you've ever eaten! I'll make it myself."

"At 1:00 P.M.," Tom said mournfully, "our jet takes off for Winnipeg."

Dismayed by the news, Neil Raj looked solemn as they entered the humid air of the waterpark. No volleyball players were on the big court; at the ping-pong tables there was only one pot-bellied man who called *wanna game?* but they turned down the offer and continued to the beach.

Not a single person lay under the palm trees or rode the inner tubes of the Raging Rapids. Three teenagers waited in the wave lake for a blasting horn to announce *surfs up*, but their cheer was nothing to the usual delighted yells of the waiting mobs of surfers.

"What a pathetic scene," Liz said.

"I don't know about that." Dietmar pointed high in the air. "There's no waiting for the Sky Screamer."

Neil Raj looked at the others. "Who's your fastest?"

"Him," Tom said, looking at Dietmar. "Believe it or not."

"Want a race?"

"Of course."

At the highest platform, nine stories above the wave lake, the swimmers below looked like ants. "What a drop," Liz said, staring at the double-tracked Sky Screamer that fell a long way straight down. "You guys can go first."

With a happy smile Neil Raj stepped forward. When Dietmar had swung onto the twin slide, Liz gave them a countdown. Then, with rebel yells, they dropped from sight.

Tom watched the water below explode into a million crystal diamonds as the pair hit the splash-down pool. Jumping on the slide, he looked at Liz on the other path.

"Let's go!"

Feet together, hands behind his head, Tom dropped into emptiness. For a few heart-stopping seconds he was free falling, then he made contact again with the slide while plunging straight down with the wind screaming in his ears. At the bend he winced as his feet hit the water and the first silver bullets slammed into his sinuses, then he was in the pool, swimming toward the others waiting on the deck.

"Who won?"

Neil Raj laughed. "Dietmar broke my personal best. When we saw our times on the scoreboard I couldn't believe my eyes."

Dietmar shrugged modestly. "By the way, Austen, you also lost . . . to your own sister."

Tom glanced at the results on the scoreboard. Avoiding Liz's eyes he said, "Which slide next?"

"Let's play some volleyball. I saw a ball lying on the court."

Within minutes they'd been joined by the pot-bellied man and a few other people, and soon after that the ball was spiked off Dietmar's head by Liz. He kicked it at her but missed, and they watched the ball fly into a stand of nearby trees.

"Nice move, Gomer." Liz ran into the trees and then reappeared to call, "Hey, Tom. Come and look at this."

The other boys ran with him into the trees. Liz stood over an opening in the ground. Cool air blew into their faces. "The ball fell into this air conditioning duct," Liz said. "See it down there beside that package?"

Tom and Liz dropped into the opening. Standing with their heads just below ground level, they glanced through a metal grill into the darkness of the duct, and then Tom bent to examine the package.

"It's a bomb!" He looked up at Neil Raj and Dietmar. "Call security on a hot line phone." As they disappeared he turned to Liz. "How'd the bomber get this package here?"

"Through the duct?" She shook the screen and it fell open. "Look, the hinges have been cut with a hacksaw. I bet this is how the bomber's been sneaking around the mall."

Tom looked into the darkness. "What do you think?"

"I'm not sure. It's so black in there."

"Maybe . . ." Tom stared at his sister. "Did you hear that?"

"Yes!"

They crawled into the duct, then waited. Seconds later the sound came again. Somewhere in the darkness a voice was shouting for help.

11

Tom moved further into the black duct with Liz right behind him. The metal was cold and there was just enough room for them to crawl slowly forward. Again the cries for help sounded, followed by silence.

Tom and Liz continued on for some time. To the right was a wire-mesh grill; through it they saw the orange light on the conning tower of a submarine. "I think it's in the tunnel," Liz whispered. "But it isn't moving."

"I hear a thumping sound. Somebody's kicking a wall or something."

Tom and Liz moved toward the sound. They turned a final bend in the air-conditioning duct, then climbed a short ladder to another dark space. Slivers of light leaked in through cracks in a wooden wall. The faint light showed a man tied to the wall. A piece of cloth had been shoved into his mouth. As Tom tore it away he recognized Benn Dunn. His eyes were desperate as he gasped, "Quick you kids! You've only got a few minutes. There's a bomb at my feet, set to explode. Go through that opening in the wall and set Mr. McAndrews free, then he'll get me out of this mess."

"Set him free? What's that mean?"

"Shut up and get moving! I don't want to die!"

Tom and Liz raced to a narrow space that led between rough boards. Not knowing what lay ahead, they followed the darkness until Tom's hand touched a dark velvet curtain. Pushing it aside, he saw more slivers of faint light. In the centre of an open space was a large tank where fish could be seen; stingrays, groupers and tarpin. Above the surface of the tank Mr. McAndrews hung from a rope around his chest: his hands and feet were tied, his mouth was gagged, and he had a blindfold over his eyes. The big man twisted slowly on the rope that led from the roof to the wall, where it was attached to a bracket.

Near the bracket stood someone in a scuba outfit, face hidden behind a mask and head covered by black rubber. Hearing Tom and Liz, the unknown person turned in their direction, holding a speargun.

With a gesture, they were ordered forward. Tom went to the left of the tank, Liz immediately went right. The figure in black was forced to swivel the speargun back and forth, trying to keep them both covered. Then a blast of sound came from somewhere distant, vibrating the glass of the tank and making the tarpin flash into hiding. At the bottom of the tank, beside its glass wall, Tom noticed a package among the ferns.

Then he saw the shark.

Coming from distant water, it moved swiftly in his direction. As it reached the glass wall below and turned away, a second shark appeared. Then, at last, Tom realized a bomb had torn open their tank, freeing the sharks. They were in the sea now, and would get into the tank below if the package near the wall exploded. After that, it would be only a matter of time until Mr. McAndrews was attacked.

Just then there was a muffled cry as Liz crashed into the figure in the scuba suit, hitting the black shape from behind and knocking the speargun into the tank. Tom managed to grab the gun; lifting it clear of the water, he threw it to Liz as the black shape came at him. Then, as they struggled, Liz loomed above, pointing the speargun at the mask.

"Leave my brother alone," she shouted. "I know how to work this gun."

Tom broke free of the strong hands as they were raised in surrender. Racing around the tank, he grabbed the rope and pulled with all his strength. It was on several pulleys so he was able to raise Mr. McAndrews a short distance and then . . .

BLAM!!

Water flew everywhere as the tank was blown apart. Tom was knocked down, but managed to keep his grip on the rope. Struggling to his feet, he raised Mr. McAndrews a bit higher as a shark smashed its way into the shattered tank. A stingray was helpless before it, and then a grouper fell victim to a second grey attacker.

Tom stared at the evil eyes of the sharks in the tank, knowing that they'd soon see Mr. McAndrews dangling above. Then his sister cried out as the black figure broke away from her.

"Tom, I can't do it! I can't shoot that person! Look out!"

He only had a second to think, not knowing how to defend himself without dropping the rope. Then a spear slammed into the wall, briefly creating a barrier between Tom and the attacker.

Liz dropped the gun and ran to help pull Mr. McAndrews higher, just as a shark exploded from the water, its savage teeth coming menacingly close. Again they pulled as a second shark made a desperate bid, barely missing the man's feet. The black figure darted under the spear and tried to knock them away from Mr. McAndrews' lifeline, but they held on desperately, refusing to give up.

Out of the corner of his eye Tom saw feet appear on a nearby ladder that connected to somewhere above. With lightning speed a police woman in uniform came down the ladder with a gun.

"Don't move!" She carefully approached the figure in black, the gun steady in front of her. "There's reinforcements right behind."

"But," Liz said, "how'd you get here so fast?"

"We were already at the mall because of the bomb in the waterpark. Someone heard the blast under the *Santa Maria* and alerted us." As other officers came down the ladder she pulled the scuba mask off the attacker's face and Liz cried out in shock.

"I don't believe it. Christopher!"

* * *

Liz was still recovering an hour later. She sat on the deck of the *Santa Maria*, leaning against a cannon. Tom was nearby, listening to the questions being asked of Christopher Dixon. The blond man was in handcuffs. He sat near the open hatch leading to the ship's hold below, where the sharks had nearly ended Mr. McAndrews' life.

The police had arrived in time to save Benn Dunn from the bomb in the forward hold of the *Santa Maria*. "Tell me again," Inspector Winter Eagle said to Christopher. "You built a secret headquarters in the empty forward hold, but how did you get all the bomb materials into there?"

"I volunteered to help Lisa feed the fish. When we went on board the *Santa Maria* I was often carrying a package, but Lisa didn't notice how many times I left the ship without it." He smiled without warmth. "Later I crawled through the ducts from my store to the *Santa Maria* and collected the package from near the tank, where I'd left it."

"You used Lisa," Liz said angrily. "You fed her a line just to get a smuggling route into the *Santa Maria*. What a creep."

"Blame it on that fool, McAndrews. I was all set to marry into a California fortune when he blew in from the great white north. He used his money to impress her with roses and fancy dinners, so she married him. That's women for you."

"And you're a great example of a man."

"Shut up, kid." Christopher pulled against his handcuffs, trying to force them open. "You think I should respect a woman who dumped me?"

"What about Carroll?" Liz said. "How'd you use her?"

The man laughed. "That poor girl! Her old man's fling with wealth left her so lonely. She tried to get him to pay attention but all he could think about was this mall. Maybe he'll be different now, but I doubt it."

"It sounds to me," Inspector Winter Eagle said, "like you almost care for her. I'm surprised you're capable of such emotions, but it certainly didn't keep you from plotting to kill her father."

"I wanted to destroy McAndrews and his businesses, so I flew up here and got a job as a tour guide. That was the perfect way to learn all the secret details of how the mall worked. At night I stayed late in the office to study the blueprints."

"So you could figure out how to use the air conditioning ducts to get from the *Santa Maria* to any place in the mall?"

"That's right. I took the first bomb through the ducts to the Café Orleans. I hid it on the balcony, then phoned in an anonymous tip after I'd dropped from the air-conditioning duct into the storage room of my store."

"Why the bomb at Full Fathom Down?"

"To set up Benn Dunn as the bomber."

"And the waterpark bomb?"

"If those stupid kids hadn't found it, the blast near the volleyball court would have kept you cops busy while the other bombs were exploding."

"The ones attached to the shark tank and the *Santa Maria*?"

"Yeah. I planted them last night."

"At the hockey game you deliberately acted strangely so the kids would follow you and find the skate bomb. Right?"

He nodded. "I wanted you to suspect Benn Dunn. That's why I put the initials B. D. inside the skate. As soon as the store closed I knocked him out and hauled him through the ducts to the *Santa Maria*. I knew you cops would search his apartment and eventually find the wire I hid between the sofa cushions. It was the same wire used in all the bombs, so Dunn would have looked real guilty. Especially since I knew he'd spent time in prison. Then, after the sharks killed McAndrews, Dunn's body would have been found blown apart, apparently because of an accident in his secret bomb headquarters. The case would have been closed."

"Meanwhile, where would you be?"

"As the sharks enjoyed their snack I'd have crawled through the ducts to my store. Looking all nice and respectable, I'd be establishing my alibi while that creepy little clerk met the death he deserved."

Tom snorted. "I know why you hated Benn Dunn. At the store I remember your face turned white when he refused your order to obey the police. You didn't like him standing up to you, so I bet you enjoyed setting him up as a suspect when you faked that underwater attack. You cut the air hose yourself! That was a dirty trick."

As a police officer took Christopher's arm to lead him away he shook his handcuffs again. "I hate these things," he snarled.

The officer laughed. "You'd better get used to being locked up. You're going to be in prison for a long time."

When Christopher was gone, Liz looked around the mall. "It'll be a different place without those code reds sounding."

Tom snapped his fingers. "Code Red at the Supermall! How's that for a title?"

"Let's go ask what he thinks." Leaving the *Santa Maria*, Tom and Liz walked over to a crowd of people watching from behind police lines. "Excuse me," Liz said to a man in glasses who was making notes. "Have you picked a title for your new mystery?"

"Not yet! Got a suggestion?" He wrote Tom's idea in his notebook, then took a final picture of them. "So long," he said, shaking hands. "Thanks for your help!"

"You're welcome," Tom replied.

"It was fun," Liz added. "I'll keep my fingers crossed that your book sells a million."

The man laughed. "Wouldn't that be great?"

12

Festival Supermall!

Banners announced the gala event in huge letters. They hung outside stores, across corridors, everywhere above the crowds jamming the mall to celebrate the capture of Christopher Dixon.

One of the biggest banners was at the waterpark, where crowds of kids cheered each blast announcing *surf's up!* Free during the festival, the waterpark was bedlam with laughter, and music from big speakers.

Dietmar Oban continued to defeat all challengers on the Sky Screamer. Watching from below, Tom and Liz saw Dietmar drop from nine stories beside the current second-best, Neil Raj Gill. The challenger fell as swiftly as a barrel over Niagara Falls, but it still wasn't fast enough.

"He's won again!"

Dietmar swam across the splash-down pool, grinning happily. "I'm taking up a petition," he said, climbing out. "This waterslide should be called the Dietmar Drop."

"With your luck it'll probably happen," Tom muttered.

Later he and Liz left the waterpark with Neil Raj, who had invited them to visit Luggage Unlimited during the celebrations. "One of the big festival events is the cooking of traditional foods from other countries. I'm making my famous curry. You've got to try some."

"We'll be there for sure."

The corridors were jammed with tourists, shoppers and sensation-seekers. Clowns performing tricks passed among the people, and a juggler twirled flashing blades. Elsewhere, a woman coaxed her parrot to speak in three languages, while her husband's seal played notes on rubber horns.

Enjoying themselves enormously, Tom and Liz were trying on sombreros at a brightly decorated cart when their parents came out of the crowd. "We're going to Full Fathom Down," Mr. Austen said. "Carroll is giving us a scuba lesson in the indoor sea. Come and say goodbye to her."

"I wish tomorrow would never come," Tom said sadly. "This place is a total adventure."

Benn Dunn was the new manager of the scuba shop, and he looked a lot happier. "I never got along with that guy Dixon," he said to the Austens. "It's thanks to you kids I'm still alive."

Just then Carroll appeared from the storage room. She, too, seemed happier. "Fooled again by another

Mr. Beautiful! Maybe I should start listening to my father's advice."

"Are you moving back to the Caribbean?"

"Not for a while at least, and maybe not at all. I'd miss him too much."

"Will you be going on the morning sub rides with your Dad?" Liz asked.

"Oh yes. It's really important to him."

"I remember watching you in the sub. You didn't look very happy."

"A little voice inside of me kept saying Christopher was involved with the bombs. It was so depressing. Now I wish I'd said something to the police but I had no proof."

"I did," Liz said. "But I didn't even notice it."

"What do you mean?"

"Well, Christopher told me he'd managed a restaurant near Sea World. Later I learned it's in San Diego, which is where your father stole his bride from a jealous boyfriend."

After saying goodbye to the woman, Tom and Liz hurried through the crowded mall to catch a special dolphin presentation. Those showboat mammals—once again watched by a large and adoring audience—gave a great performance. Afterwards the Austens had a chance to speak to Lisa deVita.

"I'm feeling pretty bad about Christopher," she said, then smiled. "But I still believe in love. Hey, I'm Italian! I was born optimistic."

"I'm glad you weren't ever in any danger," Liz said.

"I guess that was my imagination working overtime." She looked at Tom. "Congratulations on nailing that creep at the luggage store. Did he have anything to do with the bombs?"

Tom shook his head. "No, there was never any connection."

"Well, I'm still glad he was arrested."

Not far away, Mr. McAndrews was one of the people taking passengers on festival submarine rides. Between shifts he came up from the dock. "Hi there, you two." He thanked them again for his safe release, then added, "I'm not proud of losing command of that sub."

"But you never had a chance," Tom said. "When it went into the tunnel you couldn't have known Christopher had come through the air-conditioning duct to wait for you to arrive."

"But to be taken by surprise!"

"What could you have done? He dropped the canister of knock-out gas down the conning tower before you could defend yourself, and you weren't wearing a scuba outfit like he was, so you didn't have the protection of a face mask and air supply."

"I guess you're right. If only I'd known that my daughter had fallen in love with the very man who was my enemy. I still can't believe he followed me from San Diego just to get revenge." Mr. McAndrews turned to greet a group of smiling people who'd come out of the crowd. "Tom and Liz, I'd like you to meet the family who built this mall. Years ago they came to Canada and built a successful business in Montreal before coming west with their vision of a supermall."

"You sure succeeded," Tom said. "On behalf of the world's kids, thanks!"

"I'll second that," Liz said.

As they talked to the friendly family members, Mr. McAndrews said, "Where's your friend Dietmar? He told me he's fond of exotic food, and I've made a special dish for the festival: haggis."

"What's that?"

"A traditional dish of Scotland. The innards of a sheep cooked in the skin of its stomach. Delicious!"

"Well, I don't know. Dietmar will eat anything, but . . ."

"If you see him, extend my special invitation. Of course, both of you are included as well."

"Thanks Mr. McAndrews, but no thanks!"

* * *

Soon after, Tom and Liz went into a store called Lots of Fun Stuff. They made a special purchase, then hurried back to Bourbon Street to hear who'd won the Rock the Mall contest. On the way Dietmar joined them, then they saw Heather's manager, Mr. Sutton.

He was on the edge of the crowd waiting for the announcement, still wearing his old-fashioned suit, but with new shoes. "These are for luck," he explained. "I'm really hoping that Heather wins. I've already booked a studio to make her first record."

"But," Liz said, "didn't you say she's not ready yet?"

"Well, I've had second thoughts. She's a great talent and I can't hold her back. I think Heather may be ready for the big time."

"Terrific!" Liz smiled at him. "Remember when I met you with my mom? You'd been talking to Benn Dunn. I kind of wondered about that after he disappeared."

"Years ago I volunteered to help ex-prisoners. Benn's one of the people I meet on occasion, just to make sure that everything's okay. He was pretty upset when the bomb was discovered in his store, kind of thought he'd be blamed because of his past. But it's all fine now, and he'll make a good manager of the scuba shop."

As several people appeared above, all eyes went to the balcony of the Café Orleans. Inspector Winter Eagle said into a microphone, "This is a perfect place for the contest announcement. The first bomb was discovered here and things looked bad for a while. Now everybody's smiling again, and I'm honoured to have a small part in today's big event." She looked at the others beside her. "The announcement of the winner will be made by someone who's special to us all. I've been asked to introduce him, and it's a real thrill. Ladies and gentlemen, please welcome Cayley Wilson."

As cheers and whistles rang out, the blond hockey star stepped to the microphone. "It's great to be making this announcement! We're all expecting wonderful things from the winner of the contest. Please welcome an Edmonton girl who's on the way to success. Here she is: Heather!"

She stepped out onto the balcony to deafening applause. Her face was radiant as she waved to the crowd, then went to the microphone. "There's lots of people to thank, but one person is very special." Pausing, Heather looked in the direction of Tom and Liz. "His name is Mr. Sutton, and he's the world's greatest manager."

As the crowd applauded, Mr. Sutton smiled at Heather. Then after a trophy had been presented to her, Dietmar turned to leave. "I'm out of here."

"Hold it, Oban," Tom said. "There's a special invitation for you from Mr. McAndrews."

After hearing the details of the haggis feed Dietmar said, "It sounds weird, but I'll chance it. After all, my family name comes from a Scottish town."

"Good luck! I'm glad we're going to McDonald's tonight, not McAndrews."

* * *

Long past midnight, Dietmar lay snoring on his bed. Out for the count, he didn't hear the door open between his room and Tom's. A dark shape stood for a moment, listening with unbelieving ears to the decibel count, then the mystery figure swiftly carried out his mission.

* * *

The next morning Mr. and Mrs. Austen were organizing their suitcases. Tom and Liz had finished their packing and were lounging on the sofa, both reading mysteries. Suddenly the door of the Roman Suite burst open and Dietmar stumbled in.

"*It was the haggis*," he screamed. "I've been destroyed!"

Mr. Austen turned slowly, expecting another of Dietmar's gags, then he stared in horror. "I don't believe my eyes! Why did this boy come with us? He's trouble!"

Dietmar ran to the bathroom mirror. "They're still there! I hoped it was just a nightmare! I don't know how, but that haggis did this to me!" Leaning close to the glass, he stared at the bat tattoos above both eyes, the spiders in bright colours on his cheeks, and the tattoo of a tiny snake coiled on the point of his chin. "I look like a kid born into a motorcycle gang!"

"Just before the first bomb was discovered," Liz said to Dietmar, "I found a place in the mall called Lots of Fun Stuff that features quite an interesting product. Here's my map—maybe you'd better find the store and learn how to end your agony." She glanced at her watch. "But make it quick. We leave for the airport soon."

With a cry the boy ran from the suite, moving even faster than his record-breaking fall down the Dietmar Drop.